,NA CH

Jeary Joint Libraries)

TIPPERARY LIBRARIES

3 0021 00428546 6

The View from Coyaba

PETER ABRAHAMS

The View from Coyaba

faber and faber

LONDON · BOSTON

First published in 1985
by Faber and Faber Limited
3 Queen Square London WC1N 3AU

Photoset by Wilmaset, Birkenhead,
Merseyside
Printed in Great Britain by
Redwood Burn Ltd, Trowbridge Wiltshire
All rights reserved

© Peter Abrahams, 1985

British Library Cataloguing in Publication Data

Abrahams, Peter, 1919–
The view from Coyaba.
I. Title
823   PR9369.3.A2

ISBN 0–571–13288–X
ISBN 0–571–13489–8 Pbk

COUNTY TIPPERARY
Joint Libraries Committee

Acc. No. *D 80255*

Class No. *F*

Price *9 : 95*

Vendor *O' MAHONY*

Catalogued *F.B.*

This book is for the Africans.
It is also for my Daphne,
the present-day keeper of Coyaba.

1
Prelude: He/She

COUNTY TIPPERARY JOINT LIBRARIES
County Library
Thurles.

The Arawaks, the first inhabitants of Jamaica, buried their dead in secluded, tranquil places not easily reached. That is how the story goes, for no one alive today knows the truth. The story says that the Arawaks were gentle people: civilized enough to show the value of leisure by inventing the hammock; creative enough to make songs and to play and to leave behind their artifacts. But civilization, in the form of the Spanish opening up of the New World, wiped them off the face of Jamaica in less than fifty years. When the Spaniards under Columbus landed in 1494 and 1503 there were, the story tells, between fifty thousand and sixty thousand Arawaks in the island. The Spaniards enslaved them and worked them to death; the sicknesses of civilization, like the 'flu, killed many, and by an extraordinary act of will the Arawak women stopped producing children to be enslaved; their numbers dwindled until there were none. Now there are a few reminders of how they once lived and worked and walked and played and loved in the sun. The places where they took their dead they called Coyaba, the places of tranquillity. We have found one such, high up in the Red Hills, near a cave and close by a deep, dried ravine that must once have been the basin of a river trapped in the hills two thousand feet above the level of the sea. It is not difficult to imagine this as the look-out spot, or the place of meditation to escape to, away from the daily rounds of a busy Arawak village. But for the village to be this far into the Red Hills, this far from the sea, the Spaniards must have been in occupation of the land and the numbers of Arawaks must have already dropped to that point of no return, at some point in the 1530s to 1540s. . . .

The woman climbed the steeply winding narrow track with a slow, even pace. She breathed easily, body braced against the slope of the lush green land. The bush immediately beside the track rose a good eight feet; beyond that it was thick dense forest. The woman was a little less than five feet tall. She was round-

11

faced, soft-featured with a hint of sharpness to the nose-bone. Her skin was finely textured, with a glowing hint of red in the rich dark brown. Long, thick black hair, tied at the back with a piece of wiss framed her small face. Her small dark eyes darted from side to side, then ahead, then up, where a lone John Crow rode the silent wind with easy powerful grace, casually, lazily, flapping its great wings every few seconds. With each step the woman balanced the hamper on her head by a slight movement of her neck. At a point halfway up her climb she paused and looked down to her right. The land had been bushed here for new planting and below it she saw a cluster of women, her sisters of the village, selectively reaping the first green corn. Beyond them, on more sloping, more rugged cleared land, a group of men were at work on a yam and cassava and sweet potato field. Further below, on the banks of the river was the cluster of huts that made up the village. She could see the children of the village at play, far up at the western end where the flow of the river narrowed to little more than the width of a tall man. There the men of the village had in an earlier time diverted a stream to make a playing pool for the children. Not so long ago, there were so many more children that the playing pool was overcrowded and they had to use it in turns. Not so long ago, the whole village was overcrowded and there had been talk among the elders of founding a second and then, perhaps, a third village still further up in the hills, if water could be found. She remembered how the eyes of the old man had glowed as they sat by the fire and dreamed of more villages, nearer and nearer the skies and further and further away from the intruding whites with their cruel and graceless ways and their pleasure in hurting people.

The woman continued her climb. The sky was a clear bright blue without any hint of cloud. The sun had passed its peak and was halfway between the sky and the sea. Now the woman could see the sea, a long way to the south and the west. Fleetingly, she remembered the happier times. There were so many of them then: a whole world of her people living happily by the sea under the warm sun. She remembered laughter. Then she put these thoughts firmly from her.

She came to the end of her climb: a broad plateau that commanded a view of all the world. From it you see the land, you see mountains, you see the sea. And on a flat stone in the shade of a broad-leafed tree sat the old man to whom she had come with the food and drink.

"It is good to see you!" he called. "I thought I was forgotten!"

The banter in his voice light as air, warmed her.

"Not you. Never," she called back. She hastened toward him.

"Come sit with me."

"Why do you think I climbed this hill?" she snapped in mock anger.

"For love of me," he mocked, but gently now.

She reached him and he rose and helped her lift the hamper from her head. Their hands touched, lingeringly, and she looked into his eyes.

"What do the gods tell you? Do they offer comfort?"

The man's lips curled in a gentle smile. He was small like the woman, perhaps an inch or two taller, no more; his reddish–brown body as smooth and sheeny as hers, with only a looseness of skin from flesh suggesting age. The face was unlined, the grey in the hair mere flecks; only the eyes and the very dark lids confirmed the gap of time between the man and the woman.

"Why should they be concerned with us," he murmured as he watched the woman unpack the hamper and lay out the food on the broad flat stone. A tiny dog came leaping from the bushes and dropped a rat it had just killed at the man's feet, dancing and whimpering in high-pitched excitement. The man reached down and touched the dog's head. It was calmed immediately, licked the man's hand and lay down, waiting.

"Good," the man said absently, "take it, eat it. Go."

The tiny dog grabbed up the rodent and flashed away back into the bushes.

"He did not even notice me," the woman said.

"Like the gods," the man said.

"If I had struck you, he would have."

"Not the gods."

"Oh you!"

13

She pushed a bowl of food at him. Her eyes, now, were laughing too. He wiped his fingers on a broad damp green leaf and picked a piece of meat from the bowl; it was brown and crisp and juicy soft. He chewed it slowly, savouring the smoky taste, then he cupped four fingers to make a spoon and scooped creamy ground cassava to his mouth.

"There is no reason for them to notice us any more than my little friend noticed you just now. The hunt was good and he had other things to do. When there is no hunt, nothing to eat and nothing else to do, he will notice you. So it is with the gods."

"The gods are not dogs," she protested.

"How do you know? Who told you? When did you meet them?"

"You are mocking again; but the gods are not dogs."

"The food is good. The meat melts. Did you prepare it?"

"Yes."

"I see. So as not to shake an old man's loose teeth. Thank you. You are right. The gods are not dogs because we do not want it so and there is love for you in my mockery."

"I know that." She was a little impatient now, anxious to talk seriously. "But what are we to do? Where are we to go? Who is to guide us if, as you say, the gods do not notice us? What is the purpose of it all? What is to happen to our people? To our young? They have driven us from our old grounds. Our numbers are drying up. We are dying. And you say the gods do not notice. . . ."

He put down the feeding bowl, wiped his fingers on the broad leaf and pulled her to him. She resisted briefly then relaxed and allowed him to comfort her. He held her in the folds of his right arm and with the left he pointed to the southern plain far, far down below them.

"That is where we came from. That was our home and our hunting and fishing grounds, the place where we played and worked and loved and danced. Then they came with their death-sticks; they made our land a place of desolation and the gods did nothing. What manner of gods are they who do nothing when their followers are broken and destroyed and driven from their hunting and fishing and playing grounds?

14

From their homes? Even from their places of burial? What manner of gods?"

"Hush," the woman murmured, and touched the lean bare chest with the back of her hand. "The ancestors taught us not to question the gods."

"They did not know our desolation," he retorted.

"They did," she said. "They did. Have you forgotten their long journey to this land in an earlier time?"

"The enemies they fled then were people like us."

"But fierce and destructive as these are. Remember?"

"Not with death-sticks; and not with great canoes as big as hills; not bringing the sickness that kills our people; and not with chains."

"You are right. But those others were fierce and destructive, and the ancestors did not just give in and wait to die. They built canoes and made the long journey from the great land to this place. They did not sit down and wait to die."

"As we now do?" The heaviness of spirit was in the open now.

She steeled her own spirit against the impulse to tenderness.

"Yes. As we now do."

She sensed the stiffening of his body. Her eyes darted up to his face then away quickly. He rose and walked away from her, toward the edge of the plateau. Far to the east and reaching even further up into the heavens the great mountains were still bathed in the light of the sun, made a hazy purplish blue by the light and the air and the great distance. Puffs of white smoke rose from the settlement far down on the plain where those who had been put in chains were preparing food for the intruders.

The man turned and looked at her, measuring the distance between them. There was a hard edge to his voice now: "So. . . . And what would you have us to do, woman? Go down and fight them? Embark on another great journey, as the ancestors did?"

"Fight them," she snapped back, simulating anger. "Or embark on a great journey. Do the one or do the other."

"But do something," he mocked, his voice gentle once more.

"Yes. To do nothing is wrong. To do nothing is to be part of the thing they do to us; is to be part of the destruction of our people. And that the ancestors will not forgive."

15

"The ancestors. The ancestors. Always the ancestors. They become a burden on a man's spirit, these ancestors. They did not prepare us for this time of desolation. They did not forewarn of the coming of these brutal strangers. These ancestors on whom you are forever calling, woman, they taught gentleness and peaceful ways. They did not teach us to fashion the fighting weapons of those other enemies, the Caribs, who drove them from the great land and followed them through all the small lands. How are we to fight the death-sticks of these new enemies who know nothing of gentleness? And where are we to run to? Up into those mountains? Already the cold here is more than we can bear when the season changes and the sun cools down. Every time the cold comes some of our people die. To take them higher up into the mountains is to find a quicker death, even if we find water." He waved his arm to the Blue Mountains. "I know there is water up there. A long time ago, in the days of our youth, a party of us went up there and found much water and much meat for the hunting; but the cold drove us back and killed some of our party."

"I remember, you told me," the woman whispered.

"And that was in the days before the sickness these strangers carry and let loose when the sun cools down and the earth turns cold."

He walked back to her and took her two small hands into his own not much larger ones. He looked tenderly into her eyes.

"Listen, woman," he whispered intently. "To build new canoes we have to be down near the sea. We have to fell trees and dig them out and shape them with fire and stone. It is a labour that will need time and many men and women from many villages. It is not a labour that can be carried on in secrecy down there. What do you think the intruders will do? Let us be? They will do what they have done many times before. They will swoop on us; they will kill those who resist. They will put our men in chains and use our women for sport. And our children they will turn into creatures ministering to their every need." Then, knowing the unfairness of the question, he asked: "Is that what you want?"

She fought off the overwhelming sense of helplessness.

"We must do something," she insisted. "To do nothing is wrong."

"To wait is not always to do nothing," he said.

"To wait?"

"Yes. To wait."

"What for?"

"Come," he said. "You have shown me I was wrong not to talk before now. I will go down with you and we will talk with all our people and make them understand why we must wait and what we must wait for."

"Make me understand," she insisted, "and I will tell you if they will understand. I am nearer to you than anyone and I do not want to wait. If you cannot make me understand you will not make the young ones understand."

They returned to the flat stone, shed their sandals of tree bark and climbed on the stone, both warming feet and buttocks from the heat the stone had absorbed through the long sunny day. The woman reached into the hamper and passed the man a honey brew. He took a long drink then handed it back to her. She took a few sips, recorked the earthen vessel and replaced it.

"Do you remember the last of our people who came up here from down there? The one who had escaped from the intruders and who had learned of their plans?"

"Yes. I did not feel at ease with him. He had too many of their ways."

"He had been their prisoner for a long time, woman."

"You know that the weak always take on the ways of the strong; if they do not the strong destroy them. Remember that one told us the intruders had not found the gold they had come to seek. Well, he also told me that his master had heard of a land where the gold they sought was in abundance. The plan was for them to use this Jamaica as a stopping point on the way to that land of gold. From here they would provide the great canoes with food and water to complete the journey to the land of the gold. Later, when they no longer needed to do this, they would leave this land."

"Leave this land?" the woman whispered.

"Yes. Leave this land."

She examined his face searchingly.

"Do you believe they will leave this land?"

17

"I do not know. I do not know *them*; and he who told me had become half part of them. So I do not know. But their ways and their greed for gold tell me it is possible. On this I have built a slender hope. And to hope is also to do something."

"But if they do not go . . . ?"

"Then we will surely die; not in the way you or I die. As a people."

"Then what?" she said softly.

"Then nothing," he replied. "When there is nobody left to remember us as we remember the ancestors there will be nothing. It will be as if we were never here. As long as you live, even if I were to die now, you will remember me and so I will be alive in your memory. So it is with each of us, with you, every one of our people, even with my little friend the dog whom you do not want to see as a god; as long as he remembers me, I am alive for him and he for me, and so we do not die."

The woman touched the man's body, as if with a new consciousness, feeling the skin and the muscle and the bone.

"And if we die, all of us, everywhere in this land, will the intruders remember us? Will we live through them?"

"I do not know. I know I would not want them to."

"Because of what they have done to us?"

"Not just that, but that is part of it. To be remembered as things in chains, as creatures to be enslaved and broken, is to be robbed of the feeling and love which made us the people we are. For them to remember us they will have to impose a different kind of being on us. Remember the one you did not trust because they had half changed him into one of their kind? Well, it would be like that. They would remember us not as we are but as they have made us." The man's voice suddenly trembled with anger. "And I will not be remembered thus by them! They are not worthy of safeguarding the memory of our people. Better it be as though we never were!"

"Peace, my man," the woman murmured. "Peace, wise one. Have you not taught us that all things live, not only man? And what lives will be remembered as they should be remembered?"

18

"Not by them!"

"Then by the earth and the air and the wind and the forests."
He remained deeply serious. "Remembrance is the thread of life.
Without it there is no meaning. It linked the ancestors with their
ancestors far back into the great land, and with us all their
descendants into the small lands. They live in our remembrance
as their ancestors lived in their remembrance and so their
ancestors now also live in our remembrance. If we die then all this
thread of remembrance dies with us. The ancestors die; their
ancestors die; the ancestors of their ancestors die; the past dies;
everything dies."

"You grieve yourself, old man."

"It is a thing of grief, woman. See it, woman! All that past. All
the striving. The fleeing from the wild ones. The building of new
homes in a strange land. There were so many of us once. Vast
numbers in all the small lands. There was so much tenderness, so
much laughter. And, oh, the games and the songs we made! and
now. . . ."

"And now there is need to do something," she spoke firmly.
"Tell of the waiting. How will we wait? Where will we wait?"

Far out to sea a Spanish galleon appeared on the clear horizon.

"And still they come." The man gestured, almost violently.

They both looked out intently to sea, across the nearer slightly
lower hills, then further down across the foothills, then across the
thickly forested plain that sprawled in all directions until it was
stopped by the sea in one direction and the climbing mountains in
the other.

"You say wait, and still they come," the woman's voice was
heavy.

"That is why I have not spoken," he said. "It is a slender thread
on which to build hope. If it is false. . . ."

"If it is all we have," she said.

"A man must believe in the hope he offers, or he lies."

"If it is all we have?" she repeated.

"A leader must not lie to his people. That is the law."

"Our laws were not made for such times."

"Good laws are for all times. A leader must not lie."

"It is no lie to tell them the hope is slender."

19

"And if they say to me, 'Cacique, do you believe in this thing you tell us to wait for: do you believe the intruders will go away?' Am I to tell them I do not know? And if they press and say: 'But what do you believe, wise one?' Am I to answer them again and say I do not know? A leader must not confuse his people. That, too, is the law."

There was a long silence between them after that. To the west the setting sun, just below the horizon, threw pale orange fingers of light into the darkening sky. The blue mountains to the east were dark but clearly defined silhouettes. There was the slightest of breezes. The great John Crow had left off his lazy graceful circling; but the small birds of the evening were out in force, darting and whirling, screeching and quarrelling over hunting territory, catching insects in midflight, playing perilous games of aerial near-collisions, then swooping down, like a dropping stone to grab some insect on bush or ground.

Not even the perspective of distance could reduce, for the two humans on the flat stone, the enormity of the Spanish galleon gliding into the natural harbour, and the portent of its presence. The woman broke the silence.

"Perhaps they will go," she insisted.

"Do you believe they will?" the man murmured.

How terrible the world has become, the woman told herself.

"Yes, I believe they will."

"Do not lie, woman. You are more than just my woman, more than just my comforter. You are an elder of your people, a priestess. If the young ones ask you: 'Do you believe they will go, mother?' how will you answer?"

"Then why did you tell me of the hope in waiting?"

"The slender thread, remember. . . . Because I was weak and did not want to think of the death of all remembrance that you and I, that our people, lived and loved and were happy in this gentle land of wood and water. That kind of death, the death of the remembrance of a people, is the most terrible thing in my understanding."

"But the land will remember. The spirit of the land, the trees, the wind the stream." The woman was pleading now, passionately, insistently, determined to break through the heavy despair of the man. "These will remember us as we were when there were many of us and there was laughter in all the small lands."

It was the man, now, who would not be comforted: "Will you tell this to our young people? Will this make the waiting, the slow dying, easier?"

"To tell them that only the land will remember us is to tell them of our death. I will not do that. Just as you will not lie, I will not pass our burden of hopelessness to them. It is wrong for the young to bear such burdens."

"So you will tell them nothing."

"Unless you believe the intruders will leave. . . . Enough now, old man. You are tired. It is time to rest our spirits. Come, we will not go down to the village this night. If they see us, the young people will hope for a sign or a message and their spirits will turn to heavy matters. If they do not, they will eat by the warmth of the fire and tell tales and dream dreams of hope and make love and have laughter. And that is good for the young."

The woman left the man and walked to the northern edge of the cleared circle of the hilltop, a distance of some thirty yards; then the wild forest confronted her, dense, heavy, dark. A small path made a low entrance into it. She entered and moved slowly down a slight incline, bent almost double to avoid the heavy overgrowth. The path turned right and right again; then, with startling suddenness, she emerged in a cave, tucked into the side of the hill and facing south. She saw, at a lower level now, that the Spanish galleon had passed the finger of land pointing out to sea. Two curls of white smoke rose from the edge of the sea where the Spaniards had one of their encampments. But she could not look north now; the village, and the children at play by the pool, and the men and women at work in the fields, were all out of sight and sound.

The cave, a high-domed chamber of marl, was light and warm and airy. At the far end was a fireplace, some earthern pots and a pile of prepared kindling; at the other, the end nearest the entrance, a pile of softened animal skins formed a bed. Bits of fossilized coral, embedded in the marl stone, told that this land, two thousand feet above the sea, was once under the ocean. Though the air was clean and fresh, there was no hint of the gentle breeze here. Only an overwhelming air of tranquillity, of a place of total peace.

Some time during the day two young women of the village had climbed the hill to bring food and drink and to clean the cave in case the Cacique stayed to commune with the gods; and in these days of trouble he spent much time up on the hilltop, away from the tribe. Square slabs of marble made seats in the deepest part of the cave. The woman rearranged the bedding, then knelt near the fireplace and began the slow process of striking fire from flintstone. She worked steadily and methodically, rubbing hard black stone against hard black stone over a pile of dry leaves. The woman's mind grew numb with the monotonous motion. Suddenly, the stones, almost unbearably hot now, struck spark, dropped on the dry leaves. A tiny spiral of smoke rose. She leaned over it, blowing lightly, knowing from long experience the precise level of breath to fan the sparked smoking leaves into flame. And then, suddenly, the fire leapt to life! The miracle the gods had given the ancestors to give their descendants: the living flame and how to bring it forth and put it away. The intruders had this too, and more, and they used it to kill. Who gave them that? The same gods? Greater gods than our gods? Oh no!

"Oh no!" she said out loud. But the thought was there full-grown, terrible, terrifying.

Their gods have killed our gods. That is why our gods cannot protect us from these intruders.

"Oh no!" She cried again.

"What terrible thing do you see, woman?"

She had not noticed the quiet coming of the man. Again the man's voice reached her: "What is it woman? Why such new grief?"

Do I put this burden on him too? Without looking up or turning her head she said: "Nothing. The nightmares and memories of a foolish old woman."

"Who treats me as an old fool now. I know you, woman!"

"Please. . . ."

"Tell me: share it."

She piled the kindling on the burning leaves; first small pieces, carefully, to let through air, then bigger and thicker pieces. Then, her work on the fire done, she rose and turned to him. He was too distant for her to read his face in the gathering dark.

"Then come nearer."

He came to her and leaned forward till she could see his face in the leaping, rising flames.

She flung her arms about him. He wrapped his arms comfortingly about her.

"What is it, woman?" He was all calming tenderness now.

"Do gods die? Can gods die?"

"Tell me more, woman," he whispered gently.

"Their gods. . . . Their gods. . . ."

"Calmly, my beloved. Calmly."

"If their gods are as terrible as they are. . . ."

His thoughts reached out and met hers.

"Oh, my love. Now I see your pain. Have their gods killed our gods? That is it?"

"Yes."

"When did it come to you?"

"Now. Here at the fire. Do gods die? Can their gods kill ours?"

"And is this why our gods have not protected us?"

"Yes. Yes."

The man held the woman even more tightly. It was a long, silent embrace. Then, at last, he pushed her away and held her at arm's length and looked into her face.

"I do not know, my love." A quiet heaviness in his voice. "I have searched the heavens and the earth for answers. I have gone over all the laws and remembrances of the past for answers. I have found no answers. There was never a time like this in the remembrance of our people. And when the wise ones do not know what to tell the young or where to lead them, when there is no more belief in gods and no vision of hope to take us forward, when we ask if our gods are dead, then we are into the time of desolation. This is that time, my love."

"Our gods are dead," she murmured, all the desolation of the world in her voice. Then she began to moan in a soft, low voice, her head against his chest. A long, slow, steady moan of grief without end. . . .

23

After the disappearance of the Arawaks the high land to which they had escaped from the Spaniards and the hill with the great flat rock overlooking the plains remained uninhabited by man for almost two hundred years. Bush, then deep dense forest, over time, reclaimed the land the Arawaks had tamed and cultivated. Huge trees, some hard as rock and capable of living a hundred years and more, became masters of the land and rose above the deep dark undergrowth to reach for the sky where the big carrion birds continued to sail the soft wind with casual, almost indifferent, grace. And still the night-birds left their caves when darkness came, flying in the direction of the plain and the sea, and the gradually growing habitation far down there, and returning, in formation, with the first signs of daybreak. As the forest grew denser and reclaimed all the land that had once been a human settlement beside a deep ravine of flowing water, the water drifted up, and its level rose till it formed a deep clear pool between two hills. The land in the valley between the two hills feeding the ravine grew moist and damp till there was the constant drip of water, whether it rained or not. The land, here, was again as the early Arawak had first found it, a soft, fertile and kindly land of wood and water.

So it stayed until the coming of a new group of humans. The time would be somewhere in the late 1820s. The British had, centuries earlier, replaced the Spaniards as the rulers of Jamaica. Blacks had been carried forcibly from the African continent, first by the Spaniards, to replace the vanished Arawaks as slaves, then by the British and other European powers and by the American colonists, to work the sugar plantations of the Caribbean islands and the North American mainland. Other brown and yellow people from Asia were also brought, but mainly it had been the Africans who were imported even before the Arawaks had completely vanished.

2
Samson/Maria

1

For days the small group of half-naked people had struggled frantically, chopping through the dense bush. The first day their desperation was overpowering; they worked through the day and through the night, and far into the next day, not stopping, not resting, only pausing for a quick drink of water from a gourd one of the children always had ready. Then, the men in front, the women and children close behind, they carried on with their frantic, endless chopping. They cut a narrow path through the bush under the big trees and as they passed through, the women and children with bundles of clothes, food, cookpots on their heads or across their shoulders, those who made up the rear replaced the bush again, covering their tracks.

On the second night they stopped and rested. A woman gave each person a lump of thick porridge wrapped in a huge leaf: the biggest lumps for the men, the smallest for the children. Then each lay down where he or she was and slept.

There were a dozen in the group: three men, five women, four children – two boys and two girls.

The leader, a big, towering black man with a bullet head and a smallish face, was terribly scarred. A huge, livid, recently healed scar ran along the right side of his face from chin to forehead, passing between eye and ear. Older healed scars criss-crossed his back, arms and chest. The middle finger of his left hand was missing; and though he was in his late twenties his front teeth were missing. This one they named Samuel Brown, and on the plantation he had been known as Samson because of his great strength. It was that strength, and the impression it had made on the little brown slave girl, which had led to the trouble between Samson and the driver. The driver wanted the girl; the girl wanted Samson; the driver had the authority and the whip; he used both.

Buckra Massa approved, for that was how he got what he wanted. The older slaves had seen this situation before: a driver could kill a man with his whip. One night Samson crushed the driver's head with a huge stone, gathered his few belongings into a bundle, crept out of the slaves' quarters, and made for the hills. The others watched him go and said nothing. He knew that if he was caught and brought back they would watch with similar indifference while his body was broken as an example to other would-be runaway slaves. The brown slave girl did not follow him to the hills. Instead, when enough time had passed for her to estimate that Samson should have reached the foothills with their enveloping forests, she it was who told Bucky Massa that the driver had been killed and word from the slave quarter was that the killer had escaped. This way, she, as well as the other slaves would not be punished for keeping silent. And when militiamen were sent for and hunting teams were sent out, many of the young male slaves volunteered to join in the hunt for the killer of the driver: slaves who carried the scars of the dead black slave-driver's whip on their bodies.

Samson woke suddenly and sat up. Had he heard the distant bark of a dog? Were the hunters nearing? The moon was high. A good night for hunting runaway slaves.

"Some'n wrong?" It was the man nearest him, the short square one.

"Don' know," Samson whispered back.

They listened intently for a while longer. The utter silence fed their anxiety, set imaginations at work on latent fears.

"Better we move," Samson whispered.

All twelve of them rose instantly, wide-awake as though they had not slept at all. The moon was up and full and clear; light filtered through the thickening bush. Samson motioned to the third man, the tall thin one with the sickly look on him.

"Take a boy an' go back to near the place we came in and see if you see or hear anyt'ing. . . . You did cover it good?"

"Yeah. . . . Stay there 'n watch?"

"No, see 'n come back."

The man and the boy slipped away, back along the path they had cut. Samson raised his machete. It glinted in the filtered moonlight then sank with a swish into the soft wood, almost severing the young tree in one stroke. The short square one, Jonas, swung his machete at the next clump of bush. Then there was the softer chopping of the women. The rhythm of the work picked up and became steady. They worked steadily through what remained of the night, and into the morning and on. The thin man, Joe, and the boy, David, returned about the middle of the day. They had seen no sign of searchers; but they had found and caught a young wild hog and David was carrying it on his shoulder, trussed up, alive and gagged to stifle its squealing.

The oldest woman, Maria, angrily grabbed the trussed-up young hog from the boy's shoulder and undid the gag.

"You kill the dumb t'ing!" she protested. "Get me a piece a' wiss."

The younger of the two boys, who did not know his name, took Maria's machete and went off. The woman laid the hog on the ground, making soft grunting sounds to calm it, while she slowly undid the tight vegetable rope binding its legs. The boy returned with the wiss, an enormous roll nearly half an inch thick. The woman fashioned a neckband for the hog, with a long lead which she gave the boy without a name.

"You look after her, Noname. She will drop soon. Is a good thing for us."

Big Samson paused from his work, looked at the woman, a curious, admiring expression on his face.

"Sure? How you know?"

"Me know."

"Woman know woman business," Jonas chipped in without pausing in his work.

"Yeah," Joe, the sickly one, said sarcastically.

"I raise them." Maria gestured in the direction of the plain. "Me learn to know them and them sweet t'ings. Sweet fe eat and sweet fe friend when them know you."

Maria sensed Samson's sudden new interest in her and looked directly at him. She saw the question forming in his mind, then he shook his head slightly and said instead, "If we find a safe place you will look after the animals?"

"Yes," she said. "Me love animals."

"Time running," Jonas said and they all set to again.

On the fifth day since they entered the dense, steeply sloping bush they came, suddenly, unexpectedly, on a broad piece of level, cleared land. The others held back among the trees while big Samson moved into the clearing: cautious, alert, machete held tight and ready for instant battle. People had been here. A fire had been made. There was no one now. He raised his left arm and beckoned. The others hurried forward.

"Look!" the boy they called Noname shouted, caution forgotten. He pointed back to where they had come from; far down they could see, beyond the tops of the towering trees, stretches of the plain, and beyond that, the placid Caribbean sea. Now, for the first time, they had some measure of how far and how high they had come.

"And there!" the boy David shouted. He had moved to the western edge of the clearing; he pointed westward. Below them, a broad flat green stretch of land, bright in the sunlight, swept away until it met the sea, then distant rising hills, then past those hills till it met the sea again, and on again till it grew hazy beyond the reach of human vision.

"Aaaiy! It big!" One of the younger women exclaimed. This one was called Sarah: big heavy-bosomed and with a strong body smell made stronger by the days of exertion and heavy sweating without washing.

Jonas joined David at the western edge of the clearing. He examined the ground, moving first this way then that; then he disappeared into the bush.

"Samson!" Jonas bawled, still out of sight. "Path here!"

Samson hurried to where Jonas was; together they examined the footpath and followed it some distance into the bush. It was like the footpath they themselves had cut through the forest in their long journey to this point. And, as they had done, those who had cut this footpath had concealed the point where it came out on the piece of flat, cleared land. The further from the clearing, the more thoroughly the path had been cleared.

"It like a regular path," Jonas said.

"Coming from there," Samson pointed west, to where in the misty distance the English Governor of the island had his seat of power. "But going where, Jonas?"

"And is who?" Jonas wondered. "White people? Militia?"

"They don't make track so."

"True; but slave make it for them."

"Yes," Samson agreed. Then he repeated, "But going where?"

"Come we look," Jonas said.

They returned to the clearing. The others had piled their bundles together and were resting. Maria, Noname and the tethered wild female hog were at the northern edge of the clearing where the hog had nosed a thick juicy tuber from soft ground and was crunching it noisily; Maria and the boy were digging for more of what the hog had found.

"Come!" Samson raised his voice. "Look for a path! So. . . ." He made an arc from east to north with the sweep of his arm.

They spread out in the direction Samson had indicated. Again it was Jonas who found the new path; but it took longer, this time. This path was much more carefully concealed than the one from the west. Jonas and some of the others had criss-crossed it several times before a small telltale sign had made Jonas examine it more closely and go deeper into the bush, past apparently impenetrable overgrowth around a huge tree. When Jonas hacked his way past the huge tree he found the path, straight and clear, pointing north-east and with all the signs of regular usage.

"Samson," Jonas bawled again. All of them except Maria and Noname came rushing to inspect the new path. Jonas was proud of himself. Very few people would have found this hidden path in days of searching; this one was not supposed to be found for those who had hidden it were trackers and hunters. How to make Samson understand this?

Samson dropped his huge hand on Jonas' shoulder and let it stay there for a while.

"A big work, bredda Jonas. I could never find it. . . ."

For the first time that he could remember, Jonas felt good deep inside; it made him want to straighten up and look at the sky. So, almost furtively, he straightened up and looked quickly at the sky. No one laughed; no one looked at him with mockery in their eyes.

"Mek we go that way," Sickly Joe said. "Time to eat and rest."

"No, Joe," the thin, long woman called Flo said. "Not yet."

31

"If people there, must be our people," Joe protested. "Runaway like we."

"Maybe not," Samson said softly. "I hear of black people catch others and return them to the slavers and drivers."

"Me chance it," Joe protested. "Me tired. Me one chance it."

"No!" Samson's voice was cold now, a threatening edge to it.

"Tell him, bredda Jonas," the woman, Flo, appealed, anxious to dampen the wrath she sensed in Samson. "Tell Joe, bredda Jonas."

"If one of we catch, all of we catch; so if we go, all must go or no one go. Samson lead us, Samson will say. We all runaway slaves, Joe; they catch one they catch all."

"Me tired," Joe repeated wearily, heavily, showing it in all of his body.

An overwhelming compassion spread through the woman Flo. She wanted to do something to comfort this sick man, this weak and weary man. She had never thought she would feel like this again; would want to use her life and her body to comfort another. All that had died when they had taken the child of her body from her and carried it away. When they took the man who had bred the child in her it was nothing. That is how it had always been. When a man and a woman sleep together both know it could end any time. Bucky Massa and his driver could sell you any time, move you any time, give you to breed with another one any time. So you take it and you move and you change and you take and the feeling is not deep. Only with the child it was deep and they took the child and there was no feeling in her till this moment for this sick man. The woman walked away abruptly.

"What now?" Jonas asked.

"I don' like it," Samson said.

"Me too," Jonas said. "Better we move. But which way?"

Samson seemed suddenly to make up his mind.

"Same way as before; away from where we came, far away." He glanced quickly at Joe, then turned and walked back to the clearing. "It far enough for us to go slow now; not far enough for us to stop. And not the right place."

"How will we know the right place?" the boy, David, asked.

"We will know," Samson said.

"Yes," Jonas echoed and carefully went about re-covering the hidden pathway he had found and opened.

Samson and Jonas opened a third pathway leading northward out of the clearing. They covered their trail as carefully as the others had. They were too far away, too far up now, for hunters to come looking for one runaway slave. There was no way for the hunters to know that on his journey to the hills the one runaway slave had been joined by others as desperate as he to be free. There was talk and a little knowledge of groups of runaway slaves high up in the foothills and far up in the mountains; and there were of course the Maroons, large enough in numbers and sufficiently armed for the British army to go into the mountains to put them down from time to time. But great military sweeps for tiny bands of peaceful and settled runaway slaves would be too costly. So these were left alone, and the remote and isolated little villages of runaway slaves grew in the many spots high up in the dense forested hills wherever water could be found.

Unexpectedly, the pathway to the north dipped and fell away. They travelled downhill for two days. Samson shared his alarm only with Jonas and Maria. Perhaps they were going back down to the plains and to the slavers. Yet they were still going north. On the third day after leaving the clearing the land ceased to fall away and they came upon a slow–flowing river in a deep, broad-bottomed, heavily wooded valley. That night, after a feast of hot roasted tubers of the kind the wild hog had unearthed, after the sweat and dirt of the long journey had been washed off their bodies, they slept all through the night, lulled into deep tranquillity by the low lapping of the water.

They stayed by the river for two days. Then Samson and the boy David left the party, with Jonas in charge, and continued north by themselves along the bottom of the wide valley. When the sun began to tilt to the west, and when the land ceased to be level and began to climb upward again, the man and the boy stopped to rest, by the narrow track they had hacked through the underbush. The trees here were as big and tall as elsewhere; but the underbush was less dense, so their going had been faster. They had covered as much distance in this longer half of one day as they had done in the three days before they had come to the

33

clearing. The earth here, when Samson dug his machete into it, was a thick heavy clay, slippery in damp places, hard as rock and cracking in dry places.

The boy David eased the crude knapsack off his shoulders, reached inside and brought out a gourd of water; he handed the water to Samson and watched the movement of the big scar as the man took two measured mouthfuls of water and swallowed. Then it was the boy's turn. He tried to drink as the man had done: two precise mouthfuls and without his lips touching the mouth of the gourd. But a little water did spill over and run down his cheek and on to his chest. He looked quickly at the man and was reassured. The man smiled with his eyes. Then the boy brought out the dumpling Maria had made from pounded tubers and small soft green leaves and had then boiled wrapped in bigger, coarser green leaves. Samson ate his, coarse outside green leaves and all; the boy unwrapped the dumpling and ate only the soft savoury pancake.

The boy's colouring was several shades lighter than Samson's, a hint of freckly redness to it; his hair was more curly than kinky; the rest of him, body, shoulders, arms, legs, had that raw big-boned heaviness of those born to heavy brute labour. Samson had seen children younger than David working in the fields all day under the eye and the whip of the driver. Where had this one come from? Why had he run away? But then Samson wondered about all the others as well. Who they were, where they came from, why they ran. Especially that brown one Sarah, who looked at nobody and talked to nobody and worked with the strength of a man and then stayed by herself. Perhaps, if they reached their destination, they would all talk and know each other. Now it was better not to know; they cannot make you tell what you do not know.

Lying on his back, eyes closed, feeling the sun filtered through tall trees, the boy remembered, in a vague, dreamlike sort of way, another presence a long, long time ago with which he had felt as at ease as he felt with this badly scarred man. It was from that memory that he knew he was called David. That, and a sense of ease; nothing more. Not a face, not a touch, not a voice. He opened his eyes and willed his mind to come away from that distant presence. He decided firmly that this man Samson, who had led them safely could take the place of that distant presence . . . if the slavers don't get them . . . and if he wants.

Samson opened his eyes and sat up.

"Time to move, boy."

"Yes, sir," the boy murmured, liking the softness in the man's voice; liking the fact that it was just the two of them on this journey of exploration.

Then the man and the boy set off on their journey again. They moved much faster in the coolness of the afternoon. The boy pushed himself to keep up with the man. The man eased his pace just a little, not to overtax the strength of the boy. If a man had a son he would want him as willing and as strong as this one. . . . If a man was sure they would not take away his son . . . or whip him . . . or break him.

They journeyed through the afternoon and far into the night. The land climbed steeply now. The moon came up, big and round and full, bathing the land in a soft clear light. In the moonlight they crested a hill rising out of the valley. They could look back now and see all of the broad valley through which they had travelled. Ahead of them, more hills flowed into more valleys, and rose again and fell again; but none as deep as the valley out of which they came. Some of the hills you looked down on, others you looked up to. All green and with gently rounded tops, and with the highest hills farthest away, reaching up to the moonlit skies.

"This is the land!" Samson exclaimed, more to himself than the boy. "If there is water, this is the land! They will not come here. Rest now, boy. When day come we will seek for water."

"Samson," the boy said, and was silent.

The man waited for a long time. Then he said: "Yes, boy, what is it?"

"Nothing. . . . I just thought. . . ."

"Then tell me the thought, boy."

"It is good to be here, with you . . . now. . . ."

"It is good to know. Tired, boy?"

"Yes." How nice to be free to confess it!

"Hungry?"

35

"Yes. . . ." There was a hint of gaiety to it.

"And still good?"

"Yes. . . . Is that what it is to be free?"

"Yes, boy; it is a good feeling even when you are tired and hungry. Now rest. We will need our strength for tomorrow's search."

That night the boy slept close to another human being of his free will, without the fear of being brutally violated. Once, during the night with the moon on his face, a terrible nightmare out of the past made him cry out loud.

The man shook him awake gently.

"Hush, boy. Peace. They cannot hurt you now. Sleep. Samson will look after you."

The boy turned over and went into a deep sleep.

The man was possessed now by an enormous and overpowering anger that would not let him sleep. It had no focus at which it could be directed, nobody, nothing on which to vent it, except life itself, perhaps. The man relaxed as best he could and allowed full rein to the anger and the violence of it. Not till the sun rose again were the terrible forces of that anger spent, and still the man could not sleep. When the boy woke, refreshed, and saw the man's face, a wave of panic shot through him. He had seen people like this after they had been pushed beyond the strength of their body by the driver's whip. He had seen some just lie down and die.

"Samson, sir. Stay here and rest. I will go back for Jonas."

"No, boy."

"You are sick, sir. I know. I have seen it."

"I will not die, boy. It is a sickness of the spirit. It will pass. Do not fret. We must seek for water."

The boy worried but held his peace. They spent the day crossing the hills and walking through the valleys. The next morning before the sun had cleared the Blue Mountain they came on a narrow valley between two hills; and through the thick white mist at the bottom they could hear the sound of water running down from the wooded hills.

"This is the place," Samson said quietly.

They were on comparatively flat, gently sloping land. To their right, rising steeply, was a high hill all by itself. On its crest was a huge flat stone which time and sun and rain and wind had cracked into four pieces. It was all overgrown, as though no human feet had ever walked this way. An air of gentleness hung over the land, over the rolling hills and shallow fertile valleys, and over the deep clear pool in the misty valley.

"This is the place," the man repeated, even more softly.

Then the man and the boy walked down to the water, re-opening the path that another group of now-vanished people had trod when they tried to escape from slavery and the slavers' whips.

The long days of hard work were over at last. It was time to rest. The skies grew black and the air grew heavy, so people sweated while doing nothing. Then the skies opened and the rain fell. But they had prepared well for this. They were comfortable now, and dry, and secure. Samson had driven them, and they had been willingly driven, to be ready before the rain came. First they cleared a stretch of land where it sloped least. Then the women planted the precious seed corn they had carried with them. The earth, once they had cleared and burned the bush to kill the wild thorns, was surprisingly soft and rich, like a well-tended field allowed to lie fallow for many seasons.

"It feel like others grew food here. . . ." Maria once told Samson musingly.

Samson had grunted noncommitally and carried on, always measuring the time available to them against the changing sky.

When the land was clean and the seed planted they made their shelter. The north and south winds were the strongest up here; and when there was change the wind came from the north-east or the south-east. So the shelters had to face west or south-west.

Jonas, supported by sickly Joe, was all for the shelters facing south. South was where any intruders would come from. The women and the boys had no experience of such matters so their views were not sought. Still, Maria and David said they agreed with the leader and were scoffed at by Joe who took pleasure in showing up their ignorance with a few shrewd questions about the weather. In the end Samson exercised his right of leadership and insisted. Jonas gave in very quickly. Joe contained his anger, wandered off down to the pool and was quickly followed by Flo. So it was agreed the shelters would face west, away from the prevailing winds.

The rain started when the cooking place and only three of the planned five shelters had been completed. They gathered in the middle shelter, the biggest of the three. Crude benches and flat stones provided seating. A low fire warmed the place, and gave some light. The smoky smell of scented wood burning was everywhere. The heavy sheets of rain made a steady dull noise on the sloping thatch roof. There was not enough space; they all huddled together, uncomfortably.

"The rain catch us." There was self-reproach in Samson's voice.

"We couldn't do better," Maria protested.

"Yes," Jonas said. "We work hard and you work harder. Couldn't do better."

A chorus of other voices murmured agreement.

"Still, the rain catch us," Samson insisted. He had miscalculated, and he wanted them to know and learn from it. "Should have started the houses two, three days earlier and would be done now." He turned his head and looked at David in the flickering light. "We must be more careful in our plans; check the sun and the wind and the rain so that nothing catch us."

David nodded imperceptibly, and only the silent brown woman seemed to notice the silent communication between the man and the boy who was as big and as broad as a man.

"We will build the other houses when the rain stops," Jonas, misunderstanding, tried to comfort Samson. "Do not fret, bredda Samson."

"Tonight the women will sleep here, all together," Samson said thoughtfully. "Maria will be in control. You, Jonas, will be in control in the other place with Joe and Noname. David will be with me. . . ."

"We have another matter, bredda Samson," Maria said quietly, "So hear me. The journey is over. You have led us to this place. And it is a good place. We can make our lives in freedom here. But there are few of us; not enough to make a village. . . ."

"Others will come," the woman called Belle said.

38

"Perhaps," Maria brushed it away impatiently. "But hear me. We are few and this is our place of freedom. Any who come after us will not have made the journey with us and we must say who can stay and who cannot."

"Good," Jonas cut in.

"Yes," Samson echoed.

"But it is of now we talk," Maria continued. "What do we do tomorrow and the next day? Do we go on as we have been since the start of our journey?" She paused till Samson prompted:

"Talk, woman. What is it you are saying?"

"That's it, Samson. I am a woman and you are a man. We are, all of us, men and women and boys and girls and there is not enough of us to make a village, unless we breed. Down there they made us breed for slaves. Up here, we must breed in freedom to swell our numbers. It is that you must think of, Samson. You are our leader. If we go on as we have on the journey we will die one by one and there will be no reason to the journey. How are we to breed? Who is to breed for whom, and when it is done, how will we raise the children? I have watched you, bredda Samson, and I know these matters are not in your mind. Now they must be. Think about them. Tell us what we are to do."

There was a silence in the thatched hut with the flickering smoky-scented fire. In the silence the heavy downpour suddenly sounded very loud, though still very dull. All about them was the sound of water: the world was wet; only they, in their shelter, were dry and warm. Twice Samson opened his mouth to speak and twice he shut it again, without a sound.

Maria tried to comfort him with her mind and her voice.

"Take time and think, bredda Samson. We have time now. But we must know what to do."

They were all thinking now of what Maria had said. But it was hard to think clearly about something over which, until now, they had no control. Where they came from sex was a transient, casual release of animal urge; or it was careful, selective breeding determined by others to produce and improve slave stock. There was no element of choice; no tenderness; no endearing passion; no warm companionship; no bond made lasting by the shared joy and pain of procreation and the slow unfolding and flowering of

39

another life and another person; no sense of continuity. So it was hard to think; and yet they thought far into the night. Not clear thoughts; not thoughts that could be dressed in words and sent forth to make others understand: but thought as feeling, instinctive, which was the beginning of thought, before the birth even of language.

When the rain finally eased up and a silvery crescent moon appeared, the men and the boys left the women and the girls in the warm hut, all their minds still full of thoughts about breeding.

They began the day's work early, in the first light of the morning, before daylight was properly on the land. There were the young trees to choose and fell for the uprights of the buildings; the younger, more supple ones to be selected for the woven walls; the vast lengths of whiss with which to bind; the mounds of leaf and bark of the trumpet trees to cover the walls; the huge ancient trees to tap and bleed for the flowing white matter which thickened and held things together and kept out the wet. Because of the night's heavy rain, it was wet work, slippery under foot: dangerously slippery when machete had to deal with wet bush. They worked fast, steadily, carefully, without resting, without eating.

Only Maria, Noname and the two girls, Big Mary and Little Mary, were not part of the building gang. Maria taught the two girls how to dig tubers and choose edible green leaves. The boy, also under her instruction, was putting up a shelter in the highest corner of the pig pen, watched curiously by the now tame hog whose size had almost doubled. Maria made a fire, lighting it from the last glowing embers which had kept their hut warm through the night. She packed four clay pots around the fire, half-filled each with clear water from the pool, stoked the fire some more, and continued pounding the tubers as the girls brought them in woven baskets carried on their heads. Every now and then she rejected a tuber as too old and coarse, or as not safely edible. The coarse ones she heaved over her shoulder without looking; they all dropped on the same spot in the hog's pen. The others she stacked carefully on the ground to use as samples in her later instructions to the girls, and everyone else wanting to learn, of what not to use for eating. The water came to the boil. Maria made even-sized dumplings from her mound of pounded tubers, and then dropped them one by one into four pots of boiling water. When all the dumplings were cooked she fished them out of the water with a large wooden spoon and packed them into a leaf-lined straw basket. The boy, meanwhile, had completed the shelter and had made two trips down to the pool for water. His job was to see that all the water containers were always full. On his third trip down to the water Maria called him.

"Here, boy!" and tossed a dumpling in his direction without looking. He caught it deftly and in the same motion put it to his mouth and sank his teeth into it. The taste of it made his stomach rumble out loud.

"I hear you. . . ." Maria said. The boy shuffled off shyly.

When the girls came with their next baskets full Maria tossed them each a dumpling and they ran munching back to work.

From the distance the raucous voice of fat bouncy Belle suddenly rose in song, and came nearer. Maria smiled. That one always sang when she was hungry; they were all hungry now. They had worked through the morning with no food or drink. They all wanted to make sure that the rain would not catch them, that Samson would not reproach himself this time.

The sun was high; the clouds were beginning to build up far out at sea and over the high mountains. She measured the distance of the clouds then looked to where the men were building. The fourth hut was nearly done and there was enough material to complete the fifth. Joe was on the frame of the fifth one. Samson and Jonas were nearly done with the roof of the fourth. That quiet Sarah was packing and sealing in the walls with the bark and leaves and sticky white glue. And as Maria watched, Flo wandered over, seemingly casually, to work with Joe on the last structure. On an impulse, Maria yelled:

"Flo! Come here!"

Flo changed direction and walked more purposefully to where the older woman cooked. Without looking up Maria picked two dumplings from the now full basket, wrapped them in a leaf and held them up.

"Here, for you and him. . . ."

Flo started to protest: they lived by Samson's rules.

41

"Is all right," Maria cut in before the words were formed. "Is all right. The journey done. Is different times now. Take it. . . ."

"T'anks," Flo murmured, took the dumplings, looked furtively to where Samson and Jonas worked, then hurried to where Joe was.

Not long for him, Maria told herself, thinking of Joe.

Samson, who had seen what transpired, paused briefly to look at Maria, then carried on.

Yes, bredda Samson, Maria told herself; time different now.

They finished the last building just after mid-day. Samson was pleased and they sensed it, and felt good.

"Come," Maria called gaily. "Time to eat or rain catch us!"

They ranged themselves about the fire in the green and sunny place, each beside the one or ones with whom he or she felt most at ease. Big Mary and Little Mary; Noname almost instinctively stayed near Maria; Jonas sat on Samson's right, David on his left. Flo sat near Joe, Belle near Flo. Only Sarah received her food and then withdrew from the circle, to a spot just within earshot. Then they ate the dumplings and the savoury greens and washed it all down with cool water. After they had eaten Maria got up, motioned to Noname, and the two wandered off to a clump of dense bush. They returned each carrying a clay pot with a narrow neck. Maria placed her pot in front of Samson and the boy did the same.

"It is a day to feast." Maria remained standing, looking steadily at Samson. "It is for you to say. Taste it and say."

Samson did not have to taste it. He knew what it was.

"Not the children," Samson said. "And not much."

Maria reached down then, took one of the two pots. She pulled the vegetable stopper with her teeth and the thing hissed as it came out. She offered it to the leader. He held up his drinking bowl. She poured some of the stuff; then she did the same for Jonas, then Joe, then the women. Only Sarah turned down her drinking bowl, shaking her head. At last all the adults had it. Samson raised the drink to his lips.

"Wait," Maria said. "The children were part of the journey. Let me mix it with water for them, make it weak. They suffered with us; make them feast with us. Please. David is almost a man. It is

42

better so; or they will feast alone and in secret."

Samson remained quiet for a long time, looking at Maria, then at the children, especially David. He had not thought it would be so hard to know the right thing, to do the right thing.

"Jonas?" he asked for help.

"Follow the woman, bredda. . . ." Jonas said softly. "She know. . . ."

Samson nodded. "All right, woman."

"Come, children," Maria said happily. "Come, David, feast with us."

She mixed for each child a watered-down version of the strong brew, making David's the strongest. The others waited, watching closely, till each child had received his or her drink. Maria did it in the correct order: first David, the eldest; then Big Mary; then Little Mary; then Noname who had, by general consensus, been judged the youngest. When it was all done Maria said: "Now."

Samson raised his bowl till it was on a level with his lips but a good eight inches away; then he tilted the bowl so that some of the drink trickled on to the ground at his feet and sank into the earth.

"This is our land," Samson said quietly.

"Our land," Jonas echoed, repeating the libation of the earth.

"Our land," the others murmured in chorus, each wetting the earth with a few drops of liquor. Then they drank, each draining his or her bowl in one long draught.

They were silent after that, for what seemed a long time. The clouds were darkening over the high mountains; the rain was on its way. Directly overhead, wave after wave of small swift birds passed, going north. The strong drink warmed and relaxed the people.

"What will you call the land?" Maria asked.

Now everybody looked at Samson. But it was Sarah, the one outside the circle, who answered.

"Call it Mount Zion, brother Samson. Like the place to which Moses led the children of Israel out of slavery."

All eyes turned to Sarah now.

"It is in the Bible," Sarah said defensively, sensing the need to explain. "The book from which the preachers teach us, remember?"

43

A few nodded, remembering the preachers and the black book out of which on Sundays they talked about a God of love to people enslaved.

"Mount Zion. . . ." Maria tried it out aloud; feeling it with her mind, testing it.

"But that in the sky," Belle said. "Preacher always talk about a place in the sky where everybody free."

"First you have to dead," Joe cut in bitterly. "Then heaven."

"Mount Zion is not heaven," Sarah said.

"Then where?" Joe asked.

"It is a place like this one."

"With people like us?" Flo wanted to know.

"Yes," Sarah was a little hesitant.

"And this leader. . . ." Maria said.

"Moses," Sarah said.

"This Moses. He lead those slaves to freedom?"

"Black people like we?" Jonas asked.

"Only black people are slaves." Samson sounded as though Jonas was daft: only black people are slaves, not whites; whites are slavers, blacks are slaves.

"I don't know," Sarah said. "The Bible calls them the children of Israel."

"Must be black," Samson insisted. "Where this place?"

"Far away, across the sea." Sarah still sounded uncertain.

"Where they took us from?"

"I born ya," Flo cut in.

"Not your papa; not your mama." Maria dismissed the interruption.

"I think so; the Bible don't say."

"This Bible," Samson was intensely curious now. "It speaks to you like the preachers?"

"I can read it," Sarah said quietly, like one revealing a guilty secret.

"I seen slaves can read," Joe nodded. "House slaves; inside slaves. Is one like that help me run away."

"This place where Moses lead the slaves," Samson clung to his point. "Could be where we come from?"

"I don't know," Sarah said.

44

"That Bible thing don't tell you?"

"I will search it," Sarah said, then clamped her mouth shut.

"You have the thing?"

"Yes, bredda Samson."

"Here?"

"Yes, bredda Samson."

"Bring mek we see it!" Jonas was keyed up with excitement.

Sarah appealed to Samson with her eyes.

"No. Is her thing. We free people now. She will show us if she want to. . . . All right, sister. And this place, this name. . . ."

"Mount Zion," Sarah said, then, impulsively she explained: "I was playmate to the master's daughter and they sold my mother, the woman who mothered me. I stayed in the big house and did everything the little girl did. I learned to read with her and preacher taught me with her. When I became big I was sent back to the slave quarter. When the mistress and the daughter went to where they came from the master wanted to breed me. . . ."

"So you ran away," Maria finished for her.

"Yes." Sarah hesitated long, then added, "From the master and from the slave quarters. Driver tried to breed me and whipped me when I fight against it."

"Enough, woman," Samson said brusquely. "Tell us the name."

"Mount Zion," Sarah said. And now she felt at ease, home at last. She looked about the darkening hills and valleys, then at the small group around the fire who had suddenly become her family. Then she looked at David, half-boy, half-man, and made her own decision. Suddenly, her eyes made four with Samson's and it seemed that he knew what had passed through her mind.

"Mount Zion," Maria said, pointing up to the hill to their right. "That is Mount Zion." Maria waved her arm again, taking in the land on which they sat, the valley below it to their left, and the valley in front of them where the deep clear pool was. "And this is the valley of Mount Zion." She looked to Samson for confirmation.

"We will call this place Mount Zion," Samson said.

In the excited babble that followed the announcement they missed the approaching sound of the rain, and when it came they had to scamper to get food and drink and dry tinder and a glowing ember under dry shelter. Then they retired to wait out the rain, the women and girls in the same hut they had occupied the night before; the men and boys sheltering as they too had done before.

Samson, stretched full-length on his back, tried to grapple with the problem Maria had posed. Three men, five women: how do you divide them? How do you arrange them? Two boys, two girls, easy: David and Big Mary, Noname and Little Mary. But how arrange the men and women? Two for me; two for Jonas; one for Joe. That Flo would do for Joe. But why one for him and two for us? Not right. Two for Jonas; two for Joe, one for me. But that's not right too, and I am the leader. The two girls. That's it. If the big girl is put with the women, there would be two for each. But what of the boys? Little Mary for David. Who for Noname? And free people choose for themselves. . . . What fe do? How fe do it? He drifted off, lulled by the steady beat of the rain on the hut. On the other side of the hut young David snored rhythmically, deeply asleep, utterly spent from the day's efforts.

The rain stopped near morning. Before sunrise Maria and the children had rekindled the fire and prepared the bush-tea; the people came in twos and three to drink their tea and munch a dumpling or two, and then marched off into the bush to carry on with their allotted tasks. Jonas, Joe and David went off to clear a piece of densely forested sloping land for future planting; Flo, Belle and silent Vie went to the already cleared and partly planted cornpiece; Sarah and Big Mary went down into the valley, then westerward, retracing the course of the little river whose waters fed the deep pool. The land sloped gently upwards. Two miles beyond the pool, in a sharp leftward bend they came to the clay bank. Their crude tools were there from other times: bits of broken clay pots, shaped stones, strong sharpened pieces of sticks. They sat on the stones, facing each other, and began the day's work of digging clay, dipping it in the slow-flowing water, rolling and pounding it, then shaping it into the pots and pans and bowls and jars the community used. These two had come here and worked in silence on most days. But this morning Big Mary did not want to work in silence. Since yesterday Sarah had become a figure of mystery and Mary wanted to find out more; but how? Sarah had built up that wall of silence about her; Big Mary knew of no way to penetrate it. She kept looking up, waiting, senses alert.

When all the others had gone, Samson emerged from his hut.

"They have gone." Maria gave him his tea and a couple of dumplings.

"We must talk," he said. "Come. . . ." He waved to the high hill behind them.

"Mount Zion," she reminded him.

He finished his food quickly and they set off on the steep climb up the hill. He used his machete to cut a path; she used a stout staff as support and to beat down thin, dripping branches. They climbed steadily, following the curve of the land; every now and then it seemed they came on patches where the bush was a little easier to clear, the earth a little firmer to tread, as when other creatures had been there. At one point they came on such a clear and easy patch that Maria stopped and looked about.

"Animals here, place clear!"

"It look so, but long time gone."

They continued their climb, and then, suddenly, unexpectedly, they were on the crest. Maria let out a loud "Oooh" of wonder as all the world suddenly lay spread out before her. There it was, the place from which they had run such a long time ago: far down there, beyond the climbing hills, the houses, the trees, the smoke of fire, the ships at sea, and the sea itself; it was all there, laid out in the morning sun. To the left were the mountains; to the right another flat plain running to the sea; and behind, to the north, the near hills, higher than this one, this Mount Zion, blotting out everything else except the sky.

Samson sat on one of the four huge pieces of granite rock. The deep burning anger inside him, which matched the marks which had been burned on his body, and which was all that he could remember of life, subsided; the peace and tranquillity of the place crept into him, pervaded his body and mind; he felt a great calm, a great gentleness.

Maria came and sat beside him on the rock.

"What must we do?" he asked. "I don't know."

47

"I say, give each of the women a place; and in the first year you, the leader, will go to each. The children that are born will carry your name. In the second year the man and woman will decide and the children that are born will carry the name of the father. . . ."

"But me alone in the first year. Why?"

Maria smiled wickedly: "You don't want it? Make Jonas leader! Listen, Samson. The leader must have more children; and if all the women have children for the leader the women and the children look to the leader and give him strength. And when others run away and come here and join us, we, all the women you breed, and their children, will be one family; and the men, Jonas and Joe and young David and even little Noname, will breed from the women you bred or from their children, and we will be the strong family at the centre. We will be the people who found this place and built it. Do it so, Samson."

"Will they agree?"

"Do you agree?"

"I don't know."

A thought flashed across Maria's mind and made her smile. "Tell me, you ever breed a woman?"

"I have seen."

The woman threw back her head and laughed out loud. "Look is one; do is different. I must teach you."

"But the others."

She turned serious instantly. "Let me talk with them. Call them and leave it to me. You agree?"

"What will you tell them?"

"What I told you."

"You think they will agree?"

"It is the only way. . . . Now, you agree to let me tell them?"

"Yes." He still sounded uncertain.

She nodded, ignoring the uncertainty. "I must see to the food," she said. "Is the talk over?"

He nodded, deep in thought, staring down on the distant town.

"Come." She rose and went down. He shook his head and stayed.

Samson could find no flaw in what the woman said. And he had come to trust her, to depend on her as he searched for answers to the many questions he faced as the leader of these free people who had submitted their lives to his guidance. There was no justness, no truthfulness, with those who enslaved them and used them like animals. Up here, as free people, there must be justness, and truthfulness between them. This he must tell them, so he must remember the words with which to tell them. And this land, they must share it with justness. Of this, too, they must talk.

He explored the hill till he knew all its turns and grades. Then he cut his way down a curving sloping ledge till he came on a small cave set in the marl rock; the entrance was overgrown by hard stubborn bush which grew straight out of the rock. It was hard to chop the bush away, but at last it was done, and again Samson looked down, from a slightly lower angle this time, on the town far down on the plain and the endless sea beyond it. Again the sense of others having been here was strongly with him; but not recently, not in a long, long time, or the entrance would not have been so thickly overgrown and the things in the cave all powdery dust, except two flat stones on which those others of another time might have sat. He sat on one of the stones and again that earlier sense of peace and tranquillity overwhelmed him, but even more powerful this time. For a time Samson sat as one in a trance. Then he shook himself slightly, rose briskly and left the enchanting place, making his way back to the crest of the hill, then more briskly, down the hillside.

The rain came earlier that day; the day before it had been a little earlier than the day before that. It would do this every day until the peak of the rainy season, when it would rain all day. Then it would taper off, coming a little later each day until it finally stopped and the hard dry season would be on the land.

Maria spoke to the women in their hut that night. The two girls were included, for they too would soon have to undertake the task of multiplying and perpetuating the numbers of a free people. The women listened in silence and accepted. Choice had never been theirs, matters had been decided for them; and this decision was for the common interest. The only outward sign of concern shown by any of them was Sarah chewing her lower lip.

Then Maria scampered through the pouring rain the short distance to the hut of Jonas, Joe and Noname. The boy was asleep. Jonas sat near the fire, by its glow fashioning sandals from tough but pliable tree bark. Joe lay on his back, head cushioned on his hands, his eyes big in his gaunt face, staring at nothing. He sat up and moved nearer the fire on Maria's signal.

Again she explained the plan but this time she made it sound as though it was all Samson's idea. Then, looking steadily at Jonas, she ended up: "The mother of my mother was the one they carry from Africa. And she told my mother, and my mother told me, that is how they do it. What shall I tell the leader?"

"Let it be so," Jonas said; then he smiled crookedly. "And next year, you and me?"

"You want me fe keeps?"

"Yes. . . ."

"And you, bredda Joe?" Maria asked.

"Is not me him goin' breed," Joe snapped and returned to his bed.

"Don't pay him no mind," Jonas said.

Maria touched the back of Jonas' hand lightly, briefly, then left. Noname had slept through it all.

Samson and David were both asleep. The glow of their little fire was almost out. She shook David lightly and held her finger to his lips as he woke.

"I made a bed in the new hut," she whispered, pointing. "Go sleep there. I stay here tonight."

The big-boned boy rose, naked, and went out into the rain. Then Maria took off her wet ragged dress, dried herself as best she could, and lay down beside the sleeping Samson, trying to get a little warmth from his body and running her hand lightly over the huge scars that stood like ridges on that body. . . . Three times they had taken away the child of her body just as she had got to know it and to love it. This time the child would be hers and free and no one would take it from her. No one. But first she must teach this one who had no knowledge of it. She must teach him the joy that last one had taught her. She went on caressing him, carefully, respectfully, her own desire coming alive again as the man, still half-asleep, stirred in response. She reached down and caressed the man rhythmically. The man woke fully, fully aroused. She continued to caress him, making her body dance against his with provocative little shivers, all the while telling him quietly about those three times. And she told him what to do with the other women and how to do it, because a woman breeds most easily when she is fully aroused and the man and the woman reach their peak at the same time. Those who had tried to breed her roughly or too quickly had never succeeded, only the three who took time and were soft and caressed her body into making willing responses. The man listened, relaxed, grew warm with the woman till he, too, joined in the caressing: feeling her body, the roundness of her buttocks, the fullness of her breast, the hard flatness of her belly. And tenderness for this woman flowered in the man. This was the first one, the first time, and for him, a new beginning. So he held her close in deep motion as the warmth and the tenderness spread through him.

But for all the woman's physical warmth and sexual desire, she received him with a calm, quiet, clear-headed detachment. It was not her first time; the only difference was that this time she had done the choosing and the purpose of the choosing was hers and was clear. She, Maria, would be the mother of this free community; they would make it multiply and grow strong in these hills; and she would supervise it and make sure it was done in the right way. Only when the man's passion exploded in her, did she cry out and lose control, surrendering all thought to the blinding flash of passion that consumed her. . . . When thought and consciousness returned she was utterly spent. She sensed that this was how it was with the man, too. His arm was a dead weight on her shoulder. At some point their bodies had changed position and they lay side by side, but still locked in the embrace that had been part of their passion. She tried to ease the big, heavy arm off her shoulder, moving slowly, not to wake him. But he was awake and moved the arm for her, resting it high up on her hip.

"I will breed no others," he whispered. "Only you."

"It sweet you?"

"You know, woman."

"And I am the first one?"

51

"Yes; and the only one."

"Then hear me good, Samson. You will not have me again until you have had the others. I told you why; it must be so."

"I want only you."

"But you will breed the others?"

"Yes." His voice was heavy with sleep.

She held her peace, feeling him drift into deep sleep, knowing that he would, for all this protesting, do as she wanted; for the power she had over this man, which had grown during the long journey had been made complete this night. The beauty of the unscarred body of Jonas the hunter had stirred her often on the journey. This body, made hard and ugly by the driver's whip, had held no attraction for her. She had known that the leader would have to breed all the women. But after that, she had thought, Jonas was the one; none of the women would be able to pull him away from her even though they were all younger. Now it was different. She would be this one's woman and he would be her man; she would show him the way to be a good leader, and she would let him alone use her body to breed and for easement.

The decision was made. The woman turned her head slightly so that her forehead touched the man's chest. His body smelled like burnt leaves. She closed her eyes.

In the women's hut Sarah was the only one still awake. She knew that Maria would spend this night with Samson and that tomorrow the women would draw lots to choose the next one. It was the dread of this which had kept her awake, making her heart beat so hard she felt it in her head. All night long she had been willing herself into a state of mind that would do the thing which might save her. Now the rain had eased. Now they were all asleep. Now was the time to do the thing.

She rose quietly, went out of the hut and round to the back as though going to the bush to relieve herself. Then she veered to the left and moved quickly and lightly past the back of the hut where Samson and Maria slept. She had helped Maria prepare the place for David. Her heart pounded. She hesitated briefly, then went into the hut; then she froze.

"Who you?"

"It's me, David, Sarah." Her voice felt tight, choking.

"What you want?"

"Nothing . . . I thought. . . ." She could not go on.

"Oh. . . ." Then David's voice changed. "I see . . . come. . . ."

They made love awkwardly, messily, without skill and without satisfaction. Sarah bled profusely which frightened and worried David until she explained it to him. Then, when the rain had stopped completely and the moon had risen, they walked down to the pool in the bright moonlight. He sat on a stone watching while Sarah washed the blood away. The night air was cool and the water was cold so Sarah came out shivering, her skin chilled and bumpy.

"Come," Sarah said and took David's hand and led him partway up the now dark hill they had named Mount Zion. There, in a dry spot under a rocky overhang surrounded by a dense cluster of trees, Sarah showed David her own private place, the place to which she retreated when the day's work was done and she was free to be on her own. The others knew of this place; they knew it was where Sarah could be found after the day's work, but would only go there by her invitation which, till now, was never made. This, for them, was the outward and visible expression of freedom which did not exist in the slave village or the slave barracks where anybody could, at any time, enter anywhere. Slavery meant no privacy: slave master, driver, could enter anywhere any time. Sarah kept her treasures in the private place: the book she read from when alone; the special pots she had made; the beautiful flowers and leaves she collected daily. Some she had transplanted to make a flowering garden on a piece of level ground by the side of the overhang. There, in her private place, they tried again. It was less messy than the time before, less frenzied and, for David, more pleasurable, more satisfying. But, for Sarah, it was the absence of pain, and the sense of a flowering tenderness in David, that made it rewarding the second time around. She had to bind him to her for passion would come; bind him to her and bear only for him: forsake all others and go only with him.

David, for his part, was discovering the joys and glory of having a woman of his own. The fear when he first saw the blood had now been turned into a bursting pride in his own manhood; pride that this beautiful woman – both Jonas and Joe had said she was the most beautiful woman in the group – should want him, and want to bear his children.

The big-boned boy became a man and all through what remained of the night the woman used her body and the words from her book to nurture his newly aroused passion and pride of manhood.

As the first light appeared in the eastern sky, they woke and made love once more. When it was over, drifting into a sleep of utter exhaustion, Sarah knew with quiet certainty that she would bear David's child. They were bound together now; and now she might do the things that were in her book. They slept deeply.

They woke to the sound of the horn calling the group to the main meal of the day. The sun sat high in a cloudless sky. The greater part of the day's work would have been done by now; after eating, any further work would be light. David and Sarah had slept right through the work-day at its peak.

Sarah woke first, touched David, and he woke. They lay in silence for a while, listening to the receding echoes of the horn as the sound travelled over the hills and into the valley.

"We must go down," she said, turning her head quickly to read David's face. What she saw reassured her. He was calm, not frightened or worried as she feared he might be. She sat up and touched his chest. He sat up and touched her breast. A small smile of satisfaction tugged at the left corner of her mouth.

"We must go down," she repeated. "They will be vexed."

"Because of the work?"

"No. Because of us. This is not Maria's plan."

"No matter. It is our plan; it is your plan for us."

"They may punish us." She looked steadily into his eyes, willing him to look into hers. "They may beat us and make us promise."

He thought about it and she felt the resolve build up in him, slowly and steadily, over many minutes. Then he said:

"No," very firmly, and again: "No!"

We are ready now, she told herself; no longer afraid or worried. They dressed and then, hand in hand, went down to where Maria presided over the food.

The others saw them from a distance. They looked at each other, then at Maria, then at Samson, then again at Maria. Samson stared for a while at the two coming down, then returned to his food and ate without looking up. The others followed his example. They all knew what had happened, had known since early morning when Noname had gone to wake David and found the empty hut with the bloodstained bedding. He had called Maria and everything had become clear. Now they waited for the two, all pretending an indifference which none felt.

At last the two stopped just outside the circle of the eating group. They stood side by side, close enough for shoulders to touch, for arms and hands to brush against each other with every movement.

Maria finished eating, looked up at the two, then looked at Samson.

"Shall I speak?"

Samson nodded: "Speak, woman."

Maria stared steadily at Sarah, using the strength of her mind to force Sarah to look away. It would be easier then. Sarah returned Maria's steady stare.

"You have broken the rules we all agreed to. Why?"

"I did not wish to be part of the breeding," Sarah said.

"You said nothing when we agreed."

"I was afraid."

"So you turned his head."

"I turned my own head," David cut in.

"Who lead who?" Samson asked.

"I did," Sarah said. David's hand tightened on hers to the point of pain. Then, as suddenly, it relaxed.

"I did," David said.

"They mock us!" Maria cried angrily. She closed her eyes, bent her head, waited for the flash of anger to pass. "Hear me, Samson; hear me, all you. They break the thing we agree, then they mock us and our leader. 'I did,' she say; 'I did,' he say. Let it be so. They both lead each other to break what we agreed. And if they can do it, why not you?" She looked at Jonas. "Or you?" She looked at Joe. "Or you?" She looked at each of the women in turn. "Or me? Why not all of us? And if we break what we agreed then everything will die and we will be divided. So I say they cannot stay here again. They must leave us to live with what we agreed; they must go. . . ."

"It hard," Jonas said softly.

"Yes, it hard," Maria said. "It will be harder for all of us if they do not go. Each one will look on them say, why not me."

"Punish them and make them stay," Joe suggested. "Take her away from him."

"No!" David shouted. "No punishment! No one touch her; no one take her from me!"

"She just a woman like any woman," Belle laughed mockingly at David. "Same hole; same everything. Try and see, bet me do it better than she!"

"Stop that!" Maria tried to sound sterner than she felt.

Flo looked speculatively at Sarah.

"Think he breed you?"

Sarah nodded.

"Then give over the child to bredda Samson when it come." She looked to Maria to see how she would take the idea. "Could still be part of the family."

"And tomorrow you will want to do the same," Maria said.

Flo looked quickly at Joe then down at the ground.

Samson, whose mind had withdrawn to some distant private place of his own, came out of his reverie and looked at David and Sarah in turn.

"You will not live by what we agreed?"

Sarah straightened herself: "I will not breed with anyone but David."

"Will you give me the child to make a strong family? Maria will care and love it."

"If they stay others will want to do what they did," Maria insisted. "They must go, Samson."

Jonas nodded sadly: "The woman is right, bredda Samson."

"Better they go," Flo said suddenly. "Me go do same thing if they stay."

"Will you give me the child?" Samson repeated.

"No," Sarah replied.

Samson looked at David.

"She said 'No'," David said.

"Then let them go," Samson said with mingled grief and anger. "There is land up there," he pointed to the western end of the valley of Mount Zion. "And there is water. Let them go there. They will not live by what we agreed so we must cast them out. Let them go, now!"

Samson rose abruptly and walked briskly away, in the direction of the hill they called Mount Zion. They watched him go, then gradually dispersed, none looking at the two who had just been cast out of their community.

At last there were only Maria, Sarah and David.

"David is hungry," Sarah said.

"Then eat before you go." Maria hesitated over her pots then made up her mind. Quickly, deftly, she made up a parcel of food, wrapped in green leaves, tied with wiss. Sarah accepted the food without a word. Maria watched them in silence after that; she watched them eat, then gather their few belongings. Then she watched them climb to what had been Sarah's private place and come down a little more laden. Then she watched the two walk westward, along the bank of the watercourse in the deep valley between the two hills. Then, as the rain came she climbed the hill to find Samson and give him comfort.

There was no sleep for Sarah and David that night; no corner of the bush where they could escape the rain. After hours of searching for shelter they gave up and huddled together on the soaked earth at the base of a huge tree, wide awake, cold and uncomfortable, waiting out the rain. When the rain stopped, near morning, they continued their journey. The sun rose and warmed the wet land. They took off their wet clothes, tied them to a long slender post which David carried on his shoulder, and kept walking, naked, through the land. There was no person to see their nakedness, no need to hide their nakedness. They were out of the long narrow valley now, the settlement of Mount Zion out of sight behind the last hill they had topped. As their bodies warmed their spirits returned from the deep protective distances into which they had withdrawn; they became consciously aware of each other again, alive, caring. They looked at each other with seeing eyes now, aware once more of their nakedness and of the physical thing between.

"Water must be there." David pointed to where the sloping land seemed to end, hemmed in by another western hill. To himself, he thought, if it's not there, then we're in worries.

Sarah saw a huge dry washed stone and made for it.

"Let us rest."

They sat on the stone and ate some of the food Maria had given them and washed it down with water from David's gourd. When they had eaten David insisted that they move on. Sarah wanted to stay a while longer; her body ached from the wet and the cold and all the walking and all the passion of the night before last. But David insisted; they had to find a place and build a shelter before the rain came; there would be time for rest after that. So they went on down into the bed of the valley and came upon the water. This was a round valley, not long and narrow as the valley of Mount Zion. The land sloped less steeply. The water was trapped in a rocky place in its northern corner. Above the water, to the west of it and with the gentlest of gradients, was a wide stretch of land.

David hurried ahead of Sarah; he climbed the rocks and went across to the flat land and disappeared into the bush. Sarah sat in the sun, on the edge of the water, resting and waiting. They had found their place and her mind was at ease. The only noise was the sound of the birds loud in the nearby bushes, and the sound of water. Then she heard the hiss and clang of David's machete.

"I found the spot," he called. "Come see!"

She made sure their belongings were secure, chopped some bush to cover them, then crossed the rock wall above the water to join David. She realized he had remembered her private place at Mount Zion.

The hill, of a very hard, very dark slatey rock, rose sheer behind the wall along which she had walked to get to him. Where David was the rock caved inward, making a natural shelter.

"Here," David said, turning in a circle in the small area he had cleared.

"Yes, David, yes!" She wanted to hug and make love to him, any way to please him. "Yes, David!" Then she raised her machete and swung at the bush. She would please him! She would help him clear the land! They would work together, to hasten the work and lighten the task. Tomorrow she would go back to woman's work; today she would work like a man. She swung her machete again, all her aches and pains and weariness forgotten for the moment. Then she caught the rhythm of the swinging sound of David's machete and tried to pace herself by it. At first she tried to match his two strokes for one, but it was too much; so she adjusted it. Three strokes from David and she joined him on the fourth. One, two, three, then four! They worked steadily for nearly two hours. They bypassed the huge trees, clearing only the undergrowth; they cleared a good stretch of land, making it possible to live and move and work and grow food between the huge trees. Later, David would fell some of the bigger trees to use for building a proper home and to clear more of the land. For the present what they had done was enough, a good beginning. They built their first hut between three tall trees, the sheer rock wall sheltering it on the west from which no prevailing wind threatened; the slope of the land protecting it from the north and the south; and the opening facing east; and the water was nearby.

When they had done David and Sarah went deeper into the bush and returned with huge piles of leaf and bush bark. Some of the healing leaves David wetted and wrapped around Sarah's torn and blistered hand. They ate what remained of the food Maria had given them, and then lay down in their shelter and slept. They did not hear it when the rain came; they did not know it when the rain stopped. They slept through it all, warm, dry, worn out; they had found their place, made their home.

Samson sat on the highest point of Mount Zion, on one of the huge fragments of the enormous rock time and the elements had ripped to pieces. This high hill was a place of lightning; he had seen the lightning at work up here; he had seen it strike dead, like a flashing sword of fire, a huge and ancient tree. Time had been kind to Samson. His face had lost its gauntness, his near-black skin glowed with the good health which comes of abundant nourishment; even the scars on his body seemed softened and reduced by time.

Many years had passed since their coming to the valley of Mount Zion; good years they had been. Only the casting out of David and Sarah was the painful blemish on these years. But Noname, grown to young manhood now, had found David and Sarah in one of his wanderings and had reported that they were well, in a good place with water, and had bred three children with one on the way. One day, Samson told himself again, he would go to them and give them a chance to make their peace; what was done had to be done. Maria was right about that. . . . Yes, he had been right. He could see the faint, small, distant movement of people in the first light of morning. What had impelled him to climb to this point so early in the morning? What had made him so restless last night? A foreboding of this? Soon now, as soon as he could see them more clearly, could make out who or what they were, he would have to hurry down to join the others at the spot where the advantage would be with them if they had to fight. . . . If we have to fight. . . . If we have to fight. . . . He knew the others were in their appointed places. Only the girl was back at the settlement guarding the seventeen little children, ages ranging between seven years and nine months, that they had force-bred mostly in the first and second and third years. Samson had fathered all three of Maria's children; Flo had bred twins, a boy and a girl for him shortly after Maria's first child. Then Vie, who could not speak, had become part of Maria's household; Maria had encouraged him to breed her and a child had been born for each of the first three years. Belle had bred him a girl as loud as herself. And Big Mary had bred him a boy. Big Mary had been young and difficult and unskilled and Maria had to help and force them both. So ten of the seventeen children were Samson's.

Jonas had then taken over Belle and Big Mary as his women and they had each borne him two children and were now each carrying. And as she had done for Samson, Flo had bred twins for Joe the first time, and a single one the second time and was now so big it looked like she was going to have two more for Joe the third time. Instead of dying, as Maria had expected, Joe grew stronger and less "facety" with his chat. Only Little Mary had not yet reached the time for breeding.

There had been a small fuss between Samson and Jonas over Maria. After the first breeding Jonas had wanted Maria to move in with him, had even tried to force her, and Samson, seeing it, struck him to the ground. During that time there was a bad spirit between Samson and Jonas. So they ceased eating together as a group; and since the time of eating together was also the time of thinking together and talking together and planning together and feeling together, all that was lost. It lasted a time and then Maria put an end to it. One day when the women came to the cooking place at the end of the day's work to collect the food to take to their huts they found Maria had none; when the women returned to tell their men, they all came to the cooking place to find out what had gone wrong. Maria waited till the angry, hungry voices were stilled, then she spoke to them of her own anger. Why should she cook for all of them, mind the children for all of them, if they were no longer one family, if they no longer shared words and feelings with each other? She reminded them of how this had come about. She reminded them they had cast out David and Sarah to ensure the unity and the growth of the family tree. If that was what they wanted they had all better separate. She would cook only for Samson and the children that were Samson's. Samson would have to work the fields alone to provide for her and all his

61

children; each man would have to work alone to provide for the women and children who were his, and each woman for the man and children who were hers. "There will be no morning sport to clear the land and make the work easier; no one to help a man bring down the tough old trees. Each alone. Is that what you want?"

It was then that Samson and Jonas looked at each other and the anger left them. . . . But what would it have been like if they had separated and each family had gone its own way? If he and Maria and the little children had been alone now and those he was watching were coming, what would they have done?

Those who were coming were now near enough for him to make out individual figures: three people and a string of animals. The biggest animal came first, followed by two smaller ones, all carrying people, then three smaller animals, carrying packs.

Samson left his look-out point and hurried down the hillside to join the others. They were into the dry season and patches of the hillside land that they had cleared by fire looked bare and dry. Underfoot the path had become firm, easy and with no growth after long and regular use. The hills about Mount Zion, and the valleys into which they flowed, were now clearly marked with many such footpaths used regularly by the little community. The section of hillside near the settlement from which they chopped and collected wood was a bare patch of rock face which grew bigger with the passage of time. Each time the heavy rain came the topsoil on the bared patch was washed down with the water that flowed into the valleys.

Breathing hard because of his great weight, Samson came to where the others waited. It was a point at which one valley led into another, narrow, with the hills separating the two valleys becoming gently sloping ledges overlooking the passageway. Joe, still very skinny but much less sallow and more wiry-looking, flanked by Maria and his woman Flo, was in command of one ledge. A huge mound of rocks, packed so they could easily be released as an avalanche, was his main weapon. And each of them had a worn-down but razor-sharp machete. Jonas, his women; Belle, a fully developed and spreading to fat Big Mary, and the mute Vie from Maria's household, were similarly armed and positioned. Samson stopped in the passageway immediately below the two ledges. The people on the ledges were not visible. His voice rose softly. Sound carries in these valleys. "They coming soon now. Is three and animals. I will meet them here. You know what we do if is trouble. . . ."

Maria whispered: "Take care, you hear."

It warmed him all over; a gentle smile passed over his face.

He half-leaned, half-sat on a rock outcropping, sharp machete in hand, body and mind at full alert.

The best part of an hour passed. They waited in silent patience. The sun burned hot on the dry land. There was a sharp dryness to the air. No breeze blew. Then the strangers topped the ridge leading out of the lower valley and came fully into sight: the one on the big animal leading the way. A mule, Samson thought, a big mule; the others, small donkeys. The three people all wore broad-brimmed straw hats which shaded their faces from the hot sun. . . . Why hadn't we thought of that? Samson wondered. Instead of using leaves and wiss to cover our heads, weaving dry grass and straw. But inside he knew why: all the things which reminded him of the days of his bondage had been wiped out of his mind. Now, the coming of these strangers forced him to remember they had been slaves who had run away. And slaves can be returned to their masters and slaves can be punished. The scars on Samson's body came alive and the tranquillity he had known in these quiet hills and valleys left him and the memories, and the threats, and the fears of the past again possessed him. With a huge act of will he brought them all under control. This time, he knew, he would die rather than be taken into slavery again. . . .

Now the strangers had reached the bottom of the shallow valley and were climbing the slightly sloping land up to the passageway to the next valley where Samson and the others waited. Samson and the others could see the people clearly: a man and two women; a mule and five donkeys. This they could handle, whatever else had to come later: a man, and two women and their animals – and black as them. . . .

Samson moved into the middle of the narrow pathway, showing himself, and waited. When they came within calling distance the man on the mule raised his right arm; his animals came to a stop.

"Morning bredda," he called in a husky voice.

63

The sun had passed the high point of morning.

"Morning," Samson called, a question mark in his voice.

"We come in peace," the man said. "The animal say there is water in these hills."

"It smell our water," Samson called back. "This is our land."

"Then give us to drink and we will move on; we will pay you in return."

"Then come," Samson called, relaxed a little now, but still on guard, watching the approach of the man and two women and their animals. It would be good to have animals like those. . . . Perhaps they could exchange some of their corn for one of those.

The man on the mule pulled up a few yards from Samson and dismounted. He was small, wiry, very black, with a lined old face and a strong young man's body. Samson towered over him. Now, the others came down from their ledges to surround and examine the strangers. The two women were much younger than the man; one in her late twenties, the other in her middle teens.

"They call me Robert," the man said. "When I was a slave the one who owned me, and them," he gestured with his head to the women, "was named Mr Bagley; so I am Robert Bagley, and this one," indicating the elder woman, "is Lena Bagley, and that one is Eliza Bagley."

Samson went through the ritual of introducing his people, in order of status in the community. He ended: "So is water you want. Then what? Where you going?"

Something the man had said bothered Jonas, so he cut in: "How you get away?" He looked pointedly at the laden donkeys.

"Then you don't know," the man said.

"What?" It was a chorus of voices.

"Slavery done," the man called Robert said quietly. "Done many months now; nearly a year." He looked up into Samson's eyes. "No runaway has to fear again. It's all done. Many people are moving into the hills. After the English King free us they ask us to stay on the estates and on the plains and work for money as free people and learn a trade: some agree to stay; but more leave and go into the hills."

"Fe true?" Maria whispered in wonder,

Flo remembered that first child they had taken from her; her eyes filled with tears.

"So nobody can take us back," Jonas said.

"Nobody," the man said. Then he smiled at Jonas. "I took these things from the place of the Bagley who had been our master. They kept us working as slaves for many months after the king made us free. When we found out about it the man and his driver ran away and left us; and the slaves took what they wanted from the place to pay for what had been done. We three were the last houseslaves to leave; we took these animals and things and decided to find a place in the hills. There are many moving into the hills and some will reach here soon. Now you know."

"It over!" Joe exclaimed. "It over! I can visit Kingston now!"

They looked at each other in wonderment; they embraced each other; they laughed and they cried all at the same time. They had been free for more than seven years now; but it had been a stolen freedom with recapture and punishment always possible. While they were runaway slaves those, both black and white, who traded in the capture and return of runaway slaves, were a constant threat. Every time there were signs of the appearance or the approach of strangers, they were conscious of this danger. This was why they had tried to blot out of their memories all that had happened before they escaped to this place. Now the threat of return to that past was over; now, at last, they were free to remember the pain, the humiliation, the degradation.

"I will never go down there," Samson said harshly. "Never!"

It will come out now, Maria told herself; he will be at peace and we will have a good life in the valley of Mount Zion. Aloud, she said: "Come, let us go home. Let us welcome the strangers and give them water to wash and drink. And tonight we will have a feast to our freedom! Come."

They led the strangers over the hills and through the valleys to their home.

Samson, Jonas and Joe got gloriously drunk that night. Maria's brew had been fermenting in the warm earth for a long time. Now it went to all their heads in celebration of an emancipation that was already almost a year old. Everybody was loud, tipsy, happy.

After a few drinks even the subdued strangers, for whom emancipation was no news, joined in the heady celebration. They talked at the top of their voices; they embraced each other; they feasted prodigiously on Maria's dumpling and vegetables, which, this night, was accompanied by pieces of fat salted pork – corned pork – contributed by the strangers.

At first the talk had been subdued as the stranger, Robert Bagley, told them of all that had happened and of which they were ignorant. . . . The great slave rising in the west; the hunting and the killing of the slaves. The drying up of the riches of the slave masters. The growing numbers of those they called the Free Coloureds, and those freed slaves that were free even before the king freed them all. But it was hard to be serious for long. This was the night of freedom. No more fearing; no more waiting for the militia or the hunters. . . .

So they drank and shouted and sang far into the night. Then, because it was a warm clear night, and because they were free, they fell asleep one by one, where they were, lying in a wide circle around the eating place under the big moon and the stars. Only the children, and a few of the women, slept in the huts on that first night of their knowledge that slavery was over.

Early the next morning they came together, still caught up in the wonder of their delivered freedom, and planned for the days ahead. As usual, Maria guided the planning, making it sound like Samson's planning and looking to Jonas for support whenever some matter was in doubt. And so, while they drank their bush tea, they agreed that they would continue to work the land in common, sharing the rewards of their labour. Samson would continue to be the leader, Maria the mother of the community. But now there was no need always to be together for their safety and protection; no need always to be on the alert in case they had to abandon this place quickly to seek another. This place would now be that permanent home Maria had talked and dreamt of: for them and for their children and their children's children unto the generations yet to be born. So now, instead of huts, they would build homes that were strong and lasting; they would fell trees and cut stones. . . . And they would build a place of worship,

Maria suggested tentatively. But the hardness in Samson against anything connected with those who had enslaved them was so strong, Maria's suggestion was left to die. Each man and the people of his household would choose a piece of land on which to build a house, with enough yardspace to grow family food. Samson would be the first to choose his land and his house would be the first built; then Jonas; then Joe, Noname now was big enough for his manhood, too, to be recognized and for him to have his own house. So it was agreed and they dispersed to do the day's work.

Robert Bagley had brought many wondrous things: a dozen new machetes, half a dozen axes, four digging bars, several hammers, two reels of wire, several pliers and two small caskets of nails. There were, too, several bales of the heavy canvas-type material out of which slave clothes had been made. The women had brought all the clothing they had found in the abandoned slave master's house.

On the third morning after their arrival Robert Bagley joined Samson, Jonas and Joe as they climbed the sloping land leading to the big trees above the deepest end of the pool. Bagley was not used to this type of terrain, nor to walking distances as easily and quickly as these men. When they reached the place he was out of breath and sweating profusely, so he sat on the ground, his new, unused, unsharpened machete beside him, and watched them fell one, two, three, large tall trees before they paused for breath. By then he had recovered.

"Sorry I'm not helping," Bagley said. "Not used to this kind of work."

"S'all right," Samson smiled at him.

"You'll learn." Joe was friendly, reassuring.

"Take time for body to get used to this work," Jonas put in.

Then they returned to their chopping, and in a little over an hour of steady, rhythmic chopping, they brought down three more enormous trees. Bagley was fully rested by now and he tried his hand at a smaller tree.

"It need to sharpen," Joe advised. "Find a hard rockstone and rub so," he demonstrated.

"Can we stay with you?" Bagley blurted out suddenly, staring at Samson. "Give us a piece of land and we will give you half of what we have."

Samson straightened up. "Half the animals?"

"Yes," Bagley said.

"The big one in it?"

"The mule? Yes, Mass Samson; but it doesn't suit you. The mule can't breed. We have two jacks and three jennies; they will breed."

"We share things here," Jonas said quietly. "You heard. Everything."

"Everything?" Bagley sounded worried and uncertain.

Jonas looked quickly from Samson to Joe, his suddenly twinkling eyes telegraphing a message which both picked up.

"Everything." Jonas sounded very solemn now.

Bagley hesitated for a long time: "The women?"

"The women, too," Jonas said.

Bagley searched the ground, his head swaying from side to side as though looking for some small specific object. "Then we must leave." Bagley's voice was heavy with depression. He had so much wanted to stay here. There had been a strong sense of goodness and security among these people: something he and the two women had not found in any of the other groups they had encountered on their journey.

"Because of the women?" Samson asked quickly, Jonas' humour forgotten, his mind on David and Sarah.

"Yes," Bagley said, getting up and turning to walk down to the huts. "I promised them I would not let any man force them again. For them that is freedom."

"And you will fight for them?" Jonas was seriously curious.

"If I must," Bagley replied and began to walk away.

"Wait!" Samson said. "You can stay if the others agree."

Bagley paused and looked back at the big man. "And the women?"

"That your business," Samson said. "Jonas just running a joke."

"Yes," Jonas said.

"Not a good joke," Bagley said, hurrying away.

"Bredda Bagley!" Jonas called.

"Mek him go," Samson said, watching the little man's quick movement down the hillside.

"Him vex," Joe said casually.

"But him stay," Samson said. Then added: "If we agree."

"Yes, him stay," Joe said.

Jonas felt he had misread the little man, gone wrong somewhere.

"Why him so vex? Just because me run joke?"

"Because him frighten," Joe said. "A man doan like to be frightened."

"But he's no coward," Jonas murmured.

One of Samson's very rare smiles flitted across his face.

"That's why he's frighten, bredda Jonas."

They returned to the task of felling trees, pausing only occasionally for a brief silent period of rest.

Bagley approached Maria among her cooking pots as she prepared the day's main meal. His female companions seemed to have slipped into the community routine. Lena had gone off to the fields with the other women. Eliza had joined Little Mary in taking care of the large brood of children; their voices at play carried clear through the valley from a point where the river flowed shallowly toward the deep pool. From the steeply sloping land above the pool, came the rhythmic thud of metal against hard wood as the men felled the trees.

The community had, over the years, turned both the cooking place and the eating place into a comfortable area with a huge thatched roof on posts. The eating place had one long table – long enough to accommodate all the adults and the children – and long benches along both sides of the table. Maria had a special seat with back supports from which she presided over her pots. The once-wild hog's pen had been enlarged and enlarged again as litter after litter made the community abundantly rich in hog's meat. Just beyond the hog's pen, and manured by the waste from it, was Maria's lush kitchen garden of green vegetables; wild spinach, acid little berry-like tomatoes, pumpkins, cho-cho on a wooden frame prepared by Noname, and other edible plants carried by the birds or the wind and carefully selected and nurtured by Maria, assisted by Noname and Little Mary, who seemed to have absorbed some of Maria's uncanny feel for finding edible things and making them grow.

Bagley drew nearer, slowed down and paused hesitantly.

"Sister Maria. . . ." He had quickly realized that this one was key. "Can I talk with you?"

She looked up, a darting, birdlike flash of her eyes over his face, reading his eyes, reading his mind; then she looked down at her work, blank, waiting, her face an expressionless mask. Bagley remembered how it had been when you had to be a blank in the masters' presence so that they would not notice your black presence even while you served their needs.

"Did you talk with Samson?"

"Yes. And the other two; Jonas and the one called Joe."

"It is as they say," Maria said. "As Samson says. He leads us."

"I asked him to let us stay."

He paused but she showed no reaction. He felt forced to go on: "He said we can stay if the others agree."

"If Samson said so then it is so."

"Please."

Maria stopped working, folded her hands in her lap, turned her eyes fully on his face and waited.

Still the blank mask, he thought. He said: "Jonas ran a joke about how you share everything, even the women."

Maria's eyes came to life; a crooked smile flitted across her face, then she was blank again.

". . . Samson said that part was a joke. I want to ask you. . . ."

Maria told him how they had made their family. "That is done now. We do not need your women. If Samson say you can stay, you can stay. But you are not part of the family; not part of those of us who came together to find this place and who are now part of the leader's family. Is that what you wanted from me?"

"Yes. And one more thing. You yourself, will you let us stay?"

"If Samson say."

"But you yourself," the man insisted.

"I do not know," Maria said coldly. "I do not know you or your women. I do not know what kind of people you are. If the others say you can stay I will accept it."

"Please, sister. I will not stay if you do not say you want us to stay. I know the power is with the men but you are the mother of this place and the women and the children, while they are growing and after, and even the men, will all be guided by you without knowing it. If you do not want us, they will feel it."

"You will respect Samson always?"

"I will. We will."

"And his children?"

"And his children." The man hesitated. "Sister, I am tired and not very young and I need a place where we can live in peace. I can see you are good people here, and peaceful."

"You cannot be part of our family."

"I know that."

"And you will live by our rules even if you do not like them?"

"I promise that. I will be loyal to Samson and I will be loyal to you who are loyal to Samson."

Maria returned to her work among the cooking pots. Bagley remained seated on the huge log near the fire, not knowing what more to say but certain that without this woman's blessing it would not be worthwhile their putting down roots in this beautiful and peaceful place. Maria reviewed the talk between herself and this stranger. Did he really want to stay here for the simple reason he gave? A clever one, this, a man who thought clearly and sought to make friends where he thought power and influence were to be found. But is that so wrong? Is not that precisely what she herself had done? And if he wants to protect his women, is that, too, not precisely what Samson would do or what she herself would do for her man and her children and her household?

"What did you do down there?" she asked abruptly.

These people don't want to remember being slaves, he told himself.

"I was in charge of the big house. I looked after things."

"Then you can read and figure?"

"A little. Lena is better at reading."

"Can she teach the children?"

"Yes. And I can build things and start a store later, when more people move to this part of the hills. You will need somebody who can manage them."

He's rushing me now, Maria thought; he's trying to push things. "I will talk with Samson about it," she said coldly. "Please leave now, I want to get on with the food."

Bagley rose to go; "One more thing, if I may?"

"All right, what?" This is the main thing, Maria thought; the thing that was at the back of his mind all the time.

"When others come here and ask for land, how will you deal with them? Will you just give them land in return for half of what they have? And what if they have nothing?"

Maria suppressed her excitement, her face more masklike than ever. "What should we do? What is in your mind?"

Bagley sat down on the log again. He would not look at her now; would not do anything to provoke her suspicion or hostility. He picked up a long straight stick, lowered his eyes to the ground and doodled symmetrically on the dry ground, making the outlines of a fenced-in place with marker posts and a house on a rising.

He said: "I was thinking it would be good for the family to let the strangers use the land in return for what they call a rent; they will give a portion of what they grow every crop time, or a portion of what they have made. This way they will know the land is not theirs and they must pay and go on paying to be on it. Whatever a man grows a certain amount will come to the family. Some of it can be stored; some can be carried down to Kingston to sell or to trade for the things you need up here. This way Samson's power, the family's power, will remain and grow stronger, and you will decide who and how many people can come here."

"And you?" Maria asked softly.

"If you let me, I will plan and keep the records for you; I will keep the stores."

"Like the driver?"

"No; not like that. Like the bookkeeper of slavery days, but not robbing you, for you yourself will be here to see."

"And why will you do this? Why for us? Why not for yourself?"

Now at last he looked up, looked straight at the woman, allowing her to see the irritation on his face and hear the impatience in his voice. "I *am* doing it for myself, woman! Can't you see that? Look at me! Can I find a place like this by myself, me and two women? Can I build it up to this and then force others who come later to accept my rules and pay me rent? You and your men, you and your family, you are strong; you can make others do as you want." He waved his arm in a wide arc as though to embrace all the quiet landscape. "We made our journey to find a place like this for ourselves, but we, one small man and two weak women, we cannot do what you have done."

But *they* have done it, Maria told herself; just the two of them. Her mind was suddenly so full of David and Sarah she did not hear all of Bagley's words. But no matter, she understood him now. She would let him stay and she would use him to strengthen Samson and the family. She would use his smart brains to serve their interests. She had the measure of this one now: a smart one with a big brain, who can plan things but not bold enough, with not enough heart, for great ventures. . . . Such make good servants and managers. They are not to be feared for they have no stomach for the challenges to power. He would never take or try to take what was Samson's. A little stealing, perhaps, but no more.

Bagley realized the woman's attention had strayed. He also realized that there was now no longer need to go on talking. He was, suddenly, absolutely certain that she would let them stay and that the plan he had laid before her was how it would be. A great sense of relief and peace settled on Bagley's spirits. He tried to choke back the tears of joy that came unbidden to his eyes. You must not show tears in the presence of this stern woman; she would not understand a weeping man. . . .

He rose abruptly and walked away toward the hut which had been assigned to them. The mule and the donkeys were tethered and grazing a little distance from that hut. All their precious goods and possessions were stacked in a high neat pile by the entrance to the hut. In the long journey safeguarding their possessions had meant survival, had been Bagley's main preoccupation. Some of

73

their things had been stolen on the way whenever they encountered other people. At one point Bagley and the women had to fight off a would-be donkey thief. But since they came to this place he had not been concerned about the security of their possessions. These people would not touch them. Bagley bustled among their things, unpacking some, rearranging others, searching, until he found the long rifle tied in its canvas cover, and the wooden box of rifle bullets. He would not need this now; it would be his present to Samson, and he would show Samson how to use it. If only Lena were here with him now; someone to talk to and to tell of the lifting of the burden from his spirits.

Maria took the small horn that hung from the post nearest her seat. She put it to her lips and let out a cracked, bleating sound to summon the community.

"Mass Bagley!" Maria shouted. "Come gi me a hand!"

The children were the first to come trooping up from their playfield down by the dry riverbed. The others followed the children in, first to wash by the large communal water trough, then to seat themselves at the long table for the main meal of the day.

During the meal Maria quietly told Samson of her talk with Bagley. Bagley, for his part, ate with his head close to Lena's, whispering to her all that had transpired that day. The woman nodded from time to time and seemed relieved. At one point, on the pretext of getting more food to the table, Maria singled out Lena to help her and Noname. The two women talked hurriedly while dishing up and lingered to go on whispering for a while afterwards.

When the meal was done Samson rose and made a sound deep in his throat. Everyone became silent.

"The strangers who came among us are asking to stay with us. Jonas and Joe and I have talked about it. And I say they can stay if they pay us rent and follow our laws. . . ."

"I say so too," Jonas said, though the rent part was new to him.

"Yes," Joe added.

"They cannot be part of the family," Maria said.

"We understand that," Bagley said. "We will serve the interests of your family."

"It is to their suit," Maria said. "We will give them a home and peace. And it is to our suit. Mass Bagley will help to look after our business, like a storekeeper and a manager; and Miss Lena teach our children." Maria looked enquiringly at Samson till he nodded, then she continued: "And there is the renting of the land. Mass Bagley will tell you of that. . . ." She sat down.

Bagley rose and explained carefully what he had already told Maria and what she, in turn, had already told Samson during the meal.

When Bagley had done Joe asked: "And what happens to the rent? How will we share it?"

Nobody had thought about that. Samson looked at Maria; Maria looked at Jonas; they all looked from one to the other; then they all turned to Bagley, the man who had first come up with this plan.

"Let the head of your family keep it," Bagley said, "for all of you. There will be a record of what there is and when anybody has need of anything it will come out of his share."

"How much will a share be?" Joe wanted to know.

"Yes, Mass Joe," Bagley explained patiently. "That is what we are coming to. First you must decide if you are going to follow this plan. When you have done that then you must decide how you will cut up the land to lease, and how much each person may lease, and what rules you are going to make for those who lease, and for how long they are going to lease. You want to decide what you will do if a person leases the land and does not pay after the first crop; or if a person brings another person who is not of his family onto the land. Only after all these matters have been decided and agreed on and are working well, and the rent from the leasing is coming in, only then do you need to worry about the sharing of it."

"First you catch the bird. . . ." Jonas murmured.

"Nothing wrong with knowing!" Joe snapped.

Jonas ignored Joe and addressed Bagley: "So how we work this?"

"I propose," Samson said, and they all fell silent, knowing that whenever Samson said "I propose" he and Maria had decided on a course of action: "I propose we leave it to Mass Bagley to work out the plan for the leasing, and when he is ready he will put it to us to decide. Now, we agree Mass Bagley and his women can stay? And the work they do for the family will pay for the land we give them?''

There were murmurs and nods of assent. Then Robert Bagley hurried to the hut where their possessions were and returned with the rifle. He unpacked it and presented it ceremoniously to Samson. "And two of the donkeys, too, for you to use for the good of the family. And the women of my family will give enough cloth to make a dress for each of the women of your family. That will be for free to show our thanks. After that it will be business and trade.''

''You are good strangers, Mass Bagley!'' Maria said with a joy which did not reach her cold, watchful eyes.

''Not all strangers are,'' Bagley warned. ''We met some who are bad. Let your family beware and be strong and be on guard always.''

Their sudden stony silence told Bagley that he had over-reached himself; these people were not in need of warning from him to be on guard. He had been presumptuous, forward, pushing; he must guard his tongue. He lowered his head, looked at the tabletop, withdrew into himself. After a while, gradually, the silence was dissipated and the people talked among themselves of the day's work and the day's plans, and the new ideas let loose by the coming of the strangers. But Bagley had learnt his lesson and there was a conscious restraint in everything he said.

In the early evening Samson led Bagley up to the hill of Mount Zion. It had been Maria's idea. Samson was at peace up there, his mind seemed clearer than anywhere else. He and Maria had shared deep thoughts up there; they had looked at the world below and made their plans for the family. Now, she wanted him to think clearly about Bagley's plan; and she wanted to be there to hear and to test it again, but more calmly now than earlier. The woman, Lena, Bagley's companion – Bagley's woman? – would be there, too, to help in that testing. For how she reacted could be a guide to their true intention. So Maria and Lena followed the two men up the hill.

76

They reached the crest of the hill and Bagley let out a sigh of wonder at the sight of all the world laid out below him.

"Lordy, Lordy," Bagley murmured, then called out loud: "Lena! Lena! Come look!"

The woman hurried to his side, tall, big-bosomed, broad-shouldered, narrow-hipped, with spindly legs and long narrow feet. She was a good head taller than Bagley, with a smooth, soft-featured, near black, high cheek-boned face. The face was a young girl's; only the lines about the lips, and the lips themselves, told of harsh experience which had force-bred resilience. The normally expressionless dark eyes glowed with excitement. Without being aware of it she slipped her hand into Bagley's and held tight, aware of the returning pressure of his hand, of the man himself, and of messages of feeling. She released his hand quickly and moved away a little. Their eyes met briefly, as though for the first time.

"It brings out the truth in people," Maria murmured, half-mocking, half-gently.

"Come!" Samson called from his favourite perch on the largest piece of the huge scattered boulders which had once been one.

Maria sat on another boulder near him, watching the two who were now self-consciously a foot apart but still disturbed by the flow of feeling between them this place had released.

"Let them be," Maria spoke for his ears only. "I thought they were man and woman; I was wrong. I don't think they ever slept together."

"Hush, woman," Samson ordered, but with a gentle indulgence in his voice. "I did not come here for your matchmaking." He raised his voice: "Come, Mass Bagley! The sight won't go away!"

Bagley and Lena joined them and found stone perches of their own.

"Now," Samson said. "Tell me again of your plan for the renting and the cutting up and the storing and the things you told Maria."

Bagley went over it all again, carefully and confidently, reassured this time by the knowledge that he had the support of Maria. He had, also, meanwhile thought the whole plan through so that it was now a clear concept he could visualize and explain.

77

Maria's eyes darted from Bagley's face to Lena's then back again, registering reaction, emotion; listening intently and comparing the words he used now with the words he had used earlier; testing, weighing, judging the man and his motives against his words, and against the reaction of this woman who had been with him a long time and who had just discovered a stronger bond between them. . . . Not clever like the man; not able to manage him and guide him, unless she knows of the weakness of his spirit and how to make use of that; but a woman soon knows these things. . . . And listening, Maria found nothing to cast doubt on her original judgement. This man was as she had first judged him to be smart, ambitious, but sufficiently aware of his weakness and his need for security in the shadow of a stronger one, and therefore with the capacity for loyalty to such a stronger one, Samson would be such a stronger one for this one.

For his part, Samson listened in silence while Bagley spoke. His mind, clear as usual up here, saw the plan and all its implications as he had not seen it at the eating place. Now he could improve on the plan and guide Bagley to make it better. He was not consciously aware of when Bagley stopped speaking for his mind simply took over where Bagley left off, refining, improving Bagley's ideas.

The three of them waited in silence while Samson, lost to the world, completed his thinking. When it was done his eyes came alive, searched for Maria's, and they embraced each other with their eyes.

"Yes," Samson said quietly, speaking really to Maria only, though he included the other two. "Yes, we will do it that way. All right, woman?"

Maria nodded. It was Samson's plan now. He would know what to do; and he would tell her in his own good time.

"Night is coming," Maria said. "Better we go down."

"You go," Samson said. "Take the sister with you. We will stay and talk a while; we will soon come."

The women left and made their way down the hillside. The two men remained seated. There was a long silence between them while the light over the land changed rapidly, turning the high mountains to the east first to a dark purple then to a deep hazy blue, seen through a clear mist. In a matter of moments the light over the land changed again. The light from the sun disappeared suddenly, as though turned off; the full moon, now, came into its own. The Blue Mountains became dark shadows against the sky: the transition from daylight to nightlight was instant; but yet there was no darkness over the land, only a different kind of light.

At last Samson broke the silence: "Tell me, Mass Bagley," his voice heavy. "Why they do this to us? Why the slavery thing?"

Bagley felt cornered: "I don't know, Mass Samson."

"Because we black?" Samson persisted.

"I never see white slaves," Bagley said.

"Just because we black." Samson made it a confirmation.

"To work for them," Bagley suggested.

"So they have slaves in their own country to work for them?"

"No, I don't think so."

"So people can work for them without being made slaves?"

"They work for money in their own country; like the bookkeepers."

"So why they do this to us?" Samson pressed: "Why they don't make us work for money?"

"They do now."

"Why not before? You know how many slaves died? Where I was many were whipped to death."

"We were lucky," Bagley said heavily.

Samson pulled the tattered covering off his back. "See! They did this to me. Why? Feel it!"

Bagley ran trembling fingers across the thick welts on the broad back.

"And the one who did it black like you and me. I killed him."

"They made him do it."

"I know; but he did it. Would you do it?"

"If he didn't they would do the same to him."

"I know; but would *you* do it?"

"I really don't know, brother Samson. I am not strong like you. I could not take that kind of pain; I think I will do anything they tell me to avoid that kind of pain."

"He was big and strong," Samson said. "Like me: but he found joy in hurting. He hurt women, he hurt children, he whipped sick

79

old men till they died. I know. I saw it. I still dream about it."

"They made him do it," Bagley said heavily.

Samson was angry now: "Was he not a man? Could he not refuse?"

"And be whipped?"

"Yes! And be whipped!"

Bagley felt cornered and on the defensive, as though he had whipped women and children, and whipped old men till they died. He had heard of such things but never seen them. Would he have done it if the alternative was that he himself would be whipped as this one had been? Would he do it?

"It's hard," Bagley said. "When they own you like animal and can do anything to you, it's hard not to obey their orders."

"And when you obey them, hurting your own people becomes a pleasure. Why did they not use their own people to do the whipping? I ask you, why black people to whip black people? Why slave to whip slave? Why not white drivers to whip black slaves? It is that I will never forget! They use a black man to put these marks on my body; and so they made me, a black man, kill a black man to remove the bitterness of the shame. If these marks had been put on me by a white man it would be clear. And if I had killed him that would be clear too. This way there is the special shame that it was one like me, a black slave, who put these marks on me; and there is the special shame that it was a black slave like me that I killed for putting these marks on me. Do you understand, Bagley? Do you understand? They do this thing and they take away our manhood; and because they use us whatever we do to those of us whom they use destroys our manhood further. It is like an animal caught in a trap: the more he tries to break free, the tighter the trap holds him and the more he hurts himself. The bad thing here, brother Bagley, is that it is our minds and our spirits that they have caught in that trap. They have set a trap for our minds in order to destroy our manhood. I could not see this until I came up here where the air is clear and a man can think. It took me a long time to see it. But now that I see it I cannot see a way out, I cannot see an answer. Will we ever be free of that, brother Bagley, will we ever be free?"

Samson turned his head and looked searching at Bagley's face in the clear nightlight. "Do you understand what I'm saying, brother Bagley?"

"I think so, brother Samson."

"Then try to help find the answer so that we can be really free, free in our minds."

"I will try," Bagley said, not knowing what it was that he would try to do. But knowing certainly now that this was the leader, however strong Maria was.

They stayed on the hill a while longer, not talking, each wrapped in his own thoughts. Then Samson led the way down along the moonlit path. Behind him, Bagley wondered what he would have done if they had ordered him to be a driver and he had to whip people. He was terribly depressed by the answer his mind kept giving, no matter how he turned the question around. Perhaps Samson was right. Perhaps their former slave masters had made a prison for their minds; a prison you could not see or touch, or even feel, unless you were a man like Samson and had suffered the pain he had and had a hill like his on which to sit and see all the world and think.

Later that night, lying on the floor of his section of the hut Bagley tried to explain to Lena and Eliza, lying at the opposite wall, what Samson had talked about. Somehow it was not as clear as it had been up there on the hill; the more he tried to make them understand, the less he succeeded.

Eliza began to snore softly. His talk had lulled her to sleep. He stopped speaking, feeling depressed though everything had transpired to make him feel good. They had a home now, a place of safety among good people. Then he sensed, rather than saw, Lena leave her place and crawl over to his. It had begun up on Samson's hill and he knew it had to come to this. But here? With that other one sleeping and likely to awake? The woman lay beside him.

"What of her?" he whispered. "She may wake up. . . ."

"It does not matter," the woman said. "She has seen it before. And I told her tonight it would be so with us."

"You are sure? I am not young. You will not want another later? It will be painful for me if you do."

81

"I am sure," the woman said. "It is I who choose you. Come."

The dry season dragged on with seeming endlessness. Hot dry days gave way to hot dry nights; even the cool night wind ceased to blow through the land. In the hot days Samson and the other two worked at felling the big trees and Bagley and Noname used the mule and the donkeys to pull the trees to the building sites the women had helped to prepare. The land which had been cleared of trees and bush grew dry, parched, dusty. The water level of the pool dropped lower than they had ever known it. They blamed it on the long drought and dug steps into the claylike earth, down to the new water level, to ensure that the women and children could still reach the water. They used rocks and trees and wiss to make the way down to the water safe. But still one of the children drowned in the pool during that hard dry season. It was one of Flo's twins by Joe, a three-year-old girl. It was the first death since they had reached this place and the despair it brought hung over them throughout the long dry season. But the work continued and they built three solid timber houses during the three dry months. Joe, in particular, worked as though he were driven, as though work would ease the pain of their loss. Flo, near the point of delivering, periodically broke into hysterical screaming.

The great inflow of strangers Bagley had anticipated did not come about; a few came, but slowly, in small numbers, at long intervals. Near the end of the dry season two groups did come, one hard on the other: one a group of four – two men and two women, and the other just two young men. These told of a number of big and growing settlements scattered in places with water all the way up the hills. The nearest one, they said, was in a place called Red Hills which had a large number of people. Another, and going westward, was a place called Cyprus controlled by a man called David and his wife Miss Sarah. Many people had gone there for there was a church and David was a strict man of justice and of God and Miss Sarah was the teacher. After hearing this, when they were alone, Maria and Samson talked about going to see David and Sarah, but they were uncertain whether they would be welcome. After careful questioning they turned away the two young men. The two

82

couples became their first tenants under the lease arrangement. Each was apportioned a piece of land to work and was given seed for planting when the rain came. They were helped to settle in, helped to build their shelters, but they were not allowed to become part of the collective communal life. Bagley and his two women were the only outsiders allowed to become part of that communal life. Later, during the rainy season, other strangers came. Some they welcomed and leased land to; others they sent away. Always, they decided together whom to allow and whom to turn away. The families about whose willingness to work they were satisfied, were welcomed and helped to settle in. In the end a small community of a dozen families was scattered in the long valley of Mount Zion, all tenants of the original family of Samson and Maria and those who had been with them when they cut their way through the bush to this place in the day when men and women were still held as slaves.

In the remote hills and valleys all over the land, groups, some like Samson's who had escaped during slavery, others who had repudiated the apprenticeship they were offered after slavery, yet others who wanted to have nothing to do with the system which first enslaved them and then released them, built self-contained and self-sustaining communities of their own, close to the earth, a part of it. And except when the dry season was particularly harsh and particularly long, the earth was kind to them, sustained them, even revealed some of its secrets to them; and these, each community, each village, each family shared life co-operatively, in an old remembered way whose unknown roots were lost in the distant past that went back to times beyond the days of slavery.

COUNTY TIPPERARY JOINT LIBRARIES
County Library
Thurles.

3
Sarah/David

1

Samson was struck down in the good season of the calm and easy not-too-hot-and-not-too-cold, not-too-wet-and-not-too-dry days before the coming of the Christmas Breeze. He was partway up the hill to his favourite look-out point when a terrible flash of lightning exploded in his brain with a force that struck him to the ground, and pinned him there, unable to move any part of his body. It was late afternoon; the day's work was done and they had eaten, so no one was concerned that Samson did not return when night fell. He often stayed up on the hill far into the night; sometimes, on rare occasions, he did not come down till the early hours of the next morning. Maria, these days, was too busy managing her brood of growing youngsters, all now between eleven and fourteen, to devote as much time and thought to Samson as she had done in the early days. Only at night, when they were in the big bed he had built with such pride and care and were alone, was there time to share thoughts and be sensitive to each other's moods and feeling. And often they were both too tired for even this; so the bond between them was less strong, less close, than in the early days.

Maria had gone to sleep, expecting to find him at her side when she woke in the morning. When she woke in the pre-dawn hours and Samson was not beside her, she was alarmed. She sent one of the elder children to tell Jonas and Noname that Samson had not come down from his hill, then she, herself, set out along the familiar path up the hillside.

A small search party, headed by Jonas and Noname and including a few of the male tenants who lived nearest, found them a little over an hour later. Maria sat on the ground, motionless, Samson's head in her lap. They were two-thirds of the way to the top of the hill.

"He can't move," Maria said to Jonas. "And he can't speak."

Jonas went down on one knee, in the half-light of the oil lamp he saw that Samson's eyes were wide open, seemed aware of him and Maria and the others. "What happened, brother?" Jonas urged, trying to coax some sound out of his old friend. "What happen, man?"

"I tell you he can't speak," Maria said.

"A stroke," someone said. "Sometime it go away and he can speak again."

"Make we take him down," Noname said. He had grown into a strong-bodied young man of small size, all muscle and smooth-skinned grace. "Come. Make we build a thing fe carry him."

They chopped down bush and young trees and wove these into a stretcher. Noname tested it for strength, then they lifted Samson's big heavy body on to it, and made their way down the hill slowly, carefully, not to drop their stricken leader or shake him too much. And all the while Maria held onto that strong right hand of Samson's; but now that hand was limp, no feel to it, no response when she pressed it.

When they got down, carrying Samson's body, the first signs of daybreak were showing and the word had spread and the entire population of the valley was waiting silently at Maria's yard.

They carried Samson into the house and laid him on the huge wooden bed which filled almost all of the room. Maria fussed about, making him comfortable, ensuring that they moved him slowly, without bumping into things and jarring his body. The cluster of people remained waiting outside.

"Go, tell them," Maria said to Jonas.

He went out to the broad verandah facing south. "Mass Samson awright. . . . Only one thing: he can't move and he can't talk. Is a stroke they say. . . ." There was a collective sigh and everybody began to talk. Jonas held up a hand. "Make him rest; you go on, you will hear what happen later."

They dispersed slowly talking among themselves. One or two of the elder women lingered, waiting to be of service, for they knew that at times of trouble one hand must wash the other. After a while the men who had carried Samson down left, leaving only Jonas and Noname with Maria and her huge family. Vie and two elder girls and the women who lingered prepared the early morning food; the boys went to the fields to do the work Papa had assigned to them long before: routine distracted their minds from the terrible thing which had befallen them. Only in the room where Samson lay was there no end to the preoccupation with the disaster. Did he hear what they were saying? Did he understand? What to do? How to find out? Was he hurting? Was he thinking? What was he thinking? How to know? Maria sat on one side of the big bed, Jonas on the other, Noname leaned against the wall near the door.

"What must we do?" Maria said it again and again, each time the realization of what had happened overwhelmed her anew. This time Jonas answered.

"I will go into Red Hills. I hear say someone there knows about herbs. Perhaps they can help."

Noname pushed against the wall and straightened up, making it an act of decision. "I will find David. Maybe David and Sarah know what to do." He left the room quickly, giving Maria no time to react or gainsay him.

"That one never forgot David," Maria whispered broodingly; "like this one here." She looked searchingly at the open-eyed, motionless figure on the bed. "I bet he would agree."

"They shared much," Jonas reminded her, then softened the harshness of it. "We all shared much."

"It's a long time since them gone," Maria murmured. "Long time. Perhaps he won't want to come. He was a boy when we sent him away."

"Who had done a man's work." A small smile flitted across Jonas' face and was gone. "And he bred that Sarah like a man! When I look pon them that morning she was drunk with it, like a bee drunk up to its eyes in honey!"

Maria recalled it vividly; despite her despair, a smile of remembrance lit up her eyes. "Eee . . . I remember; she almost smelled of it. It come so sometimes and it bind them. . . . It come so with this one for me; I was his first and it bind him to me. . . ." She moved abruptly, "Hear me, Sam!" raising her voice to near shouting.

"Easy, sister," Jonas said intently, watching the man on the bed.

89

If the man heard, there was nothing to show: no change in the eyes, no hint of feeling, just a blank stare.

"I will go now," Jonas rose and went to the door. "I will try to come back quickly with good news."

Maria composed her face into a blank mask and nodded.

Noname reached the village of Cyprus in the late afternoon and was startled by how the place had changed since he first came upon it, many years before, and found David and Sarah. Then it was a long quiet wooded valley with one little shack, very little cultivation, and only David and Sarah and their three children; a lonely place, he remembered thinking at the time. This time, reaching the crest of the last hill, he looked down on more houses than in their own valley at Mount Zion; more houses than he could count, some tucked away in well-cultivated fields of corn and cane and shaded by huge breadfruit trees in the bottom of the valley, near the water, others dotted on the sloping hillside land. There were regular pathways, and packed stone or wooden fences marking off some of the land. And dominating all this, on the highest south-western crest, was the church that David and Sarah had built. In moments of quiet, moments of rest when no others were about, he and Samson had talked often of making the journey to see David and Sarah and look upon this widely known church of theirs. Now Samson was paralysed and would never make the journey. But what a huge building that church was! And what a sharply sloping narrow roof! He must find out how David did it. And this prosperous and flourishing land, with all these houses, and all the people moving around, was founded by David and Sarah, who had been sent away from their settlement so long ago. The big house down there, near the water, with all that green land rich in food trees, that was where David and Sarah had their shack when he first saw them here. Noname walked briskly down to what he knew was David and Sarah's home.

The young man who opened the door to Noname was the spitting image of David – as David had been in the days of their long journey up into the hills: tall, big-boned, broad-shouldered; the same rich dark-brown skin drawn tightly over the high cheek-boned face, the same light grey eyes, the same reddish tinge to the hair which was a cross between kink and tight curl, the same feel of contained strength Noname remembered. The likeness startled him into a long bewildered silence which the young man finally broke: "If it's my father, he's not home yet. He'll be back soon." The young man turned his head slightly, indicating a long bench on the verandah.

Not the same voice, Noname told himself; softer, quieter, weaker; then it came to him: like Sarah's, though deeper, being a man's. "I'm from Mount Zion; they call me Noname. . . ."

"Oh yes," the young man was warm, interested now. "Please come in. My mother is home; I will call her."

He flung open the door and turned and went away, disappearing through a small door at the far end of the big room. The room was darker than the outside; only the light from the open door and the two big windows to the west prevented it being completely dark, made it possible for Noname to see. It was a bigger room than Noname had ever seen and with the same high sloping roof he had seen on the church. There was a long table in the middle; not as long as the old communal table at Mount Zion but long enough for a dozen people to sit comfortably on each of the two matching benches on either side. At the ends were two chairs, one slightly bigger and higher than the other. Over the table a large brass oil lamp hung from a ceiling beam; smaller lamps stood on the table at intervals. Benches and chairs were ranged along the walls. This room was, evidently, more than just a private living room. Noname sat on a bench near the door and waited. . . . What would she be like after all these years? How would she receive him? How would she react to what he had to tell her and David. . . ? That boy of David's, seeing him so suddenly there took him back to a time on that long journey when he, Noname, had a running belly and was too weak to keep up and still carry his load; David had taken his load and made him lean on him without letting the others know. . . . Boy like David, repeat of David; only Sarah's voice but as a man's voice; and strong-looking too, again like David.

He was so engrossed in his thoughts he did not see her till she was near the long table and raised a little the lamp she carried; then something about her made him jump to his feet more quickly

91

and awkwardly than was normal for him. She put the lamp on the table and came toward him as though floating, the long dark dress just not touching the floor, but hiding her feet completely. Her face was part of the gathering shadows; her presence filled the entire room. This was not the Sarah Noname remembered.

"Noname? Is it really you? Welcome, my dear. . . ."

This overwhelming presence and this rich, compelling voice, were not as Noname remembered Sarah. She rested her hands lightly on his shoulders, bent down and kissed him on the cheek, then stepped back to examine him more closely, all the while telling him how pleased she was to see him and how pleased David would be. David had gone on a journey and would be back later. Did he want to wait for David or would he in the meantime tell her what had brought him here?

"It is Samson," Noname said. "He's sick; he can't talk and he can't move. People say it's a stroke. . . ."

Sarah let out her breath in a long loud sigh. The light on the table was not strong enough for Noname to see Sarah's face clearly, and put a meaning on that sigh.

"When?" Her voice was without feeling.

"Sometime in the night. We found him this morning."

"On the hill?"

"On the way up."

"Or down," she added.

"Yes," Noname said; and felt tired suddenly.

"Oh please sit down, my dear . . . I'm sorry; I forgot what a long way you've walked." She clapped her hands twice. A shadowy female figure appeared in the far door. Raising her voice only slightly Sarah called, "Something to drink, please." She turned back to Noname.

"And Maria: how did Maria take it?"

"Bad."

"Oh Noname! What do you mean, 'bad'?"

"It look like she can't believe it. It's a kind of shock. She doesn't know what to do."

"Yes. I understand what you mean. He was her life, the life through which she lived; if that life is paralysed, what will she do?"

92

The shadowy female returned with a pitcher and two mugs on a bamboo tray, placed it near Sarah and withdrew. Sarah poured two drinks, a long one for Noname, a small token drink for herself.

"You will like it."

What if I don't, he wondered, putting it to his lips. She was right: all the different fruits of the earth seemed to have gone into it, blended with the refreshing mild sweetness of honey, to make a drink of heavenly delight. He took a long swig, then another, then another till the mug was empty. She refilled it for him and he knew she was pleased at his enjoyment of it.

"David and the children love it; they drink it all the time. It took me a long time to get the mixture just right. I learned it from Maria, only I'm better at it; I worked harder at it, took more time, and I had more time because I had only David and the children of my own body to look after. She wanted too much; she used too many people. Perhaps that's why. . . ." she stopped speaking abruptly.

"It is good," Noname said, sensing where Sarah's thoughts were leading and wanting to change the direction.

"Not to worry, my dear," Sarah said as though calming a frightened child. "You must never be afraid of your thoughts. Keep them clean and free of malice; but do not hide them because you cannot hide them from God. So let us say it aloud: perhaps that is why she has suffered this punishment."

The second time, Noname thought: how can she do it? Then he realized she had picked up this one too. She was laughing at him softly.

"It's really very easy, my dear; if you learn to listen hard enough, like the birds and the other little creatures do, and if you learn to look closely enough."

Startled, Noname asked: "You can know what everybody thinks and feels?"

"Not everybody. Only some people, people close to me, or people I care about; or people at the other end of it, those I do not care for and who do not care for me; sometimes I think I will always know what Maria feels or thinks if I look at her face; but not for the same reason that I know what you or David thinks."

"Always?"

"Most of the time; with David and the children my own feelings blind me most of the time because they are so strong. It all began at Mount Zion with Maria who tried to teach us how to find which plants to eat by watching the little creatures around us. When we came here and were alone, the loneliness forced me to learn Maria's lessons better than she herself did, and I improved on them. So you see, there's no obeah, no magic, except really listening and really seeing." She rose. "Come, Noname, meet the family. I know they will want to ask you about the journey we made. It is like a little story to them, exciting and hard to believe, especially that it happened to their own parents. Come, we will eat and talk about these things till David comes."

"Please. . . ." Noname wanted to return to his own family. But there was the need to do something about Samson; perhaps David knew what to do. Better to stay and wait for David. His Mary would guess the reason for his absence. . . . "Is nothing," he said and followed Sarah out of the large dark empty room into another, equally large, brightly lit and seemingly crowded with people. He nodded, not really registering names or faces, as Sarah called out the names of her children and of the other members of her household.

They were halfway through the meal when David walked into the room. Noname looked up at the giant stranger, even less like the David he remembered than the young man who had opened the door for him and who now sat beside him. This one was big and quiet in a way the land can be quiet; the same sense of peace came from the presence of this man who had been his friend and big brother David. Only the eyes were the eyes of a stranger, looking calmly, coldly, through you.

The talk at the table stopped. Sarah rose, and everybody stood up with her, so Noname did the same. David walked to his place at the head of the table, counted and examined his children with his eyes, embraced Sarah with his eyes, only then spoke to Noname.

"Welcome, little brother. It is good to see you." He took his seat; Sarah followed, then all the others. The talk resumed at the table till food was placed in front of David. The silence returned while David bowed his head in silent prayer. When he raised his head and started to eat the talk returned once more; neither he nor Sarah took any part in it. Noname was overwhelmed by a sense of being a stranger in a strange place. He used to know David and Sarah; he was not sure that he knew them now. In times of trouble you do not turn to strangers for help: are these strangers now?

After the meal the children and others dispersed. David went into the other large room, now well lit, for a meeting on church affairs. Sarah showed Noname a small room where he would spend the night; then left him for a meeting of her own to do with the school she ran for all the children of Cyprus. She had said: "We have much work, Noname: David with the land and the church and the community's business, I with the family and the school and the community's business too. They are talking about a person coming up from Kingston next week – a white man – who wants to talk about our church becoming part of their church; some of the elders are for it, some against. I think David has made up his mind so the meeting will not take long. Mine will be over quickly, too. Then we will talk about Samson. Rest now."

Noname could not rest so he found his way out onto the long verandah. Sitting there alone, looking up at the bright stars, listening to the noises of the little night creatures, the sense of disturbing strangeness left him and he felt at ease again. This place founded by David and Sarah was so much bigger, had so many more people than they had in Mount Zion. He could understand why. The valley, here, was wider, the land less steeply sloping, it could sustain more people more easily. But it was not as intimate, not as protected and cut-off and difficult to approach; and there was no high hill like Samson's hill: a rich, broad-bottomed fertile valley this, but no safe hiding place for a group of runaway slaves, like Mount Zion. Militia or slave hunters from Spanish Town or the Catherine Plain would have reached here with speed and ease. Now, with no militia to fear, with no slave hunters to avoid, the openness of this valley, its easy accessibility, had made it more prosperous, more peopled. The level of the deep pool at Mount Zion was dropping lower year by year. He knew that one day it would be too low to sustain all the people there. Perhaps, before that day, all the people would have left. But he, Noname, would not leave. That was his land, the only land he had or wanted. That was the piece of earth on which he first felt free; he would not leave it, even if the pool dried up. . . . A rich and beautiful place this Cyprus of David and Sarah; but not for him. He would talk to Mary about sending their children to Sarah's school; it's good for children to learn and he was impressed with the learning of David's children at the meal table. . . . Time passed and Noname dozed off, leaning against the stout logs of David and Sarah's home. . . .

When he woke they were on the bench beside him, a huge pitcher of Sarah's brew at hand.

"Time to talk, little brother," David said in his deep quiet voice. "Sarah told me. You tell me again, all of it."

When Noname finished David asked: "What do you want us to do?"

"That's why he came here, David." Sarah sounded testy.

"We don't know what to do," Noname said.

"Yes," David said. "What's to be done – beside prayer, that is? Well, Sarah? What's to be done?"

"I've sent word to some of the older women." She said. "There are herbs and bushes which will help and may cure. We'll have them early in the morning."

"Then we'll decide what else to do. Is he in pain?" David asked.

"Don't know," Noname said.

"Not usually," Sarah said. "The old women's herbs will take care of any pain."

"In the morning, then," David rose abruptly and walked away.

"He's very tired," Sarah said reassuringly. "And he's upset. Samson means much to him, even after what happened. And when he's upset he likes to be alone, away from people, even away from me; so don't take it any way."

"S'all right. . . ." Noname had hoped for some guidance, for some comfort.

"We will do something for Samson," Sarah assured him. "Trust us. Trust David."

But how do you trust people you do not understand, who are suddenly like strangers to you?

"I'm tired too," she said, again sensing his mood. "He still calls you little brother from the time of our long journey; so he remembers just as you remember and just as I remember. We remember how Samson took care of us and guided us; we have forgotten nothing. All right?"

Noname felt ashamed of all his doubts.

Noname woke early, long before daybreak; it had made for a restless night this sleeping in a strange place away from his own home and his own bed and without the familiar presence of Little Mary beside him. He had spent most of the night in the strange dreamlike state between sleep and wakefulness: thoughts, dreams, worries, intermingled. He lay still for a while in the half-dark little room till mind and body came together. He thought of Samson and moved his body consciously: arms, legs, fingers and toes, muscles – they all responded. He got up, opened the wooden window and dressed quickly by the pre-dawn light; from the window he saw that David and Sarah's household was already up and about. He went out, expecting to encounter only the helpers and the children. But David and Sarah were in the big back room, two very old women with them, and several little bundles of herbs tied in different coloured cloths stacked on the table in front of them. The smell of freshly brewed coffee filled the room.

"Morning, Noname," Sarah said. "See, we kept our promise. These are the Nanas I told you of and they have brought the medicine."

David filled an earthen mug with coffee and pushed it to the space near the empty seat beside him. "Sit here, little brother. Now explain it all to him, mothers."

"This one," whispered the most wrinkled and leathery of the two old women, putting a gnarled hand on a bundle tied in the red cloth, "is the first to give him. Pour boiling water over it. Two *yabas* full so," she shaped them with her hands in the air. "Then you strain it into one big *yaba* and cork it. Give him a cup in the morning and in the middle of the day and before he goes to sleep.

Know how to hold his tongue and put it in him? Know how to get food into him?"

"Oh, Lord. . . ." Sarah sighed. "I didn't think of that."

"Does Maria know what to do?" David asked and they all looked at Noname.

Noname shook his head uncertainly. "I don't know. I don't think so."

"Then he will die," the second old woman said in a slightly more robust voice than the first.

"Then one of you must go with Noname to make sure he lives."

The two old women looked at each other, then the younger of the two nodded. "As you will, Pastor."

"But we will go together," the elder said.

"To help and support each other," the younger explained. "There will be much to do if he's not to die."

"If he's not already dead," the elder added.

"All right," David nodded and turned to Sarah. "Two donkeys and provisions. Do we send anyone with them? Or will Noname bring them back?"

"I'll bring them back," Noname said.

"One of us must go and see Samson later," Sarah said. "We can bring them back then. How long will you need to stay there?"

"Three-four days," the elder said. "If he's still alive."

"He's alive!" Noname exploded suddenly.

"Easy, little brother," David murmured.

"I'll see to the preparations," Sarah said and left the room.

Again, as abruptly as the night before, David got up and walked away, only pausing briefly to lay his hands lightly on the shoulders of the two old women. This time Sarah was not there to soothe away Noname's distress. David did not even look at him as he left.

A little before sun-up all was ready. The two old women had been lifted onto two amiable and equally ancient donkeys. Behind them hampers of provisions balanced evenly on the hips of the donkeys. Noname himself carried the parcels of precious herbs in his shoulder bag. Sarah saw them off. There was no sign of David and Noname was not even sure he was still at the house.

"They will take care of Samson," Sarah said. "One or the other of us will come and look for Samson and take them back when the time is up. Tell them that; and tell Maria to do everything the Nanas say; they are the only ones who can help us now. Tell her if she doesn't he will surely die."

"Even with that he may die," the elder cut in.

"But I know you will do everything to prevent it," Sarah said very firmly, making it an order.

Then Noname led the two donkeys, quickly and purposefully, out of the valley of Cyprus in the direction of Mount Zion. At the crest of the land, before dipping out of sight of the wide valley, he looked back. Sarah was still standing where he had left her, tall and straight, her long dress down to the ground, radiating a feeling of power. She raised her hand and waved, and he knew that that was what she had waited for; she had known he would look back, and she had waited to wave when he did, to make up for David. He turned again and led the animals into the next valley and out of sight of David and Sarah's prospering Cyprus.

Samson was still alive when Noname and the women reached Mount Zion. Desperate, not knowing what to do, Maria allowed the two old crones to take over as though her house were theirs. They brewed a nourishing broth compounded of meat – fresh, not salted, they insisted – and vast quantities of green vegetables and yellow roots. When this had been reduced to a thick soup, they ordered help and propped up Samson's great frame, forced open his mouth and wedged it; one held down his tongue while the other spooned the broth down his throat. It was a long, slow process. When the feeding was done they stripped him naked and bathed his body in hot water made strong-smelling by the herbs they had soaked in the water. Then they took turns at massaging his stomach and lower abdomen in firm downward movements, on and on and on till the elder sighed, dress soaked in sweat, "It move. . . ." The younger went to the door and again summoned help, but only men. Jonas and Noname came in and were told to raise the lower part of Samson's body and hold it while the old women spread a pile of broad leaves under his buttocks. Then, with the two men holding Samson in a crouching position, the elder pushed her hand, oiled and shaped into a pointed spatula, up his rectum. She pushed and heaved till it seemed her whole hand was gone; she worked her hand, groaning and grunting, eyes closed, sweat dripping down her face. Then she withdrew the hand, slowly, and with it came a foul noxious smell which filled the room and all but choked those in it for all the open door and open window. When the hand was finally out the elder held up for the younger to see, a hard, stinking, rocklike little black ball. "The cork!" a hint of tired triumph in her voice. Then Samson's body voided itself.

"He will live," the elder said, wiping her hand on a clean edge of the mound of leaves.

The younger held his tongue and poured a dark brew down his throat while the elder removed the pile of fouled leaves from the bed.

"All right to put him down now," the younger told the men. "The drink will make him sleep for a long time."

"They lick him bad," the elder said. "I saw one take licks like that in slavery time; he died. This one is strong; they lick him so and he lives. That why they call him Samson, like in the Bible?"

Neither Jonas nor Noname knew but Jonas said: "Yes."

"You can go," the elder dismissed them. "Tell the women to come clean up."

Maria did all the cleaning herself, refusing to allow anyone to help her, refusing to allow even Vie or any of the children into the room till all the muck, all the smell was removed from it. The two old women cleaned themselves and went to the room provided for them and immediately fell asleep, side by side, utterly worn out. When Maria came looking for them to find out what would happen next, they were in deep sleep, holding hands, the younger sucking her thumb.

The strangers came up to Cyprus from the Catherine Plain end, as though coming from Spanish Town, though they really came from Kingston. The journey was easier on the animals by way of the road to Spanish Town, turning off at Ferry for the steep climb to Cyprus. This way the climb was much shorter than by way of

Liguanea. There were two of them, both on horseback; a small, thin, white man with the dull yellowish colouring of one long in the tropical sun, dressed in black, black trousers, shirt and coat with broad-brimmed black hat; the other was tall with a burnt-copper black skin, dressed in canvas trousers and shirt bleached white by wear and weather, with a broad-brimmed straw hat that kept his face permanently shaded. The black rider was armed, rifle cradled easily in the crook of his arm, machete dangling at his knee on the right side of the saddle. He stayed a horse's head behind the white rider, only going ahead when they encountered people or approached some point of limited visibility: a sharp blind turn in the track, the crest of a hill, a cluster of trees. When these were cleared he fell back again. They had started the journey early but the hot sun had caught up with them, so the white rider sweated profusely and kept mopping his face with a large snow-white handkerchief.

When they reached the outskirts of Cyprus there was no need to stop and ask the way: the magnificent church on the slope of the distant hill, and the sprawling house near it was their destination.

"What a beautiful place, Joseph!" It was a surprisingly big voice for that sized body, deep and rich.

"Yes, sir," Joseph said noncommittally.

"Now let us go and take the measure of Pastor David, if Pastor he is." The white man spurred his tired horse to a gentle canter; the black followed suit. The people of Cyprus stopped what they were doing to turn and stare. This was the first white man to come to Cyprus. White people stayed on the plains and the big estates; black people stayed in the hills. As they neared their destination the white man slipped on his pastor's collar without slowing his horse, with the ease of something done again and again till it became instinctive.

By word of mouth passed across the landscape by men in their fields, by little boys running with the word from one household to the next, the coming of the strangers was made known to David and Sarah long before their arrival. So they were waiting when the strangers arrived.

The white man sprang quickly from his horse and hurried

forward, right hand extended, a warm smile on his face. He doffed his hat when he saw Sarah. What a striking woman, he thought as he tilted his head to look into David's eyes.

"Pastor David! So glad to meet you at last. We've heard about your great work. I am Pastor Rae, John Rae, travelling secretary for our churches' Council of Elders."

David took the extended hand and noted the firmness of the little man's grip.

"David Brown," he said formally. Samson had given him, all of them, that surname; he wondered momentarily how Samson was. "This is my wife Sarah."

The man bowed slightly and took Sarah's hand: "Mrs Brown . . . I hope you do not mind too much my coming like this. Our President, the chairman of our Council of Elders did write twice." He paused.

"Yes, I got the letters," David said. "I do not go to Kingston much."

"We thought so, which is why they sent me."

Something about the man's companion nagged at the back of Sarah's mind; something familiar, something that went back to that painful past of the days of bondage. She had seen him somewhere, much younger but still him or someone so like him as to be a twin. And the man, too, it was apparent, was trying to place Sarah.

"Your companion, Mr Rae," Sarah said. She would make the man introduce his bodyguard.

"Oh I'm sorry, Mrs Brown. That's Joseph. He looks after me when I travel. He's a good and faithful servant of the church. We're very proud of him."

Sarah was not listening. Joseph: that was the name of the young boy she had tried to protect. "That you, Joseph?"

"Yes, Miss Sarah," the man said, as he had said it as a frightened boy long ago. His face remained impassive; only his eyes glowed.

"Come into the house," David said to Rae. "You've brought my wife a piece of her past. Let them be for while."

Rae followed David, suddenly less certain of himself than he remembered being in a long time.

"You really my little Joseph of long ago? The one I used to give food out of the window?"

"Yes, Miss Sarah." Still only the eyes shone with feeling.

"Oh Joseph! I never thought I would see you or anyone from that place again."

She took the man's hands, squeezed them and led him round to the back of the house where the horses would be stabled. And in her mind she rejoiced; Joseph would know more of Rae's plans than Rae thought. The past had sent them an ally.

All day long the two men fenced with each other, feeling each other out, testing reactions and responses, mentally exploring each other's possible strengths and weaknesses. They talked about the land and what grew best on this part of it; about how David and Sarah began building their church long before the first settlers came into the valley.

At one point, as they crested a slight hill that led to Elder Jones's home, they paused to look back at the church. Unexpectedly, David said: "You know, we were runaway slaves and our leader, Samson, had killed a man, the driver who had hurt him cruelly. Do you think God will forgive him?"

"I don't know; I am not one of those parsons who knows the thinking of the Lord on every matter. Tell me, what do you think?"

David countered with another question. "Can you put yourself in Samson's place? Can you think of yourself as a slave?"

"No; and I cannot know the true feelings of a man who was."

"Can the Lord?"

"What do you think?"

"Like you, I don't know; all I do know is that his son was cruelly whipped, like Samson, and hung on a cross where he died. The feelings and pain of such a man Samson knows and I know. Such a one must know how it feels to be a slave."

"White men have been sold into slavery too," Rae said. "And to this day, in Africa and the Arab countries brown men and black men are holding other brown men and black men in bondage."

"Slavery," David said softly. "Slavery."

"Slavery," Rae conceded. "Cruelty and injustice are not confined to one people or one race or one nationality."

103

"I agree; but is there no difference between the cruelty and injustice within one people or one race or one nationality, and the cruelty and injustice of one people or race or nationality against another?"

"I have not thought about that," Rae said honestly. "Perhaps I should have, but I haven't. I will now. My first instinctive reaction is to say that all cruelty and injustice are the same, no matter the circumstances."

"Think about it and we will talk about it again."

Perhaps this is the time, Rae thought. Aloud he asked: "Has this to do with our invitation for you to join us?"

"Think about it and we will talk again." David turned the surefooted mule abruptly and led the way down the sloping land to Elder Jones's house. A small, slightly ironic smile flitted across Rae's face. This encounter was proving very different from any of his other encounters; nothing simple or straightforward about it, this man was in control, whatever Jones had told the Elders. Would be interesting to see how Jones behaves in his presence.

It was Saturday and as was customary people had stopped working and left their fields in the early afternoon. This valley reminded Rae of the land of the Shonas in Africa where he had served briefly before being sent to Jamaica; it was a miniature version of that long Shona valley in which he had first discovered his gift for learning African languages and his ability to get on well with black people: not because they were childlike, as most of his missionary colleagues seemed to think, but because they were, for the most part, devastatingly straightforward in their dealings with each other and with everyone else. The ancestors of the people here in Jamaica were brought from another part of Africa and their ways, overlaid no doubt by the bitter experiences of slavery, were very different. His experience belied the assumption that all black people are alike, and if you can deal successfully with one group of them you can do so with all of them. David's voice cut through his reverie.

"Do you want to talk about your business?"

"You mean with Elder Jones?"

"Yes."

"I'd prefer to talk with you first." As he said it, Rae knew he had walked into a trap. He extricated himself as best he could, knowing the futility of it after his long awkward pause. "I met Elder Jones in Kingston."

David turned his head and looked into Rae's eyes: "I know."

"Wanted to find out if I'm a liar as well," Rae murmured.

"As well as what, Mr Rae?"

"As well as your enemy."

"Are you my enemy, then?"

"You've treated me as such; all this feeling and fencing."

"But are you?"

"That's a hard one, my friend."

"To think about and talk about later?" David suggested. "Like the purpose for your visit?"

"It is my duty," Rae said thoughtfully. "If I don't do it, someone else will. If I refused to come they would send someone else."

They travelled in silence after that, the surefooted mules moving easily over the uneven land and the rock-strewn track to Jones's house where the land dipped sharply.

Jones waited for them on his verandah, a big, hearty man, not quite as tall as David but as broad and as strapping. He was still in his field clothes and these clung tightly to his body. A small thin woman poked her head out of the door then disappeared again.

"Greetings, brother Jones!" David called. "I think you know Mr Rae. I'm showing him around."

A wide ingratiating smile that did not reach his eyes cracked Jones's broad face. "Welcome, Pastor David, Pastor Rae!" His voice had a hearty booming ring. "Just back from the fields! No time to change! But come in, please!"

Rae spoke quickly, cutting off whatever response David was about to make. "We're just passing, Elder Jones; just wanted to pay my respects; not stopping. I understand we'll have a proper meeting tomorrow after church. Pastor David and I have much to discuss."

"Yes! Yes!" Elder Jones boomed. "I understand!" He pounded off the verandah and wrapped both his huge hands around Rae's small pale extended hand, face beaming, eyes calculating. "I hope your discussions are fruitful!"

"I'm sure you do," David said drily.

"Greet your good lady for me," Rae said, seeing the small figure among the dark shadows just inside the door. "I look forward to meeting her tomorrow." He looked at David and they turned their mules together, as though by prearrangement.

As soon as their backs were turned Elder Jones's beaming smile was replaced by a thoughtful frown. "They're close," he said to nobody in particular. "Too close. . . ."

The two men rode in silence for the best part of half an hour. At last Rae said, "You're a patient man, Pastor David."

"You will tell me if you want to," David said.

"And if I don't, you won't ask? I deal with people like that most of the time; it's part of my work. I'd prefer to deal only with you and Mrs Brown."

"And if you get nowhere with Sarah and me?"

"Oh we'll get somewhere. We always do." Rae sounded depressed. "I think it is time for us to sit down and talk. My friends – the very few I have – call me Jock; I'd like you to."

"Are you our friend?"

"I'd like to be."

"By taking what is ours?"

"Not taking; putting it in a larger context."

"Against our will?"

"No; preferably not."

"But if you have to?"

"I think your wife should be in on this now."

"I'm glad you see that."

"I see more than you think, my friend."

"Then you should see we do not want this union."

"I see that, and more; and I would like you to see what I see before you close your minds, for your sakes as well as for our sakes."

David held his peace and they rode all the way home in silence. Sarah met them at the door.

"It is time to talk," David told her.

"The three of us, please," Rae said.

David caressed her cheek with the back of his hand, a rare show of affection in the presence of a stranger. "Let us eat together; just the three of us. Tell the children."

David led Rae to his workroom, a long narrow room attached to the back of the house, jutting out like a landlocked peninsula. The two long walls, east and west, had open shutters running almost their entire length, and reaching almost from floor to ceiling, so letting in both morning and evening light; by day the room was permanently bright. A large oil lamp hung from a ceiling beam directly above the large desklike table which contained Sarah's Bible, some writing material, three books and a number of magazines. A smaller table against the east wall contained a straw tray with a huge *yaba* of Sarah's nectar and several mugs; four chairs made up the rest of the furnishing.

"What a place to work and think!" Rae exclaimed. "I envy you." He picked up Sarah's Bible, black clothbound, finely printed, much used, some of the middle part coming away from the back binding, but clearly handled with much care and love.

"Sarah brought it with her," David said softly. "She used it to teach me to read and write. And she used it to teach our older children when we were alone, before the others came into the valley."

"How long were you two here alone?"

"About ten years," David said.

"A long time."

"Didn't seem so then; there was so much to do and to learn. We needed the time to get to know each other."

"Never lonely?"

"No."

"She must be a wonderful woman."

"She is."

Sarah came in at that point. Rae sensed a quick momentary confusion in David.

"What is she?" Sarah asked. "And which she?"

"He said you must be a wonderful woman."

"And you?" Sarah laughed at him with eyes.

"Not fair," Rae said quickly, suddenly sounding very Scots.

"Time to talk," David said brusquely.

"Yes," Sarah said, continuing to laugh at him with her eyes.

Sarah filled three mugs with her nectar; the men made themselves comfortable in chairs. The mood and atmosphere in the room changed. Sarah stood by the wide west window, watching the changing light in the orange sky.

"Where to begin," Rae said thoughtfully.

"Why you want to take us over," Sarah said. "That's as good a point."

"You know our Elders would deny that they want to take you over."

"I thought *we* were going to be honest," David said.

"I think it is important that you understand them, their reasoning, their motives. In your own interest."

"And you care about our interest!" Sarah was scoffing.

Rae held up his hand and nodded acknowledgement of the jab.

"All right," David brushed it aside. "What is their motive?"

"Growth and survival, survival and growth; they interact. Just as weakening and death interact. You are not singular in your church here. There are others like yours all over this land; indeed, all over the world where the Christian message has been carried. There's a bitter struggle going on about it in Africa. Some of them are true Christian churches, like I believe yours is; others are distortions, admixtures of Christian faith and paganism, or superstition or animism. Among some Africans we found attempts to graft Christian teaching on to ancestor worship and spirit worship so that rivers and trees and rocks assumed odd Christian shapes. . . ."

"There are no such problems in our case," Sarah said.

"No," Rae agreed. "But until you are within the fold there is no assurance that it may not come to that one day. The purity of God's message must never depend for its survival and perpetuation on any one or two persons. A day will come when you two will not be here and others who may not be like you may inherit your church and your responsibilities. All your work may then be distorted and your church may be used to serve someone's wish for personal power over others."

"And this is not possible within your fold?" David cut in.

"You know it is. The history of the Church of Rome is replete with instances of men using the power of the church for personal power over others. That was one important reason for the Reformation and the Protestant breakaway. But even there, the

108

fact of the all-embracing nature of the Roman Church ensured that those who used the church for personal power would, sooner or later, be brought under the control of the true meaning and teachings of the church. It is that structure which we talk about as the fold which is the strength of the church. The church must maintain and strengthen that structure. So we must bring all the independently established little churches into the fold."

"And if you don't?" Sarah asked.

"Then the structure will be weakened. To the extent that the so-called independent churches are allowed to grow and flourish, to that extent will the corporate Christian community be damaged. That is the nature of things."

"Wait," David said. "Let's make sure we understand you. Are you saying that the survival of your church demands the destruction of ours?"

"Not the destruction. The taking into the fold."

"And that is not destruction? You say you must take what is ours and turn it into what is yours, and that is not destruction of what is ours?"

"Peace, my friend. To destroy is to wipe out. We do not want to wipe out your church. We want to bring it into the wider fold of all other like-minded churches practising the same form of worship. We offer you the greater strength of a wider community. We can send you preachers and teachers to help with your work. We can see that your school has more books and other supplies for your children; that your mothers get regular help and instruction."

"And for those benefits we must give up our independence?"

"We all of us surrender our independence, or a measure of it, to the greater whole and derive the greater benefit. Surely that is reasonable."

"If it is your choice," Sarah said.

"If it is your free choice," David said.

"But it is," Rae said. "We cannot force you to join us."

"And what if we don't?" Sarah slipped into a chair and braced herself. Better to get it over with.

"I would be very sorry," Rae said softly, his big voice just above whisper. "I came here not caring, doing my duty because it is my duty. Now, because I've met you and seen this place and know something of how it came about, I care."

"But not enough to tell them to leave us alone. . . ." Sarah said.

"If I did they would not listen; and I can't let my caring interfere with what must happen. And they would not let me. Please understand. They can't just leave you alone and pretend this place does not exist. If they did a score of independent churches would refuse to join the fold and a score more would pop up here and there . . . ."

"And soon the fold of which you speak would be too weak to impose its will. And that cannot be allowed to happen, right?" David's voice was bitter now, and tinged with suppressed anger.

"What will they do," Sarah asked, remote and deliberate and cold. "What will they do if we refuse?" She looked searchingly at Rae in the fast gathering gloom, trying to read his mind but his eyes where in shadow.

"You will not notice it immediately but things will begin to happen. Another place of worship to begin with, a place like Elder Jones's; then a visiting pastor and more help and things than you can give. You may know we've already got a piece of land where we can build a church and school, thanks to your own generous allotment policy. . . ."

Sarah nodded, Joseph had told her of the parcel of land they had bought from Elder Jones.

Rae continued quietly. . . . "It will be slow and steady. And in the end we will win. We've done it all before; we have great experience at it. Whatever you decide, be sure of one thing: we will win in the end because we are stronger than you."

"And the Christian justice of it?" Sarah asked.

"Is there really such an issue involved? Think of it. You have founded a good community here, a Christian community, and you have brought that community the message of the Lord as best you can, and I think you have done a wonderful work. But the church will tell you you are not qualified to minister the Gospel; it needs more than just the will and an intimate knowledge of the Bible. And the church says to you, 'Well done, thou good and faithful servant, we are now ready to take over the work from here; come into the fold.' And if you say 'no', the church begins its own work which it must do. Where does the matter of Christian justice come into that? No, Mrs Brown, I see no question of any kind of justice or injustice involved."

"Only of power," David said bitterly.

"Yes; the power and the survival of the church."

"And those who were slaves are not good enough to manage their own churches; only those who were once the slave-owners!"

"Your anger is just," Rae said heavily. "But it will change nothing."

"And you care nothing."

"I do care, my friend, but. . . ."

"You are not my friend!" David's rage was towering now.

"David, my dear," Sarah's voice caressed him, and Rae was startled by the effect; the man's rage dissolved instantly. Then she moved her head slightly and spoke to Rae: "You say you care. If you care, tell us what to do. Or would that be a betrayal of those who sent you, of your side? What are we to do to be left alone?"

"You will be left alone," Rae said.

"With your rival church in our valley. . . ."

"Yes; neither you nor I can stop that."

"So we can do nothing?" Sarah pressed him.

"You can do nothing. . . ."

"She does not mean surrender," David said.

"I know that; neither do I, certainly not in the long run."

"David," Sarah appealed. "Yes, Mr Rae. . . ."

"Please bear with me," Rae said. "It's not easy to explain, but you two have learned patience here, and this requires patience to understand and patience to carry through successfully."

A member of Sarah's extended household came in and lit the lamp; she was followed by two others carrying trays of food which Sarah arranged on the table. The helpers withdrew; Sarah motioned the two men to the table. David said grace, and then they ate the meal of succulent smoked hog, roasted breadfruit, callaloo and avocado pear. Near the end of the meal Sarah said: "Please go on, Mr Rae."

"Call it what you will," Rae said slowly. "Call it the official church or the establishment or the white church – and it did, however willingly or unwillingly, collaborate with the slave system, as you say – it is, at bedrock, part of a system of order, a way of doing things in a managed and organized way which ensures stability. Anything outside that system which threatens the strength of that system also threatens the stability. Do you see what I am trying to say?"

"I understand," Sarah said noncommittally.

"If you do then you will understand that within the system all things are possible; it is even possible to change the system itself from within. That is what the Reformation was all about. Our protest was against the dogmatic domination of Rome. It took time. If you want to protest against the domination of the church in the colonies by white people from Europe then, as we have done with our Reformation, you must first be within the fold."

David, coldly thoughtful now, said: "You are telling us to give up the independence of our church we now have, to submit to you, become part of your fold, and then try to change you. Why should we?"

"Because," Sarah cut in, "he says that is the only way we can survive."

"More than survive," Rae said. "Take over, in time, something bigger than you could ever build by yourselves. You, and people like you could, in time, become the Council of Elders. You yourself could become the President."

"But you are not part of the Church of Rome," Sarah said. "You broke away to be independent."

"We were of the fold, in the fold, till we were driven out. You must be in the fold, you must be part of the system, if you are to challenge it, to change it successfully, even to break it up. You cannot stay outside and do so; it will destroy you."

"So we are back at the thing of power," David said.

"All of life has to do with power," Rae said impatiently. "You yourself are reacting to a challenge to your power."

"We did not build it at anyone else's expense; we took nothing from anybody else."

"And," Sarah said, "we always used it morally, as the Bible teaches."

"You were fortunate. Things were clear and simple for you for a longer time than for most others. That simplicity cannot continue. The use of power is complex and difficult and the church, in all its forms, has a greater experience in the use of power than any of the other systems on earth. That is why we know your independence threatens our power even while we admire you for it. That is why we say, come into the fold and shape us to your desires. That way we will not have to destroy you."

"Having taken away our independence," David jeered.

"And if we join," Sarah said, "what will we have to do?"

"Submit yourselves to guidance; some instructions, perhaps. We manage these matters carefully so there will be no loss of dignity, no loss of respect. Your case would be special, this I can promise you. It would suit us for you to sit on the Council of Elders but there would first have to be the special instruction and ordination."

"I was a member of your church as a slave," Sarah cut in. "I was baptized after instruction. I gave David that same instruction and I baptized him as I was baptized. The laying on of hands is unbroken. Christ's apostles who first preached the Gospel did not have licences or black suits or white collars."

Rae nodded and smiled. "That was before the church became a power system, Mrs Brown. Today it is a power system, the greatest in the world, and it must have rules. We will apply them with due care."

"As you rob us of our independence with due care!"

"Please, David," Sarah calmed him again. "And where will it lead then, Mr Rae? What would happen to our church? Our school? Who will be in charge?"

"There are different ways of handling these things. . . ." Rae stopped abruptly, peered at the woman's shadowy face in the lamplight. "Why are you asking these things when the answers do not really interest you, Mrs Brown?"

"To try and understand you, Mr Rae; to understand what manner of man can come and do these things and say they are done in the name of God."

"In the name of the church, Mrs Brown; in the name of the church."

"The church of God or the church of man?"

"They are one and the same. But about me, ma'am, it is simple; I'm a cog in a great machine, conscious of the power of that machine

113

and the rules for the using of that power. Within the rules I can use that power, even to make things easier and more bearable for people like you; outside that great machine I am nothing. If you can see that then what I feel or what you feel is only important within the framework of that machine."

"But you are a man," Sarah protested. "You have soul and conscience. You have choice, free will. . . ."

"I'm beginning to think he's right, Sarah," David cut in. "Think about it. Remember our long talks about the church and slavery? They wanted us to be good Christians and good slaves at the same time. Remember Samson's anger about that."

"And yet," Rae said, "it was the work of the church, more than anything else, that led to abolition."

"Not here; not among us," David objected.

"But still the church," Rae retorted. "To be tolerated here, to be allowed to do its work here, the church had to appear to acquiesce."

"The parson visited the great house," Sarah said. "I saw it. He was the friend of the owners, not the slaves; they entertained him and he saw the slaves through their eyes. The one who came to our plantation had no feeling for us, no Christian love. I was young but I saw it."

"He was part of the system," Rae said.

"And the system was slavery," David said.

"And yet we ended slavery," Rae said. "Without wholesale slaughter or murder. We ended it by using the system. But there is point to your criticism. It would have been easier now if the church had made it plain to the slaves then, especially the Christian slaves, that accepting the fact of slavery did not mean that the church approved of it. We made the mistake, we still make the mistake, of confusing illiteracy with ignorance. We dealt with you as wise parents with foolish children. I think that was wrong."

"You still do it," Sarah said.

"Really? Is that what I am doing now? Telling you the harsh truth about power and the use of power that the church might survive and flourish? I don't think you are being fair this time, Mrs Brown!"

Sarah exploded: "Fair! You talk to me about fairness! You come here and tell us you are either going to take over or destroy our church and then you talk to me about not being fair! No, Mr Rae!

114

That is treating us like children!"

"You *are* being unfair, Mrs Brown," Rae insisted quietly. "I think I understand why but it is still unfair. You are turning an argument of reason into one of feeling; and I can no more argue with your feelings than you can with mine. We can try to understand each other's thoughts, we can even try to understand each other's feelings. What we cannot in conscience do is argue the superiority of one set of feelings over another. I have told you the intentions and methods of our church and I have laid it out before you openly and in good faith, holding back nothing. Would you have preferred me to make it less open, less forthright? I could have done it, you know. I've done it before now, God help me. Would you really have preferred not to know all that is involved in the choice you make?"

"Peace," David said. "It has become too personal. We are not seeing as clearly and calmly as we should. Let it rest for now. We will talk again tomorrow."

David rose and lit a small oil lamp, went to the door opened it. Rae and Sarah rose and faced each other. She towered over the little man. They seemed awkward with each other. Impulsively, Sarah offered him her hand.

"I'm sorry, Mr Rae. This means much to us; it is all our life."

"I'm sorry, Mrs Brown; sorry to be the one to bring these tidings, sorry there is no way I know for this not to happen."

Sarah straightened her back, raised her chin, seeming even taller, more statuesque. Rae turned and followed David out of the room. Sarah remained, putting the used dishes together. David led Rae to the room where Noname had slept. Rae knew this would be one of those restless nights which afflicted him from time to time, whenever his faith was disturbed and his spirits troubled.

"I am not likely to sleep," he said to David at the door.

There was no bond of understanding between them now; yet they seemed unwilling to part with each other.

"Then why do you do this?" David asked.

"Someone has to."

"Not necessarily you."

"Someone with less feeling, perhaps?"

"You know what I mean."

115

"We do not want to destroy what you have here."

"Does it matter?"

"I think it does; and so do others. They know more about you and your work than you think."

"It won't be the same; it can't be the same. It's already started changing."

"I know. That's why I didn't want to stop at Elder Jones's. I look at him and become afraid of what might come. Change can be terrible at times, and the worst part is that you cannot stop it even if you see that it is not for the best."

"Not even through the power of your system?"

"I'm not arguing our case now."

"Sorry. There's rum in the house; want me to bring you some?"

"No. Can I walk out to your church?"

"Yes; it's always open."

"Expected it to be."

"Want me to come?"

"I'd like to be alone."

"All right then, goodnight. Stay out as long as you like. The house will be open. There'll be someone about if you want anything."

"David . . . Pastor David."

David stopped and turned back.

"If you could manage the change, if they agreed to leave you to do it, only helping where help is needed, would you join us then? Don't answer now; think about it."

"All right. I'll think about it; but you know it will not be our change: It will be your change, whoever manages it."

"It is the damage I fear," Rae said.

"Then leave us alone," David said softly.

"You know we can't. I've explained that."

"Then the responsibility for the damage must be yours too."

"That is easy. Systems of power find no difficulty taking responsibility for damage and destruction; that is why wars are made so easily, why people can be put in chains, why even the church can be so brutal at times. And still we cannot function without systems. Systems are faceless, conscienceless, heartless;

116

but they impose order and keep the peace and make the future possible."

"Then why worry about the damage?" said David.

"Why will you not understand?"

"You mean, why will I not surrender? That is what you want. It is not enough to take what is mine. You want me to tell you it is right for you to do it. Well, I will not. If you have any more conscience than the system in whose name you excuse this wickedness, then let that conscience eat into your soul! I will not understand! I will not see with you! I will not give you my mind!" David walked away, his big body a moving monument of contained rage.

For a long moment John Rae stood by the door, the little oil lamp growing hotter in his hand, a quiet depression over him. How often he had done this sort of work; and each time it was different. This time it was more personally painful because these two had revived old spiritual doubts. The strength of their faith was its simplicity: do what is right and thou wilt find favour in the eyes of the Lord and his blessing will fall on thee and protect thee all the days of thy life. Or is there more to it? We, the body of the church, are the conscience of the system; we do what we do for the greater glory of the church. Then why do the good ones, the best among them, resist us so hard? Why is it only easy to win over the self-seeking and the crooked; why do we often have to break the good and the upright and destroy their works? "Oh, Lord, give me the strength to persuade these two to come into the fold, to walk with us and continue the work they have started here. For thy name's sake, Amen." John Rae placed the little lamp on the bedside table, and found his way to the back door and up the hill to the church. The moon had not yet risen. A dog barked nearby, half-announcing, half-challenging his presence. A voice growled: "Is all right; is parson, hush." The dog was silent. He felt and smelled a fine mist coming down on the valley. And suddenly he remembered his lonely childhood in a crofter's cottage among the Scottish hills. Not the same, really; very much colder and very much bleaker. So why this strong remembrance? At other times of deep depression his mind had slipped back to those hard yet tranquil childhood days. But never as sharply and strongly as this

117

night. Beyond the strength of our system, beyond the harsh logic of the need for the survival of that system, what right have we to destroy the work of good people like these? Is survival justification enough? He talked of "our" change and "your" change. They needed no guidance from us and our system to get to this point. Would they get beyond it, perhaps beyond our system, by themselves if we left them to themselves? But how can we leave them alone? Guide us, Oh Lord, that we may do thy will. . . .

David stood at the open window of their bedroom.

"He's entering the church," he said. "His spirit is really troubled."

"If he is a good man," Sarah said thoughtfully, "then he should let others do this dirty work."

"Not dirty, my dear; not from their standpoint. Painful, perhaps, unpleasant perhaps but, again from their standpoint, very necessary."

"Then why his distress? He's not going back to them to say: 'Don't do this', or, 'I think it is wrong to do this'."

"You are being unfair to him, Sarah. You know that doing what you are sure is right can still cause you distress. Want me to remind you of some of the times you yourself were so distressed?"

Sarah's mood changed, and her voice with it. "You're suddenly very clear-headed. Why, my David? What are you seeing?"

"Think of him," David's voice was almost impersonal. "Think hard about him and all we said to each other."

"All right; now what?"

"For all the power of his system, for all his knowledge that we cannot resist it and win, he still wants our agreement. Think. They didn't ask for our agreement to turn us into slaves."

"But they did use some of the slaves to become drivers," Sarah said.

"Now you are thinking," said David. "And the drivers had to agree because they were the only slaves with some sort of choice. They could choose to drive the others and get the benefits of being drivers, or they could refuse and remain like the others and often suffer more punishment for having refused. Did you know Samson refused to be a driver?"

"You never told me. That why they hurt him so?"

"Partly. But you see now why Rae is so anxious to win us over? They want drivers to drive the souls and spirits of our people into obedience to them. It is a kind of slavery of the mind instead of the body."

"A slavery of the mind; a slavery of the spirit. David, it's a terrible thought. Does he understand this?"

"I don't know. We must find out; make him understand."

"Then what?"

"Then nothing. He must understand, that is all; and we must understand."

"He told us himself," Sarah said. "They don't want to destroy what is here already if it can be avoided; take over and build on it. That is what they want. And that part of it is reasonable, even to me. What is not reasonable is to take it against our will."

"You do not need reason when you have power."

"Then why the attempt to reason with us?"

"Because the conquest of the mind is the most complete victory."

"Then it is not just our church?"

"No. He told us so himself. He was honest with us."

"To make us over, not in God's image but in their image."

"So that we see the world and ourselves through their eyes, as they see us. We must make him understand that, Sarah."

"What makes you think he does not already?"

"Because he's out there, my dear. Because his spirit is troubled. Because I think he is a good man."

"Oh, my David," she protested in exasperation. "What makes him a good man? His good language? The good manners with which he tells us they are prepared to build another church here and turn the people against us? No, my David. A good man would see that what we are doing is good and give us his help or leave us alone. You know that."

"This is something you and I have not really thought about until now. It is not simply good men and bad men, Sarah. This is the thing we have not seen and could not see as long as we were here alone. What we did not see is that their system will not leave us alone. Perhaps it cannot leave us alone. Perhaps their system has to take over and take over until it has control of all the world."

"And turn everybody into drivers for their system or else destroy them?"

"Perhaps that too, my Sarah."

"But why, David? Why?"

"Because anything not under their power threatens it. He said so."

"I know that; what I want to know is, why do they have to have this power? Why is it such a terrible fire in them, driving them to such terrible things?"

"I don't know," David said heavily. "Let us see if he does."

There was a long silence in the room after that. Sarah snuggled deeper under the light bedclothing. The high-pitched whine of a solitary mosquito was cut off suddenly as it passed too close over the lamp and was instantly scorched to death. Sarah allowed body and mind to relax.

"Come to bed," she murmured sleepily, as she had done countless times over the years, and then, drifting off, half-heard him adjust the shutters of the window, half-heard him move across the room to his bedside chair, half-heard the heavy thud of the big boots, the rustle of the shedding of clothes, felt the bed sag with his weight, then felt him and leaned her head against his chest and, feeling safe and secure, slipped into a deep untroubled sleep. David lay thinking and brooding for nearly an hour more, then he deliberately put all thought out of his mind and fell into a deep sleep.

Only John Rae, alone in the austere high-ceilinged church, was too disturbed and restless for sleep.

The morning sun cast a warm spell of tranquillity over the church on the edge of the wide valley. People in their Sunday best came strolling to the church from miles around, the gay bright colours the women wore challenging the gentle warmth of the sun. They came in twos and threes and in larger family groups, men and women, boys and girls, and a large number of old grannies, their heads tied with the coloured bandanas of slavery times. The younger women wore woven straw hats decorated with coloured ribbons of white and red and blue and pink. The men looked awkward in jackets and ties and unfamiliar Sunday hats, the boys uncomfortable at having their usually bare feet enslaved in heavy shoes and boots.

Sarah and David and John Rae received the congregation under a huge breadfruit tree near the church door, surrounded by the Elders of the church. Each member was introduced to the visiting white Pastor who had a handshake and a word of welcome for each. Then they gravitated to friends and acquaintances and the talk became spirited and lively and the atmosphere that of a Sunday morning outdoor party.

Elder Jones and the three Elders who were his supporters in the move to join the greater church based in Kingston on whose behalf the Pastor had come, stayed self-importantly close to the visitor, ensuring that all the congregation saw where they were. Rae tactfully kept his distance, speaking to David and Sarah when not greeting a new member of the congregation.

At one point Sarah leaned toward Rae and whispered: "You must not ignore your supporters, Mr Rae."

"Wish I could," Rae whispered back, a wicked twinkle in his eyes.

"Mr Rae!" Sarah protested, only half in jest.

"Mrs Brown!" Rae mocked back in perfect mimicry of her, and roared at his own humour.

"You're very cheerful this morning," David said.

"There's a time to weep and a time to laugh," Rae said. "I want to laugh on this beautiful morning. I wept enough last night."

"Let him laugh for now, Sarah," David cut in. "Come, it is time to begin."

The very old man whose duty it was, rang the church bell for the last call and the people trooped into the church. . . .

At the end of the service David told his congregation: "You know Pastor Rae has visited with us these past two days. We have talked and we will talk again and the Elders will be a part of that talk. Some of you know what this is about. You will hear more. Now Pastor John Rae will give you his message of greetings from his church."

121

He's very sure of himself, Rae thought as he mounted the pulpit, very sure of his people: not at all the secretive possessiveness of a man jealous for his personal power Elder Jones had hinted at down at the Kingston office.

"I bring you greetings of the President of our Council of Elders and of all the Elders and of all our congregations all over this land and all over the world in the name of Christian love and Christian unity." The church's huge wooden rafters intensified the deep richness of Rae's melodious "preaching voice".

"Amen!" Elder Jones led; "Amen!" many voices echoed in unison.

"We are very impressed with your work here. The fame of your pastor has travelled far and wide. Men speak of him as a good and wise and Christian leader who walks in the footsteps of our Lord. And now that I have seen it for myself, now that I have had the privilege of speaking with him and his good and gracious lady," Rae looked at Sarah and his eyes twinkled momentarily, "now that I have seen and felt the spirit which inspires your efforts, I understand why men talk of yours as the most united and productive Christian community in all the land, and I can say, from the fullness of my heart: Amen. So be it; let it always be so that the blessing of the Lord may always be on you and on those who lead you into the paths of Righteousness for His name's sake. Amen."

"Amen!" the congregation said; and it was a warm appreciation of both the meaning of the words and the preacher's art with which they were delivered.

"I come to offer you the hand of brotherhood, to invite you to share with us the wisdom and the goodness you have found and brought about here, and to receive from union with us the strength and the support which comes with the greater power of greater numbers. Alone, you can do only so much. Together, united in one great congregation which embraces the whole country and all the countries of the world, there are no limits to what the church can do in your name and our name and in the name of Jesus Christ. Amen." Rae stepped back dramatically, eyes closed, both arms raised.

There was a momentary hush, then vociferous "Amens" and

"Hallelujas". David waited till the hubbub died down, till the congregation was silent again; he waited till the people became restive, concerned and uneasy over his silence, till they started turning to each other enquiringly; only then did he rise.

"We thank Pastor Rae for his strong message of Christian love and brotherhood." His speech was soft, casual, conversationally quiet as his people had grown over the years to expect of their pastor. "I am pleased that the pastor's words moved so many of us. We must be moved and stirred by words of unity and love and brotherhood. But afterwards we must think calmly and ask hard questions. And there are questions to be asked; not about Christian love and Christian brotherhood, for we all agree on that. But who is my brother? He who say so or he who shows so? And how does he show it? These are questions to which we must seek and find our own answers. These are not questions others can answer for us. We welcome the hand of friendship that is offered. Friendship is a good thing if it is a thing on which two decide; it is not a thing one forces on another. Otherwise it is not friendship. And just as a man cannot force a woman to love him if she does not want to, so any love which is forced by one side on the other is no love. And as it is with people, so must it be with what Pastor Rae calls systems. There must be love from both sides to make the bond. All this we of this church must think and talk about. When we have done so and come to a point, we will let you know, Pastor Rae. That is how we have always done our business here. That is how we do the Lord's business in this community. We thank you for coming and we thank you for your message of Christian love and Christian brotherhood."

A woman in the church choir, it sounded like the one with the melodious voice which had impressed Rae under the breadfruit tree, raised her voice in a Christian song of joy and praise and all the congregation joined in, filling the church and floating out into the broad valley till it was filled with the joyous Sunday morning sound of praise to a God unknown.

Again, John Rae was overwhelmed by the haunting feeling of being very close to the bleak Scottish hills and valleys of his distant childhood. He closed his eyes and allowed the music to wash over him. And watching him, and the single unbidden tear

123

that rolled down his cheek, the former slave boy, David, felt compassion for this man who had come here to take over or else undermine all that they had built. Then David felt Sarah's mind tugging at his consciousness. He straightened up, touched John Rae, and they led the singing congregation slowly out of the church.

The early morning mist hung low in the valleys between the hills, giving the green earth an ethereal, almost unearthly appearance. They rode in pairs, David and John Rae ahead (Sarah and Rae's bodyguard, Joseph, behind) and a spare mule, extra big and strong, behind them. They had been riding for nearly three hours and the brightness of daylight was beginning to show behind the Blue Mountains.

John Rae wondered whether he would ever be able to make those leaders down in Kingston understand what he had seen and experienced here with these two. Could he make them understand that he had deep philosophic discussions such as he had not had since his university days with two people born into slavery and with no formal schooling? How could he, when he could not have such discussion with the Elders themselves? To them he was useful because of his skill at dealing with the former slaves and at bringing them into the fold, but he was also far too clever to be fully trusted. If he told them of these two in straight and truthful terms it would be seen as part of his cleverness, part of his skill at dressing up simple things to make his work appear more important and exciting than it really was. Some of it was a charade, what these two would call a thing of show. This detour to their original home to see the legendary Samson, now stricken and paralysed, was such a thing of show. It would make the journey down to Kingston that much longer and slower. But he wanted to see this Samson and the place where all those runaway slaves had first settled.

"We are nearly there," said David. "You'll see it after the next hill."

Sarah spurred her mule forward till she rode beside David on the narrow path. Rae sensed the excitement in her and her need to be near David. He reined in his mule and fell back to ride beside

Joseph. Sarah and David rode side by side, almost touching, as they climbed the last hill before the valley of Mount Zion.

At last the long narrow valley lay below them. They halted and looked down.

"Oh, David," Sarah murmured. "Such a long time. We should have come before. It looks so small now, so dry. What's happened? Not many houses or people."

The sun was up now and the mist was gone. The valley looked parched. The river that Sarah remembered was now a deep dry yellowish gully. What was once a permanently moist and dense forest of huge and ancient trees on the slopes of the hill leading to Samson's look-out was now a barren place of shrub and rock. The deep pool immediately below where the sloping forest had been was now a dark waterless hole. The village was still there; a dozen houses or so. As they rode into the valley people came out to look at the strangers.

Nothing was as Sarah remembered and David sensed her mounting dismay. He tried to comfort her.

"It is a long time, Sarah. It cannot be as it was, as you remember it."

"It's so dry," Sarah said.

"They burned it too hard," David said. "He shouldn't have allowed that."

They rode in silence the rest of the way. Sarah and David remembered the valley as it had been when they were sent out of it all those many years ago: a green place of tall trees and rich damp earth and gurgling water.

David turned his head to Rae. "It has changed since we left. I thought it was only Samson. . . ." His voice trailed off. Sarah took his hand and held it tight as they rode on more slowly.

An impulse to offer them comfort rose up in Rae. He raised his voice: "The last time I visited the place where I was born and grew up, there was no one left whom I had known. The house where I lived with my mother after my father died was a ruin with only some of the walls standing, and weed had taken over the rooms where we had spent our days and nights. I wept because I knew there was nowhere to go back to for the rest of my life. . . ."

"Change is not always good," David said coldly.

125

"But it cannot be stopped," Rae said.

"There is Maria," Sarah said, letting go of David's hand and spurring her mule on.

The others were there too: Jonas, grey, big-bellied now, but still the same; Noname, Big and Little Mary, both pregnant and both grown fat from eating too much starch; but most of all there was Maria, unchanged physically, an ageless, firmly held-together black presence. And there were many others, adults and children, unfamiliar to Sarah and David.

Sarah slid off her mule and embraced Maria. There was no responding embrace from Maria.

"Forget the past," Sarah murmured. "It was a long time ago, Maria. Please be as glad to see me as I am to see you. Where is Samson?"

Maria turned and led the way round the house to the sunny side of the verandah. David, meanwhile, introduced Rae and Joseph to the welcoming group.

Samson, dressed and normal-looking, sat in his huge chair catching the morning sun. One of the two old women had fed him and had just finished wiping his face.

Sarah slipped into the chair facing him. "How is he?"

"Awright now, Miss Sarah; but he not going change."

"Not getting worse?"

"No; and not getting better."

"Can he hear? Can he understand?" Sarah got her answer from Samson eyes. "It's all right!" She cut off the old woman. "He hears; he understands."

"How do you know?" Maria sounded angry.

"Look in his eyes," Sarah said.

"I've looked in his eyes every day! I've begged him for a sign!"

"Not anger, Maria, please. Look with love."

"Still the same," Maria said bitterly. "Always love."

David came up with Rae. The old woman suddenly grew agitated.

"Something wrong! He's getting a fit?"

Sarah looked intently into Samson's suddenly very bright eyes. Then she said urgently: "Take him away, David! Take him away now!"

"Who?"

"Rae! Take him away right now! Samson doesn't want him here!"

David grabbed Rae's arm and led him away.

Sarah put her hand on Samson's. "I'm sorry." She watched the fire go out of his eyes, sensed the agitation leave the caged body. "I'm sorry," she repeated. "We should have remembered. I should have remembered. Try to talk to me; tell me with your eyes. I will try to understand. Please try. . . ."

The old woman gathered her things and moved away quietly.

David led Rae from the cluster of houses, in the direction of the hill that was Samson's look-out. On either side of the worn footpath were mounds of rock, piled up to make planting space for yam. The trees which shaded the way to the top during an earlier time were all gone and the short dry shrub offered no protection against the bright morning sun.

"Did not expect this to happen," David apologized. "My fault for forgetting. He was hurt badly; the marks they put on his body will remain till the day of his death."

"We must pay for the sins of our fathers," Rae murmured. "I think it would be better to move on. What will you do about your. . . ?" Rae was lost for a way to describe Samson. "Will you accept our help? Bring him down for one of our doctors to look at. We may be able to help."

"No," David said. "You can see he will not want that. He swore he would never have anything to do with Kingston."

"And white men. . . ," Rae said very softly.

"And white men," David agreed. "He was a proud man."

"And they put chains on him. . . ."

"On all of us. And now you want to put chains on our minds."

"If being in the fold is being in chains then we all are, black and white alike. You must see that."

"There is the difference of choice," David said, his voice grown cold and remote.

"Choice!" Rae exploded. "Who has choice? What choice have I got? What choice has anybody got but to function as part of the process and the system or be destroyed? Choices are made before we are born."

127

"Your system, not ours; and that is the difference. Your fathers and forefathers created your system so it is easy for you to talk about being a part of it. You had choice through your forebears. We had no part in the making of your system just as we had no part in the turning of men into slaves. Our forebears had no part in it either."

"Oh my brother in Christ!" Rae said heavily. "You know and understand what I am saying and you will not reach out to help me. Why? I told you they – we – cannot leave you to succeed. The change must and will come. You either go with it or are swept aside by it. I do not want you to be swept aside. . . ."

"So you would take away my choice, our choice, as the price of survival."

"There is no other way."

"There is Samson's way," David said.

"Then there really is no more to say," Rae said.

They turned and retraced their steps to the village in silence. The people had dispersed; only Jonas and Noname and Rae's bodyguard, Joseph, were with the animals outside what had once been Bagley's store. Sarah was still with Samson and the others were about their business. Rae, grown depressed and desolate by both his failure to win over David and Sarah and by his sensing of the slow dying of this place, was anxious to be gone. And Joseph, who understood him better than the little white Pastor realized, knew it and was ready. Noname instructed Joseph on the quickest way to Red Hills, from where the journey would be straightforward. Bagley in Red Hills would fill their water gourd and sell them whatever food they might need for their journey down. Rae wanted to go without seeing Sarah, but David sent for her and she came quickly.

"Is he all right? Pastor Rae is leaving."

"He's calm now. . . . I'm sorry about what happened, Mr Rae. I'm sure David explained."

"Not to worry, Mrs Brown, he did. I am sorry to have to leave you in this way. I would have preferred it another way. I hope you will think of me as a friend; I will always think of you both as such. And believe me when I say I will never forget you."

"David and I will remember you, Mr Rae."

"I know you understand what is bound to happen. Is . . . there. . . ?"

"We do, Mr Rae, and there really is nothing you can say to change matters. You did what you had to; we must do what we have to."

Rae took Sarah's hand. . . . Impossible to think of this woman ever being anybody's slave; and yet she was. Then he took David's hand and resisted the strong impulse to embrace him. Then he mounted his mule and hurried away down the drab path that led out of the narrow valley to Red Hills.

Sarah embraced Joseph. "Come back to us, Joseph. Come back any time you want to. There'll be a home for you. No matter what they decide, you are part of us."

"I know what they decide, Miss Sarah," Joseph said. "I will take him down then I will return. Then I will come home." Joseph looked into David's eyes, a quick, brief, glancing embrace of commitment. "Mass David." Then he mounted and followed Rae out of the valley.

Rae waited for Joseph at the last point from which he could look back at the village. When Joseph reached him, he said: "You want to remain with them?"

Joseph's face was expressionless. "I will take you down, Pastor. That is my duty."

"But you want to stay?"

"I don't know. It is good up here: quiet, cool, no fighting, no heavy rum drinking."

You have made up your mind, Rae told himself; but you will not tell me. You're not yet as forthright as those two back there; but then, I've never thought of you as anything other than a good and faithful body servant so I've never tried to talk to you. Now it is too late, you will evade me with oblique responses which do not offend and give away nothing.

"But tell me, Joseph. Wouldn't you like to come back up here? I thought Mrs Brown would ask you to."

"Maybe one day," Joseph said.

"Yes, Joseph. Maybe one day. Let us go." Maybe one day it will be possible for people like you and me to talk to each other instead of using words as weapons to probe and barriers to repel the probing.

Rae spurred his mule forward. Joseph followed, a horse's head behind his master, the rifle cradled in his arm, the machete hanging from his saddle. It was a long ride down to Kingston; longer this way than had been the climb up to Cyprus by way of the Catherine Plain; but it was downhill all the way.

Sarah and David walked slowly back to Maria's house, using the time gained by their pace to talk.

"I don't think Maria can cope," Sarah said.

"She can cope," David said. "She can cope with anything she has to."

"Or wants to," Sarah added.

David stopped and kicked at the ground. "Are you saying she does not want to?"

Sarah stopped a little distance ahead of him. "Yes."

"Why?"

"I think we should ask her."

"Are you sure?"

"Yes. I think he knows it too."

"But she loves him."

"She loved him strong, David. She loved him and made him our leader."

"He was our leader before."

"Yes. But not in the way she made him. She made him the leader who built the community and drove us out when we broke the rules. Remember, David, he was the leader but it was Maria's will that made him make things happen."

"You could be wrong, Sarah. This is a heavy blow for her. She may have lost control for now."

"Let us talk with her."

They found her alone in the kitchen at the back of the house. There had been no time for David to greet her properly, no time for him to go and look at Samson. He had not seen her in many, many years, this woman who was the nearest approximation to the mother he had never known. Now, he towered over her, broader and taller than Samson in his prime.

He took both her hands, hard and bony, and held them tightly. She was as he remembered her from those early years, physically unchanged. Only the eyes were changed: the knowing, at times laughing gentleness he remembered was not there; a sombre bleakness instead.

"It is good to see you, Maria. You have not changed."

"You have changed. I hear your Cyprus is better than here. I hear you," she used her eyes to include Sarah, "have done well and prospered. We tried to build a school here!"

"We were fortunate," David brushed it away.

"I hear she has given you many children; she alone and you have as many as all the women bred for Samson."

"You remember," Sarah murmured in the background.

"I remember everything," Maria said sharply. "What we did was right. We were alone; we did not know of the freeing of the slaves."

"That is in the past," Sarah said. "We are not here to judge the past."

"About Samson," David said. "We want to help."

"What can you do? The Nanas you sent stopped him from dying. But they cannot make him walk again, they cannot make him talk again. So what can you do with a man who lives but is like a man who is dead? What can you do?"

"We can help to look after him," Sarah said quickly. "Nurse him, care him, make him know we love him; we can make him happy and pray he will get better."

"And if he does not? Your old women say he will not."

"We will just care him. . . . Till he dies."

"No matter how long?"

"No matter how long."

"And you," Maria's eyes searched David's face. "You agree? You agree with this. . . ."

"Yes," David said, letting go of her hands, suddenly bitterly depressed to find Sarah was right.

"But he is not a man again!" Maria flashed with anger. "He's not my man again! My man was strong! He could do anything! I know if he could choose he would choose to die; to be left to die."

"He has not chosen yet," Sarah said.

131

"You know?" Maria grew very still.

"I know."

"He makes you understand?"

"Yes."

Maria nodded, accepting the truth of it in spite of herself and against her will. "I cannot understand him." Her voice was distant. "I cannot understand this one who fouls himself and cannot move or speak. I look on him and I see only what he was, the proud strong man who was in that body."

"You must be patient, Maria. It takes time." Sarah moved a step toward Maria. Maria's body swayed back, refusing the offered contact and embrace.

"You just came here and you understand him." She was colder now, more withdrawn.

"What do you want to do?" David asked in an equally cold and impersonal voice, examining Maria's face closely.

"What can I do?" Maria countered. "You say care for him till he dies. We will care for him. Will you leave your old women?"

"No," Sarah said quickly. "They have their own families."

"Then they must teach Vie what to do," Maria said. "Let the dumb look after the dumb."

Sarah started to protest but David cut it off. "We will take him to Cyprus," he said sharply. "We can care for him there . . . if you wish."

There was a seemingly endless silence among them. Maria held on to herself tightly, using the force of her will to keep her body calm and relaxed. They thought she had no feeling for him, she knew that, these two who had done what she had planned for them to do, what she and Samson should have done. Let them think what they want to. Only she knew how she felt. To see your man die and then to live with the empty shell of him.

"If you wish," Maria said at last. She left them abruptly. She walked round the house to Samson. She sat down and stared into his eyes, looking for some sign of recognition, some understanding, anything that would tell her of the link of life between them. She saw nothing.

"They will take you to Cyprus," she said. "You hear me? They will take you away from me and your children and your place.

Do you want that? Do you want them to take you away? She says you understand. She says you made her understand. Now make me understand. Show me a sign. Make *me* understand! Do you want to go with them?"

Just the blank stare. She sighed heavily. "Down there on the plantation when a man grew sick they looked after him to make him well so he could return to work. But if they failed; they put him away to die, for the work must go on. We must raise the children and find food and water and work the land; that is how it is. If you are not part of this, you are nothing. If you will get well, Samson, we will wait and we will look after you till you are well. If you are not going to get well you are a burden we cannot bear. If you make a sign to tell me you will get well I will believe you and we will all work and wait; I will even clean the smells away myself. You hear me, Samson? You hear me? show me you hear me. . . ."

She leaned forward, staring intently into his eyes, willing him to respond, to show some sign that she could cling to. That Sarah had said, calmly with love. . . . Calmly, with love. . . . Hear me, Samson, please. . . . Still only the blank, empty stare. Abruptly, Maria got up and walked away, body held erect by the strength of her mind, seamy matt black face an expressionless mask, dark eyes almost as blank as Samson's.

What remained of the original members of the family met at the old gathering place, now part of Maria's extensive yard, in the early evening, when the day had grown cool but yet with still enough light by which to hold a meeting. They had carried Samson in his chair to his customary place at the head of the table; so it was as it had been when this place had been the centre of all their decision-making. Jonas and Noname, and now David, were there. Only Joe had gone away to Kingston and never returned. Among the women, Belle had died in childbirth less than a year before, and Flo and a new man with a family of his own had abandoned their Mount Zion lots and moved nearer Red Hills with its flourishing community of small peasants and artisans. So of the women there remained Maria, Vie, the dumb one, the two Marys and, now, the returned Sarah. There were of course others too: the large number of children of the original family, people who had come to settle later under Bagley's not very successful tenancy plan, and a few who had drifted into the valley and attached themselves to this or that household as helpers in exchange for food and shelter. These were on the fringe of the meeting of the family, away from the long table, able to watch and hear, but taking no part in the proceedings.

Jonas, the proud hunter, Samson's right-hand man of the old days, grown fat and heavy and old now, opened the proceedings by welcoming David and Sarah and remembering, mainly for the benefit of the onlookers, the days of that long journey out of bondage when Samson guided them to this place and was their shield and protector, with Mother Maria as the nurse and the provider. He remembered the good days when they were building this place, and the joy of working together in the good place with good people; the stories they told on warm nights when the moon made the world soft and Maria's brew warmed their bodies and made men feel sweet toward their women. He remembered cold nights when they huddled around warm fires; and he remembered the wet days and nights of torrential rain before they had built their sturdy homes. And somehow, looking back, it all seemed more exciting, more adventurous, more fulfilling than he had found it at the time. . . . "And now we get a blow," Jonas concluded. "Our leader get a lick that is too heavy for the mother of the family to carry alone, even with the help we who live here can give. So David and Sarah come forward and say they will take Mass Samson to Cyprus where they can care him better than we can. It is Maria's wish that he go with them, if the family agree. We know David and Sarah will care him good. And maybe he will come back better one day. We moved well together. . . ." Jonas, overcome, stopped speaking and looked at Maria.

Maria felt dry and empty. She shook her head slightly and waited for others to speak. No one wanted to speak. So she said coldly, so that no one should know her feeling: "It is hard but he must go. We cannot manage him here. We must care for the living."

"It is hard indeed!" David said harshly, unable to hide his anger. "In slavery days when a man became useless they cast him out. Those days are done and still we cast out a man because he is useless!"

"David!" Sarah said softly, urgently, taking his arm. "She's hurting enough."

"We did not ask you to come and take him," Maria said. "You do not have to."

"We are taking him," Sarah said quickly, "if the family agrees."

"I agree," Noname said quickly, to avoid any further argument, and so did the others.

"We leave in the morning," David barely controlled his anger. "First light."

"We will travel with you, Noname and I," Jonas said.

"Come!" David said to Sarah and walked away from the meeting place.

Sarah paused beside Maria, laid her hand lightly and briefly on Maria's, looked into the expressionless eyes, and whispered: "Forgive him. He's angry because it seems you don't care." Then she hurried after David as he walked briskly up the slope in the direction of Samson's look-out.

She found him there, sitting on one of the huge boulders, staring into space, seemingly unaware of the world about him. She leaned against the rock, careful to keep her distance and careful, also, to be able to see his face fully in the fading light. She waited till some of the bleak remoteness passed from his face, the tautness from his body.

"You were hard on her," she said.

"No harder than she is on him." He was calming down and she relaxed and felt at ease.

"Hardness for hardness," she murmured. "Like an eye for an eye?" Something about this place that she remembered from long ago; some soothing quality that caresses the spirit and makes you feel at peace.

"She learned nothing. She's driving him out as she drove us out. And not one of them protested; just as when she drove us out. Nothing's changed."

"Oh, David. We made the decision this time, you and I. Not Maria; not the others."

"Because he is useless and she does not want him here. She said so."

135

"But they would have kept him if we did not propose to take him."

"And put him aside to die as they did the useless old slaves. . . ."

"That, yes. But they would have kept him."

"All right, so they would not have driven him out; they couldn't because he can't move. They would have left him to die slowly."

"No. Maria, perhaps. Not the others. No need for you to be angry with Maria. She has lost control. She does not know what to do without him as he was."

"She can accept him as he is."

"I do not think she can," Sarah had a moment of panic at the thought of perhaps having a paralysed David one day. She fought it back. "I don't think she can live with defeat. To accept what he is is to accept defeat."

"So she casts him out."

"No. We take him away."

"And what does she do? Pretend it never happened?"

"She puts it out of her mind. She remembers him as he was. She chooses the strongest of his sons and she dreams through him as she dreamed through Samson. It is the only way she knows, David."

"It's a hard way," David mused. "As hard as the slavery way.

"It is also the way to survive, my dear; for some, like Maria, the only way. To be defeated you must admit defeat. Is she really so very different from us? Is our answer to John Rae really so very different from Maria's refusal to admit defeat?"

"You are straying now," David protested. "Straying far and wide. The comparison is false. And we are prepared to face and deal with defeat."

Sarah laughed. "For the same reason that we were prepared, all those many years ago, to be driven out rather than submit to Maria's plan. She was right then and we were right then. You said so yourself."

"I am not sure about this time," he countered.

"It took you years to see her rightness the first time. You are the one who always tells people to take time and think, Pastor Brown. So you take time and think, and judge not lest ye be judged. Look at the mountains, David! They don't look the same as from Cyprus."

They looked at the mountains in the fading light of the dying day. Sarah moved nearer David till their bodies touched. She took his hand and they sat on the great boulder, allowing the peace and calm of the place to wash over them.

In the fading light they both recalled the early days and the sense of Samson's presence a protective shield over all they did, wherever they walked. And now, David thought, he cannot even come up to his hill again and see the view from here; to again see Kingston and through it, all the cities of the earth. Sarah picked up the thought and answered it:

"He does not need to be up here again. The memory of this view is with him always. He can always come up here in his mind and look and see all this again."

"Yes," David agreed, thinking: If you were to die tomorrow I would remember you always; I would see your face clearly always, sharply as I see and feel it now. Impulsively, he flung his arm about her shoulders and held her tight. She turned her head and kissed him, gently, tenderly, as a mother kisses a disturbed child to give it comfort.

"Duppies?" she whispered.

"One slipped through," he said. "I'm glad he can come up here in spirit. I'm very glad I found you, my Sarah."

"You forget I found you, my David. You forget I made you take me."

"So no one else would," he mocked. "You used me to upset Maria."

"And how you enjoyed it! I close my eyes and still see it; you wild as a bull."

"Shameless woman!" He held her closer. Remembered passion stirred renewed passion in him. "I want you."

She grew still, serious. "Up here?"

"Yes. Now."

She began to ask why then choked back the question. The duppy that had slipped through must have been a terrible one; the kind you do not talk about until much later. She straightened up, took his hand and led him along the path which took them to the small room-like cave immediately below the look-out. The sleeping and cooking places were still there though they had clearly not been used in a long time. Weathering had crumbled the stones and clay of the fireplace; cooking pots were reduced to bits of broken pottery, only the neck of the water *yaba* was identifiable; termites had reduced the kindling logs to small mounds of dust most of which the wind had blown away. The more sheltered sleeping area was a bed of dry leaves giving off a faintly scented burnt-leaves smell.

They stripped and went down together on the brown leaves and made love; not with the passionate heat of other times, but gently, tenderly, as an act of devotion and commitment. When it was over they stayed close to each other for a long time, unwilling to break the bond. At last the air turned chilly till Sarah began to feel it. So, reluctantly, they rose and dressed and went back up to the look-out.

Kingston, far below, was in hazy darkness now. Here and there a thin swirl of white smoke spiralled up into the darkening night. Beyond Kingston the sea was a curving sheet of dark green glass, stretching away as far as the eye could see. The mountains, to the east, were a massive dark presence over the land.

Sarah took David's hand once more.

"Duppy put to sleep?"

"Yes. . . . Please don't die for a long time, Sarah."

So that's it; but of course, all that talk about remembering.

"Oh my dear! I will try to live as long as I can, David. You know that; but we don't control these things."

"I know. My foolishness."

"No, dear. Just preparing yourself. We all do it. I did it earlier when I thought of you being like Samson. I wanted to ask you never to get a stroke."

Again David embraced Sarah, but without the earlier hint of desperation. One day he might have to go on living without her, or she without him; one day he or she might be stricken. To live with the conscious knowledge of the shadow of uncertainty, with the knowledge that disaster or tragedy could strike at any time; to be afraid and to know and acknowledge your fear, and still to live creatively and with unstinting love: that is to live with grace.

138

Holding onto each other, alone on that high hill, David and Sarah shared a heightened momentary consciousness of the grace they had won.

In the morning they would take Samson out of this valley, and he and they would never see it again, or stand on this hill and look down on the world below. Yet they would carry the memory with them for all their lives, and perhaps beyond. There can be no death as long as there is remembrance of person and place; there can be no life when person and place are no longer remembered.

All these things David and Sarah sensed and felt up there. Always, in the times ahead, David and Sarah would share a remembrance of this place because they had shared the mood it created.

"Time to go down," David said.

"It makes me sad," Sarah said, "to leave. It's like leaving friends. What will happen?"

"The place will remain," David said. "It will always be here."

"Will others come to it? Will it be as special? Will they feel what we feel?"

"I don't know."

"No more runaway slaves."

Not the only thing to run away from, David thought. "But there always will be," he said out loud.

"What you talking about?" Sarah's voice implied he had been touched in the head by this place.

"I was thinking of Rae," he said.

"There always will be what?"

"Independent churches," he said. "I was wondering what he would do when there were none to take over."

"And that's something to run away from too. . . ."

"Or fight. Come," he said insistently. "We must go down."

"Please don't be afraid of my death, David. It is life that is important. And ours has been good. We've been happy together and raised good children and loved our neighbours as the Bible said."

"And we've built a church," David added.

"That too," she said. "So don't be afraid when the day comes; I promise you I won't be afraid. Lonely, yes; but not afraid."

She tucked her arm under his, turned her head in one lingering examination of the details of Samson's look-out, then she moved with him to the path that led down to the little village in the narrow valley. The world, all the world they could see, was soft and unutterably beautiful in the fast gathering darkness. They knew the land and they knew the way so the darkness held no threat and there was no need to hurry against it.

David died first, quietly and peacefully, sitting at his desk in the narrow room, business papers in front of him, Sarah's Bible to the right of them. He sat as though he had just leaned back to take a breather from the numbers on one of the papers. Sarah found him thus and stayed alone with him in the little room for nearly an hour before letting the rest of the household know. By then she had composed herself and no one, not even her children, saw her grieve for David. That had been more than thirty years ago; years of terrible loneliness without the companion of her life beside her. But she had kept faith with him and with the promise she had made that last time on Samson's hill. She had not been afraid and she had carried on their work as though he were still there; and he was still there, always with her in spirit. As time passed and Sarah grew older her remembrance of David grew stronger till, in the end, he was more alive for her than all her vast household of children, grandchildren, great-grandchildren, great-great-grand-children and all the surviving descendants of the large extended household she and David had built up over the years. With time, events, too, merged till there was no distinction between the past and present, only the continuous present in which the living and the dead and what happened thirty or forty or fifty or ten years ago all had the same relative value and immediacy. Time moved to a point of timelessness for a very old woman; and Sarah's memory in very old age became a very small, very clear pool on which sunlight and shadow played magical tricks.

The battle with Rae's church had started a few months after they brought Samson from the valley of Mount Zion. Another white Pastor, not Rae, had come to Cyprus for what was clearly a final attempt to make David and Sarah see the error of their ways: a fat, well-fed, comfortable looking young man who did not bother to hide his condescension toward black people whom he called 'my children'. When David and Sarah rejected this final invitation to join with the larger church in Kingston Elder Jones led the break. About a third of the congregation went with him, and there was a great coming and going between Elder Jones's home and white folk from Kingston. Then he started the building of a new church and one of his sheds was quickly turned into a store from which all manner of goods and food from Kingston could be bought for very low prices.

It was Joseph, now part of their household, wise in the ways of the Kingston church, who warned Sarah of the importance of securing their land before the church laid claim to it. So David and Sarah and Joseph went down to the colonial administration office, and after much time and effort came away with papers giving them title to nearly half of Cyprus. They had been just in time. The land which Jones had worked and on which his house stood had already been bought from him by the church, which was using the sale papers to seek title to that particular parcel as well as to all unregistered land adjoining and abutting it. After this setback the Kingston church redoubled its efforts: it built a house and installed a bright, stern, very light-skinned, young Pastor and his equally light-skinned wife in the house. The young wife started a school for the children of the breakaway congregation. The Cyprus community became divided: those who went to David's church were divided from those who joined the new church, which its leader called the old and true church. In the end the divisions ran so deep that those who worshipped in one church would have nothing to do with those who worshipped in the other. On Sunday mornings, when the church bells rang, and the people of Cyprus marched to their two churches as soldiers of opposing armies march into battle, the depth of the divisions were clearer than on any other day of the week: the day of the Lord was the day of the outward and visible manifestation of a community divided in the name of the Lord.

Then, early one morning, some six years after Pastor Rae had first visited David and Sarah and invited them to join the greater church, the battle was resolved. David and Sarah's great wooden

141

church was on fire. The huge beams, the long rows of wooden seats, the beautiful wooden altar, all cured and made dry and moistureless by time, blazed in a riot of living fire that all the effort of David's congregation and all the water they hurled against the flames could not quench, though they fought the blaze for more than four hours. In the end it was David who ordered his followers to give up the hopeless fight, when a part of the high ceiling collapsed with a great explosive woosh sending massive tongues of fire leaping at the sky. The long lines of men, women and children, making four conveyor-systems between the river and the church, continued to work for a while after David signalled them to stop; then, hesitantly, reluctantly stopped moving the buckets of water up the line. People went on their knees where they stood; others, too worn out and weary to pray, lay on the ground; some wept, some were dry-eyed, holding themselves in.

Sarah held David's hand, tightly, as though it were a staff to hold her up.

"I did not think of this," David said, a great desolation in his voice.

She wanted to comfort him so she said, knowing he would not agree: "We can rebuild it, my dear. It would be easier and quicker than the first time; then we were alone, now we have an army of helpers."

As she expected, David said nothing.

It took all that day and most of the next before the fire finally burned itself out, leaving what had once been the most beautiful church in these hills a huge mound of ash and charcoal. No one knew how the fire was started; no one ever found out; no one talked about it again after David refused the offer of his congregation to rebuild the church on the same site.

David and Sarah withdrew from the life of their community for the remaining months of that year. Gradually David's congregation drifted to the imposing new cutstone church which had been started before the fire and was completed a few weeks later. Most of the children who had been taught by Sarah were now attending the new church school which had a building of its own and two teachers. Although a few of the defiant Elders of David's former church continued to hold services in their own homes, and tried to keep alive the spirit of their old church, the battle for the control of religious activity in Cyprus was over; and the outcome was as the little Scots missionary had told David and Sarah it would be.

In the new year David turned his vast energies to business. They already had a forest of pimento trees and coffee bushes on the sloping land above the burnt-out church. Now, he built a factory for extracting the pimento oil, and a series of marl and clay platforms for drying the coffee, and a series of huge clay and brick outdoor ovens. He mobilized the members of this extended family and put them to work. Sarah kept the records. Their eldest son, John, he put in charge of the pimento and coffee operations. They put more land under coffee, under citrus, under banana. Sarah's protégé, Joseph, was put in charge of a farm of pigs, goats, chicken; two of David's younger sons were put under Joseph to learn all about livestock farming. Some of the girls had been sent to boarding school; for Sarah was determined that her daughters should have the best training available and there were places in Kingston where such could be had at a price. But mainly Sarah herself taught their daughters, and helping her in the management and record-keeping side of the business was part of their training. As time passed they brought more of the land under cultivation, produced more pimento, more coffee, more citrus, more bananas, huge quantities of pineapple, vast amounts of ginger, till David's farm became the largest and most prosperous in this part of the hills. In time the mule tracks gave way to wider cart roads to carry the greater volume of David's produce down to Kingston to be sold to the merchants and traders who in turn shipped these to the markets across the seas. And David and Sarah prospered and grew rich.

Through it all, until he died ten years after coming to Cyprus, Sarah looked after Samson. The two old Nanas had long since died, but they had taught a younger woman how to look after him. She was Samson's constant nurse: looked after him, washed him, fed him, exercised his muscles, until a bond grew between them as between a mother and a helpless child. Each morning, no matter how busy or what the pressures, Sarah spent at least half an hour sitting with Samson at his favourite spot on the verandah. Each evening before retiring, David and Sarah sat with Samson and discussed the day's affairs, making him a silent part of the discussion. To the children he was the casually accepted and honoured silent living presence of their parents' history. He was "Papa Samson", to whom you could tell things you could tell no one else; to whom you could complain about real or imagined injustices; to whom you could safely reveal outrageous thoughts and deeds. And it seemed to Sarah and David that Samson was at peace enveloped by all this love, jealously guarded by his young Nana. Once only there was a little movement in his left hand, and his young Nana worked on his muscles as though she could, by an act of will, bring them back to active life. Neither Maria, nor any of Samson's children, ever came looking for him. Jonas, for all his promises, never came. Noname came once; but he was preoccupied with the increasingly arduous struggle to win a living for his family from the now parched and barren valley of Mount Zion. David sensed that Noname had come in a moment of desperation so he offered him the job of overseeing his just-started twenty-acre coconut farm. The offer cheered Noname's spirits enormously; both David and Sarah expected him to accept, but at the last minute Noname found it impossible to abandon his piece of earth in the valley of Mount Zion, no matter how hard the struggle. He tried to explain: but how to tell people, even these people, that a piece of hard parched earth has become part of your life? Then he looked into Sarah's eyes and knew she understood.

Noname sat with Samson for the last time in the fading light of the late evening, and spoke of all that had transpired in the valley of Mount Zion. Sarah had urged him to give Samson all the news, so he spoke steadily, even though he did not know whether Samson heard or understood any of it. They sat there on the verandah at the ending of the day, the big stricken silent man and the wiry little one. Samson's Nana periodically came to the door to see that all was well then retreated again. The members of the household went about their rounds. Whenever anyone came home after the day's absence, they paused to salute Samson. Some, the menfolk, would touch his shoulder or hand and nod or mumble some greeting and carry on; the womenfolk would touch him, kissing his forehead or cheek and

144

linger a little longer than the men. At such times Noname would stop talking till the person had gone, then he would start off again.

Noname decided to return to the valley of Mount Zion after supper that night. It was a time of the full moon and he and his donkey knew the way. When Sarah could not persuade him to stay till morning, she instructed Joseph immediately to have a donkey loaded with produce for Noname to take with him. So Noname took his leave of Samson and, a little later, of David and Sarah, and set out for home. He had told Samson that the numbers in the valley had now dwindled to five families. The other families had moved to where there was more water and the land was easier; some to the higher hills to the north-east of Mount Zion; others to the growing and flourishing community developing in the fertile valleys of Rock Hall; others down to Red Hills; and others further down to Lime's Kiln or the higher ridges of Sterling Castle. There was more water in these places and the land was easier to work. Of those who remained there was Maria's family or what was left of it, since half of it had moved to Red Hills; there was Jonas's family, but Jonas had already found himself a good piece of land just above Red Hills and was building a house there, so it was just a matter of time before he would leave; and there was he, Noname, and his family. Like him, Little Mary did not want to leave the valley, even though she was growing terribly thin with the hard work. The other two families were newly arrived strangers, attracted by Maria's low land rent. Noname had no time for them: the man of one was a thief whom he caught stealing yam; the other was lazy and did nothing for his family. All this he had told Samson but not David and Sarah. At the crest of the hill he paused and looked back. They had gone into the house. He would have seen their shadowy figures if they had waited for him to go out of sight. Their not waiting for the last farewell wave brought a sudden, unexpected ache to his heart.

"Mek we go home," he said, lightly nudging the flanks of the donkey with his heels, and tugging the rope of the second one, weighed down with two panniers laden with all manner of food. "Them doan even want you back, donkey, them so rich; rich to rahtid. . . ." So Noname rode home through the night, talking to the donkey, remembering, aloud, how Samson had been before he was stricken and how he and David had been boys together, and the chores they had done together and the things they had learned together. And now David was a big and rich man, while he was a small poor man, even though they had started out together from the same place. Not many years between them either; maybe four-five, not much more. We all wrong, donkey, we all wrong from the beginning. We all thought Maria was the strong one; and it not so at all, at all, not so. That Sarah turn David into a king and a rich man and a preacher man too. Hard woman, that one! Me ca'an handle anyone like that, not even to grow rich; only me sweet likkle Mary – soft and gentle and easy to move with and loving the land same as me. But Maria shouldn't a done that and we shouldn't a agree for them to go. Now it is them caring Samson and him not lonely at all, at all. . . . So he talked aloud to the animals, to the land, to himself and ceased to be alone, and ceased to be lonely.

Samson died in his sleep. His Nana found him when she came to prepare him for the day. His eyes were open but she knew he was dead. So she called Sarah, and Sarah called David from his little office. David closed the staring eyes and felt the hands and moved the arms; the paralysis which had gripped Samson in life was gone in death, his arms and legs and body moved easily.

The women prepared him quickly for burial and the men prepared the burial spot in what was once the churchyard. Many of his former congregation and their relatives had been buried there so David and Sarah had turned the place into a quiet burial park, fenced-in and surrounded by a grove of grapefruit, oranges and limes. By sunset all the preparations were ready and Samson was buried in the shadows of a young ebony tree, no more than thirty years old, twelve feet tall and in full flowering. The birds had carried its seed to this spot where it rooted and start its life. With David's voice sounding the familiar parting words to the dead, Sarah thought about Maria. Even David, with all his understanding, could not forgive Maria. She would try again, that night, to make him see, try again to soften the hard edge of his thought and feeling about Maria; not for Maria's sake, for his

146

sake. "Oh, Maria, how I wish I could comfort you!" That silent man imprisoned for so long in his great brutalized body, he understood and forgave her and she didn't even understand that. Now, at last, he is free, free of remembrance of bad and bitter things. . . . David's voice came to her as they shovelled the earth into the hole. . . . Tears ran down her face. She would not sit with Samson again. Oh Maria!

David's death made no difference to the family's growing fortune even though the island was in deep political and economic trouble. The events in St Thomas in the East, and the trials and the killings and the business between the British Crown and the local planters' Assembly had only marginal impact on the self-contained and self-sustained lives of the black communities of the hills. They wanted to have as little as possible to do with what went on down there, so they lived in self-imposed isolation and only went down to the plains when they had to. The young who came from very poor homes went to seek work on the plains. The better off, like the young of Sarah's sprawling and much enlarged household, only left the peace and security of the hills for special schooling or training, but even this was rare. Sarah and David's grandson Jacob, the first son of their own first-born, John, was one such. He had gone to America to study at the black university at Atlanta in Georgia, a place of such racial hatred and bigotry that white mobs hung and burned black people to death. Both Sarah and her son, John, were at first bitterly opposed to his going there. But Jacob was stubborn, and Sarah, in old age, was particularly fond of this strong-minded young man, so she gave in and prevailed on his father to let him leave the hills and go to a strange land of savage whites. Jacob was eighteen and in his second year at Atlanta University when Sarah died, twelve years into the new century.

By the time the letter reached him, she had been buried for more than a month. They had dug her grave as close beside David's as could be done without disturbing the older grave. John, David's and Sarah's first-born and now head of the family and in his middle sixties, had spent all his life witnessing the close, and exclusive, bond between his parents; that closeness had set up resentments and jealousies among the children but time had washed these away as they put Sarah to rest beside her beloved David, a little distance from the grave of the legendary Samson. Now they remembered only the good things and the good times and the warmth and the gentleness that had radiated from them. So the children and the grandchildren and the great-grandchildren, and those they had taken in and made part of their family, built private shrines within themselves as personal remembrance of David and Sarah, and of the legend of Samson leading them up into the hills, away from bondage.

2

Something about the big young man's bearing disturbed the professor, made him slacken his pace, keep his distance and follow. There were many other people about, strolling in twos and threes and in larger groups; others sprawled on the lush grass off the paved walkways; some sat on the benches scattered at intervals under shady trees on the vast campus grounds. Daylight was fading and in the Georgia twilight there was a fresh fragrance to the warm still air. A sense of peace and tranquillity hung over the place. The professor had been here for two years now, and still he could not reconcile its peace with the known reality of violence and brutality just beyond its confines and all through this land. Perhaps, he thought, this was the augury of how it would one day be in this fair land, when our white fellow countrymen will see us for what we really are, good patriotic Americans like themselves, with the same abilities, the same passions and weaknesses, and with the same dreams and hopes. This is what the highly educated and gifted minority among us must show them till they respect us, and through us, in time, all Negroes and accord them the equality of opportunity which is their just due.

The big young man turned off the main path and down a slope to a thick cluster of trees. The professor hurried after him, drawing closer, no longer wanting to follow unobserved. It was time to be seen and heard now, he judged, if this young man was as desperate as his bearing suggested. The young man paused at a huge fallen tree, leaned against it, and waited.

"Why are you following me. . . ." Then he recognized his follower. "Oh, professor. . . ."

From the islands, the professor decided; that lilt to the speech could only come from the islands of the Caribbean.

"You seem to be in trouble," the professor said in a quiet voice.

"A personal matter," the young man said. "Nothing to do with this," he waved an arm to encompass the little world of the university.

"Personal and very deep," the professor said. "They're the most difficult to live with at times; it usually helps to let it out and sometimes to a stranger is best."

There was a long silence in the Georgia twilight; not a sound as though all the world had held its breath.

The young man wished this busybody would go away and leave him alone; he wished he had the nerve to tell this smooth-faced, handsome little copper-brown man with his pointed beard and curled moustache and Englishman's ways of speech and manner to mind his own business and go away. He was not even one of this man's students. But he was a professor and you cannot just tell a professor to mind his own business; especially one like this, whom everyone seemed to hold in awe. The professor sensed the changing mood in the young black man, saw the slight squaring of the shoulders and raising of the chin, and felt quiet satisfaction. Distraction is the first step.

"It is my grandmother," the young man said reluctantly, the mood changing again; he lowered his head. "She died. . . . And I was not there."

"Can't you still go? How far?"

"They buried her; a month ago. The letter reached me today."

The professor had guessed at the Bahamas, but a month would put the place much further; Jamaica, perhaps. Aloud, he asked: "Jamaica?"

"Yes, Jamaica; far up in the hills."

Tears suddenly welled up in the young man's eyes, and rolled down his cheeks. He let them, unchecked.

"My grandmother and my grandfather were runaway slaves, part of a group that went up into the hills." Despite the tears the voice was calm and even. "They went alone into the bush as young people and built a world for us. And now she's gone and I wasn't there."

"And your grandfather?"

150

"He died long ago. . . . We used to sit under a tree near his grave and she would tell us about all that had happened from the time they ran away right up to the time we were born."

"She sounds like a wonderful woman. How many of you are there?"

A smile flashed across the young man's face. "She called us her army, there are so many of us. They had eleven children and the eleven had eight and nine and ten and twelve and fifteen; my father and mother had the smallest number with eight; and now their children are having children. We are her army! And I was not home to bury her; all the others were there."

"I'm sure she understood. I will leave you now to your remembrance. Come dine with me this evening and tell me more about your grandma and Jamaica. Know where to find me?"

"Yes, sir."

"The name is DuBois. . . ."

"I know, sir."

"Come, young man; I am trying to find out your name."

"Oh, yes, Brown, sir; Jacob Brown."

"All right then, Mr Brown. I'll expect you in my rooms about seven this evening – that is, unless you do not want to come. You do not have to, you know. I really want to hear about Jamaica."

"I'll be there, sir; I want to come. I'll tell you all I can about Jamaica."

"And I'll tell you of my travels in England and France and Germany and some of the people of colour I met there."

Professor DuBois rose from the trunk of the fallen tree and walked briskly away, leaving the young man still seated. He thought the mood had changed and the young man would be all right. He thought: and so the grandson of a Jamaican runaway slave woman, just died, will dine and talk with me, one of the mulatto offspring of the often strange liaisons bred by American slavery.

Except for the bottle of wine and the table napkins and the china crockery and, of course, the privacy, it was the same as in the large student dining hall; the food was the same, but somehow Jacob Brown enjoyed it more than he remembered doing in all of his two

151

years here. He had found the food bland, not rich and spicy as he was used to; these people did not seem to use pepper and ginger and garlic in their cooking; and it all seemed cooked in water, not in the rich coconut oil which brought out the full flavour in a piece of meat.

"You are far away, Mr Brown," Professor DuBois murmured; his eyes, normally guarded and with a touch of sadness, twinkled brightly now; a gentle smile tugged at the left side of his mouth, softening the remoteness and austerity the world usually saw. He seemed a kindly, concerned man now.

The second glass of wine had relaxed Jacob so he smiled at DuBois, a wide, open smile: "I was remembering our food at home. It's all rich and hot and greasy."

"And delicious, I'm sure."

"Yes sir! Very delicious."

"Not bland, like this."

"It's different," Brown said quickly, not wanting to sound complaining.

"You'll find this kind of food in every institution you go to, anywhere in the world. It is as different from our folk-food as it is from yours. What we call soul food is as spicy and full of flavour, as rich and gooey-gummy as anything you have down in Jamaica, believe me!"

"Then I must try it, sir."

"You will; have no doubt, Mr Brown. Institutional food is something completely apart from the food people eat in their own homes. But enough of food, I see in the registry records that you are studying theology?" DuBois paused, passed the dessert and topped up Brown's wine glass.

"My grandfather was a priest. . . . I don't know if you would accept him as such. My grandma taught him to read and write out of the Bible and because she was the one who had been baptized in church as a slave, she baptized him and later ordained him. They all say he was a good priest; I spoke to some of the old people who remembered him as their pastor. His church, which he and my grandma had built, was burned down when he refused to become part of a Kingston-based circuit."

152

"Everywhere," DuBois murmured. "Even in Jamaica. Why? So you will carry on your grandpa's work?"

"That's been it ever since I can remember. Grandma Sarah was a strong and determined old lady, and we just agreed that I would carry on. . . ."

The younger man hesitated, lowered his head and thought deeply. Should he tell this Professor DuBois of his and his grandma's agreement on the importance of having independent churches guided and controlled by black people, not under the control of whites, not used by whites? He said, tentatively: "We agreed, Grandma and I – and he would have if he'd been alive because she says it was his idea – that we need churches not controlled and used by whites; not telling us what to think and what not to think, what to feel and what not to feel."

"What of the moral side?" DuBois asked, thoughtfully. "The church is a political power force in the world. Is it also a brand of imperialism? Is it being used to guide black minds into accepting prevailing dominant white values? Mind you, it's not the values that are necessarily wrong; it is the use of them to impose a certain domination. . . ." DuBois stared speculatively at his young guest. "And this is what you and your grandma talked about, out there in the hills of Jamaica?"

"Yes, sir."

"I wish I had met your Grandma Sarah," DuBois said.

Jacob Brown smiled and nodded; he had made the right decision about this man. And each right judgement, Grandma Sarah had always said, will lead you to others.

"I would like you to join my social studies group," DuBois said. "We meet every Thursday at five in my office. Tell me: apart from your promise to your grandma, do you yourself want to be a priest? Are you sure of it?"

"Oh I am sure of that all right, sir. Grandma was strong-minded but she never forced anything on anybody. She raised the same questions you are raising now, and many more. It's hard to explain but that is the only thing I want to do; it is like a calling. Of course what they did to Grandpa and his church is important: our own church, free of domination or control by whites is one driving force, but. . . ."

153

"But vengeance is not the reason," DuBois suggested.

"I do not know," the young man spoke as if to himself. "All I know is that the God I know, the God my grandpa and grandma raised us all, and the people in the hills, to worship, is a God of truth and caring for each other, and of respect and grace. He does not set up one people over another, and he does not measure men by the colour of their skin. That is the God whose gospel I must preach."

"How can your God of love condone so much cruelty? Slavery?"

Jacob Brown began to answer, then saw the twinkle in Dubois' eyes. He relaxed, shook his head, smiled: " I don't know; many things I do not know, sir. That's why I'm here. Can you tell me, sir?"

DuBois threw back his head and laughed, a lilting gaiety to his laughter, "Well done, Mr Brown! Like you I do not know. But I find it strange indeed that so much cruelty and brutality has been done by men to men in the name of the God of love. It is a terrible thought, you know, this idea of the colonization of the human mind by way of religion. Cannot your God of love do something to stop it, to disassociate His name from it? No, do not answer. Let me guess what your answer will be and then tell me if I am wrong. Your grandma's religion, in the end, provided and provides the key to the rebellion of the slaves. Ultimately, the teaching of Christ provided each converted slave with a sense of his own humanity and therefore with a measuring rod against which to judge his status; and the result led to rebellion. And this makes your God of love a revolutionary, a fomentor of discontent, dissatisfaction; He causes a questioning of the status quo, He causes self-examination and a posing of what is against what could and should be; and hey presto! an explosive revolutionary situation is brought into being. Is that what you would have said, Mr Brown?"

"Tell you the truth," Brown chuckled, "I had not thought of all that; but I wish I had."

"Well, man! Think about it now and tell me if that is what you would have said if you had thought about it."

"If I had thought it out as clearly, yes." Brown could contain neither his laughter nor his sense of high excitement.

"But here's the rub," DuBois said, suddenly sombre. "He creates the will to freedom and dignity and what you call caring and grace, this God of love; and yet, it is in His name that they have created slavery and racism with its lynchings and burnings, and colonialism. So it would seem He can be used to serve both good ends and bad ends, this God of love. Is He indifferent? Has He made no choice? Is it all some grand game He is playing with puny little humans for pawns? For surely, a God of love, a God of goodness should tilt the scales in favour of goodness and love and against wickedness and hate?"

"Has He not done so?" Brown asked, equally serious now.

"Has He?" DuBois asked. "Go out into the world, away from your protective Jamaican hills and away from the artificial peace and tranquillity of this university campus: complete your studies and go and spend ten or twenty years out there in the world, and then let us meet again and see if you give me the same answer."

Jacob Brown was very serious now as he asked: "Do you really believe God is indifferent to the suffering of people?"

DuBois' mood changed. He gestured with body and hands as though to be rid of an unpleasant shadow of the mind. He divided the remains of the bottle of wine into the two glasses.

"I'm the one who asks the questions, remember. You, especially when you are a priest who has to guide the minds and souls of a congregation, will be expected to give the answers. I am the man of questions and doubts, which is the true business of scholarship. Leaders, parsons and politicians, must deal in certainties. That's the difference. As to your question: I do not know, for I have no way of knowing. I know what men say of Him but I suspect that they have no more way of knowing than I have. This is not a matter of knowledge, it is a matter of faith, and I was not raised by anyone like your Grandma Sarah."

They talked for a while longer and then Jacob Brown left. He walked briskly to the student quarters. It was a clear moonlit night, comfortably warm and still, with the faint scent of Georgia pine on the air. How his Grandma Sarah would have enjoyed the banter and the challenge of this night's talk! What a sharp, clear brain this man DuBois had! But then, he is not a Doctor of

Philosophy at thirty for nothing. Something sad and lonely about him though, this brainy young brown professor with the French name. . . . Grandma, Oh Lord, Grandma's gone and I wasn't there to kneel beside her bed and touch her for the last time and kiss her for the last time! Last time we walked, just before I left, we went to where the church had been and she talked about Grandpa and Samson. Last time she leaned on me for support; last I heard the fading, whispery old voice and felt the great strength of mind and spirit caged in that very frail old body. Oh Grandma, did I tell you how much I love you? Never enough; we never tell it enough until it is too late. He made it easier, this Doctor DuBois; easier when I first got the letter earlier today, and again tonight. A thoughtful, kind man behind all that sharpness. I think I like him; I'm sure you would have. You would have taught him something for all his great book learning. Well, I will get some more of that learning and then . . . then I'll go to Europe as he has done and then I will go to Africa, the place where the slaves came from. A black missionary to Africa! How I wish I could talk to you about this! But you know. All I have to do is think about something and you know it, as you always have. Oh, Grandma, I'll miss you so!

DuBois' Thursday evenings social studies group were a revelation to Jacob Brown. There were some seven or eight other young people at each meeting of the group which DuBois had limited to ten, with the women outnumbering the men. Jacob Brown became the fourth male in the group, the other six were women. On that first Thursday evening only one of the three other men was present; he discovered, at later meetings, that male attendance was erratic but it was exceptional for a female member of the group to be absent; there were rarely more than two men present. And as with attendance, so with performance: the women carried out their assignments with more care and consistency than did the men. Often, the men, if they came, brought some excuse for a task not carried out. Dr DuBois usually accepted these without comment but Jacob Brown noticed the professor always seemed a little more withdrawn and melancholy, a little physically smaller, whenever this happened. He noticed, too, that the young women went out of their way at such times to do the kind and quality of work that raised the spirits of the professor and restored the approving twinkle to his eyes.

From those Thursday evenings Jacob Brown began the painful process of learning what it meant to be black in America. Things he had never thought of were laid bare for him: how black men were convicted on the flimsiest of charges and then leased by the prison authorities to white farmers and entrepreneurs much as machines or animals. Up to 1874 the lease term of such prisoners had been two years. The Governor of the State of Georgia then argued for an extension and it was increased to twenty years. He learned about lynchings: how black men, women and children were set to the torch by mobs of whites for real or fancied crimes like rape or theft or being "uppity". Rape could be simply the way a black man looked at a white woman; assault could be a black accidentally bumping against a white on a pavement, or protesting against being short-changed in a store. He learned about the defencelessness of blacks: how blacks could be cheated and robbed by whites in business or trade or commerce with no hope of redress in the courts of law. Homes built by blacks which were considered too pretentious would be set on fire and a wooden cross burned as warning to other blacks; the law never found the arsonists, even when they boasted about having done the deed. When black women were raped neither the law nor the white mobs paid more than lewd attention to the event. All this DuBois' team of young women researched and reported on those Thursday evenings with much statistical support and documentary evidence from the newspaper accounts and the reports of the proceedings of local, county and state authorities. Jacob Brown noticed that neither DuBois nor anyone else ever enquired how any one of the young women came by some particularly sensitive document. And so they built up a picture of the social, economic and political conditions under which black people lived. Later Jacob Brown found out that these studies were not confined to the University or the State of Georgia. Information, as carefully documented, came from all over the South, and further afield, with DuBois at the centre of it all: examining, sifting, questioning, collating and, forever it seemed, writing.

To Jacob Brown it became clear that being black in America was totally different from being black in Jamaica, especially in the hills. He had never doubted his own manhood, his own humanity in the way he had found the black Americans, especially the men, seemed always to be doing. Professor DuBois was the exception but even he seemed driven by a need to prove their humanity; to show, by scholarship, by achievement, by quality of character, that blacks were the equal of whites. We in Jamaica, Jacob thought, even after slavery, never had to prove anything to anybody because we knew ourselves. The whites were on top because they were stronger, more cunning, more unscrupulous, more aggressive: not because they were better. One day things would change: blacks would get stronger and become as cunning and aggressive and unscrupulous and take over; no question about that. We are many more than them, and time longer than rope. So we never have any of this black American self-doubt. The trouble in the United States was the numbers. He had talked with DuBois about it once. Even though their numbers were greatest in the South, and there were places where they outnumbered the whites, the American blacks were still a small minority in a vast sea of white people, just one tenth or thereabouts of all the American people; and they were a minority that looked so strikingly different. Elsewhere, in Jamaica and, from all accounts in Africa too, the strikingly different looking minorities *are* on top, which ensures change one day; here, the minority is at the bottom which ensures its permanence at the bottom. DuBois had talked of making the majority accept the simple fact of the Americanness of the minority. That, for him, seemed the answer to the problem. But even as he put it forward Jacob Brown sensed a certain dissatisfaction in the man. It was as though heart and mind were in conflict, tugging against each other. Once, when this dissatisfaction seemed at its strongest, and almost in anger at it, DuBois muttered to himself; ''There is no other way.''

Jacob Brown was the least active of DuBois' small group. He was not assigned to any of the weekend investigation trips on which members of the group went, usually in pairs, from time to time; he was not asked to follow some special court case of more than individual significance. It was understood that his presence in the group was part of his own education. So he made notes for himself of some of the salient points of the often heated arguments and discussions which followed the presentation of reports and statistics. Under DuBois' discreet guidance, the little group took nothing for granted: everything was questioned; everything was tested; every statement, every figure, had to be justified. And after several months Jacob Brown found himself caught up in the habit of testing and questioning the merits of every proposition. From time to time it led to problems in his theological classes. The Dean of his faculty once had words with DuBois. According to DuBois' dry witty account of the encounter it came to a question of whether the plenipotentiaries of the Almighty could produce evidence that He preferred His followers to be blind morons rather than intelligent and questioning human beings. Jacob Brown was more restrained in his questioning of the theological statements after that. But even those teachers who were disturbed by some of the explosive ideas DuBois planted in young minds were impressed by the new questing intellectual vigour he had let loose in the tall young man from Jamaica.

Among those in DuBois' group impressed by the young Jamaican was Harriet Bruce, a tall, big-boned, strong-minded young woman with a glowing copper-brown skin and a rich deep voice. Jacob Brown met her at DuBois' group on Thursday evenings, at church choir practice on Saturday afternoons and at church on Sundays. The friendship between them grew slowly, over time, fostered by regular meetings and shared activity. When, as part of his training he was sent to some nearby rural black church to conduct Sunday School classes or deliver a sermon, Harriet Bruce usually went with him to ensure that he did not, through ignorance, violate the racial rules of the American Deep South. And because there was now no one back home to whom he could confide he turned to Harriet Bruce to talk of the things he had once talked of only with his grandma. The letters home to his father were informative but formal, as were the letters he received in return; there had never been great intimacy between them. He had hardly known his mother, a thin, gentle little woman, always with child, who seemed permanently overshadowed by Grandma Sarah and her throng of physically towering and assertive children. Winning Grandma Sarah over to his coming to America was more important than winning over his father. But then she simply told his father: "John, I don't like it; but he wants to go and I think he should go." Just like that. And so it was. All this and more he told Harriet Bruce in the quiet moments when they were alone. He told her of the joys of growing up in the hills: the carefree play of children in a world of peace and warmth. He noticed her eyes light up when he talked of the special taste of melon eaten in the shade of an old tree near the river after hard bushing in the warm sun. And, hesitatingly to begin with, but with more passion and assurance when he saw her deep interest, he told her the history of Mount Zion and of what had happened to them. She usually listened quietly, head down when they walked or hands folded on her lap when they sat on the soft grass in the shade of a tree. He liked the quietness about her; it made it easy for him to talk and let his thoughts flow. Only her change of expression and the rhythm of her breathing told of her interest in what he said, and so he came to know when she was excited or moved or agitated by what he told her. She spoke little when they were alone, yet she seemed pleased to be with him. Coming from a place where everybody talked nineteen to the dozen, her silence, when he thought about it, which was not very often, puzzled him. She chatted enough, and with animation, in the presence of others; but always, she fell silent and was content to listen when they were alone.

Then one Saturday near Christmas she and one of the young men went to investigate a lynching near Atlanta. They were to go to the Negro section of a small farming community, find out as much as they could of the details, and report back. Somehow, something went wrong and they were followed by four rough young whites who beat up the young man dreadfully and then turned on Harriet Bruce. One of them knocked her down, splitting her lip and cheek, and started to rip off her clothes. She fought and screamed at the top of her voice, possessed by a combination of fear and panic and rage. Her screams attracted a white man on horseback, grey-haired, obviously affluent and known to the four young whites. The assault ended. Harriet

Bruce helped her battered companion to his feet, and together they hurried away while the man on horseback marched the four young ruffians in the opposite direction.

When Jacob Brown heard the story that night, and when he saw Harriet's cut and battered face, and the badly beaten young fellow student in the infirmary he was possessed by a cold rage which stayed with him for days. He did not go to church the next day, and he did not see Harriet. Till that moment being black in America had been an abstraction. When it ceased to be an abstraction, you had to grapple with anger and bitterness and hate almost choking you. Black is what you are because you are born that colour. Black people are turned into Negro slaves; black slaves may be freed but Negroes are not free. Now he could understand the hatred Grandma Sarah said choked up in Samson when he saw that white man in the valley of Mount Zion!

Harriet came looking for him that Monday evening. Her cut lip was still swollen but looked less terrible than it had on Saturday night. The cheek split showed faintly. The eyes were no longer bloodshot.

"I've been looking for you," she said, taking his hand.

She had never done that before. He remembered he had thought of her as his girl; she was his girl now. He would take her away from this place, right away from America and its brutality that did not even spare women.

"I don't like America," he said coldly.

"I'm part of America," she said. "Don't you like me?"

"Not what they did and tried to do to you."

"Which is why we are here; to change that." She hesitated, then added: "This is shocking and terrible to you, Jacob. It is not to us. It is part of life here. It happens all the time. We were lucky; he was not killed, I was not raped. Some black person somewhere in this country is being killed or raped as we now talk. Do you see why the others were so calm about it?"

He said: "No!" explosively.

"You must; you will," she said, caressing the back of his hand,

"Come with me when I have finished here," he said impulsively. "We'll visit my home in Jamaica and then we'll go to Europe and Africa. You'll see my people; you'll see our hills! Oh,

161

come with me, Harriet! Be my wife and come with me!" It was out now. He put his free hand over hers and allowed the warmth of his feeling to flow over her. Briefly, she rested her forehead against his chest; but for a long time she would not allow him to embrace her, resisting gently by holding on to his hands. Then, suddenly, she relaxed all of her body and he folded his arms about her. He held her tight and felt her warm softness, and sensed the cool scent of slightly damp dry leaves it gave off. He could not kiss her cut and bruised lips so he kissed the undamaged cheek. After a while she freed herself of his hold and led him on one of their favourite walks to the old fallen tree in the dip of the land where Professor DuBois had first spoken to him. The Christmas night air was cooler than usual. When they reached the spot and sat on the trunk he said: "Well? Will you?"

She seemed faraway and lost in thought. "Will I what?"

"Will you come with me? Will you marry me? Not now; later, when we have finished our studies."

"Oh Jacob, sweet Jacob. You're sorry for me and you want to protect me. But you can't, my dear."

"Why not? And I'm not just sorry for you. I want you to be my wife."

"And what will you do if one day your wife is raped?"

"I'll kill. . . ," he began harshly.

"And be killed," she cut in quickly. Then she laughed, her rich voice tinged with harsh bitterness. "Oh Reverend Brown, you must not talk of killing; it's not Christian!"

"I'm sure Christ would want to kill if He were here."

"He'd be lynched before He could do anything," she said coldly.

"Then come with me, away from this place. I know you'll be happy in our hills. If you don't want to go to Europe and Africa, I will rebuild Grandpa's church and we could stay in Jamaica. Nothing like this would ever happen to you there."

"Your whites so different – so good?" She was teasing him now.

"No. Just they wouldn't dare. There are too many of us; and besides, we're in control up in the hills."

"What a wonderful thought," she murmured. "To be in control. You're very lucky, my Jacob; never thought I'd meet anyone like you, a really free spirit. But they fear that here, my dear. They will

162

hurt you if they see it. So you must always be on guard and not let them see how free you are."

"You have not answered me," he said, impatient now.

"Give me a little time," she said. "Better still. Come home with me for Christmas and meet my folk and I will give you my answer on Christmas morning. Will you?"

"Of course," he said, certain that he knew her answer already; it was there in her voice, in the way she leaned against him and took his hand and tucked it more securely about her waist; it was there in the new intimacy of touch and speech and openness, an unexpressed commitment which required words only for confirmation. But he wanted to hear her say the words so he said: "I love you, Harriet."

He felt the tremor shake her body, then she said in a small voice of pain: "Oh Jacob, I love you too."

"You make it sound like pain!" He laughed. "Love is supposed to be joy and fun! When a man and woman choose each other up in the hills they have a party and there is all night dancing and drinking!"

She laughed with him and snuggled closer. All the night and all the world seemed beautiful, and as if to share the joy of love the big Georgia moon came from behind a high white cloud and bathed the land in a glow. Harriet Bruce's mood changed, her body straightened. The man felt and responded to the changed mood.

"Do you know about sharecropping?"

He said: "No?", making it an enquiry.

"My family are sharecroppers," she said. "We live on white people's land and work a piece of it and in exchange they take half the crop. There's a whole village of us, my family and other families, and we are all dirt-poor. And I didn't tell you, Jacob, my mother was not lucky as I was. She *was* raped by a white man and there was nothing my father could do. You will meet the child of that rape, if you will still come with me. Will you?"

He said "Yes," soberly, heavily, all joy of love vanished now.

The flat, reddish land had sloped upward all morning, forcing the train to labour hard for every mile it gained. It puffed and rattled and strained against the slopes making slow but steady progress. Twice, at some point where the single track joined another, smooth and sleek express trains shot by, one minute flashing out of the distance with a high-pitched sustained scream of warning, the next minute gone in a woosh and a rattle, seemingly unaffected by the slope of the dry red earth, as they rushed on to the great cities, to Washington and Chicago and New York and Boston. Then the little local train was on its own again, straining against the vast sloping landscape, and stopping at every small station and siding.

The two first-class carriages were at the front, spacious and clean with well-upholstered seats and a white neatly starched little cover for the headrest of each seat. They were sparsely occupied: whites travelled first-class. Then the baggage carriages where the white guard, and his black porters, functioned. Finally, the four other carriages with bare wooden benches, crowded with passengers of all shapes and sizes and colours – except white. These carriages were hot, made steamy and dank by many bodies in a confined space, and uncomfortable and noisy.

Harriet Bruce and Jacob Brown were in the last and best of the crowded carriages. It had compartments with the corridor running down one side; the others were rows of benches with the centre aisle as the corridor.

When they had boarded the train at Atlanta in the very early morning they had the compartment to themselves for a time. With each stop passengers had joined the train, mostly to crowd into the four rear carriages. By mid-morning Harriet Bruce and Jacob Brown shared the compartment with four women, two men in their not very comfortable or accustomed best suits, and three very boisterous children. Intimate conversation was impossible; everybody made such conversation as there was at near the tops of their voices. But the racket was all amiable and good-natured and there was an easygoing quality about the hot, noisy discomfort. They were all black people together so they were safe. There were no whites around so there was no need to be on guard; no need to hush the children or be on best behaviour.

Harriet Bruce and Jacob Brown sat in silence side by side near the window, their backs to the engine, safe in the hot uncomfortable embrace of the numbers of their own, watching the land flow past. Terribly flat and terribly parched it was to Jacob Brown, used to the near high mountains and lush green hills of Jamaica. The scrublike clay earth was cracked, in places red dust stirred into quick swirling clouds by gusts of wind. But it was the flatness that struck him most. He wanted to talk to Harriet about it; but how to do it against this noise? He wanted to take her hand; but the two women on the other seat would stare. So he remained silent, watching the landscape flowing by.

Harriet was absorbed in the open book on her lap: *Suppression of the African Slave Trade* by W. E. B. DuBois, published three years earlier. The flyleaf carried an inscription from the author to Miss Harriet Bruce, "In salute and admiration of her brave investigations in the interest of her people".

At one point gnawing hunger and thirst had shaken Jacob out of the stupor into which he had lapsed; but Harriet was asleep now, her head held in place by the sharp corner where the seat met the frame of the window. No use waking her, he decided; besides, how could they eat and drink from the hamper she had prepared for the journey while others watched them hungrily? So he got up and found his way down the corridor to the little toilet. But the place stank so much his stomach began to heave, and the water container was empty. He hurried out and stood in the corridor near an open window till his stomach calmed itself again. Then he returned to his seat, careful not to disturb Harriet.

In the late afternoon, but with the sun still high, the train drew into the border siding between Georgia and Alabama. There was a long delay and a great to-do over the changing of drivers and guards and the taking on of water by the giant engine, then the shrill whistle screamed again and the train moved into Alabama. As far as Jacob could see, there was no change in the landscape. But Harriet was evidently excited: he felt it in the new tension she gave off, saw it in the new brightness of her eyes. Ignoring the stares of the women opposite, she pulled his head down till his ear was close to her lips.

"Soon now," she said. "The second stop coming up."

He nodded and tried to smile; the effort was sickly. He was hot and hungry and thirsty and tired and uncomfortable; the muscles of his body ached for movement. And still the red clay earth fell away in flat mile after mile.

The train stopped then moved off again. A half-hour passed, then Harriet stood up and reached up to the luggage rack above their heads. Jacob helped her bring down their suitcases. Then they eased their way out of the compartment to the now friendly smiles and nods of those who remained. The woman who had shown the most forbidding expression throughout the journey relaxed into a beaming smile. It was irresistible and Jacob Brown's face broke in warm response. He grabbed her hand, shook it vigorously and followed Harriet out of the compartment.

The train lumbered to a halt. Harriet pointed: "There they are!" Jacob saw a cluster of nondescript people around a long, large mulecart. Then they were on the dusty earth at the end of the train, a good twenty yards from the little siding platform. They were the only people to get off. Harriet took Jacob's ticket from him, told him to wait, and marched off to the siding platform where two white men, as red and faded as the clay earth, waited. Not till she had handed the tickets to one of the two white men was there any movement from the group by the mulecart; then all but one of them came forward. The one who stayed back sat on the driving seat of the cart, a long rifle cradled in the crook of his left arm, his right hand resting near the trigger. The others bunched themselves about Jacob, a group of strapping young men and women in faded old homemade clothes, floppy cloth hats and barefooted, showing their friendliness in awkward welcoming smiles. The young men took up their cases. Then Harriet ran happily towards them. She embraced her own family and called out each name for Jacob's benefit. Jacob could not take it all in; he could not, in that first flush of meeting, connect any face to any name; but he smiled happily. These were Harriet's family and friends and the tedious and exhausting journey was at an end; and there had been no trouble. Unknowingly Harriet had transferred some of her own undercurrent of anxiety to him so that he too, was possessed of a subconscious alertness against the possibility of an ugly white encounter. He could relax now. He knew these people would look after him. That one over there with the rifle was the earnest of it.

"Come meet my big brother, Abner!" Harriet bubbled, taking his arm and pulling him to the mulecart.

One of the other young men took over guard duty so brother Abner could meet the stranger. Brother Abner jumped off and offered a huge calloused hand. He was a fraction taller than Jacob and much broader; all his body the hard muscle and strong sinews of a human workbeast.

"Hiya!" Abner said in a deep rich lilt. "Glad to see ya!" Then he turned, wrapped his huge arms about Harriet and lifted her off the ground as though she were feather-light. "Hiya, sis! Good to have ya back!"

They all bundled into the cart, Harriet and Jacob up front beside Abner and the young man riding guard with the rifle. The two whites came to the edge of the siding platform to watch them drive off along the narrow dirt road, laughing and joking among themselves, secure in their numbers. The mulecart raised a small cloud of fine yellow dust. Far ahead a clump of tall trees stood out. As they neared it Jacob heard the sound of flowing water, as familiar to him as breathing itself. The river, when they reached it, was broad and shallow and slow at this point; the noise came from further up the land where the flow had to be faster. They crossed the river by a crude but sturdy wooden bridge and saw the vast sweeping stretch of land in cotton, as far as the eye could see.

"That's cotton," Harriet said. "King Cotton," an edge to her voice. The dirt road ran straight with the trees on its left and the acres of cotton on its right. As they crested the rise Jacob saw a village ahead of them. A series of drab wooden shacks clustered near each other in a slight hollow. Some distance beyond it, perhaps another two miles or so on a rise, were bigger, more solid-looking structures, glowing pale in the light of the setting sun.

"That's home, Jacob," Harriet said, pointing to the cluster of shacks.

"And that?" he asked.

"The owners," she said. "They own everything you can see and much more you cannot see." She pointed as though through the trees. "There is at least as much land again and three other villages

167

like ours over there. Ours is the oldest and the children over there come to our school. I didn't tell you, our mama is the teacher here. . . . That's why they did what they did to her. To show everybody."

Abner turned his head and stared coldly at Harriet.

"I told him," she said. "He's from the islands, from Jamaica; he doesn't know these things. I had to tell him when somebody tried it on me." She answered Abner's unspoken query. "No, nothing happened. We got away."

Abner sighed softly. "That the mark on your face?"

"Yes."

Abner looked at Jacob.

"He wasn't with me," she said quickly. "It was another student. They beat him badly."

"He'll be all right?" Abner asked.

"He'll be all right," she said.

Every now and then they passed small groups of people working in the cottonfields who stopped to watch them pass. Those nearby called out, welcoming Harriet home; those further away waved their greeting. He had, Jacob realized, entered another island of security, like the university. Here again, the black people of this country seemed to have built about them an invisible wall of self-protection by isolating themselves from the whites and by avoiding, as far as possible, all contact with them. You protect yourselves by segregating and isolating yourselves, by being armed against any possible encounter. This was what DuBois was trying to overcome. He wanted to bring down the barriers and make the white majority understand that the black minority had, as of right, the same claim to everything in the land as the whites had. But what if people do not want to understand? Yet they are Christian too, as we are. They worship the same God and pray in the same way for forgiveness by saying "Our Father".

They entered the village and the wooden shacks were set further apart than appeared from a distance. Close up, they were also larger than they had seemed, each had ample yard space at the sides and the front, and a larger space at the back with chicken runs and pig pens and heavily cultivated vegetable patches. Jacob recognized the familiar farming community smells of animal

168

dung, vegetable matter, turned earth in which human waste was used as manure, and the pungent smell of dry leaves turned to mould. This, at least, was the same as up in his Jamaican hills. But the Christmas breeze would be blowing up there now, wilting the leaves of the trees with their force. Harriet's touch brought him back from his Jamaican hills. She pointed and he saw a tall thin black woman in front of the very last house, waiting. He was sure that was her mother. And he noticed the absence of children and dogs. The first things you saw as you entered any Jamaican village were the children and the dogs.

"Where are the children?" Jacob asked.

Harriet stood up in the cart, waving to her mother.

Abner said, "Picking cotton."

Harriet jumped from the still-moving cart, stumbled and was saved from falling by her mother's arms. Now, at last Jacob could distinguish Harriet's brother and sisters: they came off the cart, the others remained on it. The young man who had ridden guard gave Abner the rifle, took the reins and urged the pair of large mules back down the empty village street. The young folk in the cart called out greetings and goodbyes to "Mizz Bruce" and "Hetty" and Abner and Jacob of whom they talked as "Hetty's quiet young man in the fancy city clothes". Abner gathered up the suitcases and went into the house.

"This is Jacob, Mama," Harriet said. "Remember? I wrote."

"Welcome, Jacob," the woman said. She held out a strong hand and gripped his firmly. Her dark face was unlined, her thin body ramrod straight in the long plain dress which had long since lost whatever colour it once had. The kinky hair, nearly all grey, was pulled back in a bun at the nape of her long neck: not an old woman, but not a young woman either; until you looked into her eyes and then she seemed older. Jacob found it hard to think that this woman had been forcibly violated by some brute white man. If this were his mother . . . but it was Abner's mother and he knew how Abner felt, had seen it. He had sensed some of it in Harriet too.

"Thank you for having me," Jacob said, unsure of himself.

"We're dying of hunger!" Harriet exclaimed. "Couldn't eat on the train with all those people!"

169

"Then we had better feed you," the woman laughed, making it sound like singing, as she hustled them into the house.

This was where Harriet got her beautiful voice from, Jacob decided; from this woman who had been brutalized and who gave you the feel of a cool breeze touching you. He felt glad, suddenly, that he had asked Harriet to marry him. He wanted to see her up in his Jamaican hills, see how she would respond to being really free.

It was a small drab room, a truly small living room for what he had seen of Harriet's family this far: her mother, her brother Abner, and the two teenage girls who looked like twins. Still to be seen were the father and the boy who was the bitter fruit of that rape.

Abner took Jacob to the back to wash while the women prepared the table. Abner watched as Jacob washed and changed his dark suit and sweaty shirt for pale slacks and a fresh open-necked shirt. Without his jacket and tie Jacob fitted more neatly into the surroundings: he could be a young man of Alabama or of Georgia.

Abner admired the sharp crease of the slacks and the gay colours of the shirt. "That what they wear in your island – what's it called again?"

"Jamaica," Jacob said. "Yes."

"It like here?"

"No. Different."

"How?"

"We have mountains and hills and everything's green all the time."

"We have mountains and hills too."

"Yes; but they are very near with us; most of us live in the mountains and the high hills."

"White folks too?"

"No. They live in Kingston, on the plain."

"Same as whites here?"

"I don't know; I don't know any whites there or here. Few at the university but I don't know them. What I do know is that they will not lynch us or molest our women because they know there will be war. So they don't trouble us, especially in the hills. They did trouble my grandpa a long time ago. They burned down his church and took away some of his congregation.''

''They no different,'' Abner nodded. ''Same as here; maybe not so many, but same as here. . . .''

They were interrupted by Harriet's voice, calling. Jacob started to lock his suitcase; his valuable papers and clothes could not be left open on a section of a verandah partitioned off with canvas into sleeping quarters.

''S'all right,'' Abner said. ''Nobody will touch them.''

Jacob felt shamefaced suddenly, as though he had thoughtlessly hurt Abner.

''I'm sorry.''

''S'all right,'' Abner said. ''Come.''

The woman had prepared a small feast of cornbread and gummy pig's hock, sweet potatoes and a mound of fresh greens cooked lightly in a deliciously savoury gravy. The others took token portions and watched Harriet and Jacob eat with the relish of the truly famished. Then, near the end of the meal, very politely and carefully, but very searchingly, they questioned Jacob about where he came from, the size of his family, the land they owned, what they did, and what life was like in Jamaica. Jacob told them everything they wanted to know, as simply and clearly as he knew how. He had asked Harriet to marry him and it was right that her people should want to know all about him and his people.

One of the twins asked: ''Is there no colour line? You said nothing about it.''

It was Abner who answered: ''No white folk around where Jacob's people live so they don't need to have any truck with them.''

''Not even for work?''

''Not if all that land is theirs,'' Mrs Bruce said softly. ''Here. . . .'' And she told Jacob much of what he had already learned from DuBois' Thursday evening group. But he heard it as fresh new information because Mrs Bruce told it from the inside of the lives led by black folk; not as some carefully researched and documented piece of scholarship. She talked of being raped and of at least a score of other cases of which she had personal

171

knowledge. Some of the women had gone to school with her, others were strangers; all understood that it was part of a deliberate exercise in racial humiliation so that they and their men and their children should never forget their place.

"Do you see, Jacob," Harriet said when her mother paused. "It is not a moral question for them; it is as clearcut as lynching, only, you lynch black pride and black self-respect instead of black bodies. You leave the bodies themselves to go on living and walking and talking and hurting as reminders of what can be done to black folk any day and any time anywhere in this country; and those living bodies are the bodies of your mother, your sister, your wife, even your grandmother. What kind of pride can you have if they can do this to your women and you can't do anything about it?"

"What kind of people are they?" Jacob wondered aloud. But somehow he could not get quite as angry about it as these people were. Why couldn't he? It seemed that they knew he was not as angry as they were and the knowledge created a mood of awkwardness. To try and get over it he told them about his family history. As he talked he realized why he was not and could not be as angry as they were: theirs was an anger of despair, and despair was alien to the hill folk where he came from. When he had done Mrs Bruce said, a world of detachment in her voice:

"They had somewhere to run to; we had no hiding-place."

"Ya," Abner said. "Your mountains."

The sudden awkwardness was not dispelled, so Harriet changed the subject and they talked about plans for Christmas, two days away. The twins cleared the table, Mrs Bruce got up and moved about the room, Abner withdrew into blank silence; and so the awkwardness was gradually dissipated in everyday routine.

When darkness fell Mr Bruce, a tall thin man with a round-shouldered stoop, returned from the cotton fields. With him came the boy, Martin, twelve years old and several shades paler than the rest of the family. He was also physically different. Whereas the others were long-boned, tall and lean, young Martin was thick-set, almost squat, with big, not yet fully grown but already heavy bones; in contrast with their long narrow faces tapering to small chins, his was round and square. Only his pale grey eyes were like their dark ones, the same quiet, sadly withdrawn quality about them in repose.

There was no awkwardness between the boy and the man he called "Paw"; nor between the woman and this offspring violently forced on her. Jacob had wondered about it but there was nothing to see. And yet they had made it clear to him that they were conscious of this young yellowish boy as the living symbol of their racial humiliation.

The man mumbled something when his wife introduced Jacob, Jacob was aware of a husky rasping voice and sensed difficulty in breathing; but he did not know what the man said as he shook the gnarled and totally inert hand. Then the man and the boy disappeared into the back to wash and clean up. Abner went with them leaving Harriet and her mother and Jacob alone in the front room. When the room was in complete darkness Mrs Bruce lit the big oil lamp they used on special occasions only, the one with the glass shade with "Home Sweet Home" on it, which could burn all through the night.

"Some of our neighbours coming by later to welcome Harriet home," Mrs Bruce explained. "And you too, of course. First time she's brought a boyfriend home so everybody wants to see you, especially as you're a foreigner from the islands. We've never seen a foreigner, you know." Her smile, made gentler by the softness of the lamplight, made being a foreigner seem special.

Jacob held on to himself, on guard, not knowing what to expect and anxious to win the approval of this woman. She, it was clear, was the head of this household. Whatever was done here, whatever was decided, would be with her approval. Not all that different from Jamaica, and yet different. Men and women worked together and decided together, especially where their children were concerned. Here it seemed men left things to the women, elected not to be in control; no, not elected. That implies choice. Was it part of the humiliation, of the destroyed pride being expressed?

Jacob turned to Harriet: "Remember what you said about black pride?"

"Yes," she thought for a long while. "You thinking about Pa and Martin?"

Jacob looked quickly at Mrs Bruce who said, "It's all right."

"About your men, about black men in this country."

"Dr DuBois' group has been looking at that," Harriet told her mother.

"I see," the woman said. "So what's the question, Jacob?"

"Not a question, really, more a thought. As long as they have your men in this position of being without self-respect and pride there is little you can do to change things."

"Unless we counter that," Harriet said.

"And we will," Mrs Bruce responded, at ease now. "We the women have a special task. As they destroy our men's pride so we must build it up again. We must use our minds and our hearts and our bodies to give them back that pride and that self-respect that will make them want to fight back. Our love is the only weapon we have to support our men. If we do not give them that support and make them strong then the day when equality comes will have no meaning."

"The day when equality comes. . . . When is that?"

"I don't know; you and Harriet must tell me, your Professor DuBois must tell us. We are prepared to carry on until it comes, however long that is. Does that explain Pa and Martin to you? Martin will grow up learning to hate what they did to his Pa through me and to all his family, for we are his family and his bastard blood will want to avenge us and him too. . . ."

"In the name of love?" Jacob asked softly.

"Yes!" the woman said. "In the name of love! You will learn, my young pastor, that love can be harsh and even cruel when there is need for it. Your grandparents were slaves! Have you forgotten that already in the name of your Gentle Jesus? He was not always gentle." The dark eyes glowed with passion.

"Has she talked with DuBois?" Jacob asked Harriet.

Harriet's lips curled in a happy smile. "No."

"I wish your professor could hear some of the talk in the cottonfields. It would buss his big brain."

Harriet chortled. "I think he hears of it, Ma. I think you'll get a big surprise if you ever meet that refined and over-educated little

174

brown gentleman from Boston; and I'll see that you do."

"I hope so." A small smile flashed across the woman's face and was gone. "You think as much of this Professor DuBois as Harriet does, Jacob?"

Before he could answer there was a shout from outside; then the sound of many voices. Mrs Bruce turned up the wick of the lamp and they all hurried out to the verandah. A cluster of people, the first of the visitors, had arrived. From the verandah Jacob could hear the familiar sounds of the night: the bark of dogs, the calls of the little night creatures, and the kind of stillness country people listen to.

The people, mostly women and mostly elderly, greeted them one by one in the semblance of a ceremonial line-up; first, Harriet's father, who had appeared at the door when they arrived, then Harriet's mother, then Harriet herself, then the stranger; the rest of the family were not subjected to such formalities. For them the greeting was a nod or a pat on the arm or a "Hiya, Abner", "Hiya, Cissie", "'Lo, Merl", "Hiya, Martin." Then the visitors spread themselves on the verandah, the older people on the long benches, the younger ones on the verandah steps and on its rails. All the chairs and stools were brought out of the house as more people came. The talk flowed freely. After a time the young people naturally found themselves a little apart from the older folk. A half-gallon earthern jug of corn liquor appeared and was passed from one man to another. The women and younger children shared cookies and a non-alcoholic punch. Abner and two young men disappeared into the night down the dirt road and returned, ten minutes later, with their own corn liquor, half a dozen more young people and two banjos, a mouth organ, and a long reed flute. Before long everybody, old folk as well as children, were dancing on the bare earth outside the Bruce home. Those who did not dance sat clapping their hands and stomping their feet to the rhythm. The morrow was the Sabbath, the day of rest so they could sleep late. Christmas was two days ahead and its spirit was all about them.

Mrs Bruce came over to where Harriet and Jacob sat in the shadow of a huge tree. She took both Jacob's hands and pulled him to the dancing circle. Then, in mid-dance, another motherly

175

woman relieved Mrs Bruce of Jacob, after that, another and another and another; and then at last Harriet came to his rescue, danced a few turns with him and took him back to their shadowy spot under the tree, to rest and to recover his breath.

Mrs Bruce brought them each a thick slice of corn bread with a piece of smoked hog resting on it. She raised her voice so Jacob could hear her above the music: "You are one of us now, Jacob. If you want to be!"

When they had eaten Harriet led Jacob a little distance from the sound of the music, but not so far that they could not still be seen by the others.

"You know why they all danced with you?"

"An endurance test," he jested; then: "A sort of welcome."

"Yes; a special welcome. They all like you. Ma was telling you that just now. Do you understand us, Jacob?"

"Understand what? You are people like all other people. You are angry about your status, how you are treated and you want to change that. That's normal. That's how people are; all people."

"All these people help to pay for my being at university, Jacob. My family can't do it alone. When I finish another child from our three villages will be sent to college and university. Because I am expected to earn more with my university degree than their combined earnings they look to me to help that next child as they have helped me. That is my debt to them. And when that other child gets through college and university there will be two of us to support two others. Later there will be three of us then four of us then five of us. . . ."

"I see. . . . When does it end? When do you finish paying your debt?"

"Never. Oh, it will change. When I have children of my own my first responsibility will be to them. But I must always help the others as these people have helped me. . . ."

"What is it you are telling me, Harriet?"

"That if you still want to marry me, you take on my responsibility too. If you marry me, you marry a sharecropper's daughter and a bunch of sharecroppers who want to free all their children from sharecropping. We see schooling and education as the way

176

out. Not tomorrow or next week or next year, but still as the way out one day, no matter how far away that day."

"That is the struggle of all black people," Jacob said. "It is my struggle as much as yours."

"In the abstract, yes, Jacob. In this particular instance, no. Mine is a specific obligation and commitment to a specific group of people in a specific little corner of Alabama. Dr DuBois could depend on his brains and ability to get him through those Northern public schools and universities; you could depend on your family who could pull themselves up because conditions are different in Jamaica. You see how it is here. There is no way out for anyone among us such as you and Dr DuBois could find. If the day comes when we do have that way out my specific obligation will come to an end and I would become committed, like you and Dr DuBois, to the wider struggle of all black people. Now it must be to this place and these people."

"What does that mean for us, for you and me?" He forced himself to speak calmly: "What does it mean to our marriage?"

"Oh, my Jacob! I just want to marry you and be your wife and have your children and. . . . Oh, so many things!" She, too, now forced herself to be calm: "I will marry you if you understand that I cannot leave Alabama until. . . ."

"Until there is a way out for everybody here?"

"For every child, Jacob. There'll never be a way out for the old folk, not even for Ma who has had more schooling than most of them. For the children, yes."

"That is really saying you won't marry me!" He was hurt and angry now.

"No, please, Jacob! I will marry you; I will marry you if you will stay here. You can do your work here; here in Alabama or in Georgia or even Mississippi. We would be in touch and I would be able to do what I must do. Please, Jacob!"

"So," Jacob said, slowly, harshly. "You would give up nothing but you want me to give up everything. What kind of love is that?"

Harriet Bruce moaned softly and wrapped her arms tight across her belly as though trying to hold it together; she seemed shrivelled up and small. Her voice, however, was calm and steady: "Oh Jacob, I am so sorry. I did ask too much. But not because I would give up nothing; I thought you would at least understand that. Just to go off with you would be to give up nothing, to take everything from them who have nothing and give nothing back. I couldn't do that and still live with myself. That's why I asked so much of you. I'm so sorry . . . I'm sorry. . . ." She turned and walked away, to the house, but so that she would avoid the people dancing in front. "Tell them I'm not feeling well; tell them it's the excitement. . . ." She still held in her belly as she went, round-shouldered and small-looking.

Jacob remained where he was till the hurt and rage left his heart and mind. He tried to think calmly but rational thought was not possible now. He felt empty, depressed, unhappy over Harriet's unhappiness, unhappy over his own unhappiness. The music was still playing, the dirt-poor black sharecroppers on the sprawling Alabama cotton plantation were dancing away happily, their sorrows, their hopelessness forgotten for the moment. Christmas was just two days away.

Jacob Brown felt suddenly very lonely, very homesick for the hills of Jamaica.

And in his study at Atlanta University, Professor DuBois re-read an essay which began: "The problem of the twentieth century is the problem of the colour line. . . ."

COUNTY TIPPERARY JOINT LIBRARIES
County Library
Thurles.

4
Jacob/Dan/Liberia

1

He came struggling out of a hot dank swirling green fog, fighting his way free of an unseen force, overpowering and determined to assimilate him into its darkness. Suddenly it was over: the fog was gone, the fighting ended. The green, now, was peaceful, dispersing in waves, each a lighter green than the wave before it. He relaxed in the world of receding green waves, utterly spent, unable to move, hardly able to breathe, aware only of an overpowering heat and thirst. From a great distance far beyond the green waves a voice reached him at last. It said: "Jacob! Jacob! Are you awake, Jake? Can you hear me?" He felt a hand on his head. He tried to open his eyes.

The man bending over him saw the movement of the eyelids, and, taking his wrist, felt the more even rate of the pulse. He turned to the nurse behind him. "The fever's broken; I think he'll be all right. Better change his bedding very quickly before the chill sets in; then we'll let him sleep."

"Yes, doctor." The nurse left the room and returned almost instantly with two strapping young men, barefoot and in faded khaki shorts and shirt. Her voice became authoritative as she told them to lift the semi-conscious man from the bed to a trolley. She stripped and remade the bed quickly. Then, instructing the men how to hold him, she stripped the patient of his sweat-soaked hospital gown, rubbed his body down with dry towels and supervised his return to the bed. "You can go now," she ordered. "Mattress to the steam room, rest to the laundry, understand?"

"Yes, lady nurse," one of the young men said, bowing his head.

The doctor, who had been watching from the window, cleared his throat so the others all looked at him. His face broke into a smile as he pointedly recognized the two young men with his eyes. "Thank you. Dr Brown will be all right now; thank you for helping."

The one who had answered the nurse bowed again, showing his teeth this time. "Thank you, doctor, sir." The other one echoed him. "Thank you, doctor, sir." Then they bowed themselves out with their bundles.

The nurse made no attempt to hide her tight-lipped disapproval. These Afro-Americans did not understand how to deal with the natives, and they would not learn from those who knew. A doctor praising these boys directly would spoil them; they would want to talk directly to doctors, and then to other people as well. No use talking to Dr Brown about this either; he was the same. Afro-Americans and West Indians all couldn't understand.

To himself the doctor muttered: stew in your rage and damn you. Aloud he said: "Prepare this sedative for Dr Brown and then let him sleep. Have a nourishing soup ready for him later. I'll come and take a bowl with him. He hates eating alone." He scribbled on a piece of paper and handed it to the nurse as he walked out.

"Yes, doctor," she said to his back.

When the doctor returned at sundown the patient was awake and free of fever or chill. The room had been transformed from its earlier hospital-room appearance into a pleasant airy bedroom: a small table beside the bed with a vase of delicately arranged flowers; Jacob Brown's favourite big table within reach; an easy chair for visitors by the open window. The overhead fan stirred the air gently.

"Hiya, Jake; welcome back! For a moment back there I thought we'd lose you. . . . You damn stupid idiotic Bible-thumping ass! Why the hell didn't you take the quinine I went to such trouble to get for you? You realize you nearly died, you fool! Even the so-called natives have more sense than that! You bloody Jamaican monkey-chaser, you!" The doctor's anger went as suddenly as it came. "I see Mrs Jones has taken over from Nurse Symes. Symes turns every room into an intensive care unit. You should have seen the state of this room; but you were too demented for that, you fool." His voice held only affection now. "How you feeling?"

"Tired, weak, thirsty, hungry and glad you've done with cursing me. I just misplaced your quinine, that's all. Only realized when I got up country that I'd left it behind. Tried to get some from the Frontier Force people but they didn't have enough to share, or wouldn't share." The voice was cracked and whispering.

"So you decided to go on. . . ."

"What else could I do?"

"Turn back and save a whole lot of people a whole lot of trouble."

"What do you mean?"

"How do you think you got back here? Frontier Force brought you? If it were up to them you'd be long dead and buried."

"What happened?"

"Bush people carried you back here in relays, running night and day to get you here before the fever burned you up. They kept you cool with their bush medicine. You reached here wrapped in more leaves than I've ever seen. They saved you, Jake. Not the prayers and the services and the 'get well' messages. . . . Tell me, who is Harriet? You kept on calling for her. I went through your papers but found nothing, no letters, no address, nothing; but you kept on calling for her like your life depended on her coming. Who is she? Where is she?"

"Goes back a long time," Jacob Brown said weakly. "A very long time, Dan."

"It sounded fresh as yesterday," the doctor said, studying the face of the man on the bed closely; "charged with immediate pain, not the pain of a long time ago. We've been friends a long time, Jake, shared many things and secrets, yet you never mentioned any Harriet."

"It was in the past," Jacob Brown said wearily. "The dead forgotten past of youth."

"And young love," the doctor murmured. "And came alive at the moment near death."

"All right, Dan, I'll tell you; but not now. I'm too tired and thirsty."

The doctor poured a small amount of cool water from a

heavy, covered, earthern pitcher, raised his friend's head, and helped him drink it.

"How cool and sweet it is! Reminds me of the cool spring water of our hills."

"Same principle. The tribesmen say the earth from which this pitcher is made purifies and cools the water and gives it the minerals of a spring, only they call it the magic of a spring."

"True?"

"How do I know, Dr God-man? That's your territory. All I know is it is good for you and the tribes people are right about it. Don't tell Symes though, she will want to boil the germs and everything else out of it. Being civilized and hygenic can be such a bore."

A knock on the door interrupted them. The doctor called: "Come!" Then, as the tall and very handsome and scrubbed-clean young man entered: "Ah, Jones, our reverend doctor is back in the land of the living and screaming for his chop. Got it?"

The young man's eyes twinkled. He nodded and approached the bed. Jacob Brown felt the warm affection and great relief of the young man wash over him.

"Hello, sir. So glad you are better."

"Not better yet," the doctor said sternly. "Just back among us. And damn lucky, too; thinking he can roam the bush with only his God-cross and no medicine. I'm telling him now and you are my witness. Try it just one more time and we'll watch you croak."

"Oh, shut up, Dan," the man on the bed smiled tiredly, but spiritually at ease.

There was another knock and this time a young woman entered pulling a tray table on wheels, followed by an older woman pushing and steering. The young woman made way for the older woman to approach Jacob Brown first.

A round, dumpy, black woman, face shiny and creasy, eyes laughing from a world of experience and shrewdness. She carried the air of self-assurance found only among women who have survived, unbroken in spirit, in the slums of the great cities of world. Mrs Willis was a product of Harlem, USA, come to Africa in the service of her church. Her bishop had told her that one of her most important chores at the mission station would be to look after Dr Brown so that he could look after the business of God. If he had died of the fever she would have blamed herself and Dr Daniel Lee for not making sure that he took the quinine when he went to that awful bush country where mosquitoes are as big as flies. Only the Lord knows why He made such terrible and deadly things and placed them where they could attack and kill His servants. But then, nobody knows what the Lord knows. . . . She tried to shake free of these thoughts; the Lord's business always confused her mind, better just do what she knew best. She took Jacob Brown's hand.

"Good to see you, Rev'rend. You should have. . . ."

"Yes, Matron; doctor's already told me all about it. He says you'll all leave me to croak next time!"

"Well, I never!" Matron protested, eyes wide in mock horror.

Young Mr Jones and his wife, Dorothy, giggled by the window.

"I will, too," the doctor said defiantly.

"We'd better eat," young Mrs Jones said.

"You've all heard him," the patient said.

"He's getting better now, Jonathan," the doctor said. "The tyrant returns. Better make sure everything is in order."

The young woman came to the bedside. "I have a lot of mail for you. Can we go over some of it before school tomorrow morning?" She looked at the doctor who nodded. Jacob Brown agreed with his eyes. Mrs Willis set about dishing up thick, very nourishing soup for all of them.

This group of five was the core of the team with whom Jacob Brown ran the mission; all five of them from the States. The rest were locals: Nurse Symes, an Americo-Liberian, and half a dozen teachers. The mission was a good twenty years old, but the members of his team had been here for a little over five years and they had nearly doubled the size and capacity of the mission in that time.

Jonathan and Dorothy Jones ran the school and the mission farm and workshop. Dr Daniel Lee ran the hospital with the help of Nurse Symes, who had a string of young trainee nurses and male orderlies under her, all of whom she treated atrociously because they were "natives". On this point neither Jacob Brown,

185

the doctor, the two Joneses nor Mrs Willis could budge her. Natives were different from other people: backward and savage and uncivilized and would remain so for a long time to come. Until then they should not be confused into seeing themselves as the same as people who had been exposed to civilization for centuries.

The difficulty they had all found was the passionate sincerity with which Miss Symes held and expressed such convictions. Her ancestors, two brothers and their wives, had been among the first one hundred and fourteen pioneers who had landed on the coast way back in 1822. For black Nurse Marjorie Symes, as for the other descendants of the freed slaves who had landed in Liberia, the gap between the natives and the Americo-Liberians was deep and permanent for as far into the future as they could see. This often caused grave problems between Nurse Symes's people, the Americo-Liberians, who saw and thought of themselves as the only true Liberians, and the more recent arrivals from the United States who called themselves Afro-Americans. Relations between the true Liberians and other blacks were uneasy, with the black American missionaries being the most difficult. Bringing schooling and the rudiments of good health habits, and teaching them trades, was welcome. Planting false notions about their status and the rights they were supposed to have was sheer trouble-making. This the Liberians, their President, and their True Whig Party, would not tolerate. The most troublesome of these new arrivals were told, politely at first, then more sharply, that they were not suited for Liberian settlement and citizenship, and would not be given the piece of land to which every accepted settler is entitled. None who were unwelcome remained for long; when any new arrival did not adjust quickly enough and was advised to leave he usually left immediately.

Dealing with the missionaries was much more tricky. Behind each missionary enterprise in the country was a powerful and influential church back in the United States. Pressure on the head of a local mission had, in the recent past, led to stern warnings from the US State Department that further harassment of any American missionaries would be viewed as unfriendly acts which could have grave consequences on the good relations now existing between the two countries. Word had gone out to the Provincial Commissioners, the District Commissioners, and Sub-District Commissioners, and the Commanders of the Frontier Force to be careful and circumspect in all their dealings with the missionaries, and only to act, in even the most flagrant abuses of Liberian national interests, after consultation with Monrovia. So the missionaries were distrusted and resented, but left alone, or else the pressure exerted on them was covert; nothing sufficiently tangible for them to be able to complain to their governments of being persecuted or obstructed. The American Government was not only the guarantor of Liberian sovereignty, American remittances and loans and investments kept their country afloat. The American dollar had replaced the English pound as the Liberian national currency; American missionaries brought large amounts of dollars into the country to finance their efforts and thus into the general pool of available dollars. The missionaries were important and powerful; they were needed enough to be handled with care, whatever they did and however much the Liberians resented their presence and their influence on the natives.

When the five had eaten their soup, when the small talk was done, and when the African darkness had crept over the land, Mrs Willis and the young Jones couple departed with the used dishes and the table-on-wheels. The doctor stayed with Jacob Brown, relaxed in the comfortable chair by the screened open window. The noises of the little night creatures flowed through the room in circular waves, rising to a peak of intensity then fading away only to return again. There was a slightly damp chill to the air, not as sticky as it would be down at the coast, but enough to be noticed even at more than seven hundred feet above sea level. At a thousand feet or over it would be cool and comfortable, but that would mean being much further into deep bush country. The mission stood on the highest point of the land here, overlooking a swampy, forested stretch of land sweeping down to the coast and the capital city of Monrovia, sixty miles away.

Jacob Brown had dozed off; now he woke.

187

"Dan. . . ."

"I'm here."

"The truck. What happened to it?"

"Don't worry. We've sent Sam for it."

"Hope they don't wreck it before Sam reaches."

"We have to take that chance. I hope they have not stripped it of everything."

"How long?"

"Should be back sometime tomorrow, if things go well."

"I mean how long have I been like this?"

"Hard to say. They say they carried you for two days, but if they carried you from where they say it couldn't be done. You've been back three days."

"And the boy Smiley?"

"He stayed to guard the truck and its contents. He should be back with the truck."

Jacob Brown sighed and closed his eyes again.

"About Harriet, what did I say?"

Dr Lee turned his face to the window. "You called for her again and again and you wept, Jake, as you called. That's all. It went on for a long time."

"Just calling. . . ."

"And weeping, Jake; pitifully. I told Matron you'd called for Harriet in case she knew her."

"She didn't."

"I know; she told me."

"It was a long time ago, Dan. Thought I had forgotten all about it. More than twenty years ago."

"That why you didn't marry?"

"Probably. I'll tell you about it one day."

"You'd better."

"What d'you mean?"

"It needs to come out, Jake, desperately; it's choking you."

"My friend the psychologist!"

"I mean it, Jake. I heard your desperate weeping."

"Perhaps you're right," Jacob Brown said softly. "I really thought I had got over it. Such a long time ago."

"Time is as relative as life, my friend. You haven't gotten over whatever happened between you and Harriet. You were not weeping for some dead twenty-year-old experience; your pain was here and now."

"All right; but not now."

"To yourself, Jake; let it out to yourself, not to me or anyone else. Face it. That's the thing."

Jacob Brown put the glass on the table and slid lower down into the bed.

"Time for sleep," Daniel Lee said briskly.

He helped Jacob Brown swallow a pill, turned down the lamp, gathered up the empty glasses. At the door he paused for one quick careful survey of the room, then he went out, leaving the door open. The night "boy" appeared and settled down outside the open door. He would stay there through the night, keeping watch over the patient while the doctor slept in the next room.

The low mission buildings lay white in the moonlight in a neatly arranged but irregular circle, with the church at the highest point. The cemetery was behind the church, on gently sloping land. The quadrangular hospital structure was to the south of the church, along a walkway marked off with large lime-washed stones. Beyond the stones flat broad-bladed grass clung close to the reddish sun-bleached earth. Prodigious effort went into keeping the grass alive and green. The after-classes work on planting, keeping, and spreading the lawns provided scholarships of free board and tuition for at least a score of young boys each year. They were the ones whose homes were too far back in the hinterland for their people to send ground provisions or livestock or coffee beans to pay for their schooling. All the work in the mission, from housekeeping, cooking and laundry to clearing the land, putting up buildings, and terracing and landscaping the land, was done by the worker-students who often made up as much as two-thirds of the student body. In return they were taught to read and write, wear western clothes, and become Christians – followers of the gentle Jesus who was killed on a cross.

The worker-scholar system in time made the mission near economically self-sustaining. The coffee, cola nuts and other exportable crops were shipped back to the States; their sales contributed to the home church's remittances which sustained the mission. There were times when the mission's enterprises made a profit for the home church. On such occasions there were great celebrations back home; the successes of the mission stirred home congregations to even greater Sunday offerings and inspired many young men and women to opt for missionary work. The mission under the Reverend Jacob Brown was having a period of such prosperity. The hospital was more than paying its way in addition to winning the trust and confidence of the native tribes for the church, thanks to a highly successful campaign against yellow fever in which Doctor Daniel Lee had saved the life of an important hinterland chief, and then, by introducing live fish into their water source, held down the disease. This, to the natives, was powerful and convincing juju; any god that could do that was worth following, at least with one's mouth and in public where he could hear and see.

The whole hill of the missionary village was a neatly laid out combination of buildings, gardens, trees, walkways, manicured lawns: an efficiently managed, well-organized bit of America deep in the African bush. It was surrounded on all sides by that bush, dark and heavily forested, with small native villages tucked away everywhere in it. Mr Jonathan Jones, the gifted young missionary teacher from Ohio had, in his first year and after careful questioning and many journeys into the surrounding bush, estimated that there must be upwards of five thousand people living in the hidden villages within a radius of ten miles of the mission. Dr Jacob Brown had warned the young man not to pass that figure on to the Frontier Force people: they would want to relate the taxes they levied on the tribal folk to the highest figure they could get. So young Mr Jones kept his estimate to himself.

On the fourth day Jacob Brown was strong enough to resume his full normal workload. Dr Lee had moved back to his own bungalow and Brown's spare bedroom was again reserved for important visitors. He was moved by the spontaneous cheer that went up on his reappearance at assembly, and amused at the sternness with which one of the teachers from the coast, Mr Johnstone, hushed them. Almost every other detribalized coastal native family was called Johnstone – pronounced as it was spelled.

Then Mr Johnstone told him that a delegation from two of the farther villages had arrived the night before and was waiting to see him, if that was all right, if he was strong enough? Jacob assured Mr Johnstone he was strong enough. He guessed that some of the delegation would be members of the tribe to which Mr Johnstone's people had belonged before they moved to the coast. Mr Johnstone would come with the delegation and "speak for" it since none of its members spoke English. Each of the local teachers spoke one or the other of the many tribal dialects; some more than one.

Jacob Brown looked in on the hospital where Dr Lee, Nurse Symes and a couple of young men were wrestling with a huge man, stark naked, who was violently resisting an injection. The half-dozen other inmates of the cool thatch-roofed ward, as well as the four trainee nurses present, were in paroxysms of laughter which added to Nurse Symes's quiet determined fury. After a while they held the man still long enough for Dr Lee to push the needle into the rump. The man let out an almighty bloody yell then relaxed, allowing the doctor to complete the injection.

"Up to your old trick, I see!" Jacob Brown laughed.

"Subject for your next sermon," Dr Lee said. "The needle is not the spirit of the devil. It is a good juju, sent by the gods to drive out the spirit of the devil."

"Superstitious nonsense!" Nurse Symes snapped, glaring at the grinning trainee nurses who fled to their various tasks.

"I'm seeing a delegation," Jacob Brown said to Dr Lee. "Mr Johnstone's bringing them. Can you come?"

"I've one operation, gangrene; and a delivery."

"I'll take care of the delivery," Nurse Symes said.

"I'll come after the operation," Lee said. "It's a bad one; they left it too late before bringing him here. An old man. Is he under, nurse?" Nurse Symes looked at one of her trainees. A silent signal passed between them.

"Yes, doctor."

"See you later," Jacob Brown said; then from beyond the door he called: "Good luck."

Brown walked to the administration building in the centre of the mission compound. The early morning sun cast a tolerable, almost gentle heat over the land. There was the hint of a breeze which barely stirred the leaves on the trees. Again, as so often since he had come to this part of Africa, Jacob Brown had a sudden longing to see a dog scampering across the grass or between the buildings. There were no dogs here and it was hard to accept their absence. Wild dogs, lean and hungry and nondescript sometimes attached themselves to a village and stayed on its fringes, scavenging and cleaning up and having an arm's-length relationship with the people of the village. But the intimacy between dog and man with which he had grown up in the hills of Jamaica was rare here, for dogs were few and not often seen.

The delegation was waiting. There were four old men; three of them tall and thin, one short and rotund. They wore white seamless cotton robes which made them look like people out of the Bible. The robes were so clean they had obviously not been worn on the journey. Mr Johnstone had not yet arrived and the young man who acted as office boy and office manager was in class so no one had received the delegation; it waited patiently outside even though the office was open and there were benches where they could have sat.

Jacob Brown had met many such delegations so he bowed ceremoniously, smiled warmly, shook each by the hand and ushered them into the office, noting the order in which they went in. The eldest and most senior would enter first, so Jacob would know whom to address and show most respect to even if someone else were the spokesman or linguist. Nothing could begin till Mr Johnstone arrived so they waited, examining each other politely and showing their teeth in token of goodwill.

Mr Johnstone arrived shortly after, breathless and apologetic for being late. For all his learning he showed great deference and humility toward these illiterate elders. They, for their part, showed to Mr Johnstone the thoughtfulness and kindness of the good master or overseer for the good servant. Again and again Jacob Brown had been impressed by the easy authority which illiterate tribal elders invariably exercised over even the most educated coast natives.

"Can we begin now, sir?" Mr Johnstone asked in English. "The elders want to start the journey back as soon as possible."

"All right," Jacob said. "Tell them I greet them and I welcome them and the mission is their home for as long as they wish to visit."

The short round one, who had entered the office last, was the spokesman. He spoke in what Jacob Brown guessed to be the language of the Mendi.

"We are grateful for your welcome, lord of the mission, and for the graciousness with which you welcome us without notice. Your District Commissioner will not receive us in this manner. To have audience with him we must send a messenger to beg for audience; then, no matter how urgent the matter, he sets a distant date and time when he will receive our elders. If any elders arrive as we have done here today, your District Commissioner will not see us. So we are grateful to you. We had heard you would receive us so, which is why we came; but we were prepared to return home without seeing you."

"It is my duty and my pleasure to welcome you and to do whatever is in my power." Jacob Brown spoke directly to the most senior of the elders. Mr Johnstone translated smoothly. "And please permit me to make one thing clear. It is this: there is no connection between the District Commissioner and our mission. We are the servants of Almighty God; the District Commissioner is the servant of the government of Liberia."

The eldest of the elders spoke up in a dry soft voice:

"And are not those who are the government also servants of your Almighty God? We hear they worship at your shrine, at the shrine of your God."

"There are many who say they are servants of our God, many who worship in his temples, who violate the spirit of His teaching."

The eldest elder's face broke into a half-smile. He nodded slightly. A flash of understanding passed between him and Jacob Brown. "It is so among us too. And you teach our children this?"

"We do."

"So we hear from others. It is good to hear it from you."

"But they – your District Commissioner and your government – will not approve."

"We do not seek their approval; we serve only our God. We do not seek their enmity either. We do not violate their laws. We do only God's work."

The elder nodded and smiled again. "We must talk about this God of yours another time; and about our gods, too. But now for the business that is at hand."

The rotund one, the spokesman, took it up: "We ask of you to intercede on our behalf with the government. Taxes and tributes are traditionally collected once every year. We paid our taxes at the usual time this year, no more than three months ago, and the burden was heavy. But we paid. Now eight days ago, the soldiers have returned and are demanding more taxes and are taking our people's food; they are threatening to destroy our fields and burn our huts if we do not give them more tribute. We are a people of peace and we prefer the ways of peace. . . ."

The eldest of the elders cut in: "But even people of peace must fight when the locusts darken the skies and swarm down on their fields; no man stands idle while the locusts destroy his crops. . . ."

". . . So we seek your help," the rotund one ended. "Will you help us?"

"I will try," Jacob said promptly. "What is it you want me to do?"

"They say you interceded on a matter such as this one in the past when your District Commissioner dealt unjustly with the people of another village."

"That village was in this district where we of the mission are under the rule of the same Commissioner. Your village in the land of the Mendi. . . ."

"Not one village, lord of the mission, four. We are each the chief of his village."

Jacob nodded, acknowledging the correction. "Your villages, chiefs, are in another district, under another District Commissioner whom we do not know and with whom we have no dealing and who does not rule over us."

"So?" the eldest asked.

194

"So we must find another way to intercede."

"So?" the eldest pressed.

"I could ask our District Commissioner to intercede with the District Commissioner of your land."

The chiefs consulted among themselves; Mr Johnstone did not translate for Jacob Brown. Instead he, too, took part in the consultation. When it was over he turned to Jacob: "They are not sure that would be the best way, sir."

"Why?"

Mr Johnstone hesitated, seemingly reluctant to pursue this line of thought.

"What is it, Mr Johnstone?"

"It is difficult, sir." He was uncomfortable now.

"I must know their thinking if I am to help."

Mr Johnstone told them; again they consulted among themselves. Then the eldest spoke, measuring his words.

"It is not our wish or intention to be disrespectful of you or of your District Commissioner, especially if he is also your friend. We speak only from our experience. If you send a thief to plead with a thief you may end up having to pay tribute to two thieves. We know nothing of your District Commissioner, we know much of others, and there is a sameness about them. They will show respect for you because you are the lord of the mission and we know they fear you; but if your eye is not on them all the time they will turn on those who sought your protection and punish them for it."

"So how must I proceed?"

"Only a fool tries to teach his teacher," the eldest said.

"We are all teachers and we are all students," Jacob replied warming to the exchange now.

A wintry little smile flitted across the face of the eldest. "That is true, but a truth few know; it is only seen when we learn wisdom."

"So how should I proceed?"

"I. . . ." He turned his head to include the other chiefs. "We see two ways. First, for you to come among us bringing your authority and the fear it instils in the hearts of the wicked, and telling us, and through us the soldiers, what to do and what not to

195

do; and after that for you to be our linguist as we meet the District Commissioner, for he will meet us if you are with us. We know the journey is long; we will pay for it and for your time in much produce and in diamonds that will buy you all the things you want. And then," the eldest paused for effect, "and then we will swear to follow your God and be Christian as you are. All the people of all our four villages. That is the first way." The eldest waited for Jacob's reaction.

"And the second?" Jacob asked.

"For you to go to the coast and ask their big chief, the one they call the President, to stop the soldiers from robbing our people. They say the soldiers and the District Commissioners fear him as much as they fear you."

"Much more," Jacob cut in.

"But we do not know if you can see him."

"I can see him," Jacob said; probably much more easily than your District Commissioner, he thought to himself. "So which would you prefer?"

They consulted among themselves again, a little more excitedly. Then the spokesman said: "To do both would be ideal; to get the President to instruct the soldiers, and then to have a big palaver and feast at our villages: that would be good. All the tribes would know of our victory then."

"We have not won yet," Jacob said drily.

"And only a fool trumpets his victory," the eldest added. "Better to be humble and win the friendship of the vanquished."

"I will do the second," Jacob said. "If it is successful, there will be no need for the first."

"Then it will be so," the eldest said, rising. "The journey has been fruitful; the gods have been kind. We will add your God to our gods and we will pledge allegiance to Him and build a temple to Him whenever you are ready to come among us."

"That is not the way of our God," Jacob said. "We plan to start a school if you will help us. And we will send people to teach your children and to make clear the ways of our God. Only after that can the matter of allegiance begin. Our God is a different God from your gods."

"You know of our gods?" the eldest asked. "Of our river gods, and our tree gods and our land gods?"

"No."

"If you come I will tell of them and you will see that the gods are not really all that different. They pretend to be because all gods are vain. We will leave you now, lord of the mission. You are indeed as they have said. One day you must tell us why the others are so different, more like the white men who would take everything from us."

"Stay and rest and eat before you leave."

"We thank you; but the journey is long and our people wait anxiously. We will eat and rest on the way."

Ceremoniously the eldest brought a little pouch from the folds of his robe. He opened it and tilted it so that four marble-sized but irregularly shaped diamonds rolled into his cupped right hand. The early morning light made them send off sparkling shafts in all directions as they turned in the old man's hand.

"A small token of our gratitude," the eldest looked straight into Jacob's eyes; a look of embrace and blessing all at once.

"It is not necessary," Jacob murmured.

"Not for you, perhaps; for us, yes. There is a need to show thanks. That is our way."

"I know."

"You do? That is good. Not many who are not born here do."

"My grandmother told us. She knew your ways."

"She came from this land?"

"I do not know. She was a slave. Perhaps she did. She knew your ways."

"Yes; I heard of the terrible times of the slavers from those who were old when I was young. Perhaps that is why your people and your soldiers are so harsh with our people. Perhaps they blame our ancestors for what happened to them."

"Perhaps it has just corrupted them," Jacob said.

The eldest shook himself as though to banish that thought pattern. "We must deal with the troubles of this day. Thank you for receiving us." He pushed the diamonds back into the pouch and handed it to Jacob. "We will hear from you. We will tell the world of your kindness to us." The eldest shook hands solemnly and led the way out. Each of the chiefs, in order of seniority, did the same. Mr Johnstone bowed to Jacob and hurried out after the tribal chiefs.

Jacob weighed the diamonds in his hand. Must be a good many thousand dollars' worth. He sighed heavily. No way not to accept these without insulting them; but the line between the genuinely voluntary gift and the "dash" for services rendered, or anticipated, was so thin as to be almost invisible: there was a price even to God. No, not that; where there are many vain gods there has to be a different perception of God. . . . River gods and rain gods and tree gods and land gods. They didn't prepare us for this so we have to learn on the job. Perhaps they didn't know how to. Must find out from the young men from the hinterland.

He went into the inner office and put the diamonds in his desk drawer. They would probably fetch enough to pay for the building of the girls' wing. Mrs Willis had long pressed for a girls' dormitory so that girls, too, would be able to receive the benefit of a good Christian education. You cannot, she insisted, educate the men and then send them back to marry tribal bush-girls. In black America the women were usually better educated than their men, which is why there had been so much progress; until the same happened here there would be little.

He pushed these thoughts from his mind, took up pen and paper and started to write, beginning: "Dear Mr President. . . ." It was a request for the President of the Republic to please receive him on an urgent matter two days later. He sealed the letter, put it aside, and took up the monthly report he had half written before that journey into the bush which brought him down. He wrote quickly and steadily for the best part of an hour, spelling out all the details of the mission's operations for that month. He ended with the visit of the chiefs and his intention to appeal directly to the President on their behalf. He was satisfied, he reported, that the Frontier Force soldiers of the district were indeed extorting tribute over and above their legitimate tax collection from these distant tribes. Then he signed the report, gathered all its many pages together, added the pouch of diamonds, and put them all in a large envelope with the mission's head office address boldly printed on it. The United States government's representative in

Monrovia would send this report back to Washington in his own diplomatic pouch; from there it would be sent to the mission headquarters. Good friends in high places always helped things along: which was one reason why the Liberian President would see him.

Dr Dan Lee arrived a little after ten, followed by a young trainee nurse with their morning coffee.

"Sorry I missed them."

"How did the operation go?" Jacob asked.

"I don't think we can save him. Too far gone."

"Pity."

"Yes. If only they wouldn't leave it to the very end."

"Can't you do anything about that?"

"Not yet; but soon I hope. When my young fellows are trained enough I want to send them into the villages in pairs to explain such basic things, to deal with minor ills, and be our eyes and contacts to get serious cases to the hospitals quickly. I'm going to need your support and some money."

"You'll have it."

Dan Lee paused midway in pouring the coffee, his eyebrows raised in question. Jacob waved, indicating the bulging envelope. Lee finished pouring the coffee then took out the contents of the envelope. He let out a long sigh when the diamonds rolled sparkling onto the desk. "Wow! At least five grand, if not more. Your visitors? What for?"

"They're being held to ransom by the Frontier Force. Seizing their crops; threatening to burn their huts if they don't pay more and more."

"Goddammit!" Lee exploded in a sudden paroxysm of rage. "Is this what Garvey's Back-to-Africa means? Blacks exploiting blacks instead of whites? And is this DuBois' Pan-Africanism? Yankee Nigger on the neck of tribal black man in true white bwana style? Jesus, Jake!"

"Easy, Dan."

"What you going to do?"

"I'm going to see the President. I'm going to ask him to stop this. He will."

"Of course he will – this time. And he'll curse them out for not

199

being more discreet; and they'll do it better next time."

"Oh come on, Dan! Your rage is becoming a self-indulgence. They're no worse than what we've seen in the States; different perhaps, not worse."

"They're black, Jake! Black like us!"

"So?"

"They should know better. They have suffered; their ancestors were slaves."

"And suffering is supposed to confer wisdom and understanding? Come on, Dan! Have you ever seen anything brutalized into wisdom and understanding? Man or beast?"

"Isn't that the teaching of your God?"

"I refuse to argue with irrationality. Give me some more coffee. We'll stop this thing this time. And each time it comes up and we know about it we'll try to stop it again. That's all we can do. You get your young men trained and send them into the villages. Those diamonds will get you some of the drugs you need and Mrs Willis her girls' dormitory. That's how we do it: step by step. One thing at a time. White people have just finished slaughtering each other in the most awesome bloodletting the world has ever known. I don't think you want to go on judging Dr DuBois' ideas and dreams, and Marcus Garvey's, through the eyes of white folk. They've made too much of a mess of things for you to accept their values as a yardstick for everything everybody else does."

"What other yardstick is there? Even your friend DuBois uses what you call a white man's yardstick."

"He'll get away from it. You wait and see: I am sure of it." Jacob Brown's mind went back to those days in Atlanta. He could almost see those hooded eyes forever searching. "For what he wanted to do, for what he wanted to understand, he started late, even though he was only in his early thirties. You need two or three lifetimes to do certain important things like charting new ways of thinking and understanding. Usually those three lifetimes are spread over several generations. When a man has to begin from nothing and chart what is a completely new way of seeing it is a long and lonely process."

Dr Daniel Lee looked searchingly into Jacob Brown's eyes, there

200

was that sudden stillness between them which came in high moments of mental intimacy.

"You really believe this business of the generations, don't you? A kind of apostolic succession of understanding and perception?"

"Why not? What's wrong with it?"

"You're dodging, Jake."

"All right, I believe in it."

"Experience is the one thing people do not inherit, which is why anything that is not recorded is lost. Even your Bible tells you that."

"Lost to whom, Dan? As far as I know those chiefs who were here have no written records of their past; does that mean they have no past? Not by the way they spoke to me. The senior one even offered to introduce me to their gods. Does that sound like folk without a past, or without a knowledge of that past?"

"How will your DuBois' or Garvey's ideas reach them?"

"Like all ideas have travelled through the ages. You have the legends, the songs, the poems which are spoken songs; and those that grip the human imagination most forcefully are passed on from generation to generation. Surely I don't have to tell you."

"No, Jake. But what about science and technology? Those do not fit into your oral tradition."

"Come, Dan. Aren't you passing it on to your young men now? Won't you send them back into their villages to pass it on? And won't one of them one day want to be a doctor, just like doctor Dan?"

"I thought. . . ."

"We exclude nothing, Dan. Nothing that can be put to the service of our people; certainly not your science and technology."

"But you, my employers, your church, have excluded others who have offered to serve because they look different."

"You are shifting ground, Dan. Science and technology as against the message of DuBois and Garvey, that was the argument. I say there is no conflict unless you invest science and technology with a sort of exclusive copyrighted Western European character and quality. Is it all really so exclusive? Even the written language of which you make so much: is that really a West European invention, any more than explosives are, or the philosophies are? We hold that there is nothing exclusive to any set of people about any aspect of world civilization. The uncivilized barbarians were not always the darker races of mankind; the rulers were not always the lighter races of mankind."

"If you see this much, Jake, then why exclude?"

"White missionaries who offered to join us? And the white man who went through med school with you and volunteered to join you here?"

"Yes. Why do you – or, rather, your church – exclude them by refusing their help?"

"Jim Crow in reverse, thinks Doctor Dan."

"Well, isn't it?"

"There are many white missions here and elsewhere in Africa, Dan; many more than there are black missions such as ours. So there's greater opportunity for whites to be missionaries in Africa than there is for blacks. There is also a history of takeovers. Wherever there is contact and co-operation, they take over sooner or later. To be in control of our own we must exclude them."

"Like they exclude us."

"Not quite the same, Dan. We have not yet developed, as a race, that arrogance of power that wants to control whatever it touches. Perhaps we will one day. I hope not. That is the key difference now."

"Even in the face of an extortionist Frontier Force?"

"Yes."

"And venal and corrupt black administration?"

"If and when they come, yes. We don't have all that many yet. And Lord, how the dice are loaded against them, Dan!" Jacob Brown reached out across the desk and held his friend's hand in a gesture to take all personal sting from his words. "That med school made you a good doctor and a very good American, Dan. I hope this mission and Africa will help make you a good man and a free black man. . . . That is the mission of our black churches in the twentieth century. If it's any comfort to you, Dr DuBois is as sceptical about us as you are. But the logic of the path he is on will bring him to our viewpoint; not in religious terms necessarily, but there will be a meeting point."

"Because of his Pan-Africanism?"

"No. Because he's a good and great man in search of true independence for black people."

"And that is the one criterion?"

"Before a man can belong properly to the world or even to his God he must first belong to himself; he must know himself as a man on this earth."

Daniel Lee rose and said "Amen!" but only half in jest. He put the coffee tray on a side table, raised his hand and went back to his hospital and the old man from the village whose gangrene had spread too far to be arrested.

Jacob Brown turned to the accumulation of paper work on his desk. Things had piled up heavily in the course of ten days. For one hour, two hours, he worked steadily, totally absorbed in his work. He paused once to straighten his back and ease the cramp in his body by walking briskly round the room. He tried to think about Harriet. Dan had said he needed to bring her out into the open. Twenty years is a long time and time filters memory leaving only the essentials remembered. There was the memory of being deeply, passionately in love, and, surprisingly, especially for a Jamaican, of not having made physical love to her. That was all. If she walked into this room now, he would not know her. So what was there to bring out into the open? He couldn't cut off his life at twenty and restrict it to struggling on behalf of the black folk of Alabama. To do that would be to break faith with the dreams that were nurtured in the high hills of Jamaica with his Grandma Sarah. This was his life; being here, doing what he was doing. Helping to strengthen the independence of his church and spread its message was a double fulfilment: for himself and for his grandparents whose church had been burnt to the ground because they resisted the white religious establishment. If this were done well, if he could give to these people here a fraction of what his grandparents and the other founders and leaders of the black independent churches had given him, then his life would be fulfilled. Harriet was a beautiful and painful interlude of his young life. DuBois now, there was a man you could never forget. He had met him twice since, once in Europe immediately after the war, and later in New York when he was a leading figure in the

National Association for the Advancement of Coloured People and the editor of its magazine *The Crisis*. But even without those meetings he would have remembered DuBois. Odd, he had loved Harriet to the point of wanting her for his wife. Now he could not even remember what she looked like. Yet Dan said his subconscious cried out for her in his fever. . . . And we talk about knowing ourselves. . . .

Jacob Brown returned to his desk and worked steadily till the church bell rang announcing the end of the morning work period and time for lunch.

Jacob Brown took over the driving some ten miles from Monrovia. The road here was easier and less bumpy and jarring. It was also much more dusty. The red dust rose and swirled in their wake. He had shared the driving with Sam, the handyman who usually travelled with him and had become quite a good driver. But it was wiser for Sam not to be seen driving in or near the town: some nonsense about "natives" not being allowed to drive until they became "civilized" taxpayers. Same sort of thing goes on in South Africa, he had heard. They approached the town. From a distance and from the rise of the land the town looked flat and drab. A heat haze hung over it at even this early hour of the morning. Its outstanding feature was the Executive Mansion, the home and office of the President, which rose higher than all the buildings gleaming white in the sun. Beyond the Executive Mansion was the sea. To the right on slightly rising land was the bluff, the residential quarter of the affluent. Jacob Brown turned the truck in the direction of the bluff. He would find a bath and breakfast among church connections before calling on the President. It would be no real imposition on them, only on the army of "native" house boys who did everything for every affluent "civilized" Liberian household.

Jacob Brown had used this particular household many times in the past so the head "boy", a clean-scrubbed, greying old man, tall and straight and dignified, welcomed him and ordered other "boys" to do the things he knew had to be done. There was no need to check with the master or the mistress of the house and they, in any case, were still in their sleeping quarters.

His host, a senior government official whose precise job Jacob Brown had been unable to pinpoint even after asking of it directly, came from his sleeping quarters just as Brown was finishing breakfast: a fruit salad followed by a deliciously fried freshly caught fish. The head "boy" had remembered his preference from those other early morning visits.

"Ah, Dr Brown!" the host beamed. "Don't get up! I see they are taking good care of. . . . Just coffee for me, Charley One. . . ." The head "boy" went away to get the coffee. "Had a bit of a night last night. Thought you might be coming. Word about it at the palace yesterday. . . ." He sank into his chair at the head of the long breakfast table, making it something of an effort. He was big and heavy, thick around the waist, with a puffiness to his face, especially under the chin.

This man had come to Liberia as a missionary teacher, one of the first black missionary teachers, some twenty years earlier. He soon discovered that the good life in Monrovia was more to his liking than teaching backward tribesmen in the hinterland. He had married a daughter of a very rich descendant of one of the original settlers and had become a member of the True Whig Party, and thus an important member of the upper crust of Liberian society. His sense of obligation to the missionaries who sent him to Liberia in the first place was said to be why the people from the mission station were allowed to use his home as a rest-house.

Charley One brought his coffee. The host changed his mind and ordered a dish of bacon and egg "quick-quick". Charley One hurried away again.

"There was speculation about the reason for your visit. Nothing wrong, I hope?"

Jacob finished, put down his napkin, looked at his host and shook his head slowly.

"Nothing wrong at the mission. We're fine."

"Oh. Good. . . ."

Go on fishing, Jacob Brown said to himself. He waited.

"Something else?" the host said tentatively.

"Something else," Jacob agreed. "I expect you'll hear about it after I've seen the President. He will see me?"

"Oh yes! Oh sure!"

Charley One returned with the bacon and eggs. Jacob got up.

"Thank you again for letting us use your rest-house."

"My duty," the host mumbled and tucked into his breakfast.

Charley One poured more coffee. Jacob rested his hand briefly on Charley One's shoulder. Their eyes met. Then Jacob went out into the already fierce sunlight and down the path to the modern little outhouse the mission people used as their rest-house.

Two other Charleys – he did not know whether they were Two or Three or Four or Five – were helping his handyman, Sam, put water into the truck radiator and remove the worst of the dust. He knew that Sam would have been well-fed. He looked at his watch. It was time to go and see the President.

They drove out of the beautiful garden, past other equally beautifully kept homes and gardens, the startlingly bright blue sea on their left and the ramshackle town straight ahead. The town's buildings were mainly faded wooden structures, bleached a drab uniform earth-brown by the constant sun. The main street, wide and lined with tall palm trees, and the Executive Mansion in well-kept grounds, added up to the one saving grace of the drab West African coastal town.

It was reported that there were moves afoot to close the main street and the area around the Executive Mansion to trucks and animal-drawn carts, and to allow only the few cars in the country passage on the street and past the Mansion. It had not yet gone beyond talk, so Jacob Brown drove his truck slowly along the main street, passing a few other trucks, but mainly people on foot, the important ones in striped pants and black jackets, for all the world like business people or government servants in London or Paris or Berlin or Washington.

Jacob stopped the truck by the huge gate and waited for the armed soldier with the list of the names of people to be admitted. It took a while before one of them rose from his camp chair and approached while two others covered him with long rifles.

"Dr Jacob Brown to see the President."

The man sprang to sudden attention without looking at the list.

"Yes, sir!" He saluted briskly. The two others lowered their rifles and stood at attention.

"Can I park where my man may have some shade?"

"Yes, sir!" The soldier motioned and the other two opened the great gate. "Under the tree to the right, sir." He pointed to a shaded spot just inside the gate.

Jacob Brown drove the truck in and parked it in the shade but so that any other vehicle would be able to pass.

"They don't want us any nearer their mansion, Sam."

Sam showed his teeth but there was no hiding his unease in the presence of the soldiers. Jacob Brown made a point of handing Sam the keys to the truck while the soldiers watched.

"Just in case you need to go anywhere before I come out, Sam."

Sam smiled a little more boldly this time. The first soldier handed his list to the next one, snapped to attention again, and escorted Jacob Brown up the long walk to the Mansion. Had he come by car he would have been allowed to drive up to the Mansion door. At the door another soldier took over and led him inside. There a secretary met him in a cool room filled with flowers.

She greeted him and went through a thick polished ebony door and came out followed by a tall jet-black man, dressed in an elegantly cut black suit. The man bowed slightly and disappeared through another door. The secretary murmured, "This way Dr Brown," and ushered him into the President's office. Jacob Brown shook hands with the tall brown man. This man, he knew, was likely to be the last brown man to be President of Liberia. A dark group, an ultra-conservative faction of black Americo-Liberians, had just captured the leadership of the True Whig Party from the brown-skinned group who had dominated the party and the government up to now. When this man's term was over that black conservative group would take over. Would they treat the natives and their concerns any better? Jacob Brown was not sure, though their leader, a man called Tubman, had made some interesting noises.

"Morning, Dr Brown. Take a seat, please. When did we last meet? Let me see. . . ."

You know damn well, Mr President, Jacob thought, but said nothing.

"Ah, yes; a year ago. That unfortunate business with our soldiers and the girls of that village. I confess that when I got your request this time I was so alarmed I ordered the Commissioner here to report. He said there was nothing. He's on hand in case we need him."

"Nothing like that, Mr President," Jacob Brown said.

"I am relieved. But not totally; you don't make social calls. Not on us; though I hear you do make them on the tribespeople. We were all very concerned about your illness. Glad to see you looking so well. There would be much less risk of fever if your social calls were on us."

"The bush telegraph," Jacob murmured.

"Knowing these things is our business, Dr Brown."

I will not be toyed with, Jacob Brown told himself. He smiled easily and said: "Then perhaps you already know what I am here for."

He saw the flash of irritation in the President's eyes; then it was gone. The President shrugged, pursed his lips in a smile that did not reach his eyes. The poker player's smile, Jacob thought, glad he had got under the man's skin.

"You have the better of me, sir," the President murmured. His mood changed. "I'm sure you are eager to tell me."

"I wish I did not have to, Mr President."

"Tell me anyway. That's what you are here for." The President looked down at the notes in front of him.

Jacob Brown told him of the visit of the delegation of chiefs. The President listened without raising his eyes. He made notes occasionally. His face remained expressionless. When Jacob had done the President leaned back in his chair and fixed his eyes on some point on the far wall. "And you believe what these chiefs told you?"

"Yes, sir."

"Of course, otherwise you would not be here. So what do you want me to do, Dr Brown?"

"To stop it, Mr President."

"And if my men deny the charges?"

"I am sure they can be proved, Mr President."

"And who will do that? The tribespeople? They always lie."

"We will; if we have to."

"But it is not your business. It's not missionary work. Tax collection has nothing to do with converting and educating natives."

"Unjust and unfair treatment is our business, Mr President."

"So you say, Dr Brown."

There was a long uneasy pause. In the silence the big overhead fan whispered endlessly. The President shifted his eyes to Brown's face. They looked directly, frankly, at each other.

"How will you prove what you claim if my men deny it? Will you close your mission, or leave it to the women, and you and the doctor and your other young man spend weeks or months in the hinterland collecting evidence? How will you do it, Dr Brown?"

"I will be sorry to have to do it, Mr President."

"But you will do it?"

"Yes, sir." Jacob paused for effect then added. "I would have to call for skilled help from our headquarters."

"And you are sure you will get it?"

"Yes, Mr President. I think you know that too."

The President sighed and relaxed suddenly. He pressed a button and the secretary came in.

The President rose from the desk and went to the big window. He pulled the curtains aside and light streamed into the shaded room. The President looked out at his beautiful garden.

"Do you understand our position, Dr Brown?" He spoke without turning his head.

"I don't know, Mr President. Which position?"

"Choose any you like, sir!"

"Like the matter that brings me here?"

"You are persistent, sir. All right! We have no money. Our treasury is empty. The European bankers give us credit under the most extortionate terms. Your government is only a little better. How are we to pay our civil servants? Our soldiers? Our police? How are we to maintain and to spread civilization without money? You know they all want us to fail. They want to use us as an example that no black sovereign state is possible. We need the Frontier Force to keep the peace. Without it your mission out there in the bush would not be possible. The tribesmen would swoop down on you and burn and loot and kill. And the truth, sir, is that there are times when there is not enough in the treasury to pay even the small monthly salaries of the Frontier Force. So when they help themselves to food and crops, we may not like it but we cannot be hard with them. Do you understand that, sir?''

The President swung about and glared at Jacob Brown. "Do you think it's easy to confess this to you? I am told you have little sympathy for us because you think we are unjust to the natives. Are we any more so than are the British and the French and the Belgians? You are a man of colour, Dr Brown, you know the state of men of colour in our world and in our time. Surely you see our difficulty."

"I do, Mr President, believe me, I do."

"By threatening me?"

"Mr President!" Jacob Brown protested, surprised and angered.

"Oh, not improperly, Dr Brown! I would not stand for that. You have been perfectly correct and proper. But you know and I know that if you made this matter public it would be more fuel for the fire of hatred against the Republic of Liberia by those who do not want to see black folk ruling their own country."

"Mr President, must we then close our eyes to wrong because it is done by black folk and because the enemies of black folk would exploit its revelation?"

"You do me an injustice to even ask that question, Dr Brown. That is not what I am saying."

"There is nothing personal about this, sir. The question asks itself and we must face it. . . ."

The secretary came in with coffee and while she poured and served it there was silence in the room and the whisper of the fan could be heard again. When she had gone the President said: "Not all questions have simple direct answers, Dr Brown. And justice and injustice are not always as clearly separated as you make out. We cannot afford to pay our Frontier Force. Do we demoralize it by severe and heavy punishment – education, perhaps – for those who do what you say they did? Is it acceptable for the whites in neighbouring territories to do what they do in the name of bringing civilization but not for us to do the same?"

"Neither is acceptable," Jacob Brown said.

"Both are realities," the President retorted.

"Slavery was a reality once," Jacob Brown said softly, bracing himself for the reaction he was sure would be explosive.

The President returned to his seat behind the big impressive desk and sat silent for a while. Then, instead of the explosion Jacob had expected, he said quietly: "They told me that you were a great scholar, Dr Brown, and studied under the famous Professor DuBois. Now you make it sound as though slavery was ended by Christian goodness. Well, sir, slavery was not ended because it was not acceptable to you gentlemen of the cloth, and neither will our present realities end because they are not acceptable to you. When there is time and cause for change, the change will come, with or without the approval of all the Doctors of Divinity in the world. Slavery came to an end, sir, not out of any goodness in mankind but because it became too costly and the needs of the times were for cheaper and more economic forms of labour. The time came when an army of sharecroppers, who must find everything for themselves while still working for their former slave-owner, became much more economic and profitable than an army of slaves which had to be fed and clothed and housed and nursed. So slavery was ended."

"As simple and clear-cut as that," Jacob teased, reminding the President of his own earlier words.

The President nodded acknowledgement of the point.

"Not as simple; but the essential reason why Mr Lincoln and the abolitionists prevailed. The time was ripe for it and they seized it. If there were no need for the change they would have failed, for all their high-mindedness. Anyway. . . ." The President made a gesture of dismissing the subject. He had, he thought, made his point and at least engaged the sympathy of this particular critic. He looked at the clock on the wall. Jacob Brown rose and so did the President. Again the soft sound of the fan filled the room with its hum. The President came round his desk and put on his beaming official smile.

"It was good talking you, Dr Brown. I wish you would come to one of our balls or receptions. We could provide you with good comfortable overnight quarters. Or you could stay one weekend as our guest.''

"I thank you, Mr President.''

"Then you will come?''

"I am no good at balls and receptions, sir.''

"So I've heard. We will not ask you again, sir.''

"I'm sorry, Mr President.''

"You can send a message to those chiefs, sir. Tell them from me that I do not approve of what has been done and I am sending strong instructions to their District Commissioner that there be no more of this.''

"And the damage already done?''

"Do not press me, Dr Brown!''

"I think their livestock should be returned.''

"Where it has not yet been consumed. They cannot return what has been eaten and they have no money to pay compensation.''

"Accepted. But I also think that where there has been needless destruction of homes as a form of coercion your men should make amends by helping with the rebuilding.'' The President was on the point of protest, but Jacob Brown carried on quickly: "This way, the men of the Force can develop better relations between themselves and the tribespeople, that could be of benefit in future sir, even in the matter of collecting taxes.''

"All right, Dr Brown. I am persuaded by you. In return you will use your influence to make the tribespeople understand the importance of paying their taxes.''

"In return for services they can see and understand.''

"Tell them the missionaries and their schools cannot operate without our permission. That is one of the services! And we keep the peace, that is another!''

The President went to the door and held out his hand.

Don't push him any more, Jacob Brown told himself. He took the President's hand.

"I've spoken to you as a friend and brother because we are both men of colour, Dr Brown. I do not expect to hear from others what we have spoken about. I would not speak in this way to missionaries who are not of our colour, even though they give us less trouble. You understand?''

212

"Yes, Mr President."

"For all our differences, we have the same ends, Dr Brown. We want freedom and dignity for all people of colour. . . ."

Hold it, Jacob Brown told himself.

"Yes, Mr President."

The warm official smile was now fully lit up. There was a benign twinkle in the small dark-brown eyes which looked too widely set apart for the big heavy brown face.

The President opened the door and emerged into the anteroom, an arm on Jacob Brown's shoulders. A dozen or so people rose. The tall, smooth young black man in the black suit came forward, whispered to the President and then, after another warm handshake between the President and Jacob Brown, he escorted Jacob Brown out.

The President nodded and beamed at the people in the outer room; except for two white people, they were all familiar faces. This morning's meetings looked like being good. The first one had gone off well, better than he had expected. It was clear he had impressed the missionary. It was all worth last night's careful preparation, especially the bit about slavery which his personal assistant, the young man in the black suit, had come up with after the best part of an afternoon spent at the library run by the American representative's office. Must make more such preparations for difficult interviews. Must warn that damned greedy DC that Brown and his people will be watching them all the time from now on. Best thing would be for Brown to be transferred elsewhere. He's getting too interested in the tribespeople and that could mean trouble. He's been here longer than most of the others who ever headed that mission so they should be transferring him. Unless they made him their bishop here. . . . O Lord, what a thought!

The President hurried back into his office and signalled for the secretary to bring in the next visitor so that he could stop thinking about the visit of Jacob Brown. But it had gone better than he had feared. The damn-fool action of the Frontier Force men in those villages would not be reported to Washington or the foreign press. Of that he was sure.

Back at the mission, after a late supper Jacob Brown, Dr Daniel

213

Lee, Mrs Willis and the two young missionary teachers, Jonathan and Dorothy Jones, gathered for what Dr Lee called a "strategy session": a reminder of his days as a medical officer in the American army in Europe during the war.

Among the mail Jacob Brown brought back from Monrovia was a letter from the Chairman of the Council of Bishops. It was a familiar letter, polite, friendly, nothing officious about it; all missionaries of this particular church had come to recognize it as the prelude to a new posting. The one difference was that instead of just the advance warning which would be followed, a month or two later, by the formal notification of a new posting, this one required his presence at headquarters as soon as it could be arranged; this meant rather special promotion. When Daniel Lee had finished reading it, he grinned wickedly at Jacob Brown and did a little mock genuflection: "His Grace, my Lord Bishop Jacob Brown, I presume."

Jacob joined in the laughter but sensed a subtle change of attitude, especially in the young Jones couple. A bishop was, somehow, not quite of this earth. So Jacob told the story of a tippling bishop under whom he had served for a year in a hopeless mission in a tiny Eastern Caribbean island. It amused Mrs Willis and Dr Lee, but embarrassed the Jones couple. So Lee helped him out with one of his funny war stories which made them want to laugh and cry at the same time.

Now they sat on the most exposed part of the verandah to catch whatever hint of moving air stirred in the still, heavy, hot night. The sky was an immensity of limitless blackness in which no star showed. The moon had not yet risen. To keep the mosquitoes at bay a series of little oil lamps, in an enveloping wing, burned a mixture of kerosene and a pungent soapy smelling concoction which, to the surprise of everyone, including Dr Lee who had invented it, worked.

At last the night-duty houseboy had brought out everything: the drinks, the big thermos bucket of ice, the glasses, the fruit punch for the women, the plates of cookies and freshly roasted nuts, and Mrs Willis's specially baked little meat pies for later.

Dr Lee served the drinks. There was some sort of concert going on in the students' dining hall and every now and then the sound came up to them, but softly, not disturbing. Jacob Brown again marvelled at the quietness of the Africans compared to the noisiness of the Americans and West Indians. If that were an American students' hall affair or a Jamaican village fête, the noise from it, at this distance, would be almost overpowering.

"It had to come but it's still a shock," Dr Lee said. "I always had the foolish hope that we might stay together as a team."

"Especially the three of you," Dorothy Jones said, looking from the doctor to Mrs Willis then to Jacob Brown.

"They sent me here to look after the doctor," Mrs Willis protested. "Who will I look after now?"

"There's your girls' dormitory," Jacob Brown said. "It will soon be built and you'll have to look after the girls. They will need you."

"And so will I," Dr Lee said softly.

"But if they make you a bishop you will be able to call him – the doctor – to work with you," Mrs Willis said.

"I will not leave here," Dr Lee said. "I will not leave till my work is done."

"Which will never be done," Jacob said.

"Then I'll never leave," Lee said. "I've found what I want to do."

"Your bush orderlies?" Jacob asked.

"Yes; and proper health for all the tribespeople we can reach. And one day a really good hospital here."

"If you're right about this bishop business I'll see that you are left alone to get on with your job. And you, Mrs Willis?"

"I can't go back to Harlem. Not after this. They do need help, Dr Brown. Especially the girls: I can't reach the women, but the girls. . . ."

"So you want to stay? Or shall I try and get you to join me wherever they send me?"

"Where d'you think you'll be sent?" Lee cut in to give Mrs Willis a little time for thought.

"Probably elsewhere in Africa: East or Central."

"What you've always wanted."

"Yes," Jacob said. Mrs Willis would have thought her thing through now, so he looked at her.

215

"Long time we've been here," she said. "And you get used to a place and to people. And you know something, doctor, they really do need you. It's good to be needed." She lowered her head, seemingly embarrassed at showing this much feeling. "They love learning to cook and to bake. They're such beautiful girls. It would be hard for me to start again, doctor. Hard to make new friends and learn new ways."

"You won't have to, Mrs Willis." Jacob Brown thought back to when he first met this tough-minded product of Harlem some six years ago. Coming to this part of Africa had softened her, made her look at life in a new way. And for a person to change that much in her middle years is something special. "I think you belong here now," he said.

"You and I," Dr Lee beamed, reaching out and touching her hand.

"But who will take care of you, Dr Brown?"

"Don't worry," Dr Lee said, the old mockery back in his voice and bearing. "Before they make a man a bishop they marry him off. Haven't you noticed all our bishops have strikingly good-looking wives, and all our bishops are big, tall men with what they call 'presence'? You can't have one without the other!"

"Oh, doctor!" Mrs Willis protested.

"Think about it, Willy, love; are any of the bishops not married?"

"None that I know."

"There you are! Are any of their wives plain retiring home-bodies?"

"No."

"There you are again! There's a special school of wives for bishops and our friend will have to take one of these before he becomes Bishop Jake!"

"I'm beginning to get worried," Jacob Brown said drily. "All well and good for you to joke about it. I've only just realized they don't have any bachelor bishops! But what about our plans for you two?" Jacob turned to the Joneses. "I'm afraid they will have to be postponed now."

"I hope not," the young man said earnestly.

His wife nodded. "Dr Lee could supervise us."

216

"Sure I can," Lee said. "I'll even become a member of your missionary order provided I don't have to be called the reverend anything."

"Stop the chaff, Dan."

"I'm serious, Jake. There's a golden opportunity now. Those diamond-bearing chiefs are grateful. Just the place for them to start their school. I can send two health fellows with them."

"I think you'll have to introduce us, though, sir," Jonathan Jones suggested. "It would be easier than if we just arrived there."

"And I'll have to come along, too," Lee said, "as your official representative when you have to leave. They set great store by proper and formal succession, properly and formally announced."

"And what of my religious successor? What of the man who will be sent to take over as head of the mission?"

"Oh him!" Lee mocked. "We'll do like the civil servants do. We'll brief him and guide him and prop him up as head man but we will go on running the show, just as we've done under you."

"He may want to run things his own way."

"Not if you make it clear how successfully we've run things all these years. And no God-man oversees my hospital."

"Or my housekeeping and catering," Mrs Willis added.

"And you?" Jacob glared at the very-much-still-in-love two young teachers. He wondered if they really knew how rough starting a school deep in the tribal bush would be.

They both showed smiles that made him feel at ease. He felt sure they would cope. This was their choice. Dorothy, he knew, wanted their first son – she was sure it would be a son – born deep in the African hinterland. For her that would be the proof that at least two natives had made the way back, across the centuries, to their historical roots.

"They'll be all right," Lee said. "I promise you."

"One condition. You, Miss Dorothy, will write me, no matter where I am, if things get rough and difficult. Promise?"

"I promise, Doctor Jake." She gave him a clear-eyed stare of love and trust.

A powerful wave of feeling washed over him; he knew his voice would choke if he spoke. This had become his family over the past few years. A warm intimate little family sharing a common bond of service and commitment. Now it was going to be broken up. This sturdy, self-contained young woman from the Georgia plains had been both secretary and daughter to him. And her husband, the bright teacher and quick learner of languages from Mississippi was as a younger brother-pupil to him. Now he would send them into the deep hinterland, which was what they wanted, and he would not be there if they needed his help.

As if reading his mind, Daniel Lee said; "I will be here, Jake."

Jacob took a long swig at his drink. He felt guilty at having made it necessary for Dan to say that.

"The others can manage the school?"

"Mr Johnstone can act as headmaster," Jonathan Jones said. "He's good, sir. Good enough to be the permanent head-master."

"I'll pass on your recommendation. Can we make the journey in the next two days? Or do you need longer?"

Jonathan and his wife exchanged thoughts silently, reading each other's eyes. Jacob recalled his Grandma Sarah's ability to reach and pass messages without words.

"Anxious to leave us, already," Daniel Lee said.

"Two days will be fine, Dr Brown," Jonathan said.

A pall of sadness came over the little group suddenly; its members fell silent, each recalling some special facet of the years they had shared. It would take two or three weeks before Jacob Brown would leave but this was the real moment of parting. The later parting would be a sad formality. Not even Dr Daniel Lee wanted to use words to make the heartbreak less bearable. Suddenly the moon, a thin crescent, appeared and stood out clear in the black sky. They became aware of the rising noise of a wave of passing grasshoppers. Mrs Willis and Dorothy Jones gathered up plates and glasses; Jonathan Jones went to their assistance and the three slipped away quietly.

At last Dr Lee said: "So the moment has come, old friend."

"You really staying here for good?"

"Yeah. This is my world now – if you can keep Monrovia off my back."

"That's an easy promise. Alone always? No marriage ever?"

"No, Jake. No woman for me. Something in my make up; but

218

no little boys or young men either. Not the sort of thing to tell a bishop in the making."

"Are they supposed to be such fools?"

"You mean you guessed?"

"Yes."

"When?"

"Long time ago; early on."

"And. . . ."

"And what? I watched you and realized you were under control."

"And that was all?"

"That was all. Being a Christian, being a priest, is not about sitting in judgement. Don't let me preach you a sermon now. For all your front I know you read the Bible."

"It's a beautiful book, Jake, and I love beautiful books and beautiful people. And you are one."

"So are you, Dan. I will miss you."

"I will miss you bad, Jake. Goodnight, my favourite God-man."

"Goodnight, Dan. I'll need a complete brief to present on all you want."

"You'll get it."

Now he was alone and for a few minutes Jacob Brown allowed the ache of parting to overwhelm him. Then, as he had done in the past, he put the hurt and the memories away from him and found solace in thinking through what lay ahead. This going forward in duty had always been the constant in his life: from the time he had learned about the need to serve God through serving the weakest and the most downtrodden of his fellow black men, and above all, to help in the struggle against the enslavement of their minds by white folk using the word of God. To this he had been constant. To this his church was constant; not in hostility against whites or anybody else but because that was the true spirit of the message of Christ: that all men be free in body and mind and heart and spirit, none master over the other.

The journey into the deep hinterland to the villages from which the four chiefs had come took two and a half days of steady travel by truck. The going was slow, tedious and only relatively easy on

219

the clear, higher ground. Though the track was well-worn, many parts of it were difficult for the truck to negotiate. Twice they got bogged down and, as from nowhere, men appeared out of the bush to help ease the truck out of some deep rut. Sam was the one line of communication with the men who appeared in times of need and then faded back into the bush when the trouble was over. Sam, it seemed, spoke all the tribal dialects of this part of the country. Jonathan Jones spoke a few and when he recognized what was being said he would join Sam in the palaver with the tribesmen.

The belongings of the Joneses took up most of the space on the truck. Jacob, Dr Lee, and Dorothy Jones, travelled in the truck cabin. Except when they took a turn at driving, Jonathan and Sam travelled in the body of the open truck, with the Joneses' possessions. Jonathan and Sam were permanently covered in a fine coat of powdery reddish dust, giving their hair a stiffish steel-wool texture which no amount of combing could remove. Through the journey Jonathan Jones, with the help of Sam, practised the three key dialects spoken by the tribes among whom he and his wife would found their school and mission outstation. Towards the evening of the first day they picked up three young men, all naked except for the leather strand around their waists from which hung a roughly squarish patch of soft leather which covered their private parts; this was held in place by two additional strands tied in the manner of a jock strap. They were, they told Sam, on their way home from an errand for their people: they had delivered four animals owed to another tribe to the east of the great mission station, and they had started out just a few hours earlier than the truck from the mission. The steady African trot at which they travelled had covered almost as great a distance as had the truck. Now, they could rest while the truck bumped and lurched across the wild country, moving like an alien insect along a narrow strip of land, briefly reclaimed from the dense tropical bush.

In the late afternoon the sky suddenly darkened and rainclouds grew black and heavy and hung low over the land.

Jacob pushed his head out of the cabin and shouted:

"How far to their village? Can we make it before the rain?"

Jonathan Jones shouted back: "They say not far now! They say it depends on the rain gods!"

Inside the cabin Daniel Lee, a muslin dust-mask and a wide-brimmed felt hat hiding his face, muttered: "Ask a damn-fool question. . . ."

Dorothy Jones was asleep in the far corner, her rough ride made bearable by all the cushions Daniel Lee had carefully packed about her.

The first flash of lightning and the first roar of thunder split the heavens as they topped one hill and saw in the distance, tucked between two other hills, a village in the clearing above a small river.

"That must be their village," Jacob said.

There was another, bigger streak of jagged lightning, far away, fortunately; another delayed clap of thunder. Then the rain came down: a blinding torrent of water, beating down on the earth and everything on it as though intent on hurting, bruising, damaging. Jacob brought the truck to a stop. The men on the open body took shelter underneath it. The three in the cabin shut the windows but could not keep all the water out.

They waited for an hour; then the rain stopped abruptly. The sky became clear, free of cloud, and all the African world they could see lay bathed in the clean-washed half-light of day's end just before dark. They were all wet: those with clothes soaked to the skin, the naked with water running off their bodies in little trickles. Their efforts at shelter had not kept out the wet, only staved off the worst of it. Jacob Brown tried without success to start the truck engine. Sam and Jonathan Jones raised the bonnet and set about drying plugs, points, distributor. Lee, Dorothy and Jacob came down from the cabin; above them another cloud formation began building. Lee measured it and muttered: "Another drenching in an hour."

Jonathan Jones tilted his head and looked at the skies.

"A half-hour, I would say. Heh, Sam?"

"Half-hour," Sam agreed.

"Can we get this thing started by then? Can we get to the village?"

Sam and Jonathan worked in silence. Then Sam said: "Try now."

Jacob climbed back and tried. The engine fired straightaway.

"Hurry!" Jacob called.

They all scrambled into and onto the truck. As they moved off there was the first distant rumble of a new round of thunder. Jacob looked at the skies, now darkening fast, and drove toward the village at a higher speed than was prudent: they would be in trouble if some unexpected rock or fallen tree was obstructing the track. They were lucky, there were none and they reached the village ten minutes before the new downpour fell violently out of the sky. When it came they were crowded into a stuffy but dry, hastily vacated hut on the edge of the village. This second rainwave lasted twice as long as the first. When it broke the night was black and the tiny oil lamp played games with the shadows of the five people in the oppressively humid little hut.

Two of the young men of the village came in bearing a huge calabash and several smaller ones. They poured a thick whitish liquid from the big container into the little ones and passed them around in order of precedence by age and sex: first Jacob Brown, then Dr Lee, then Sam, then Jonathan Jones, then Dorothy Jones. Dr Lee tasted the brew first and recognized it: a soupy, sweetened, sour cornmeal porridge, mildly fermented, which was food, drink and relaxant all in one: a standard nourishing standby which could be given to travellers and children at short notice. He nodded to the others and they all drank the brew. Then they were offered refills, again in the same order of precedence. The young men of the village withdrew. Dr Lee passed round anti-malarial tablets. The brew warmed their stomachs and relaxed their minds and bodies.

"Try to sleep," Jacob Brown said.

"I go to the truck," Sam said.

"No," Jacob said. "You sleep where you are. The truck's all right."

"Yes, Sam," Jonathan Jones added, stretching out on the bare damp earth and pulling his wife into the crook of his arm.

The dim flickering light made it seem that Sam's eyes glowed. Then he, too, lay down and curled himself into the comfortable foetal position.

"All's well, then," Dan Lee said softly.

"Peace," Jacob Brown said.

222

The morning broke bright and clear and the travellers slept till sun-up, later than they had intended. When they came out of the hut, the villagers were well into the business of their day. A group of elders were waiting for them under a nearby tree where a fire had been built, sipping bush tea. The most senior offered his calabash to Jacob.

"Greeting, lord of the mission," Sam translated.

Jacob took a ceremonial sip from the elder's cup. They were served breakfast of dumplings and fried fowl, softened and highly seasoned.

"We would have welcomed you more warmly last night but the rain came. We would have prepared a feast instead of sending you children's soup."

"It is the spirit of the welcome that is more important than the show," Jacob answered gravely. Sam injected the air of gravity into the translation.

The elders nodded their approval. The spokesman said:

"We have heard of your wisdom, now we hear it for ourselves. The spirit is indeed more important than the show but your people and the white people put much store by the show."

"Not all of us. As with all people, some are wise and some are foolish; some see, and some, seeing, are yet blind."

"It is good to know it is so for you, too," the spokesman said.

"Easy on the high-tone palaver," Daniel Lee said. "We have a journey to make. No translation, Sam."

"What is it your brother says?" The spokesman looked curiously at Daniel Lee. "Is he the medicine man of your mission?"

"He is, and he reminds me we still have a long journey to make."

"And the journey which is started early ends early. How can we help you? What do you need?"

One of the others cut in: "Is the purpose of your journey the same as that which lead the four chiefs from the north to your mission?"

"They rested here," the spokesman explained.

"Yes," Jacob said.

"And the word you have is good for them?"

"The promise I carry is good for them. We also carry the young man and his wife who are now down by the river, to start a school in the north."

"We have three children at your mission."

"But no girls," Dan Lee said. "Translate, Sam."

"But there is no place for them to stay separately from the boys."

"There will be, soon; it is being made ready. And the wise old woman will remain in charge of them."

"Remain? Then who is leaving?" The spokesman took over.

Daniel Lee chuckled. "How's that for a quick pick-up! And those fools down there want to civilize these people."

"Don't translate, Sam," Jacob said.

"What does the medicine man say?"

"He speaks of the foolishness of some of the leaders of the Coast."

"Is one of you leaving because of them?"

"No!" Jacob said quickly. "No. I am leaving. The elders of my church want me to return in order to send me to work elsewhere."

"And to give him more power," Dan cut in. "Translate, Sam."

The elders spoke quickly among themselves; Sam did not translate.

"Tell you not to?" Dan looked at Sam who nodded.

When the consultation was over the spokesman signalled to Sam and spoke: "We do not like what we hear, lord of the mission. We have come to know you, some of us through our children whom we have entrusted to you to teach, and some of us through our personal knowledge of you, and some of us through your deeds, for the greatest judgement of a man comes from his deeds; so we do not like to hear that you will leave us, even to gain more power. You have come among us and learned our ways and you have learned to understand us. We respect you and your God because you respect us and our gods. So why do they call you away now? Why not give you more power here, to build a greater mission? If they are not pleased with our response to you then we will send out the word and make our response greater if that will keep you here. If we call a great palaver of all the leaders of all the people and if we ask your elders not to take you from among us, will they heed our words?"

"I do not know," Jacob was visibly moved and surprised.

224

Daniel Lee came to the rescue. "You know he is a priest of his church, part of an order of priests." This, it was clear, they understood. "It is part of the rules of that order that the priest must do whatever the elders, who are called bishops, tell him to do. I believe one of the reasons they are calling him back for is to make him one of the elders, one of the bishops, so he will be one of those who make the decisions for the church and all its work everywhere in the world."

"And still they can send him anywhere they wish?"

"Yes, but as a bishop he would be part of the council that makes that decision."

"And if he does not come back?"

"They will send someone else."

"'And some are wise and some are foolish'," the spokesman quoted. "That is so even among priests."

"He will have great influence in the choosing of who is sent here. I think his will be the greatest influence. For who is chosen will be important to the work of all of us at the mission."

"So whoever comes will be his man?"

"He will not agree to a man whose spirit is not in harmony with the spirit of the work he has done and which we will carry on at the mission."

"And you?"

"I will stay here."

"Till your elders call you back?"

"No. I am not of their order. I am not a priest so they cannot order me back or anywhere."

"Then who gives you orders? Unless he is a king or a chief, a man must take orders. And even then, he cannot do as he pleases. . . ."

Jacob said: "I have promised to ensure that he stays here as long as he wants to, if he does his work well, and I know he will."

"And you can make such a promise, even for a time when you are not here?"

"Yes," Jacob said, "I can."

"And the new lord of the mission will not over-rule it?"

"I will persuade the council of our elders to make the control of the hospital a separate matter from the control of the mission so

225

that the lord of the mission and the lord of the hospital will work together but as two separate authorities. Those who have deep experience of the work they do will, if they are wise, always know how to manage when a new overseer is sent, especially if that overseer has no experience."

"It is all planned then?"

"It is all planned."

Again they consulted among themselves. Then the spokesman said:

"It is not as bad as we feared when we first heard the word. But the land and we of the land will mourn your going for you are a good friend."

"I leave good friends among you," Jacob said.

Jonathan and Dorothy Jones came walking up from the river, hand-in-hand and carrying towels. A group of village children followed at a discreet distance.

"Time to go," Dan said. "Should have been long gone if we are to reach before tonight's rain."

A line of women came from the communal cooking place with bundles of aromatic foods wrapped in huge palm leaves from which hot steam escaped. Sam received the food and packed it in a secure dry corner of the truck, under the tarpaulin which covered the Joneses' personal effects. The Joneses went through the formality of greeting each of the elders in turn. Jonathan impressed them by speaking in their own dialect. He looked fresh and young and strong, all the red dust washed out of his hair. His wife glowed with a vitality found in the young who are healthy, happy and at peace with themselves and the world.

When the parting ceremonies were over, Sam and Jonathan Jones took a last look under the bonnet and then signalled to Jacob to start. The truck shuddered and came alive. The villagers drew back from the strange machine, watched it move off spewing a cloud of bluish-white smoke in its wake; then the smoke disappeared and the noise of the machine changed, became softer, more even. Sam and Jonathan jumped on to the back of the truck. They waved as it moved off; the villagers waved back. The younger children ran behind the truck.

Dorothy Jones looked back at the last point from which the village could be seen: a tranquil village on the slope of a hill, with a little river running through the valley below it. She had felt its soft water on her body this morning, had tasted its sweetness as it splashed on her lips. No river blindness in that river, it flowed too fast. As a passing flash, her mind told her how good it would be for their school to be in that village, for her son to be born and to grow up there with the safety of clean, fast-flowing water. Then the village passed from sight and she firmly put the thought out of her mind. Their work lay ahead.

"Pretty dream. . . ," Dr Dan's voice said, close to her ear, above the hum of the engine.

She smiled gaily and took his hand. "Yes. And don't eavesdrop!"

The sun came up and the land grew hot and humid once more. They saw no people for long stretches of the journey; but they were aware of the presence of people all about them, out of sight and sound. Occasionally this was confirmed by the sound of drums, either coming from behind them or else far ahead. And Sam who told them about most other things remained silent when any of them asked questions about the drums and their meaning. Jacob, who had travelled the deep hinterland more than the others, and usually with Sam as companion, was convinced that as well as being a language, there was something spiritual in the connection between the tribespeople and their drums.

So the truck bumped and twisted its way across the vast landscape; up and down the land, round its bumps and bends, skirting deep forests, crossing rivers at their widest and shallowest parts. And over everything hung the hot sun making the humid air heavy, and draining the people in the truck of will and energy so that just sitting became wearying, and driving a heavy burden.

When the sun sat high in the sky with its heat at its fiercest they moved into the protection of a cluster of trees. There they rested in the shade for an hour, drinking tepid water but, except for Sam, not eating any of the savoury food the women of the village had cooked for them that morning. Then they moved on again, enveloped in a heat trance that made them too listless to speak.

227

In the late afternoon when the sun moved to the rim of the world the air grew less oppressive and heavy. A slight breeze blew from the north bringing a hard dryness with it. It was mild here, but further north, on the edge of the great desert, the dry winds of the *harmattan* were fierce enough to crack men's skins and bring on nosebleed, especially to those unused to it. Here, it was a welcome change from the oppressive humidity. Now they could eat a little and talk a little. But there was anxiety, too, for the first rain signs were beginning to show in the sky. So they only stopped to refill the gas tank from one of the many standby drums stored on the truck. Then the truck resumed its northward crawl across the vast green land.

When the wind dropped the air grew heavy and oppressive. The first downpour struck them twenty minutes later. It was less fierce than that of the day before, but only slightly so; it lasted a shorter time. As the rain tapered off, they saw, coming to them out of the rain, a tight formation of half a dozen tribal warriors with long spears held aloft. They were naked except for the loincloth.

"The welcoming party!" Jacob Brown shouted to reassure Dorothy Jones.

She nodded and smiled.

And seeing the approaching warriors coming mistily out of the curtain of rain, Daniel Lee remembered some lines from a poem he had read recently and said them aloud:

> One three centuries removed
> From the scenes his fathers loved,
> Spicy grove, cinnamon tree,
> What is Africa to me?

"What's that?" Jacob shouted.

"A poem. You won't find it in your Bible. Young man in Harlem name of Countee Cullen wrote it. One of the so-called New Negroes."

"Oh. . . ."

"Yes, God-man. Oh!"

Now the warriors were close up and Sam and Jonathan Jones had emerged from their shelter under the truck. Jacob Brown and

228

Daniel Lee jumped down from the cabin, leaving Dorothy behind. Sam did the speaking. The warriors were indeed from the village. The message of their coming had preceded them and the people of the villages had prepared a reception and had sent out the welcoming warriors. The warriors refused to ride on the truck and trotted easily beside it: three on each side, in single file. They ran steadily breathing evenly, moving effortlessly across the rain-soaked land, until they reached the first village. There a great throng of villagers waited, at their head the four elders who had called on Jacob at the mission. They looked less regal without their flowing white robes, but still special for they wore sandals while all the rest were barefoot.

Because another round of rain-clouds was forming, the ceremonial welcome was brief, the speeches short. Sam supervised the taking of their baggage to the three huts which had been set aside for them: one for Jacob Brown and Daniel Lee, one for the Jones couple, and one for Sam in which he would keep the more special stuff they had brought such as the truck's fuel and oil, the tools and spare tyres. People might take these if left on the truck; they would not touch them once identified as in the personal keeping of a fellow tribesperson.

The elders led them to a clearing in the centre of the circular village where a series of planted posts supported a vast thatched roof thus achieving the effect of a meeting hall without walls. In its centre was the palaver tree, the huge trunk of the dead tree in whose shade the tribal ancestors of past times had held their great palavers: the old tree which had been witness to the deliberations of the ancestors, which had heard and stored their wisdom, and which held that wisdom in trust for those who now spoke in its shade – if their hearts were open to receive that wisdom. The senior of the four elders, the chief of this particular village, told Jacob and Daniel – who sat on either side of him while they ate – of the meaning and importance of this place in the life of the village. It was the connecting point between yesterday and today and tomorrow. It was the reason why this village and its people did not, as some others did, pack their belongings and move elsewhere when the land was not kind. To do so would be to desert the ancestral meeting-place and, therefore, the ancestors themselves.

At the other end of the small inner circle of people Jonathan and Dorothy Jones were entertained by two of the other elders. The presence of Dorothy among the men, instead of in her natural place among the women, was easily excused and accepted: the ways of the strangers were different and good manners require the adjusting of your ways, temporarily, to the ways of the strangers who are your guests, if you honour them. Indeed, there were times in their own history when women had become leaders and chiefs and doctors and great warriors; so a woman among men, while not normal, was not all that unusual, certainly not as unusual as among the people from the great desert whose women had to hide their faces and cover all of their bodies. Jonathan flattered his tribal hosts by being able to communicate with them, on however limited a scale. Whenever he searchingly found a word or a phrase to reply to some question or statement, they clapped their hands and roared their approval. And the watching crowd on the outer edge joined in, not knowing what it was they were approving of, except that it was something their own leaders approved of. So the senior elder said to Jacob:

"Your young man learns our language."

It was the opening Jacob had waited for. He told the chief of their intention to establish a school and later a clinic, if the tribes would welcome these. The young man and his wife were here to start the school. If the tribes agreed they would be left behind and Sam would stay for a time to help build the school, and to organize the help from the tribes that they would need. This was why they were brought along even though the message from the President could have been delivered without their presence. And, of course, the word from the President did not depend on how the tribes responded to the school proposal. That was a separate and unconnected matter.

"But the time of our gratitude is a good time to raise it," the elder said, a hint of mockery in his voice.

"A wise man chooses his moment," Dan said. "Translate, Sam."

Sam obliged and a fleeting smile passed over the elder's face.

"We will have a big palaver in the morning and you will speak of this matter after your message from the President. And I will tell you and your people of our gratitude. A man should know he is loved before he goes to a far country – if he is loved."

"Then you know?" Jacob said.

"A word that is spoken in one village today is known in five tomorrow; we know. And we know the doctor will stay and of your plan. You did not speak of the school. There is a piece of land in my mind; we will go there after tomorrow's palaver, and your young people will have a place there to sleep and to begin before the day is done – if our people agree."

"I hate to leave this place," Jacob said suddenly; a wave of sadness shot through him. If only he had learnt to speak this old man's language. Now he was going with so much unsaid.

The old man said something that seemed to embarrass Sam.

Daniel Lee said: "Go on, Sam; what is it?"

Sam looked sombrely at Jacob. "He says he heard you crying inside. He says you are not to cry. They will not forget you. They will do as you want."

Daniel Lee got up abruptly and walked away. The crowd made room for him to pass.

The elder said: "Now he is weeping too. . . ."

Then the clouds burst and the rain poured out of the sky. Those outside the shelter of the palaver tree scampered in all directions for other shelter. Those under it pressed inward as far as they could. Daniel Lee hurried back, soaked to the skin in less than a minute. The noise of the rain drowned all other noises. A jagged shaft of lightning lit up the dark sky and was followed, forty seconds later, by a deafening clap of thunder. The people under the shelter of the palaver tree made themselves as comfortable as possible and waited for the downpour to exhaust itself.

The palaver the elder had promised the evening before, started early and ended early. Jacob delivered the President's message that there would be no more unauthorized taxes levied and that restitution would be made for the damage done. Then he spoke about the two young people he had brought to start the school if, as he thought, the people of these villages wanted a school where their children could be taught the skills and knowledge and language to make life better, to be able to talk with other people

231

from other lands, and to be able to protect and safeguard their own. "And," continued Jacob, "the lord of the hospital will soon send two of the sons from your own villages whom he has trained to deal with wounds and cuts and fevers and broken bones. They will help the two teachers and the people of the villages, and what they cannot heal or understand they will send to the doctor at the mission hospital. Perhaps one day a young man from your villages will learn enough to become a doctor himself and then return here to be a doctor to his own people. For it is our purpose to train those among whom we work, so that the day will come when they will be in control of the missions and the hospitals and the schools and the governments of their own lands. This is our way, the way of our mission. So you must help us to serve and to help you."

Then the elder spoke and from Sam's translation it was clear that he was telling the people the decision was theirs, but the way in which the elders had decided and expected them to decide was thus. . . .

And as the elders had decided so the people signalled they had decided. Then the leading elder raised a chant of praise for the lord of the mission who would soon be leaving this land to continue his good work in other lands. When he paused, the vast throng turned his last sentence into a chorus, repeated twice. He listed the deeds of the lord of the mission, and the people echoed it. He called on the ancestral spirits to walk with the lord of the mission, to protect him from evil spirits, and to guard him from the enemies who would turn aside his work – for there are always those who would turn back a man's efforts to do that which is good, and not all of them had white faces. . . .

"You'd better watch the subversion," Dan whispered into Jacob's ear. "If this gets to the President, you may not be allowed to leave."

"And offend Washington from whom all shekels flow?" Jacob returned.

"Point!" Dan conceded. "Better to be rid of the bad rubbish, heh?"

The speech came to an end and the elders led them to a gently rolling hill just outside the village.

"This," the senior said, looking at Jonathan and Dorothy Jones, "is the land for your school and your home. Choose the spot where you will sleep tonight."

Sam and a group of villagers went off with Jonathan and Dorothy Jones to choose a house spot.

By mid-morning Jacob Brown's mind was at ease about the Joneses. A small hut and a thatched shelter for their belongings had been built in record time; Dorothy and a group of women were preparing a meal for the men, women and children who were clearing the land, portering felled logs and thatching material, and building the small circle of huts that would be the new home of the young missionaries. And, somehow, Dorothy was communicating with the women: mostly in body language and facial expression, but also by touching objects and giving them names, first in English and then in their tribal language; each time they repeated the name of the object and applauded themselves with much pleasure. Dorothy would soon learn the rudiments of their language, and would teach them hers. The real thing of importance, though, was the easy air of fellowship she had so quickly established with the women. This would be a point of strength in the days ahead, at the inevitable times of misunderstanding and of friction. The goodwill now building between Dorothy and the women of the village, and between Jonathan and the men of the village, would make those coming encounters easier to manage and defuse.

In the afternoon, after they had eaten and rested, and the women were rubbing the clay floors of the two main huts to a shining gloss, and the men were putting the last touches to the waterproofing of the thatch, the senior elder strolled up from the village alone. He summoned Sam from the work-gang and Sam then called Jacob.

Sam said: "The chief invites you to walk with him alone. I will be there as his voice but I will not be there."

"Something special, Sam?"

"Yes, doctor."

"Then let us walk." Jacob made a small bow to the chief.

The chief took Jacob's arm and steered him along a track which dipped into the valley behind the village and then rose and disappeared into a dense forest about a mile beyond, near the point where the river appeared out of the forest. Sam fell in step behind them, just near enough to translate if either spoke. They walked in silence.

The land on the hill where Jonathan and Dorothy would live and teach was rich and loamy but well-drained. But once the three men got off that hill and onto the rising land approaching the forest the earth felt damp underfoot, as though the heavy moisture could not escape; the atmosphere, too, seemed considerably damper. It was as though they had made a sudden transition from one type of climate to another.

"You notice it," the elder said. "We live on the edge of the rain country. You can stand where the young ones are building and watch the rain wrap this part of the world in darkness. To the south and the east of here you find the rain country and the rain forests. To the north is the great desert with its great winds. We live on the edge of all this: touched by all and spared by all."

They stopped at the edge of the forest, where the water came down in a foaming torrent to settle in a deep clear pond, dammed at its outlet so that, from there, the water flowed down slowly, giving life and sustenance to the three villages further down the land. It reminded Jacob a little of his Jamaican hills, but the climate there was so much gentler, so much kinder.

"To be spared by all is to be blessed by all," Jacob said.

"So it is," the old man said. "And we praise the ancestors for their choice." A smile flickered across the old man's face. "As with all good choices they had no other choice. Our people do not love fighting. We are known as a cowardly people and have ever been so. We will only fight if there is nowhere to run. So when the fierce-fighting tribes took our land near the coast the ancestors ran and ran. The fierce-fighting ones were the first to be made slaves. We cowards were left in peace for we were too far from the slavers' ships; so there is virtue and safety in cowardice too. Some of the great tribes have been destroyed and scattered; we cowards are still here. But to serious matters. This thing you bring among us, why do you bring it? Where will it lead? Tell me."

They sat on rocks a little way back from the edge of the water

234

so that its incessant roaring sound was muted and they did not have to shout to be heard.

Jacob said thoughtfully: "It is hard to know what to tell, father, when the question is so wide. What is it you want to know? Is it about the schooling? About the work of our mission?"

The old man made a small physical motion of impatience: a slight move of the head, a small jerk of one shoulder, a half-motion with one hand. "Let us not blind ourselves with words. It is not of schools and gods I talk; they are always with us. You know that and I know that. It is how men use their schools and their gods which is of moment; it is of what they wish to attain through the use of their schools and their gods that I speak. What is it you plan to gain from your school here among us? And when your school is followed by your one God, where do you wish that God to lead our people? It is of that I speak; let there be no more fencing between us. You have called me father to show respect for my age: but this is not your way. Why do it?"

"You rebuke me," Jacob said.

"A son does not fence with his father, nor with someone he calls father: not among us."

"It is a foolish son, a foolish man, who pretends a greater understanding than he has. You ask me a question and because I do not understand the full meaning of your question, and because I seek to understand the full meaning so that I might try to answer with full honesty you rebuke me. Among us, that is not just."

The old man's face cracked in a wide, appreciative smile. "Among us too. Among all people, I think. Hear me then. In my youth, which is a long time ago, I and my younger brother left our village and journeyed to the coast and then north until we came to the place controlled by the white men you call the English. We went wishing to learn and to understand their wisdom. They caught us and locked us up for entering the land without their permission. They called us foreigners and sent us to work as their slaves for a year just because we had entered what they called their colony. In that place we found other men like us, from different villages in Africa, who had gone to that place without permission and had been caught and put to work like slaves. They took away our manhood from us and they handled us as we

235

would handle beasts. My younger brother died in that place. And the white priest who had no respect for us came and prayed for him with no interest in his eyes. Many had died before and he always came and prayed with no interest in his eyes. A man in sorrow sees these things. When my time was done they offered me the choice of leaving their colony or working for them for a few of their silver shillings every month and food and shelter. I chose to leave their colony. I did not like the food or the work. I did not like to be among men who had lost their manhood. I did not like the ugly and taboo things men did to each other in that place. And I noted that it was men like me who were in that place as prisoners. The white ones we saw were always overlords. As you do now, they spoke of schools and of their one God. I was one of many who refused their work; but many more made their mark on the paper and stayed to work. Those of us who did not they carried to a place on their border; then they let us loose and chased us across the border in a desolate place where there were no villages. It took a very long time for me to reach back here again. This was many years ago now, perhaps as many as the years of your life. And I did not leave this place until we made that journey to your mission after the soldiers came among us as predators. So where will your coming lead our young? To what I saw in the place they call Sierra. . . ?"

"Sierra Leone."

"That's it."

"Then why did you let us come? Why agree to the school? You know I would have respected your wish if you had said no."

"I wanted to say no. . . ."

"But you were grateful?"

"That's not the reason. It's the children. I would be happy to spend my last days here, just as we are. But the children. . . . You understand that. No man has the right to cut them off. The things you have to offer are what they want. If we try to cut them off they will do what my younger brother and I and many others did."

"And perhaps they will return as you did."

"Leaving a dead brother behind? And with a sickness of the mind which it has taken a lifetime to cast out? I would prefer them not to. Because of the unnatural things I saw men do in that place I

236

have had no children. I feared to expose any son of mine to that degradation. But seeing you made me ask; is it possible to take what they have without the degradation?"

"We have all experienced that degradation," Jacob said slowly. "In different forms perhaps. You were never a slave, you said. My grandmother, at whose knee I learned about life and about God, was a slave. My grandfather, her husband, who became a priest and founded a church, was a slave. I met, as a very small boy, a giant of a man called Samson who was brought from Africa as a slave and whose body carried the scars of all the beatings he had endured. When I met him as a child he was paralysed and had lost the power of speech; but his anger at the degradation he had seen and experienced showed like burning fire in his eyes. We have all known that degradation, either directly or through those close to us."

"Even you, with all your learning. . . ."

"Yes, all of us who are not white. And the purpose of my work, of the work of all of us here, is to put an end to the degradation for all our people everywhere."

"Is your mission then at war with the white men's mission?"

"No; not at war. We say we serve the same God. We say we seek the same end, but as you say, men use their schools and their gods to attain their own ends. Our end is freedom and no more degradation for our own people. To strive for this is not to be against any man and not to be at war with anybody."

A sceptical smile flashed across the old man's face; but there was a touch of tenderness as he looked into Jacob's eyes.

"Will they let you be? You challenge their power."

"We do not seek their permission. We do not break their laws."

"Yet they will attack you, if they see you succeeding."

"We will know how to respond. When the Lord Jesus Christ was on earth they attacked Him and tried to destroy his teaching."

"Your own people, those who look like you, will be used against you."

"We know that too. Remember I told you of my grandfather, well, they burned down his church when he did not agree to submit to them. I decided to carry on where my grandfather left off. We want a church of black people under the control and

237

guidance of black people. All other churches are controlled by their own people. Why not ours? And no matter how many of our own people that they have degraded into tools and puppets we have to face, we will prevail in the end, as Jesus himself prevailed in the end."

"And so your school and your hospital will take care of the minds and the bodies, and your church will take care of the spirit of your people. Just like a tribe; just like a village."

"Only a new kind of tribe and a new kind of village."

"But for black people, you say."

"No, not for black people only, but with black people in control because it is theirs. Others may share but they must control."

"And this is your mission?"

"That is the mission of our church."

"Everywhere in Africa?"

"Wherever it is, in Africa or the world. And we hope to spread it."

The old man leaned back on his rock, and in the silence they again heard the noise of the water. The old man began to chuckle, a low, happy chuckle. Then it rose to laughter which grew, warm and infectious, till Jacob found himself laughing too, swept along by the old man's laughter. Then Sam joined in and the three of them laughed and laughed.

The old man laughed till he was breathless and tears streamed from his eyes; he held his sides and swayed from side to side. Between gasps of laughter he said: "They even lie about your God! He loves laughter! I know that now! He's just like some of our gods! Only more loving because he is alone, heh! I am happy!"

Their laughter rang above the roaring water.

After a time they grew exhausted. Their laughter tapered off then died. In the long silence which followed they heard again the muted roar of the water plunging into the pool. Sam looked curiously from the old man to Jacob wondering precisely what it was that had caused the old man to wrap them all in that wave of exuberant laughter. He tried to retrace the conversation: trouble was he had been just a conduit connecting the flow of words between the old man and Jacob, not a participant, so he had had no time to absorb them or think about them. So why did he join in the laughter? Because they had laughed and their laughter had carried him along and lifted him out of himself? What was certain now was that the school would be well-received and well-attended. This old man would see to that.

At last, his breathing regular again and the tears of laughter wiped from his cheeks, the old man rose from the rock and looked at the trees and the forest, and at the point where the water plunged down out of the forest. Then he turned his eyes to Jacob and they were again the hooded guarded eyes which saw everything and revealed little.

"We have talked," said the old man. "My spirit is at ease."

He led the way back to the hill where his people and the two teachers were now putting up a large shelter under which the first classes would begin in the morning. They worked feverishly because the sky was darkening and it seemed that the rain would come early.

Jacob and Daniel Lee started the journey back before dawn the next morning, accompanied by four of the strongest-looking young men of the tribe. The old man had insisted on this when Jacob had announced that Sam would remain behind until the Joneses were settled in. Without Sam to speak for them and to enlist help from the hidden villages on the way back, they might be in trouble; people who could help might hold back because they did not understand and no one asked. The young men would ensure against this. Sam and Jonathan Jones had given them a crash course in how to ease wheels out of ruts or holes and how to change tyres. The rest, drying out the engine and removing any moistness from the carburetter and filling the gas tank, Jacob and Dan could manage by themselves.

Jacob was glad of the pre-dawn darkness as he took leave of the two young people. He was leaving them deep in the African bush and would probably never see them again. If things went wrong he would not be there to help. He had encouraged them in this undertaking, feeding the dream of service and the sense of adventure of the young; and now he was cutting the connection.

He was their parent in this enterprise, anxious for them, at this moment of parting.

He would always remember Dorothy as an upright, supple, willowy shadow in the dark pre-dawn, with young Jonathan towering protectively over her, a taller, stronger tree. He wrapped his arms about her and muttered up at Jonathan: "Take care of each other. . . ."

"We'll be all right," Jonathan growled. "You take care."

"And you answer my letters, hear?" Dorothy fought back the tears. "I'll write once a month and I'll expect to hear from you once a quarter."

"You're letting him off easy," Dan's voice came from near the truck. "I'd say a letter for a letter like a tooth for tooth."

"Ignore him," Jacob said, glad of the teasing interference. He turned to Sam. "Don't come till you're sure everything is all right for them."

"Yes, doctor."

The old man had left his bed to see them off. Jacob took both his hands.

"I will always remember you."

Sam translated.

"And I you, my son."

"You will guard my young people – even when you are not here."

"As long as they do your work; in my heart I say our work."

"It is our work and they will not change from it as others have. I know them."

"Then they will be safe here, always. I promise you that."

"Thank you."

"And we thank you. I wish there were more days for us to talk more. If only we had met earlier. It is ever so. Now go, for your journey is long. Go well."

"Stay well." Jacob turned away from the old man and the two young people and reliable Sam. Of them all he would only see Sam again, for a short while. "Come, Dan!"

They got into the truck cabin and the engine came to life. The truck lights snapped on, two searching beams piercing the dawn and pointing away from the village. They waved and moved off.

. . . How it hurts, Jacob told himself, this parting. Dan touched his hand briefly.

Ten days later, Jacob left Liberia. Dan Lee, Mrs Willis, Sam, and, to Jacob's utter astonishment, Miss Symes, saw him off at the docks. There were no proper port facilities so the ship that would take him away lay at anchor far out in the harbour. Small boats, barges and canoes laden with all manner of supplies moved constantly between the dock and the distant ship riding the early morning Atlantic waters. Little boys and young men in slim canoes hovered about the ship and dived into the clear water when passengers flipped coins over the side of the ship.

The parting was awkward for everybody. It had been stretched out too long. At the last moment Miss Symes pressed a sealed letter into Jacob's hand and whispered: "Please don't read it till the ship is out of sight, doctor." Her eyes misted over.

Then it was time for him to get into the boat that would carry him to the ship which would carry him away. He put his arm about Sam's shoulder. Jacob had found him when he first arrived at the mission able to speak English but uncertain, possessed of an enormous inferiority complex that made him appear stupid and ingratiating. Now he had a quiet self-assurance and had grown into a decent kind of man. Jacob and Daniel Lee had agreed that he was ready for greater responsibility; Jacob's parting gift had been to make him manager of all mission supplies and works, and provide him with an office that had his name on it: "Mr Sam Kirili, Manager of Supplies and Works." This, too, would be a fact any new successor would have to accept. Mr Kirili was part of the establishment, not a Liberian "boy" any more; Dan and Mrs Willis would see to it; and so, it now seemed, would Miss Symes as well. Small progress, but good.

"Thank you for showing me your country, Sam, and for helping me to understand; for all the journeys we made into the bush, for all the palavers we have shared. It has been good. I will remember it and you always."

"Thank you, sir," Sam said. For a moment it seemed he would break down, then his manhood asserted itself and he took a deep breath. "I will never forget you, doctor. Never!"

"Take care of Dr Dan for me, especially when he goes on journeys."

"I will, doctor. . . . Please bless me as you do in church." Sam bowed his head, standing there on the dockside, and Jacob put his hand on Sam's head, just as he had done so often in church during the sacrament of bread and wine. Then Sam turned and walked away to where the truck was parked.

Mrs Willis hugged him, showing her determination that it should be a no-nonsense parting. "Take care of yourself and eat properly; and write when you have time."

Oh, Harlem, he thought, you have produced new black women, strong, durable, capable, who have learned to stand alone in a different kind of jungle. If she passes just a little of what she has to the young women here, then tomorrow's Liberia had better watch out.

"You take care, and let me hear about your young women. Goodbye."

"Bye, doctor."

And now, Dan. They stared silently at each other for a long time, then they shook hands, each trying to smile. There was no need for words between them, no need for promises. Then Jacob turned and went to where the boatman waited, his helping hand outstretched.

5
Jacob/Chitole

1

Jacob Brown stood alone, felt alone, for all the vast throng of people about him. They were singing now, in low, rolling notes that swept over the high green hills and down into the shallow valleys, across the fields of coffee and of cotton. Margaret always loved to hear them singing. Now they were singing their farewell to Margaret. And he was standing there alone at her graveside. It was hard to say, as one of his priests taking part in the burial service had said: "The Lord giveth and the Lord taketh away, blessed is the name of the Lord." Hard, but you must accept it. Was there any other choice but to accept it? Not accepting it would not bring Margaret back. So you accept what you have no control over; but the Lord would not want you to pretend a grace you did not have. I do not want to bless His name now.

The little English bishop and his big bony wife had come all the way from Kampala for the funeral. Now, he came up and took Jacob's hand in a surprisingly firm grip. Behind him, his wife said: "Please come and see us, Bishop Brown. . . . Whenever you want to. . . . Come and stay for a few days. . . . It will be lonely. . . ."

The bishop said: "We mean it, my friend. We share your sorrow. Of course we can't really. I mean we feel with you."

"Thank you," Jacob said. "Thank you for coming; I appreciate that."

The bishop and his wife walked down the hill, away from the cemetery, to where a number of cars were parked. The English Governor had sent his private secretary to represent him. The tall thick-set young man, very fair, now came to take his leave.

"His Excellency particularly asked me to express his personal condolences, my lord. If there is anything we can do. . . ."

Behind the Governor's personal secretary, accompanying him, were the District Commissioner and his lady. These two were less relaxed than the Bishop and his wife or the Governor's secretary. Their sense of awkward out-of-placeness tended to make everybody they came into contact with feel awkward. Yet the DC was known as a firm and decisive man in his everyday work, brooking no nonsense from the natives over whom he held authority. Both man and woman looked as if they detested where they were and what they were doing. They could not, it seemed, let down their hair and be themselves. They had to impress the natives and keep a distance. The effort seemed to sour them.

"So sorry," the woman murmured, moving as though to offer her hand and then thinking better of it.

"We are sorry, sir," the DC said and pushed out his hand deliberately.

"Thank you," Jacob Brown said remotely. He did not like the DC. They had had several runs-in since the young man had been posted to this district. He should have been posted across the border in Kenya.

Then the Indian who was the import-export agent for what the mission's business section produced and required, came to take his leave: anxious, it seemed, to be gone from this vast throng of black people as soon as it could be done with due observance of the racial mores which defined both class and precedence: first the whites. . . .

"Goodbye, my lord. I wish. . . ."

"Goodbye, Mr Patel. Thank you for coming."

"I wish. . . ."

Jacob looked into the man's eyes, silently reassuring him.

"I know, Mr Patel."

Again the Indian said: "I wish." Then he turned abruptly and hurried away to his car.

The young black Ugandan doctor, a small-boned, neat little man with sharp features, came and stood beside Jacob. The singing continued to roll over the land in waves of sorrow.

"We really did everything we could, my lord."

"I know," Jacob said. "There isn't much you can do about cancer. It was her pain that worried me."

246

"It eased up near the end, which is what gave us that false hope of a remission. Remember?"

"Yes."

"My lord. . . ." The young doctor hesitated for a long time, so Jacob said: "Yes, doctor?"

"You have brought comfort and hope and prosperity to so many of our people for such a long time. Now all the people here want to comfort you in your sorrow. There is so little they can do except be here and sing their hymns of sorrow to show that they share your sorrow. That is all we have to give you."

"That is more than enough, doctor."

"I must leave now, sir. They need me at the hospital. Can I leave something to relax you? You'll need it later."

"Nothing, doctor. Thank you; goodbye."

Then the chiefs who had come from the nearby villages came and expressed their sorrow, each in his own individual way, and left. Jacob Brown stayed there by the grave, all alone, though surrounded by a vast throng of mourners whom he had known, to varying degrees, for upwards of three decades. These were his people, had been his people for a long time. His people and Margaret's people. She had helped deliver babies who grew to young womanhood, and got married at their church and became mothers themselves. Now they were mourning Margaret's death. And still he felt cut off, as though with her death, he had lost contact with those who had for so long been his people. But he knew it was only temporary; contact would come back, that was what he was here for. Pain, hurt, is much more tolerable than this deadness of feeling. This must be what hell is: to be living and for all feeling to be dead.

How beautifully they sang! How clear and fresh the highland air, clear enough to see the distant Mount Elgon, hanging in the sky, far to the north. They say the Mau Mau soldiers sometimes escaped to the Ugandan side of its slopes when hunted by British soldiers. Nothing to prevent the British soldiers following them right into Uganda; it's all British, after all.

Jacob's secretary, the Reverend John Chitole, and Margaret's long-time housekeeper, Mrs Adina Kilu, pushed through the vast moving and singing throng to him.

"It is time for food," Mrs Kilu said.

Some of Margaret's firm managerial manner had rubbed off on Mrs Kilu and showed now as she waited to lead Jacob to the house.

"I'm not hungry," he said.

"But you must eat," she insisted. "Missy would want that." Then her sternness relaxed. "Please, sir. I promised her to look after you well."

"And I have very important news, sir, from Entebbe," John Chitole cut in. "Just got it on the phone."

"Then tell me."

"Not here, sir. Someone might hear."

"All right."

Jacob looked lingeringly at the grave, as if willing his Margaret to rise from it. Then he turned and walked briskly to the car that would take him to the big sprawling house in spacious grounds on the next hill.

The house, the grounds, the trees, the flowers, they were all Margaret's. This was the home she had created and they had shared these many years. Now, for all her being buried in that cemetery on another hill, her presence was all about the place, and it was as though the three who entered expected to see her trim figure come briskly out of one of the rooms to meet them. Jacob looked up at her portrait which hung in the centre of the wall furthest from the door: A painting in the bold, dramatic manner of the art of the 'New Negroes' of the Harlem Negro Renaissance of the 1920s. Except for a few lines at the corners of her mouth, a slight sag under her chin, and the greying of her hair, she looked much as she had when she sat for that painting more than a quarter of a century before.

. . . And now that is all I have left of her, Jacob thought. Then: no, no, there is much, much more. There are all the invisible, all the hard-to-define-or-describe things. The memory of a mood, of a look of the eye; of a passing sense of a special moment or a special smile or a special silence. She had said in her quiet, self-assured way which could be so exasperating when she was wrong, so comforting when she was right: "As long as you remember me I am alive; I will be dead only when you don't remember me any more." He suppressed a mighty impulse to talk to her out loud.

John Chitole said, facing him:

"They deposed the Kabaka this morning, my lord."

At first Jacob did not take it in; his mind was so full of Margaret. John Chitole saw it and repeated the news. Now Jacob absorbed it.

"Who did it?"

"The Governor; the British Governor."

"I don't believe it. Where is he? Is he all right?"

"He's on his way out of the country, my lord."

"Stop calling me that. But they were friends. Get me the bishop on the phone."

"Which one?"

"The one who was here."

"I don't think he's back yet, sir."

"You think he knew?"

"I don't know, sir. I think so. They say the British army is in force at Government House so the English here would have been alerted."

"So Kampala is in turmoil."

"Yes, sir."

Adina Kilu pushed in a trolley of food and John Chitole joined Jacob at the table.

"What do you think will happen now, John? How will the Baganda react? Will they rise? And will the others support them?"

"No to that last, sir. Lesser people rarely rise to the defence of superior people. The rest I can't answer."

"I thought you were Muganda."

"I am, sir; but too long under your influence to believe in the natural superiority of the Baganda. One day we must fashion a real nation instead of the present series of nation-tribes with each claiming pride of place over the other."

"Oh, John! Is that really what I taught you?"

"No, sir. You taught us pride and self-respect in our blackness, and you taught us to think for ourselves. That was enough. We are responsible for the rest."

"We?"

"There are many of us, sir. We have learned from you not to be afraid of questioning all sorts of assumptions. Even little children now ask who gave *Mzungu* the right and power to decide anything for us and to sit in judgement on us."

"No wonder they call me the subversive black American bishop!" Jacob laughed. "You go on with this and they'll expel me yet."

"They cannot expel you for being a good Christian and preaching and practising the truth of the Gospel."

"You'll be surprised, young man. If they can depose the Kabaka they can certainly expel me."

"Will the Americans allow it?"

"I don't know, John. Our friends are no longer in power in Washington. I'm not sure the new people care about us and our missionary enterprises. I suspect the State Department will now see black missionaries in faraway places as nuisances. I rather suspect black Americans in the United States will feel the difference too."

"But they have no reason to expel you." John Chitole was suddenly worried at the prospect.

"They may think they have. But that's not important. If we've done our work well then it does not really matter who goes or who stays. The work will go on. You and all the others will see to it. If we've laid sound and strong foundations and the structures are right then the removing of any one person should not matter. You know that. That's how the church works."

"We care about people, too," Chitole protested, and then wished he had not said that as he saw the change in Jacob's expression.

Jacob's spirit had slipped away, back to that hill where they had buried his Margaret earlier this day. And there was nothing, John Chitole knew, that he or anyone else could do to help make more bearable this utterly quiet and contained grief.

Chitole finished his meal and left quietly. His best service now would be to ensure that things ran smoothly till his bishop was ready to take control again. There was much to attend to for the church had grown into a big, flourishing and many-sided enterprise in its years on this piece of the East African highlands.

Chitole returned, half-opened the door and pushed his head and shoulders into the room.

"Sir." He had to repeat it twice before Jacob heard him.

"Yes, John?"

"I thought. . . . Do you think a visit somewhere. . . ."

"No, John. I'll be all right."

"I thought not," John murmured and withdrew again.

You must not do this, Jacob told himself; don't you become a worry to them when they need you, especially now with the trouble in Kampala. But how do you stop a mind and a heart that will not be stopped? So many things we've shared, arguments and coldnesses, irrational angers, explosive moods and seemingly unforgivable unjustnesses, and hard and cruel thoughts; but always also the acceptance of the shared life and the instinctive sustaining of one another when the need arose. How do you bury that part of yourself? You don't. That is what you have left, all you have left, when the flesh and bone and blood are buried deep in the ground to become earth again. Where is she now: not the body, but that which was in the body? Is it still individual and separate, the unique spirit I knew housed in that body? If it is still the same then I should surely know it and feel it. The old man of that village in Liberia said the spirits were all about, and took care of the ancestral land and those who remained on it and spoke to the wisest of the descendants. . . .

Mrs Kilu came and cleared the table.

"You should rest now. That's what Missy always made you do after food. Please go now."

He went into the familiar room and lay on the bed. And now, at last, tears filled his eyes and Jacob Brown wept for the wife he had lost to death. The clear, almost dazzling light of the highlands filtered through the curtains and lit up the room.

He woke; the room was in darkness. He lay still for a while, remembering. No Margaret to come and put on the light. Mrs Kilu would not dream of coming in here to put on the light: one of Margaret's quirks about the privacy of her bedroom. She alone tended to it: made the bed, changed the linen, tidied it, swept the floor, cleaned the windows. The one place from

251

which all the world except he and young David, their son, were excluded; and when he grew bigger, even David.

He got up and groped his way to the big French window and drew back the curtains. He must have slept for many hours. He went on to their private verandah which led straight onto the small courtyard, fenced in by a high wall of thick tall grass. This, like the bedroom, had been Margaret's very private sanctuary. Here they had been able to shed all appearances: wear sloppy clothes and play cards and listen to records that were not strictly "proper" and be unshaved or even scantily clad. Here, after work, he had been a man instead of a bishop; she had been a woman instead of a bishop's wife: ordinary folk for a time. And it had been good. . . .

Then, as from a great distance, he heard the sounds from the cemetery. They were still there, still singing. He put on the verandah light and saw that it was after seven. He turned on the lights in the bedroom, went into the bathroom and washed his face and combed his hair. Then he went into the main part of the house.

Mrs Kilu was still there though it was long past her time for tending to her own family.

"Why are you still here?" he asked.

Her eyes lit up. This was how she knew her bishop.

"Reverend Chitole asked me to stay, sir. You didn't eat much today or yesterday or the day before. He thought you may want to eat properly later."

"Where is he?"

"In your office, sir."

"All right, go home."

"And your food?"

"Leave out something cold."

"The ham sandwiches with lettuce and tomato you and Missy used to have in the evenings?"

"Yes please, Miss Adina."

"There will be a chilled beer in the ice-box."

"Good; thank you. Goodnight, Adina."

"Sir . . . I'm sorry; we all are. We'll do everything the way she taught us. We all loved Missy, sir. We know it is hard for you."

252

"Goodnight, Adina. And thank you, all of you."

Mrs Kilu left to take care of her own large family; Jacob went to his study where John Chitole worked on the books to do with the business side of the mission. He rose as Jacob entered and, as with Mrs Kilu, his eyes showed relief when he recognized the bishop's old familiar mood and bearing. The darkness had passed; the sorrow still there but the darkness had passed.

"Those people are still up there, John."

"We didn't know what to do, sir. They all loved Missy."

"So they're turning it into a Nine-Nights party."

"Nine-Nights?"

"The Jamaican version of what's going on up there."

"Same thing?" John Chitole smiled. "Food and strong drink and candles?"

"Yes, with a few small differences. Anybody supervising?"

"Two of our priests are up there."

"Come. We must stop it. It's been going on long enough. What news from Kampala?"

"Nothing new, sir." To himself, Chitole said: Welcome back, my lord. He followed Jacob out of the study.

They could see the lit candles from a great distance as the jeep bounced along the uneven road to the cemetery, like a vast number of peenie-wallies spreading their light on a dark Jamaican night before the rise of the moon. The voices carried clear across the stillness of the night, one of them rising above all the others every now and then.

Jacob and John Chitole entered the cemetery and the singing was nearer, louder, and the candles no longer like distant fireflies. They parked near other cars and approached the gathering on foot. The two priests, one thin and young, one in his middle years with a middle-age spread, came to them out of the crowd. The potent smell of *waragi*, as overpowering as Jamaican overproof white rum, mixed with the smell of candle wax and fried meat. The singing was everywhere, as it had been earlier in the day.

"Surely not the same people," Jacob said, immediately aware of the stupidity of what he had said.

"They go and others come to take their place," the middle-aged priest said.

"But there are fewer of them," John Chitole said.

Jacob went to the head of Margaret's grave. The people – mostly women dressed in flowing white – made way for him. Here and there someone touched his sleeve, kissed his hand, bowed low before him. Those nearest to him fell silent, and gradually the silence spread outward like a rippling wave till all were silent. Jacob said:

"It is late, my people. It is time for you to go home. Missy has gone on her great journey and we have gone with her as far as the living can go. She is safely on her way and we will never forget her till we all meet again in heaven. So I want you all now to go home. God bless you." He held up his hand in benediction.

John Chitole said a loud "Amen" and there was a responding rumble.

The women nearest Jacob started the march back to their village, candles held high. Someone started the singing again, and all gradually joined in the slow, dirgelike hymn to the dead as they marched away.

"They'll be all right?" Jacob said.

"The men will escort them all to their homes," John Chitole said.

"You go on," Jacob told his three priests. "I want to stay a while."

"I'll wait for you," Chitole said.

"No," Jacob said. "Ride with the others. Leave me the jeep. I'll be all right."

"My lord. . . ." the eldest priest began.

"Come," Chitole said and hustled the others away.

Jacob waited for them to be out of sight, till he heard only the receding sound of their vehicle above the now faint sound of the mournful singing. He waited till there was only the silence of the natural noises of the night and he was alone with his dead. He stared down at the grave as if to see through the earth to where she lay and look once more on that familiar face.

Wherever you are, thank you my dear.
Thank you for having shared these years with me.
Thank you for having looked at me with seeing eyes

254

For having touched my hand and kissed my lips and warmed my
    soul
For having laughed with me and cried with me and fought with
    me
For having hated me and baited me
For having roused a fuming angry rage in me
And then for having made me soft and gentle, pliant and
    bending
All against my will
Thank you for lips that moved
For eyes that mocked
And a voice of music
Above all thank you for having lived and loved with me.

Jacob Brown smiled, a mixture of grief and tender joy. Then he
said aloud, as though she were beside him: ''Sorry I didn't always
tell you how I felt about you. We never do these things when we
should and then we say sorry. Sorry you're not going to retire to
Jamaica with me. I wanted so much to show you our hills; you
wouldn't have had the frustrating problem of language you had
here. And sorry I had to stop the Nine-Nights thing they had
going here. It really does go on for nine nights in Jamaica and
people sometimes get paralytic drunk by the time they have seen
the departing spirit on its way. I went into a blind funk at the
thought of being without you, love. I'm all right now. I'm glad
David wasn't here to see it. It will be hard enough when he does
come. I think he'll come out all right. He is your son, after all, and
mine too. We have tried to lead upright lives and we certainly
have obeyed the most important of the Commandments: we have
loved our neighbours and done our duty by our people and our
God. Wish I had been able to talk to you like this, as easily while
you were with me. I can even tell you about my doubts and
uncertainties. I guess I didn't want you to see my weaknesses.
Oh, about that funk; I haven't written your family about your
death. Chitole took over and did all the formal notifications and
your Mrs Kilu and your Women's Committee managed all the
feeding and other arrangements. I was in some private dark hell
these past three days and out of control as no bishop is supposed

to be. It's all over now. I will carry on; but oh, my dear, it is going to be so lonely, so desolate, without you. So much of me lies buried here with you. I don't know how I'm ever going to leave this place knowing you lie here. I must go back now, my dear. There is much to do and I think the political upheavals which have swept the West Coast and our neighbour across the border are about to come to this peaceful place. Remember the game of speculation we played about the African future? Sorry you won't be here to see how it is played out. I'm beginning to doubt our forecast of this place as an oasis of peace in a turbulent desert. When you remove the most important symbol of stability and power you leave an awful vacuum, which is what they did today. I'm going back to write to your people and Dan Lee in Liberia. Kilu is putting up some ham sandwiches for me, and there's a chilled beer in the ice-box. . . ." He stopped talking suddenly, a tight band of physical pain gripped his chest. His head throbbed. He waited for the pain to pass, using the force of his mind to relax his body. At last the pain passed.

"I must leave you now, my love."

He turned and walked to the jeep, slowly, heavily.

As Jacob Brown parked the jeep under the shelter beside the house he saw John Chitole come out of the house and hurry away, a shadowy black-clad figure disappearing into the pale moonlit night. I must stop making them worry about me, Jacob told himself, especially conscientious John Chitole. He went into the house and felt the empty stillness of it. He knew there was someone on night duty somewhere about the place; the knowledge did not ease his sense of aloneness. All the world, now, would be like this for him. He went into the large neat kitchen, took the chilled beer out of the ice-box, poured it into an earthern mug and carried it through the dining room where the sandwiches, wrapped in a snow-white napkin, were under a fly-cover on the table. He took these up and with sandwiches and beer in hand he went to their bedroom and through to Margaret's private little courtyard. There he sat down under the African stars and ate alone. He remembered clear nights like this in the high Jamaican hills. He remembered his Grandma Sarah. And this grief was not more than he could bear.

The next morning he went back to the routine of his days. Over breakfast he discussed the affairs of the dozen district churches under his control with John Chitole. In the main things were going well but there were two serious problems. In one instance the priest in charge had taken up with the young wife of an old man who was a leading member of his congregation. They agreed that the bishop would himself have to go to the area and deal with the matter if the church in the area were not to be irreparably damaged. It was important to make the people understand that the failings of any one man were not the failings of the church.

In the second instance the priest had upped and made off with his community's money which had been put into a Mothers' Union thrift scheme, the earnings from their branch of the coffee co-operative, and the church's rebuilding fund: a total of more than five thousand shillings. The priest had taken a young woman with him and her closest friend had said they were going to Egoli – Johannesburg – to savour some of the pleasures they heard black people enjoyed there.

"But how can we turn out priests like these!" Jacob Brown lamented.

"Dr Johnson, sir," Chitole said. "Remember."

"Yes," Jacob sighed. He remembered the big, hearty doctor of divinity who had come from America by way of Liberia to head Jacob's first theology college. The man had been so anxious to be loved by his long-lost brother and sister Africans that he over-rewarded, over-indulged them to the point of buying their goodwill; and of course, they, being African, had no faults in the eyes of Dr Johnson. Jacob had endured him for two years and then threatened headquarters with his own quitting if Johnson was not recalled.

"Were these two Johnson graduates?"

"Yes, sir."

"How many more?"

"He turned out four before he left. They all had perfect records."

"Where are the other two?"

"Don't you remember one went to the Catholics when you had Dr Johnson recalled?"

"So that was why. Yes, I remember him, cocky little know-all wasn't he? How's he doing now?"

"Last I saw him in Kampala he was hoping they would send him to a college in Rome. Sees himself as one day becoming the first African Catholic bishop. He envied you, sir. The position, not the responsibility."

"And the other one?"

"He's a drunkard and petty thief in Kampala; uses his learning to prey on the ignorance of our people. I bailed him out of jail twice. The third time I refused to go when he sent word. He was turning himself into our special social cripple."

"So you cut him off. It's hard but I think you did right. So, we have no more problems with Dr Johnson's graduates."

"No, sir, just these two. If you approve I'll refer the matter of the embezzlement to the police. It is a police matter."

"Yes. But I think we'll have to make good their losses. Who's there now?"

"I sent the Reverend Michael Odera. He's young but disciplined; you taught him yourself."

"You've done well, John."

"You taught us well, sir. I think you should go back to preparing men for service in the church. There are enough of us now, priests and lay people, to take on most of your other work. We can certainly manage the business side."

"What about the college and schools in the areas?"

"We can oversee the work. You will go on being the overall head but we will carry the burden. It is in the training and preparing of people for the church that we need you most now. Let's go over the business books tomorrow and you'll see just how well they are all doing on the business side."

"All right, John, we'll try it that way."

"I'm glad, sir. Can I prepare a small class to go with you when you go and settle the wife-stealing matter? I'd like to come too."

Jacob grinned. "Agreed. And while we're making plans for the future, I want you to prepare yourself to succeed me one day. I don't think we need another foreigner to follow me."

"You're no foreigner," Chitole protested.

"You know what I mean," Jacob said impatiently. "I want you to go to the States for a spell of training as soon as possible. You won't learn much from it except the inner politics of our church, and that is important." Jacob leaned back and looked at this young man who had in some ways grown closer to him than his son David. "And don't ever forget that the Christian church, in all its infinite variety, is the oldest political movement in the world, and at times, the most revolutionary. The communists call it the opium of the people; it can be. But it can also be more revolutionary than any of their communist parties. In its own quiet way our branch of the Christian church is the most revolutionary in the world today because it is closer to the spirit of the teaching of Jesus. Don't ever become so big and so successful as to forget that. The origin and the reason for our branch of the Christian church is so that black folk should worship God as our own God and in our own way. We must use our God in the service of our freedom and in insisting on the right to make our own choices. You know all that; the important thing is not to get so bogged down by the power and the growing responsibilities that they become ends in themselves. Our church must always be the teacher and the servant of our people, serving their spiritual and economic and social interests just as the best of the white churches do theirs." Jacob stopped abruptly and smiled apologetically.

"And the state?" John Chitole prompted. "If Africans head the state, if Africans are in charge of government, what then? Do we become part of the power structure? The church of the state as the Anglicans in Britain?"

"That's in the future, John. Your generation will have to face that one."

"Which is why I raise it, sir, especially in view of your plans for me."

"You will have to face that one when the time comes. There is no pat prescription, only your basic Christian beliefs and principles as guides."

John Chitole was not satisfied but he held his peace.

Mrs Kilu came into the room and at the same time the telephone on the sideboard rang. Chitole went to the phone; Mrs Kilu began to clear the table.

"Yes," Chitole said, put his hand over the mouthpiece and called to Jacob: "The Governor's secretary. Says it's personal and urgent." Jacob nodded. Chitole spoke into the mouthpiece, "Hold please, his lordship is coming."

Jacob crossed the room and took the phone. "Hello, Bishop Brown here."

"Sorry to bother you so early, sir, but a rather delicate matter has come up." Jacob recognized the voice of the cool, self-assured young Englishman. "It is your son, sir, Dr David Brown. We only heard about it this morning."

"What about him?" Jacob sounded cold and harsh; he held on to himself.

"He flew in last night piloting his own private plane, actually not his own plane, belongs to some Algerian, and he had all the proper authority to fly it."

Jacob relaxed and closed his eyes for a moment. "So?"

"That's it, sir. Our people detained him at the airport overnight. Bit of a mix-up. Not used to. . . ."

"Not used to black folk piloting private planes," Jacob said drily.

"Especially with the trouble going on next door," the secretary said.

"So?"

"It's all right now, sir. Once we found out an Inspector went out there and apologized and ordered his release. He's on the way to you now and we've alerted the people at the airstrip at Tororo so there shouldn't be any further trouble. We promised to call you to explain and ask you to send somebody to meet him. We offered to lay on transport from Jinja but he was too angry to accept anything from us."

"I'll have someone meet him," Jacob said.

"Sir. . . ." There was a long pause; Jacob waited; then: "He was fearfully angry. I wasn't there myself but. . . ."

"Wouldn't you be?" Jacob snapped, "given the circumstances?"

"It was a genuine mistake, my lord. We all regret it. He threatened some legal action. We hope you will be able to make him understand, when he is a little calmer, that no malice or prejudice was involved. He was held when there was no British officer on the spot."

"Was his the only private plane to land at Entebbe last night?"

"I'm not sure but I don't think so." There was a pause while the man at the other end spoke to someone in the background then his voice came back, softer, less self-assured. "There were other private landings."

"But no other detentions?"

Again the long pause, then: "No, sir." In a flat voice with a hint of challenge to it.

"Thank you for calling," Jacob said and put down the phone.

"Where is David now?" John Chitole asked.

"On his way to Tororo. You got it?"

"Most of it. I'll go for him myself." Chitole looked at his watch and moved to the door. "Miss Batari has a mass of letters and papers for you to see and sign at the office. I'll try and time it so that we are back here for lunch." Chitole looked at Mrs Kilu. She smiled and nodded, following him to the door.

"Don't drive too fast," Jacob said as Chitole shut the door, leaving him alone.

Jacob thought: So he got the message, and he tried to reach here in time. Would have been too late anyway. But he did make the effort and the knowledge of that is comforting. . . . To work and Miss Batari now. Margaret would have been pleased to know the boy cared enough to make the effort to come home in time.

It had been nearly three years since John Chitole last saw David Brown. That time he was here for what turned out to be a short and explosive visit after completing his internship at some British hospital. One of the intense political arguments he always had with his parents had taken on an ugly personal tinge and ended in a flaming row, with the son trying to shout the father down, his screaming laced with obscenities. Chitole had tried to leave when he sensed the way it was developing. An angry Jacob, angrier than he had ever seen him before or since, had ordered him to stay. And Missy had withdrawn into herself, agony on her face, watching the two she loved most savaging each other. He still remembered the end of it. There was that bit about having met the great Dr DuBois after the last Pan-African Congress in England. "Your quiet, refined old brown gentleman, impeccably dressed and with the patrician air you associate with the European aristocracy. He was just as gentle and soft-spoken as you, Dad. Why are you old spades always so soft, so afraid of raising your voices? Why are you so bloody proper always? Why don't you ever scream and shout at them? Why don't you ever get drunk and screw their women as they do yours? Why don't you spit on them as they spit on you? Know why? They've brainwashed you into judging yourselves by their standards! So you all try to live up to the standard they have set for you, the standards by which they judge you, because you have accepted their right to sit in judgement on you. Among all of you only Garvey begins to sound like a man. He at least challenges them. And then he spoils it with his damnfool nonsense about dukes and princes and noblemen. You're always imitating them: their churches, their dress, their ways, even their stupidities. How you flatter them! Then you expect us to look up to you as examples of success and follow in your footsteps. 'The problem of the twentieth century is the problem of the colour-line,' your great man intones. Well, what has he, or you, done about it over these past fifty years and more? To be sure, he's gone from conference to conference making fine speeches, and you and your lot have gone from land to land converting black souls; but to what end? To become soft-spoken, quiet, well-behaved niggers like yourselves, forever flattering the world's white ego by trying to live up to the standards it sets for you? We've had our bellyful of that crap! We want to vomit it out! And with it all the shame that chokes us when we look at you and listen to you! We will beg and plead for nothing! We will shout and curse and learn to use guns until they learn to respect us and to fear us! But I don't expect your brainwashed heads will ever understand that."

It was then that Missy had groaned and wrapped her arms across her stomach as though in great pain.

Jacob, Chitole remembered, had risen from his seat, a towering pillar of contained rage. David had risen too, just as tall, just as big as his father, but younger, leaner about the middle and looking stronger. Their eyes locked in mutual anger. For a moment it seemed that Jacob would strike his son.

David had warned: "If you hit me, Daddy, I will hit you back." Then, abruptly, David had pushed back his chair and walked out of the room. Missy had given way to her tears then and retreated to her bedroom. Jacob had slumped back in his chair and stared into space.

That was the last they had seen of David for nearly three years. Now he was back, more than a day late, for the burial of his mother. But he was back. For his bishop's sake, John Chitole was relieved. David had always been a wild and angry one. People like David, thought Chitole, always died young because they were in a hurry to solve problems that had been with the world for centuries. David was forever looking for that revolution which would transform the world, forever waiting for the emergence of the great leader whom he could serve loyally in the interest of a great cause. Two saving graces about David: he did not harbour illusions about himself, and he really cared about people, especially black people because they were oppressed and exploited and he was one of them.

John Chitole raced the bishop's limousine along the wide dirt road running south with a slight westward veer. After a little over an hour he reached the outskirts of Tororo and the circle of well-surfaced roads, one of which led to the border into Kenya with Kitale to the north and Kisumu to the south. He had driven across that border with the bishop a few years back, to Kisumu and a lakeside meeting with some Kenyan Christians. An arrogant young British DC, not much older than he was, had summoned the bishop to his office to question him about his business. He had told the bishop that they did not have any time or liking for any kind of independent black churches in Kenya. The local Christians who had invited the bishop had apologized and quietly abandoned their plans to establish a branch of the church. Now the whole place was on fire.

Chitole slowed down to a crawl in the busy town of Tororo with its hundreds of bicycles; it took him almost half as long to get to the airstrip at the other end of town as it had taken him to make the journey from the mission.

David was outside the airstrip office. Tall, chest thrown out, head erect, in khaki shirt and pants, a suitcase with a leather jacket over it at his feet, dark glasses shading his eyes. He towered above the reddish young white man who stood with him. A few black workmen watched from the background. David recognized the limousine and picked up his suitcase and jacket. John Chitole came out of the car.

"John!" David boomed, reaching the small slender John Chitole in a few giant strides. Momentarily they looked at each other, Chitole tilting his head upward to look into the large brown eyes with their hint of sadness in repose. Now those eyes were laughing with the joy of reunion. David Brown wrapped his arms about Chitole and all but lifted him off the ground. "Long time," he said.

"Welcome home," Chitole said.

David pushed him away to arm's length to examine him again.

"Faithful John, still the same. How's he?"

"He's all right now. He took it very badly but he's over that."

"I tried, John. I really tried."

"I know. You are here now. He needs you."

"Did she suffer?"

"Greatly toward the end."

"Oh God!"

"Come, let's go home."

Chitole turned to the airstrip manager who had drawn near.

"His plane will be all right?"

"Yes, Reverend. I'll see to it myself; we'll roll it under shelter."

Chitole used his eyes to send a silent message to David Brown. A flash of stubbornness passed over David's face then vanished; he sighed softly. A smile passed over his face without reaching his eyes. He looked at the reddish young white man.

"Thank you. Appreciate your help; not like at Entebbe."

"That's all right," the white man said. "Did some flying in the war myself; nothing special. My real interest was always in making them fly rather than flying them."

"Out here long?" David asked.

"Coming up to eighteen months."

"Like it?"

264

The young white man's eyes lit up.

"The most beautiful place I've ever seen! And that lake of yours is like sailing on an ocean! We love it here, my wife and I. It gave us a chance for a new start. There wasn't much for my kind of mechanic to do at home after the war."

"Planning on staying?"

"Dunno. Too soon to decide, and I'm not sure we'd be welcome when you are independent. May be like over there," he waved vaguely in the direction of Kenya. "I think we missed our chance to make friends."

"We must go," John Chitole reminded David. He smiled at the white man. "Sorry I don't know your name, Mr. . . ."

"Jones, a very Welsh name."

"Thank you Mr Jones."

"I'll be taking off in a couple of days," David said.

"Want me to check it over for you? Won't cost much and I'll do a good job, even if I say so myself; better than most."

"All right!" David's smile lit up his eyes now. He pushed his hand into his pocket, took out the plane's keys and gave them to Jones.

Chitole got into the driver's seat of the limousine. David got in beside him. On an impulse Jones walked round to the driver's side and leaned down.

"I know you bring a mechanic and his helpers from Kampala regularly to check the bishop's limousine. You don't have to. I can take care of this and you won't have to pay for transport and subsistence and the like. I'm not trying to take anybody's work away but if you want to save on it I am available."

"I'll discuss it with the bishop," Chitole said.

"Wait," David said. "Why do you want to do this?"

The man lowered his voice. "I'm here on a two-year contract. About six months left to go. I don't want to renew, and they may not ask me to. If I can work up my own mechanic's shop it might be possible to stay for a while longer."

"Why won't they renew?"

"We don't mix with the bank manager and the estate and factory managers and we're not much on high church, so my wife and I go to your local pubs for a beer or a *waragi* at the weekends and keep ourselves to ourselves. I don't think they like that. Anyway," he turned his eyes to John, "if you're interested I could begin building up my own shop for when the contract runs out."

"I'll let you know," Chitole said.

"I'm sure. . . ." David began.

"I'll let you know," Chitole repeated insistently, starting the car.

Jones nodded and stood back as the big car purred to life and moved off.

As Jones entered his little bare office one of the black onlookers called out: "Bishop's son like you, bwana! That's good!"

"I hope so," Jones called back.

As the bishop's limousine slowly moved through the heavy traffic of Tororo David asked, "Why the coyness about Jones's offer? I thought you would jump at it. You've nothing to lose even if it doesn't work. That Kampala Indian importer's mechanic isn't up to much and overpriced."

"I know."

"Then what?"

"We have to work out an arrangement that will pass Jones's skills on to our own young people."

David slid down in his seat, closed his eyes, and cursed himself in a soft whisper for the best part of half a minute. He was, he said, a damned stupid big-mouthed fart who underrated those from whom he should learn which was the true hallmark of conceited shittiness.

When he had done John Chitole smiled wickedly and said: "You know it's worse than that. If you were like that with everybody we could forgive you for being what you say you are. You are not that. You've just always underrated your father. You've refused to learn from him. And there's a lot to learn there, David, believe me, I know."

"I believe you."

"Until you face him. Why?"

"Probably because he is my father."

"He's my father too; and I learn from him."

"You're not saddled with the damned biological connection."

"That's a cop-out."

"Yeah," David sighed.

They left the outskirts of the town. Chitole increased the speed of the car; the need to concentrate on the road and the steady hum of the car demanded silence. David watched the familiar landscape flash by. How often he had taken this road to Tororo, or to Jinja beyond, or to Kampala and its gay and showy high-class nightlife among the Baganda. The road home; the road away from home. Which was it now? A reminder of things past only. There was no longer the urge to flee from it, so it was no longer the road from home. Now his mother lay buried in a cemetery in these African hills. She had come all the way from the New World to die and be buried in the Old; not in the land from which her ancestors were taken in chains, for they were not brought from this part of Africa but from the hot steamy Guinea Coast which was still today farther away from here than London or Paris or New York. That is how the masters of the earth had decreed it should be; and until that was broken Africa could not be free. Nkrumah, who was shaking up the Gold Coast and all West Africa, had said that. He'd said it first at the Pan-African conference in England where David, in company with a bunch of other students, had seen the legendary DuBois for the first time; and he'd said it again when he came out of jail to become the first democratically elected Prime Minister of a British African colony. Till the political and power gravity centres of Africa are Africanized Africa will not be free. But how to begin to look inward instead of always outward? Will Nkrumah and Padmore and DuBois and their people achieve it? Or will Garvey's ideas? And how?

The well-sprung speeding car lulled David into a hazy state between thinking and dreaming. After a while, the tension and weariness of the long solo flight from Algeria, and the overnight detention at Entebbe, eased somewhat and he dozed off. . . .

John Chitole touched him; he woke. They were approaching the mission. The car crested the first and second hills, passed the school and dormitories, the huge playground, and climbed the third hill where the great church stood, its tall spire reaching up to the heavens, and near it the small seminary and the office complex; and to the right of that the bishop's residence in its vast, peaceful grounds. The car crawled up to the house. Remembrances of his childhood in this tranquil place flowed through the mind of David Brown. This place, not as for his father the hills of Jamaica, or the pine-scented air of an Atlanta campus, was the point of departure for David Brown.

The car pulled up. Mrs Kilu and many others appeared at the door. David felt anxious suddenly.

"Come in with me, John. Just for a minute."

Chitole touched his arm and shook his head. David got out of the car and reached for his bag on the back seat. Someone took it from him. Again he looked imploringly at Chitole; again Chitole shook his head. David turned to the house. Mrs Kilu opened her arms in welcome. He held her close and murmured:

"Mama Kilu, Mama Kilu."

She shivered convulsively. "Oh David, you have come!"

"Too late," he said.

"No," she said and pushed him away. "Go to your father; he needs you."

"In his study?"

She nodded. He went into the house and made for the bishop's office. The others dispersed to go about their business: Chitole to park the car and clean up, allowing father and son to be together alone; Adina Kilu to her kitchen to supervise the very special meal for David's return.

David opened the study door. Jacob looked up. For a moment they stared silently at each other. Then Jacob rose and came round the desk and offered his son his hand, an awkward uncertain gesture of welcome. David brushed the hand aside and wrapped his arms about his father. They held each other in a long silent embrace. Then David said: "I'm so sorry, Dad; so sorry I'm late. I tried."

"It's all right, David. You are here. She will understand."

They stood back, looked at each other, trapped in their shared grief and in the myth that men do not weep; so they wept inwardly, without tears and without the relief tears bring.

"Can we go up there now?"

"Yes," Jacob said and opened the door and led the way out.

He had taken off his bishop's clothes and wore khaki pants and shirt, short-sleeved and open-necked. They went through the kitchen and told Mrs Kilu where they were going; she warned them not to be more than an hour or the food would spoil. Then father and son got into the jeep and drove to the cemetery and the fresh grave of the woman who had been wife and mother to them.

A man and a boy worked at the graveside, building a headstone; a pile of cut stone and a wooden board heaped with mixed mortar their building material. The flowers and wreaths had been removed from the grave and stacked in a huge mound to the side; most of them had withered or sadly wilted. The man and the boy stopped working as Jacob and David came up. They bowed to the bishop and withdrew. Some distance away, out of earshot, a group of men were at work digging a fresh grave.

Father and son stood side by side at the head of the grave.

"I wish I had seen her before she died," David said. "Now I can never make peace for the way I left."

Jacob could not find words to comfort him for he too wished the boy had been there for her to look on him for the last time. He knew how much she had wanted that. But he is your son and you have to comfort him.

"We didn't know she was dying until it happened. It looked like a remission three days before."

That would have been the time when she wanted to see me, David thought. Aloud he said: "It often does just before the end."

"They did everything they could," Jacob said. "They spared no effort; Dr Okello was very good, very compassionate."

"And I wasn't here," David said coldly, harshly. "I'll try to see Okello and thank him myself."

"He'll appreciate that."

"And you? Do you forgive me?"

"There is nothing to forgive, my son."

"I know how close you were, Daddy."

Jacob put his arm about his son's shoulders. It was a very long time since he had been "Daddy" to this big grown man who had been both the pride and the pain of Margaret's life, and of his.

Suddenly, unexpectedly, David dropped to his knees and took two fistfuls of earth and clenched them tightly then, after a while, he opened his hands and let the earth drop, two balls made by the pressure of his grip which collapsed on impact with the ground.

"Some of the desert people pray to the earth," he said, "like you and John – and Mama before she died – pray to your God."

"Some of the people here, too," Jacob said. "I expect all the people who are close to the earth do."

"You have served your God so well; so has she. . . ."

Jacob sensed the direction of his thoughts, he said: "We won't start a metaphysical argument here, will we?"

"No," David replied softly. "Not here; not now. But I wish your God had taken me instead."

Jacob felt comforted now, recognizing that which was part of his Margaret, and, more dimly remembered, part of his Grandma Sarah, in this grieving young man who was his son. Jacob thought: perhaps this *is* the moment for metaphysical argument; but I won't tell him so.

He laid his hand on his son's bowed head; fleetingly, there was the illusion of David as the little boy, of Margaret warning them not to be late for Mrs Kilu's special lunch.

"Time to go," Jacob said, and walked away, leaving David to have his moment alone with his dead mother. There was all the time in the world for Jacob to come up here to visit. Not for David; his life had been elsewhere for some time now.

He got into the jeep and waited; and after a while David came and joined him and they drove back to the house in silence.

The people they passed stopped what they were doing, bowed their heads in show of respect, or waved, or called out. For David this had always been part of the problem of growing up here. It was never private: everywhere he went, everything he did, everything he said, was measured against the reality of being the bishop's son; he was always under scrutiny. He was never allowed to be just himself; he resented it, and the resentment grew with time till it became part of the anger he vented against his parents, which grew, ultimately, into the alienation that drove him from this beautiful place. Now, in the moment of their grief, that resentment was absent and he responded to the people they passed, acknowledging their show of sympathy.

John Chitole met Jacob and David at the front door. He quickly sensed the peace between them.

"I took the liberty of bringing Michael Odera to lunch."

Jacob nodded; David smiled and took up his suitcase from under the table near the door.

"My old room?"

"Expect so," Jacob said and went to his own quarters.

When his father was out of earshot, David said to Chitole: "Don't worry, there won't be any fireworks."

"I'm glad. He needs peace now."

"He'll have it, with or without Michael Odera's presence."

"Trust you to read my motive."

"He did too; you didn't try to hide it."

"Peace at any price," Chitole said teasingly. Then, seriously: "You all right?"

"Yes; hurting but all right. We're all hurting, aren't we? See you soon."

David went to his room and Chitole went to the dining room where Michael Odera waited. Odera was another of the many bright young men from all over Uganda, and further afield, who had, over the years, gravitated to Jacob Brown's mission because it was known as a place managed by black people where ambitious young black men could work their way through school and college. Jacob had not found another woman with the drive and determination of Mrs Willis so the young women here had not fared as well. Medical facilities here were much better than they had been in Liberia so the mission had a clinic and dispensary and regular nurse, but no hospital and no resident doctor. But the flow of eager young men to the mission was greater than ever it had been in West Africa. All the mission's many enterprises were managed by the ones who had been trained in Business Management by a bright young Chicagoan, now gone. A few of the brightest ones had been sent abroad for further training. Some had become priests, some doctors, some were rising in the public service as opportunities for Africans opened up. It was easier for them here than in Kenya, or further down to the south, where white settler communities were resentful of the mission-trained Africans competing for their jobs, especially those with the kind of self-respect and self-assurance associated with the mission headed by the black bishop from

271

America. Michael Odera had become one of the small corps of bright young priests who, under the leadership of John Chitole, would eventually take over the work of Jacob Brown. When the time came for Chitole to go to America, Michael Odera would become the bishop's secretary, the effective administrative officer running the day-to-day affairs of the church and its outposts.

"There will be peace between them," Chitole told Odera.

"Then you do not need an inhibiting presence."

Chitole sipped at his cool banana beer and smiled. "Am I really that obvious? The bishop, David, now you, all see through my little scheme."

Odera threw back his head and laughed. "You wanted us to, Mr Schemer. Why?"

"To create other points and issues for thought and attention. To distract from the main issue. So they ask; what's he up to? Why's he doing this in such an obvious way; and they think about that for a while. It's a little distraction but it helps."

"So I can go and eat in peace."

"Stay and learn. Peace does not mean an absence of challenge and stimulation. Not with these two. Don't you want to know what David's doing, whose plane he's flying, what his plans are? Stay and learn."

"Learn what?" Jacob entered, fresh and wearing a clean shirt.

"What David's been doing," Chitole said.

"Whose plane he's flying," Odera said. "I didn't know he could fly a plane."

"Neither did I," Jacob mused. He took a bottle of chilled beer from the ice-bucket on the side table. He moved quickly to his seat at the head of the table.

Mrs Kilu and one of her helpers wheeled the big trolley into the room. David came in hard on their heels and joined Michael Odera at the side table while Mrs Kilu and the others transferred the food from the trolley to the long table. The room grew suffused with the rich aroma of highly seasoned food. Mrs Kilu had used her considerable cooking skills to their utmost to conjure up the kind of meal Missy used to prepare for her family on high days and holidays. There was crisply golden "jerk pork"; fricassee of chicken, Jamaica-American-style, floating in a rich coconut sauce; a large dish of mixed green vegetables, prepared as a savoury in the style of the American blacks of the Southern States at the time when meat was rarely available to them; and there were yam and sweet potatoes and a huge dish of rice, prepared Indian style, with each individual grain swollen to its maximum, dry, translucent.

"A wonderful feast, Mama Kilu!" David exclaimed.

She glowed when the young man put his arm about her. Then she left the room hurriedly, overcome by the fresh realization of the absence of Missy. Her seat at the other end of the long table was empty; no plate where hers usually was. The four men knew what had passed through Mrs Kilu's mind and for a moment they were silent. Then David raised his glass and turned to the empty chair and the empty place.

"To the absent one."

"The absent one," they echoed, each in his own individual way.

Jacob said grace, then gestured to them to help themselves.

As was the custom at this house, the talk began near the end of the main dish. Jacob looked at Michael Odera and said: "Michael wants to know about your plane, David."

"And when you learned to fly," Odera added.

"And all about what you're doing, of course," Chitole grinned. "Every little secret like 'Are you married yet? Or courting?' You know, everything."

David leaned back, looked at his father, raised one eyebrow: "And you, Dad? No questions from you?"

"Those will do for starters."

"OK. The plane belongs to the hospital where I work; it's on the edge of the desert. It's a very small, Arab-owned hospital ill-equipped and always short of drugs. So why a plane? Because our patients are in the desert and the desert is like a vast ocean, many, many times the size of your nearly twenty-seven thousand square-mile Lake Victoria. The desert is one reason for the plane. The doctors, there are usually four or five, all learn to fly. That's how I learned to fly. Oh, the pay is good. Anything else?"

"You say the desert is one reason. . . ?" Chitole said.

"The other is political," David said. "I don't think that will interest you."

"Since when?" Jacob asked.

David hesitated for a long time, then, apparently making up his mind, he looked at the others in turn, his father last of all, so that they were staring at each other when he said:

"A war is coming. Not the white settler agitation you hear about in the news; the Algerians themselves are preparing for war."

"Against France?" Jacob said.

"No; for their freedom. Against colonialism and the settlers. The settlers have got wind of something coming which is why they're agitating to break away from France and become like South Africa. If de Gaulle resists them for another year the Algerians will be ready."

"And you're involved in that?" Chitole asked. "More than in just being a doctor there?"

"Yes," David said quietly.

"Why?" Jacob demanded. "Why there? They're not even black."

"Black, brown, yellow; what difference does it make, Dad! They are getting ready to fight colonialism in the only way open to them. They are doing what the black people of South Africa should have done years ago before the British gave independence to the whites there. I know the times were different and the circumstances harder but now, after the settlers have consolidated their power, the black people are going to suffer much more grievously when they do rise against the whites. The settler-oppressor is always more brutal when he's in control. It's happening right next door. They're not yet in full control and look at what they're doing to the Kikuyu."

"Then why not join the Kikuyu?" Jacob murmured.

"Come, Dad! Outsiders can't get involved in a tribal war."

"But in an Arab war?" Jacob pressed. "If it's anti-colonialism then the Kikuyu uprising is of the same quality as your Arab friends."

"You're over-simplifying, Dad. Of course the Kikuyu rising is qualitatively the same in the sense that it's a struggle to reclaim stolen land. But what is it beyond that? When they have regained their land, what will they stand for?"

"What will your Algeria stand for?"

"For socialism, for equality for all their people, including their women; they will not go on mutilating their women and calling it circumcision. I still remember the horror with which Mama found out about this and told us. Do you remember?"

Jacob nodded. "But their women are behind the veil; just another, more psychological, form of subjugation."

"The emancipation of their women is part of the declared objectives of their struggle. I know; I've seen the draft of their independence constitution. I've met and talked to the leaders."

"All right," Jacob conceded. "So they will free their women and inaugurate an age of equality."

"More than that, Dad. They are going to reach outward to all exploited colonial people everywhere. Nasser of Egypt, in spite of his own difficulties, has already made contact with Nkrumah in the Gold Coast."

Jacob nodded again. "And as usual, all anybody has to do is offer friendship and black brother falls all over himself to seize on it, without question, without examining motive; always ready to sell his own for the illusion of a wider friendship. Always reaching outward to others, putting ourselves at their disposal, looking to others for our salvation."

David tried to suppress his mounting anger. "This is an alliance that is being forged; an alliance of the exploited of the earth. The only alternative to such an alliance through which we will take what is ours by force is your slow, painstaking, turn-the-other-cheek way. They make alliances for their wars, why shouldn't we?"

"But David. . . ." Chitole began.

David brushed the interruption aside. "I know you don't like to talk of war and violence but that's the only thing they understand. You may think Gandhi's non-violent morality changed the British Raj. Well, if the Japanese hadn't humiliated them and put the scare of their lives into them, none of old Gandhi's highmindedness would have meant a damn. They're only a little shrewder than the others and know how to let go while the going is good and still a little profitable. The French are going to hold on too long because they believe their own propaganda."

275

"But, David," Chitole persisted, "these alliances for war you talk of, they are alliances of one group of whites against another group of whites. They're not alliances of whites against the rest."

"Oh John! Aren't they? They are fighting among themselves for the spoils of their earlier alliances. They first conquered the rest in one great alliance of whites which gave them dominion of the whole earth."

Chitole raised his hand. "Now we must make a matching alliance of black and brown. . . ."

"And yellow."

". . . and yellow. We must make such an alliance to conquer. . . ."

"Repossess; not conquer."

". . . all right, repossess. To repossess, using their own methods, what they had taken from us. Then what, David? What is to prevent us from then splitting up into black against black, black against brown, black against yellow and every possible variation on these, to do what they just did in their second so-called great war. Is this what we really want? Is this the freedom to which we are heading?"

David closed his eyes and held himself in check. "He's really taught you well!"

Chitole raised his voice a little. "Rudeness to your father is no answer, David. And you're showing the contempt that you say only Europeans have for us. I resent that, I am sure Michael does too; but put it down to the heat of the moment. We respect and admire and love your father. He is our religious father; but we think for ourselves."

"Through his perspective," David said softly, refusing to be put on the defensive. "And you of all people, John, know I hold no contempt. How could I?"

Jacob began to say something but again Chitole raised his hand.

"Please, sir. . . . The question, David: Is this the freedom you want for us? To be like them? To end up in alliances against each other for the spoils after we've won?"

"You worry about after we've won when the battle's not even begun. Let's not worry about that until at least the battle has been carried to a point where victory is in sight."

"No, David," Jacob said. "What you fight for determines how you fight, and how you fight determines how you win, and all these, together, determine what comes after."

"That is your way," David said slowly, quietly. "I've not always shown it but I do respect you for the manner in which you have stuck to your way. It is good and noble but oh, Lord, it is so slow! It will take hundreds of years and they will go on resisting you, subtly, and with shows of friendship and concern for as long as they can, but brutally and savagely if they have to. They will not allow your independent Christian communities really to prevail today any more than they were prepared to allow your grandfather's church to prevail independently. They'll find a way of burning yours down just as they burned his down. They'll find a way of making your own people do it for them. And I and my generation cannot bear to wait for that and to watch that. The only thing they really understand and respect is power and force. How a great technological civilization can be based on the use of naked power, on violence and the threat of violence, is something for you highminded Christians to explore and lay bare. We, my generation, are going to meet it on its own terms. When I go into parts of the desert where the early fighting has already begun, I carry a machine gun slung over my shoulders and my doctor's bag of healing tricks in my free hand. All the doctors at that little hospital do. And we all know how to use those guns."

Chitole said: "You must think of what comes after. Using the gun is easy. You kill or are killed. But life is not as simple as that, for life goes on after you kill or are killed; your life is part of the lives of all the people who live, who ever lived, and who will live in the future; and how each one of us lives and dies contributes to the quality of the stream of all life. You know this so you must think of what comes after."

"What could be more important than that we should reclaim our personhood?" David demanded. "They will not concede it; so you claim it by whatever method necessary. Their commitment to force and violence dictates your method. Their 'gentle-Jesus-meek-and-mild' religion inhibits, as it is intended to, your use of that method. Oh, I concede that your church is exposing and countering their blatant use of the teachings of Christ. Your Christ is a revolutionary; I accept that. But he walked the earth when the power equation was rather simpler than it now is. And his teachings were always open to the kind of manipulation we are now so familiar with. I don't think your Christ would be against my carrying a machine-gun. I think he would be sad at the need for it, sad at the lives to be lost, but I don't think he would oppose it. Do you?"

"I'm inclined to agree with you," Chitole said. "But he would be concerned with what comes after. Of that I'm certain." Chitole looked quickly at his bishop. The expression in Jacob's eyes reassured him.

"What comes after is important and is determined by how you fight," Jacob said. "If you fight and are defeated, what happens to the cause of black folk? If you are victorious, will the Arabs, later on, come to the aid of the black folk as you now go to their aid?"

"You've overlooked one part to it," David said. "I – and there are quite a few others like me – am not going to 'their' aid. I, and we, are going to our aid. I had never used a machine-gun before; I had never handled grenades before; I had never assembled bombs before; I had never been able to disable a strong man with one blow before; I had never flown a plane before. I can do all these things now. They have taught me to do these things and, as I say, I am not the only black person working and learning with them. So it isn't a one-way street. They are sharing their knowledge of the skills of war with us; they are teaching us to speak eloquently and with deadly skill in the only language whites respect. That's how another black man up there, young fellow from the French West Indies who's also a doctor, described it. Bit like you, John, small, quiet, brainy man; bit sickly, though; but you should see the skill and speed with which he can use a machine-gun!"

"And what comes after this deadly skill?" Jacob wondered aloud. "If you become so good at it that you speak of it in this beautiful language, if killing in itself becomes an act of purification, will you be able to stop killing when this particular reason for it is all over, after you have won your independence? The Europeans seem unable to stop; their history in the last few centuries has become an endless bloodletting with occasional pauses for rebuilding their manpower needs and rearming themselves. Is this where we are going? Is this what you want?"

"Of course not; you know that!"

"Not consciously, perhaps," Jacob said. "I'm sure they didn't want to be trapped in an endless cycle of wars; but it happened."

"So how do you avoid it?" Chitole asked.

Jacob said: "They talked once of beating their swords into ploughshares. Now they use bombs and tanks; how do you beat those into ploughshares? Or the atom bombs they dropped on those Japanese cities? The Japanese are not white; the next targets will be the white communists, perhaps, or the white capitalists, or the white this or the white that. It began with the 'little yellow guys'. It won't end there. Are you saying we are so superior in understanding and feeling that we can step on to this same path of violence and somehow avoid coming out at the other end just like them?"

"Of course not." David felt trapped.

"Then how do you avoid it?" Chitole repeated.

"We take our chances. We learn from their mistakes and try not to repeat them. What you are suggesting would condemn us to another century or more of colonialism and domination. That is the alternative to not taking up the gun against them."

"We are not saying you must not take up the gun," Chitole said. Then, looking quickly at Jacob, he went on: "At least I'm not saying that. I don't think your father is either. What I am saying is that if you are not conscious of it, if it is not part of your planning, you have no hope of avoiding ending up where they now are, in an endless cycle of wars and preparations for war."

"I would go further, John," Jacob said. "I would say that unless those who have to use the gun hate what they have to do, they will, sooner or later, come to joy in the use of the gun for itself, and then they will become like the enemy they fight. There can be no greater moral defeat than ending up perpetuating that which you fight against."

"What the heck are you two saying!" David exploded. "War as a decent Christian moral affair! Killing with compassion! Hating what you have to do because it is right! We'll never win if we use our guns on your highminded terms! I love you both for your highmindedness but you are wrong! We can never win like that! We must risk your fears and hope that when the war is over and we are free, there will be people like you around to remind us of the evils of war and why we had to fight in the first place, and point us in another direction. Now, we must fight them on the only terms they respect; and that we will do, whatever the price."

Chitole began to reply but Jacob held up his hand with his commanding air of a bishop; so Chitole sat back and held his peace.

"That is as much as we can hope for, John. For him to hope we will be around, or some of us, when their fighting is over. The hope and the promise is that they would heed our pointing them in another direction."

"Will they listen?" Chitole pondered aloud.

"I think so," David said; then, more uncertainly: "I hope they do."

"We cannot ask for more," Jacob said, as Mrs Kilu and her helpers came in to clear the table.

Michael Odera thanked Chitole with his eyes, chatted with David for a while, then slipped away to tend to the mission's business. A strong mood of goodwill flowed between Jacob, Chitole and David making them unwilling to break up the little gathering. The pressure and intensity had gone out of it. They wandered on to the verandah, then on to the sprawling lawn with its broad-bladed grass that clung low to the earth and hardly ever needed to be cut. David slipped one arm through his father's and the other through Chitole's.

They were all acutely conscious of the absence of Margaret.

"I've only got tomorrow," David said, thinking of all the special things he had shared with his mother. "Can we make a safari to the mountain?"

"Yes," Jacob said. "All right with you, John?"

"Yes," Chitole said. "We'll start at dawn."

"Good," David said. "I'm eager to see it again."

Jacob and Chitole knew why. A safari to the slopes of Mount Elgon had always been a special holiday treat Margaret laid on for him whenever David returned from college or university or, later, from further travels, about which he did not always want to talk.

At its base the mountain is over four thousand feet above sea level, so when they were two thousand feet up its slope there was a sharp chill to the morning air. It was an easy, steady climb with the clouds backing off and retreating higher and higher up the mountain as they advanced. They had hired two villagers from the settlement at the foot of the mountain to carry their hamper and for any heavy clearing that might be needed. None was, and the familiar path was only slightly overgrown. The two villagers marched ahead, the hamper between them, casually swinging their machetes, called *pangas* here, at the occasional vine hanging over the path. When they were three thousand feet up, over seven thousand feet above sea level, the climate changed. The rich smell of wood and leaf decay gave way to a sharp dryness in the air. The carriers loosened the blanket each had carried slung across his shoulder to make a warm enveloping cloak. David put on his airman's leather jacket; Jacob and Chitole pulled on thick long-sleeved sweaters.

The earth below, from this vantage point, was a thing of unutterable green beauty. Far to the west, sunlight struck one of the many small rivers, offshoots of the great lake, which all finally converged to start the great Nile on its way through the lowlands of Egypt. At certain angles, the sun and the water made flashing lights, as if someone were signalling.

At three thousand five hundred feet they all relaxed. Wild creatures, leopards and lions, were not likely to be this high up; and the big apes of the high mountains would avoid men as long as men let them be. They were not aggressive, would not attack unless threatened.

The mountain path veered to the right in a long upward arc and brought them to a narrow ledge, and the dry northern plains of Kenya lay below them, an enormous desolate stretch of parched earth in the far distance. Nearer the mountain and to the south and south-east the Kenyan land was more inviting and fertile. The Kenyan town of Kitale was a misty dot in the clear morning light.

They had all stopped to look. This had always been one of Margaret's favourite look-out points.

"Hard to believe all the killings going on there," Jacob said.

"That's the ugly reality," David said.

One of the carriers said, "Bwana," between a cry and a whisper, which made them all turn. And there in front of them on the narrow pathway, were two tall gaunt, wild-eyed men, dressed in rags, training modern rifles on them.

"Don't anyone move," David said softly. Then, loudly in Swahili. "Greetings, warriors of Kenya. We come in peace. You are far from your battlefield."

"Then go in peace," one of them said. "Go and speak not of this."

In Kikuyu, which none of Jacob's party understood, the other said: "They must die or we will all be discovered. Our sick will be discovered."

"No," the first one said in Kikuyu. "We do not kill senselessly." In Swahili he said to David: "Why are you here?"

"We visit a shrine," David said. "A shrine for my mother. I am a fighter too and I may not return."

"Then go before we kill you."

"Not till I have seen the shrine. Listen! I am a doctor, a healer. I see you have a bullet wound that has mended itself with the bullet still inside your body. You will die if it is not removed."

"We will all die," the second one cut in. "You will die now."

"No!" the first one said as the second raised his rifle.

"Not yet!" a third voice snapped in Swahili. The second one lowered his rifle.

A tall thin man, leaning on two stout sticks, an officer's cap of the type worn by the British military at an angle on his head, an officer's handgun dangling on his forefinger, hobbled painfully into view.

"Who are you?" he demanded in English.

"Not enemies," David said.

"What do you want?"

"I told him we. . . ."

"There is no sign of any burial place. You lie about your shrine."

They've found the place, David thought. Aloud he said: "That place is our shrine. You found some tins of food there. You also found two bottles of *waragi*. That is the shrine because some of the best days of my life were spent here. My mother, who has just died, parted from me in peace for the last time at this place."

282

"You are a doctor?"

"Yes; and you need one badly."

David moved forward.

"Stop!" the man raised the handgun. The second of the two warriors put his rifle to his shoulder.

David kept going forward till he was close to the man. There was an awful stench about him.

"You need my help."

"Don't shoot," the man ordered, lowering his gun. He turned and hobbled back to the shallow cave, followed by David, Jacob and Chitole.

It was when they reached the cave that they discovered it had become the hiding place for a badly wounded and much wanted general of the Mau Mau on whom the Kenyan authorities had placed a high price. Another healthier-looking though equally foul-smelling younger man, armed with a snub-nosed automatic rifle, stood guard over the general. The young guard seemed ready to let go a volley at the intruders till the man on crutches snapped at him in Kikuyu; he relaxed, stepped back.

David said: "Stay back," to his father and Chitole. Taking a deep breath he went into the cave and pulled back the pile of smelly rags and skins that covered the general's body. The man was far gone, his eyes dulled, consciousness of his surroundings coming and going. David choked back the waves of nausea as he examined the man.

"We need medicine," David said at last, "as quickly as possible or he'll die."

"How quickly's that?" Chitole asked, from the cave entrance.

"I don't know. It may be too late already but we must try."

"Then I'll go and get what you want. If he doesn't the others will need the help."

"Is it safe?" the man on the crutches asked. "Will he come back?"

"He won't betray you," David said. "He'll come back."

The man pointed at the two bearers with his gun. "They must stay or everyone in their village will know."

"If they do not return the men of the village will climb the mountain to find them. Better to let them go down." Chitole gazed steadily into the young officer's eyes.

"They will surely betray us," the officer insisted.

"They will not," Chitole said. "They are of our church. They will promise the bishop."

"Yes," Jacob said. "I am the bishop. I hear you hate missionaries. These men will promise, if I ask them to, and keep their promise."

"The bishop," the ragged officer mused. "The one from America?"

"Yes."

"The one they refused to allow to start a church and school in our country?"

"Yes."

"I remember it. I was a teacher then; in our independent schools."

Jacob knew about the network of independent Kikuyu schools the colonial authorities were so bitterly opposed to. "Teacher turned soldier," Jacob said. "Who teaches now?"

"They ordered the schools closed. Make your men promise."

"And make haste," David added.

Jacob spoke to the carriers who understood some English; but to make sure Chitole translated into their dialect.

"These, as you know, are some of the warriors fighting for their land over there. They are, as you can see, wounded, and the one there is a high officer. My son, the doctor, will help to try and heal them; but he needs medicine. There is no wrong in a man fighting for what he has been robbed of. We are for peace always; but there are times when peace is not possible. One such time is when a people are robbed of their land; then they either fight or give up their manhood. These have chosen to fight; it is their choice and their decision; it is a choice and a decision we must respect for these are of our people. So my son, the doctor, must try to heal them; and you must keep silent about what you have seen here this day. I wish you to tell no one about it for a very long time, not even the mother of your children when you lie with her. Not for a long time."

"Do you understand?" Chitole ended. "Do you understand clearly what the bishop wishes? Will you give him this promise?"

284

The men bowed their heads in front of their bishop and made the promise.

David and the others moved away from the entrance to the cave and the stench of festering wounds. He quickly wrote a list of his needs and gave it to Chitole. They discussed the timing of getting down and of returning with the medicine. If they moved fast they could get to the foot of the mountain in a little over an hour; another hour and a half to get to the mission; half an hour to get what was needed. Three hours there and three hours back; six hours, not allowing any margin for any unexpected delays or hold-ups. So make it seven hours. It was near on eleven in the morning now. So Chitole should be back with the needed supplies between five and six in the evening. David reminded him that the bearers would be needed again to carry the supplies up.

Jacob said: "I'll stay here and help David till you return."

"I don't think that's wise," Chitole said. "All sorts of people would be curious about a daylong absence of the bishop."

"We're on safari; everyone will know that."

"And your secretary returns without you, and gathers up supplies and goes back somewhere again. That is bound to make them ask: where? If you're back at the mission what I take and where I go has less significance."

"John's right," David said.

"All right," Jacob nodded. "You take care."

"Don't worry. Hurry back, John."

They left the hamper of food and drink and water with David and hurried down the mountain in the bracing morning air, the Kenyan Rift Valley to the left of them and running all the way to the Sudan; the gently rolling highlands far below to the right of them.

David opened the well-stocked hamper and fed the four Kikuyu who were on their feet; they were desperately hungry and wanted to gobble down all the food they saw. Indeed, the youngster with the automatic rifle wanted to forcibly take what he wanted and even defied the orders from the former teacher to desist. There was a difficult moment till David relieved him of the gun. The other two instinctively wanted to help their fellow fighter; the handgun of the ex-teacher held them at bay long enough for David to do the disarming. Disarmed, the young man became peaceful and co-operative; he remained so even after the automatic rifle was returned to him. He was, after all, the designated bodyguard of the wounded general and the special gun was his badge of authority. David's ability to relieve an armed man of his gun established his authority; they obeyed his orders when he told them to get bush and sweep out the cave, make a fire to smoke out the insects, and move the general out into the sunlight and air his foul-smelling bedding.

They made a small fire and David diced up bits of chicken and tomato and lettuce to make a broth which he fed the general in small sips. Then, very carefully, since all he had was a knife and some pieces of cloth, he began to attend to their wounds, dealing with the easier ones first, those that needed to be opened to drain off the pus. He extracted two bullets near the surface of the skin: one from one man's shoulder, the other from high up in another's thigh. The worst wounds had to await the return of Chitole. The ex-teacher hobbled away and returned ten minutes later with a fat cactus-type aloe which smelled of stewed beef and dripped a thick transparent gum.

He offered it to David: "It seals cuts."

David sniffed it, tasted it, applied a bit to his own skin and felt it dry into a firm flexible coating.

"We used it whenever a student got cut; it stops the bleeding and it heals. If I had not put this on the general's wounds he would have died of bleeding."

So David used the gum from the aloe as bandage and tackled some of the more serious wounds.

About noon a plane appeared in the Kenyan skies coming from the direction of Kitale. They put out the fire, spread bush over it, moved the general and all their supplies into the shelter of the cave and took cover themselves. As it neared the mountain the plane climbed, to about twenty thousand feet, David judged, then swung north-eastward, up the Rift Valley, as though in the direction of Lake Rudolph in the far north. But then, just where the main road from Kitale to the north crossed briefly over into Uganda, the plane, a tiny dot now, banked sharply and made an eastward and then south-eastward curve that would carry it down to the White Highlands of Kenya.

"It comes this time and just before sunset," the ex-teacher said. "Every day."

"It flies too high for them to really see," David said. "You don't see much at that height."

"That's better for us." The ex-teacher smiled for the first time.

"What's your name?" David asked, adding: "I'm David."

"I am Wathugu. You can call me Joe."

"I prefer Wathugu," David said.

"And you can say it!" Wathugu laughed.

David thought: And just a couple of hours ago they were wild animals ready to kill. I know a Kikuyu called Wathugu, not a Mau Mau; a man who had been a teacher now compelled to fight. He turned to Wathugu.

"If they didn't close your schools would you have fought?"

"I don't know. They did close the schools, I did fight."

"All the teachers?"

"No. Some joined the British and we killed them."

"Why?" David asked, knowing the answer.

"As a warning to others. You know about the chief we had to kill. We had to kill him or many people would have co-operated."

"And you personally? Is that why you fight?"

"Yes. Unless you are assigned another task you must fight. That is how it is. I cannot stay home with my wife and four children while others fight. They will not allow it; and I will not agree to another man staying home while I fight. We must all do it or do the assigned task."

A tribe at war, David thought; the only issue at stake, ownership of the land: the land is the life of the tribe.

"And after you've won?"

"The land will be ours."

"And what then?"

"What do you mean? When the land is ours it will be over."

"Nothing more?"

"We will own the land; we will work the land; we will be free."

"You'll be the tribe that won the war," David murmured. "But I don't think it will be over, my friend, Wathugu."

287

"For us, it will be," Wathugu insisted. "For me it will be."

"I will go home to my village," the youngster who had first spoken to Jacob's party said. "It is near Fort Hall and my mother is looking after the one who will be my wife."

So very human now, David thought, and wondered if the British ever saw them thus.

"It may be a long time," he said. "The Englishman is a fierce fighter and they want to hold your land."

"No matter how long," the teacher said, "we will win; they have hurt us too much; we cannot make peace now till we win."

"Many will die," David said.

"Many have died," Wathugu said. He rolled on his side and stretched himself out at the mouth of the cave. The two with the rifle went some distance down the narrow mountain path and made themselves comfortable on the ground. The young bodyguard with the special automatic rifle propped himself up against the wall of the entrance to the cave, on duty even as he dozed off in the midday sun.

They've not asked me a single thing, David thought. They're not interested in anything outside their own special world. . . .

David made himself comfortable under a shade tree and immediately fell asleep. The sun was all over the land now, over the mountain too. There was no breeze and, seemingly, very little cool air even up here. The special bodyguard aroused himself sufficiently to remove the covering from the general when the heat was at its greatest and the air at its stillest.

The stillness in the atmosphere lasted a little over an hour; then it was gone. The air moved again; a cool freshness came over the mountain and all things on it. The people on the mountainside woke as from a trance. The bodyguard replaced the covering over his general. David got up and made it a little lighter. Wathugu hobbled over to the place where they had used big broad leaves and vines to fashion a watercourse which channelled drips of water from the higher vegetation into a big calabash; the calabash was half full. He dipped both hands into the water, scooped out some, drank and dashed the remains over his face.

288

David followed him and said: "It is safer and healthier to use a utensil." Then he saw the hollowed-out dried nut beside the calabash. "I see you have one. You should use it. Your hands and fingernails can carry germs."

"We used it at the start," Wathugu said.

"Use it again. All the time. See that everybody does."

Wathugu nodded and turned away.

I've offended him, David thought. But they must be clean if they are to survive. He went back to the cave mouth, called them together and lectured them on the importance of cleanliness for survival. They were not interested till he said: "That is the only way you will grow well and strong enough to fight again." They paid close attention after that.

The day dragged on, a long day, one of the longest David had lived through. Longer even than that terrible day he had spent in the stinking fetid jail cell in Algiers when he was picked up with a group of Arab revolutionaries by the Algiers political police. Only his stubborn bluff that he was an American tourist and the fact that somebody at the American consulate knew of Bishop Jacob Brown had saved him. That and the American passport his mother had insisted he should have. He never saw any of those Arab revolutionaries again. Until this day, that had been the longest day of his life. Then, there was waiting charged with fear: the fear of not knowing what would happen, the fear that you may not be able to stand up to what might happen. There had been reports of brutal torturing. Now there was no fear to charge the long day with tension, and now you were more sure of yourself than you were then. The absence of tension made this long day tediously, doubly longer than that other. . . .

They heard them coming from a long way down as the sun was setting. Each word spoken, no matter how softly, rose up to them. Each sound – each time a small stone was dislodged and rolled against another, each time a dry twig snapped underfoot – carried up to them in the still air. This is how the small band of Kikuyu must have heard them when they came up in the morning, David thought. He made a mental note to tell others how well sound travels, especially upward, in high altitudes; could make all the difference between life and death.

The four Kikuyu were tense and alert now, the first two separating and moving lightfootedly, half-crouching, to meet the newcomers.

"No!" David whispered. "Those are my people."

"Not sure," Wathugu said softly. "Must be on guard."

"Give me your gun."

Wathugu hesitated. David held out his hand. The two covering the path stopped and turned their heads to see. The young bodyguard caressed his automatic rifle nervously. Wathugu closed his eyes then opened them and handed David his gun. David signalled the other two back. They stood their ground, but passively now, without any sign of hostility. He went past them, down the path, lightly, looking at the ground each time before putting down his foot.

"You gave him your gun," the second Kikuyu accused Wathugu.

"He could have taken it," the bodyguard said. "He's a fighter, that one; remember how he took my gun?"

"There are four of us!" the other snapped back.

"And he could have killed us all when he had my gun," the bodyguard whispered.

"And he did not," Wathugu said.

"He is not our enemy," the first soldier said. "Listen. . . ."

The sounds from the bottom grew fainter so that they had to strain to hear them. There was no sound of David. Wathugu went into the cave and returned with the general's gun in his hand. He was sure he could trust David, at least he thought he was sure, but they had to be prepared, just in case: just in case they were enemies and got the better of David.

"On guard!" he whispered.

The two soldiers seemed to fade into the bush. The bodyguard went down on one knee. Wathugu leaned his back against the cave wall entrance, let go of his right-hand support and waited, gun hanging down in his hand, finger on the trigger.

Then the voice rose to them, softly, tinged with tension.

"David! David!"

290

Then David's voice, nearer but a goodly distance down: "John! Everything all right?"

Then Chitole's voice, more at ease: "Yes."

"You hear, Kikuyu warriors?" David's voice floated up to them.

"We hear, my brother," Wathugu called out.

They relaxed and waited for John Chitole with his two bearers and the supplies. Nightfall was an hour, or slightly more, away.

David went to work immediately Chitole arrived. He pumped a massive dose of antibiotics into the general, then he opened the biggest and most serious of his wounds. He was lucky and got out the two bullets in the man's side and shoulder with relative ease. He cleaned and sterilized the wounds and bound them. The general should be all right. Then he attended to the others, removing bullets, cleaning out the wounds, binding them up. It looked as though they had all received their wounds at the same time in a very close encounter. Night fell and David completed his task an hour after dark by the light of a torch held by John Chitole. At last it was all over. In four or five weeks, this group of five Kikuyu warriors would, if their hunters did not catch up with them before then, return to their bush army to carry on the war.

At parting, Wathugu said:

"Will you come back to change the bandages, as they do in hospital?"

"No," David said. "I must leave in the morning to go to my war. A bigger war than yours though it has not yet started properly."

"No war is bigger than any other," Wathugu said. "Men die in wars. There are no bigger or smaller deaths."

"True, but the reasons are different. Some fight and die for land and to take back what has been taken from them, as you are doing. Others fight for king and country and empire. Yet others fight for a vision, for an idea that would make the world a better place."

"What kind of idea?" Wathugu asked. "The world is what the world is. How can you make it a better place? Or a worse place?"

Listening, Chitole smiled to himself in the dark.

"Time to go, David. You haven't got the time to settle this one."

"Yes," David sighed and offered his hand.

Wathugu took it. Then the other three each shook David's hand, each calling out his own name as he did so. The general had gone into a deep drugged sleep. David looked at him for the last time, checking him for fever. "He should feel better in the morning," he told Wathugu.

"We are grateful," Wathugu said. "I hope we meet again when the land is ours. If we do, I will make a great feast for you."

"I would like that," David said.

"Come, David," Chitole called and led the way down the dark path, the still apprehensive bearers close on his heels. For them an ordinary day's safari which would earn them a few shillings had turned into a nightmare experience about which their bishop had ordered them not to talk; their friendly mountain had changed to a sinister place harbouring the fierce Kikuyu who were at war with the white men of their country.

The Kikuyu warriors watched till David and his companions faded into the darkness. Then they listened until the sound of their going too, was at an end, until the mountain was shrouded in its own silence again.

Wathugu said: "One will watch till moonrise while the others rest. When the light is clear enough we will leave this place. It is no longer safe. We will find another, higher place. We have enough to eat and drink, enough medicine to last till we are ready to return, if we use it with care. That is how it will be."

They agreed among themselves who should take the first watch. The rest went to sleep, each with his weapon in his hand.

It was pitch dark when Chitole, David and the bearers reached the foot of the mountain. They were glad to be down safely without having encountered any of the night prowlers, especially the silent leopard. They had no weapon other than the bearers' pangas. David had given back Wathugu's gun, and even though there were four of them the darkness would give a leopard an overwhelming advantage; so the sight of the bishop's limousine brought great relief. They dropped the bearers on the edge of their village. Chitole counted out ten East African shillings for each and each protested that it was too much, too great a fortune for a small work.

"Then share it with your church," Chitole advised. "But remember your promise not to speak of this thing."

The bearers repeated their promise, saluted, and slipped away to the security of their village and their homes. Chitole started the car again, put on its bright lights and took the road to the mission.

"They will talk," Chitole said, half-turning his head to David. "Not immediately, not because they intend to, but they will talk."

"I know," David said. "I expect our friends up there are already moving. It is one of the rules of survival."

"I thought they trusted you."

"I think they do."

"Of course you're not the only one they have to worry about."

"They would have moved even if I were."

"Then why the request for you to return?"

"For information mainly; and even if I'd said yes they would have moved. Someone would have met me at some unexpected point and taken me to their new hiding place. I would have treated them and they would have moved again as soon as I had gone."

"Rules of survival?"

"Yes."

"And human trust? And community of interest? And the unity of the freedom fighters of which you boasted?" There was a bitter teasing edge to Chitole's voice.

"Think, John!" David exploded. "Use your imagination! Supposing we had come down into the waiting arms of a bunch of the King's African Rifles for whom there are still no territorial boundaries in East Africa, I'm not sure that you and I and our bearers would have been able indefinitely to resist pressure to tell where we had come from and who was up there. Nothing to do with trust; just a matter of survival. You say 'What if so and so happens?' and you act accordingly; you do not say 'I trust so-and-so so I will not worry!'"

"That what all of you are taught in these political–military schools of yours?"

"Ours is just a variation of what is taught to all men who have to kill or be killed. Our friends up there know it. That's why they're probably moving now, or will be as soon as they can see. That's why I wanted you to bring all that food and drink."

"Will they make it?"

"I think so. The scouting plane that came today flew too high ever to see them. They say it always does and it's regular."

Chitole said, as though to himself: "It frightens me. It's all so calculated, without feeling."

"It has to be," David said, sinking down deeper into the comfortable seat. He closed his eyes, relaxed mind and body.

"Sleep," Chitole said, and stepped on the accelerator, making the big car surge forward through the night. The road was straight and wide and Chitole knew it well. The powerful headlights lit it up brightly for miles ahead. Chitole turned on the shortwave radio and a voice in London told him what was going on in the rest of the world.

. . . The Kabaka, whom the British called King Freddie, had started his exile in London. . . . There were mass arrests of blacks in South Africa as the anti-apartheid Defiance Campaign moved to a climax. And there was trouble between the French Government and the white settlers of Algeria and the first stirring of the coming war in which David was involved. . . .

He switched the dial nearer home and a voice on Kenya's radio, in Swahili, invited members of the Mau Mau to lay down their arms and surrender and turn away from the evil customs into which they had been misled before they were destroyed, as they surely would be; those who laid down their arms and turned themselves in would be rewarded with many shillings. He switched the dial again and picked up soft French music from Radio Brazzaville. He left it there as the car sped through the night. A huge continent of black people and the only sounds in the African air were the sounds made by whites. He would talk to the bishop about this. Perhaps they should experiment with a private mission radio station. He would get young Odera to look into the laws about broadcasting.

The land, meanwhile, was changing. The darkness eased so that Chitole began to see shapes flashing past, blurred at first, but gradually more clearly defined till he could identify trees, an isolated homestead, a circular cluster of huts signifying a village. Then the moon rose and the African earth lay bathed, all its details mutedly visible, in the soft cold light. Chitole dipped the very bright light and slowed down as he entered the village at the foot of the hills on which the mission stood.

"We're home," David said.

Jacob was waiting for them for supper. They washed and changed quickly and joined him. Mrs Kilu supervised the bringing of the food then left to take care of her own family.

When they were alone Jacob asked: "Are they all right?"

"Yes," David said.

"The leader too? The one you thought might die?"

"Once the stench and filth were removed he wasn't as bad as he seemed. The wounds had festered badly, but the antibiotics will take care of that."

"And you?" Jacob was surprised at the absence of any sign of tiredness or tension in David. Chitole was clearly and obviously tired. Jacob had never seen David at work, never thought of him in any other way than as his and Margaret's son. Today he had seen David for the first time as he would see any other man. This doctor man who dealt calmly and firmly with armed men was wholly admirable, and made him feel proud to have anything to do with him. "Still leaving tomorrow?"

"I have to," David said. "That was the condition on which I was allowed to come."

"How near is this war of yours?" Chitole asked.

"Almost too near. We are not sufficiently prepared to avoid taking heavy losses, especially in the beginning."

"And you will go into the fighting line?" Jacob asked, trying to hide his anxiety.

"There'll be no lines, Daddy. It's the kind of war they are fighting in Vietnam; the only kind of war the people of our world can hope to win against the armies of the rich imperial powers. The frontline is everywhere and nowhere."

"Then why can't you do your fighting here? As you did up

295

there on the mountain. Why not have a secret hospital for the wounded Mau Mau?"

"Would you support that?" David stared at his father.

Jacob looked at Chitole, a small smile tugged at his lips.

"No. Not officially."

"But we can find medical supplies and raise money and provide food," Chitole said.

David continued staring at his father.

"And you Bishop Jacob Brown, and you Reverend John Chitole, you two would do that?"

"If we have to," Chitole said.

"You heard the man," Jacob said. "Some people have weird notions about Christianity. I've told you all again and again and still you won't believe it: my Lord is the greatest and the finest revolutionary who ever lived. I learned that from my Grandma Sarah who had been a slave."

"Oh yes," David said. "Great-Grandma Sarah."

He raised his glass of sparkling banana beer, first offering a silent toast to his father, then to John Chitole. Then, eyes turned skyward, only half in jest, to Great-Grandma Sarah.

"So will you try that hospital here?" Jacob pressed.

David shook his head. "Only up there that we are going to learn the skills and tactics which we must use if we are ever to defeat the South African racists. Only there, Daddy, can we learn for Africa what Vietnam is teaching the people of Asia about fighting for freedom. Do you see?"

"All right David. If you must, you must."

"I'm still worried about what comes after," Chitole said.

"And still you'd help," David mused.

"If we have to," Chitole said. "I thought of something on the way," Chitole spoke to Jacob now. "Wouldn't it be good if the mission could have its own private radio station?"

"They won't let us, John," Jacob said.

"No harm in trying," Chitole said. "I thought I'd get young Odera to look into it. What's wrong with our having a good Christian radio station on which people can hear their own voices?"

"Try it," Jacob said.

David roared with laughter, caught between awe and despair at the simple directness with which these two approached complex and difficult problems. Here they were proposing as no big thing a breakthrough in imperial control of subject minds.

"Better for you to set up a secret transmitter on the mountain," he suggested. "They'll never allow a mission radio station."

"The fact that we tried might in itself be good news," Chitole said.

"It's a waste of time, but good luck," David said.

Jacob pushed back his chair and got up. He always took a stroll after dinner.

"Anybody for a walk?" he invited.

"Yes," David said.

"I'll turn in," Chitole said. Since Margaret's death he had moved into the guest room so that Jacob should not be completely alone in the house at night. There were things the household helpers who stayed overnight could not be expected to do. But he would soon be able to return to his own cottage. These two needed to be alone now; he watched them go out of the French windows and walk away into the moonlit night.

"Crack of dawn tomorrow!" David called back.

Chitole rang the little bell for the night helper and went to bed.

They reached the Tororo airstrip before dawn but the Welshman, Jones, was there already. He had filled the tanks and warmed the engine and taxied the plane to the runway.

"It's a little beauty!" the Welshman exclaimed. "And what power! Bit like our wartime Spitfires. I've done everything. Here's your checklist."

David took the list and he and Jones went over the plane once more, checking everything Jones had already checked and serviced. At last they were done and the young Welshman glowed when David expressed his satisfaction and appreciation. The bill, when David gave it to Chitole, looked enormous, but David said it was much less than he had expected. He

297

handed Chitole a fat wad of US dollar bills of high denomination.

"A last chore, dear John. Convert and pay and put up the rest. Okay? Time to go now. . . . Thanks again, Jones. You're a firstclass man."

"Any time," Jones said, walking some distance away so the friends could part in privacy.

David and Chitole looked at each other in the dawn light, not knowing when they would meet again, not knowing if they would meet again.

"Take care of yourself," Chitole said. "You're all he has now."

"No. He has you, John; you and all the others who love him so deeply."

"Yes; but there's nothing quite like family. So you take care. I'll write regularly. I'll let you know everything important. He wants me to go to America; Michael would have to keep in touch then till I return. You know I want him to stay here even if I succeed him."

"He won't be happy anywhere else. I'm not sure even Jamaica could replace this now. His roots have gone too deep: his child was born here, his woman is buried here, and he has served most of his life here."

"Then we are agreed," Chitole said.

"Did you doubt it?"

"No. But it had to be spoken. A man can change."

"Very little, dear John. Perhaps, if I'm lucky, I'll return for this is my home too."

"That would be very good, David. Now I can dream of a mission hospital at the foot of the mountain, one day."

"I don't like fighting any more than you or he does. But your way is so terribly slow. I see no other way."

We will not argue now, Chitole decided.

"Please try to be lucky and come back to us. . . . That address will reach you always?"

"Always; remind Michael all letters that pass through have to be opened."

"I will."

"I'll try to be lucky. I want to see him again and talk to him again. We were only just beginning to talk again. It took my mother's death to bring us together again. Look after him for me.

And get him a puppy from me for Christmas. He loved dogs as a boy in Jamaica. A female puppy, a bitch.''

''We will.''

The time of parting had come. They held each other in tight embrace. Then they separated. David Brown swung about, climbed into the small plane. Chitole moved back from the runway to the point where Jones waited. Suddenly, the plane roared into life; it moved forward, slowly at first, then gathered speed as though chased by some terrible force. Then it rose from the earth and soared into the sky, taking a northward direction.

''Please be lucky,'' Chitole murmured as the plane faded and blended into the sky.

''Beg your pardon?'' Jones asked.

''Nothing,'' Chitole said. ''Just a thought and a prayer. Will the mission cheque be all right, Mr Jones?''

''Yes, sir.''

They walked to the little office.

''And we will use that mechanic's shop of yours if you will agree to train some of our young boys. You could have all the mission's work.''

''That would be wonderful!''

''Good. The Reverend Michael Odera will come and discuss the details with you one day soon. Remember the condition is that you really train our young people. You don't have to pay them. We'll pay you for the training as well as giving you our work.''

Chitole wrote a cheque to cover David's bill then he got into the limousine and headed back to the mission. There was much to do, much to be reviewed. David had taken up most of his time over the past two days. There were two trips to deal with the problems left by the defaulting priests in those outstations. And there was the preparation for when he left for America. Young Odera would have to be very carefully rehearsed so that not too much detail had to be referred to the bishop. The bishop had to spend more time preparing the young men for the priesthood if the work of the church was to continue to bear fruit in the difficult days ahead.

Jacob Brown sat at his big mission office desk writing a letter to his old friend Dr Daniel Lee, Medical Director of the Mission Hospital in Liberia. The outer office was quiet. Miss Batari and her clerical assistants had not yet arrived. The wall clock showed that it was a little before seven. He ignored his little portable typewriter and wrote by hand:

Dear Dan, It was good to get your cable. Your words of comfort, and those of so many others from all over the world, made the grief a little more bearable. And David came back, which also helped greatly. I will put it all down for you in detail in our regular once-a-year letter at Christmas, which is just around the corner. I wish you were here to comfort an old friend in his hour of greatest need. But as I write it I realize the selfishness of the wish. I should really be grateful and happy instead of miserable and depressed. We have shared many wonderful years and I think we have built something good and lasting and Christian here, though I had to nip in the bud what could easily have developed into a Nine-Nights orgy. The women loved her so very much (they all called her Missy, her childhood American nickname) and I gather there is a move afoot to call the church women's guild the Missy Guild! I'm going to have to squash that one pretty firmly. Oh, David came in flying a plane; I'll tell you more about that later. Something happened that surprised me and made me see him in a totally different light. He *is* a man, Dan! And there's nothing romantic about what he's doing. When somebody can handcarry it, I will write you the details. He left early this morning and I don't know when I'll see him next. There is harmony between us now and I know Margaret is happy about that. I'm sure now that John Chitole is my logical successor and am planning accordingly. So we move. Peace and love. . . .

Emma Batari, John Chitole thought; and the thought startled him. He turned his head slowly to look at the bishop beside him. Jacob was fast asleep, his head carefully wedged into the corner where the backrest of the seat curved into the upholstered side. His long legs were stretched out, a pillow supported the curve of his back, his hands were on his lap, holding in place the book he had been reading before he dozed off. Chitole knew the bishop would wake if he tried to remove the book; he slept lightly on long journeys, and woke instantly at any disturbance. So Chitole let him be as the limousine moved at an even pace across the green and very fertile-looking landscape. Let him rest, Chitole thought; he had sorted out the problem of the two out stations, settled the money issues involved, installed a new priest at each station and then conducted two stirring services; he deserves his rest.

Emma Batari would be the answer, would solve the problem. . . . If she were agreeable, that is. Ever since the bishop had told him, this matter had worried him. He knew the bishop's own marriage to Missy had been managed by the church in America; a bishop of the church had to have an acceptable partner to work with him. The choice of Missy for the bishop had obviously been absolutely right, and there would be no problem if they were to help him find a wife here in his own country. But they could only find a wife for him from the church women there. This was not what he wanted, if it could be avoided. Emma Batari could be the answer, unless the bishop felt her problems of the past would harm church interests. Never thought of her in this light until just now, yet it seems such a logical solution.

He gently eased the book out of Jacob's fingers; Jacob woke, as Chitole knew he would and wanted him to, and sat up. Chitole looked at his bishop and smiled wryly.

"Emma Batari," he said.

"What about her?" Jacob asked.

"Would she make an acceptable wife for a bishop of the church?"

Jacob thought for a long time, face calm and expressionless. At last he said: "Do you love her?"

"I like her. We get on well. She's a good person and works well."

"Do you love her, John?"

"Did you love Missy when you first met? When your marriage was arranged?"

"You've got it wrong, John. Sure it was arranged but not like

301

that. The church elders introduced me to a number of acceptable young women and I chose Margaret. They didn't choose her for me."

"But were you in love with her when you chose her?"

"It's a long time ago; I don't know. . . ." Jacob tried to remember. "I remember I felt more at ease with her than any of the others; I was more myself with her and she laughed easily."

"Love grew," Chitole suggested.

"Yes, I suppose." He opened his eyes: "Yes, love grew. . . . What was it you wanted to know?"

"The church, and her past."

"Yes. Talk to her, my son; and if it goes well then we will deal with her past."

"But, sir. What if. . . ."

"Trust me, John. Margaret was very fond of Miss Batari."

"I don't want her to be hurt again."

"Talk to her and if it is all right we will deal with it."

"Do you really know all about her – what happened to her?"

"Oh, John!" Jacob protested.

And John Chitole was shamed into silence which lasted until they reached home.

In the late afternoon, one week later, John Chitole returned to his office just in time to catch Emma Batari and her two assistants on the point of locking up. The bishop had gone off to a class at the seminary.

"Could I talk with you, please?" Chitole said and was surprised by his own calmness.

Emma Batari inclined her head slightly and waited.

"It is private," Chitole said.

Batari sent a message with her eyes to her two assistants, and they walked away.

"We will wait for you," one of them called back.

"No need," Chitole said. "It may be a while. You go."

Batari reached into her handbag, brought out the key and began to insert it in the door.

"No need for that either," Chitole said quietly.

It was only then that she turned a curiously searching look on

302

his face, and some of his calm deserted him under the intensity of her stare.

"What is it?" she asked in her quiet controlled voice.

He said: "It is a personal problem on which I would like your advice. Shall we walk?"

Again she inclined her head. He indicated the way to the bishop's house and they walked in that direction slowly. Chitole was small; Emma Batari was smaller. But whereas Chitole seemed shaped from a series of lines, Batari seemed shaped from a series of circles, tiny, trim and very feminine. Widely spaced, dark eyes in a round, bronze face with strong undertones of yellow pigment, and tightly curled black hair, cut short, made her seem younger than her twenty-two years. Only the eyes belied the youthful appearance: the eyes of an animal which had been bruised and wounded, which had, through pain, grown wise to the ways of the world, and had learned to keep that world at bay. Those eyes, now, were expressionless, on guard, waiting to hear what John Chitole had to say. She had worked for him, for the bishop really, for four years now, and she trusted him as much as she was able to trust anybody other than the bishop and his wife. Those were the only two she had been willing to trust completely. There had been no outward sign of the utter devastation she had suffered with Missy's death. Missy was the one who had brought her to this place when her own people would have no part of her. Missy was the one who had helped her through her trouble. And the bishop had supported everything Missy did and had not sat in judgement. Now there was only the bishop and he had his own grief and she would do anything in the world to ease that grief.

"The bishop, he's all right?" Emma Batari asked.

"He's all right," Chitole said. "I need to find a young dog for him for Christmas. David asked me to do it. You saw him?"

"Yes. I saw him for a little. He told me what he's doing. I think it is right for him. I'll look about for a puppy and let you know. That all?"

"No. There's something I find difficult to talk about. . . ."

They entered the grounds of the bishop's home and took the path that led to Missy's favourite tree at the back of the house. The sun was far to the west now and the shadows were lengthening.

Mrs Kilu waved from the window as they walked past the back of the house.

"Is he going to leave us?" Batari asked.

"No," Chitole said. "I don't think so. This is his home now."

"I know he plans for you to succeed him," Batari said, trying to make it easier for him if this was what he wanted to talk about. "And he wouldn't do it unless he's certain it is right. Is that what's worrying you?"

"Yes, in part. If I am to succeed him I have to find a wife; we have no unmarried bishops."

"Of course; I had not thought of it. But they'll find you a wife. They found Missy for the bishop and it was a wonderful marriage." Batari smiled, a rare occurrence that made her look very young. "She told me how they were brought together; she made it sound such fun."

"He came from that part of the world," Chitole was serious. "And so did she. I don't. If they find someone for me it would be someone from that part. I don't want that; I want someone from here."

Emma Batari stopped dead in her tracks. It came as a blinding flash: He means me! Oh God! He means me!

Chitole stopped and waited for her; when she remained on the same spot he walked back to her.

"So you see what's on my mind," he said softly.

"I must go back," she said. "I must go home."

"Please, hear me first."

"No! There is nothing to talk about. Nothing I can help you with."

"I talked to the bishop today and he said I should talk to you. Let's go and sit down and talk for a little while at least."

Her face was drawn and ashen now, and she looked older than her years.

"I can do nothing to help you." Her voice was low and firm. "I have no experience of these things; my experiences are uglier."

"At least hear me," Chitole insisted. Then, as an inspiration, the sight of Missy's spot put the idea in his mind. "Do you think Missy would have brought you here if she thought you had done wrong? You had sinned? Think! Was she that kind of person?

Would the bishop have you here if he thought so? You have done no wrong. You have not sinned. You were sinned against! Wrong was done against you. Now, if you do not like me, if you are not interested in me, then the matter is over. But if it is only because of what happened then I suggest you hear what the bishop has to say."

They walked to Missy's place and sat in the shadow of the flame tree and felt the cool breeze.

After a long time Batari said: "You told him it was me you were thinking of?"

"Yes."

"And he didn't tell you how impossible it was?"

"No."

"It is impossible!"

"He didn't think so."

"I don't believe you."

"I'm not a liar!" Chitole snapped, angry suddenly at the irrational stubbornness of this woman. "I don't tell lies! You wait here!" He stalked away toward the house.

Batari sat as though in shock, trying to think but unable to be calm and rational. The only clear thing was that she would have to leave this place that had become her home and her sanctuary, leave the people who had become her people, and go out into that cruel world again. What would she do? Where would she go? Shouldn't be difficult to find work. Missy had trained her well and she would be able to manage in any government office. But the old problems might come up again. The thought of the violence of men struck terror into her, made it impossible for her to think beyond that terror.

One of Mrs Kilu's young helpers came across the grass carrying a tray of fruit juice. On her way back the young helper passed Chitole and the bishop. Emma Batari tried to clear her mind and to relax her body as she waited for the men, as if she could diminish the pain of the punishment by trying to absorb it rather than resist it. They seemed a long time coming, a long time for her to hold on.

The bishop's voice came to her from a great distance: familiar, quiet, understanding.

"He did talk to me, Miss Batari. . . ."

"I did not really doubt it."

"Then why. . . ?

"Please leave us now, John." Jacob sat beside the woman.

Chitole hesitated for a moment then left them.

Jacob filled two glasses with juice and gave one to Batari.

He said: "You understand his problem. He must either marry here or marry there."

. . . And I must go, she told herself. . . .

"And whether it is here or there, the church has to be involved to some extent in the kind of person who is to be his partner. If he was already married then whether he is chosen or not will not only depend on the kind of man he is but also on the kind of person his partner is. If he is not married the church will want to have some influence in the kind of partner he chooses. These are the restrictions on all of us who would be elders of the church; we either accept them or forgo being leaders of our flock. That is how it is for all of us. I do not think I have to explain to you why a bishop of our church has to be a man with a stable family life which can be a living example to all his congregation and all the people outside who look and judge the way of our church. John knows all this, so he had to talk to me when he thought of you. Now, if you are not interested in him then the matter is over. There is no way anyone here can or will force you to do what you do not want to do. Understand that clearly."

"I understand," she murmured, head down. "And now I must leave here."

"My dear, if you think you must leave here then you do not understand."

"But how could I stay?"

"Simply by staying; if you want to."

"But he will remember. And if he comes back and I'm still here it will be difficult; it will be more difficult if he is married."

"Then you are not interested at all?"

Her voice sank lower: "I can't be. You know that."

"Because of what happened all those years ago?"

She seemed to grow even smaller, to shrivel up: "Yes." It was a whisper.

"How old is the child now? Five? Six?"

"Five," she whispered. "She is boarding with some people in Rhodesia, people like her, Coloureds, near Salisbury."

"Suppose I would be called Coloured if I were born there, only just, though!" The attempt at lightness fell flat. "Keep in touch?"

"I send them a money order every month."

"Do they look after her well? Does she go to school?"

"Yes. They have five other children and she's treated as one of them. My friend – the one who helped me when it happened –"

Jacob felt cruel but he felt it should all come out for her sake: "Wasn't that the friend who tried to help you get rid of it at the time?"

Batari's voice grew faint and weak: "Yes. She found these people and she writes from time to time and tells me how the child is. She says they are kind people who treat the child as one of their own."

"Will they adopt her?"

"I think they prefer the money. They are very poor."

"And the money might stop coming if the child were legally theirs?"

"That is what they think, I'm sure."

"What if they were reassured or received a lump sum?"

"I don't know. I think they want the money desperately but from what my friend writes I think they would go on caring for the child even if I stopped sending it."

"So they may be willing to adopt? Especially if it means no loss."

"I don't know; I can ask my friend."

"I think you should. As soon as possible. Tell me, have you seen the child? What's her name?"

Batari let out a soft low moan. He put his arm about the woman and drew her to him. He felt the convulsive shaking of her body; he held her and remained silent, waiting for the moment to pass.

At last Batari said, her voice under tight control: "I've not seen her all these years and I do not know and do not want to know her name." Then she wept.

When the weeping died down Jacob pulled away so that there was distance between them. He refilled their glasses with juice.

He said: "I was in love with a girl once. Younger than you are now and very bright. I remember she was nearly raped by young whites on her way into Atlanta with a fellow male student. She only escaped being raped by the appearance of an older white man on horseback who seemed to know the young whites and drove them off. I was very angry when I heard of this and my strongest impulse was to go out and do harm to the first white person I saw. They calmed me down, those black Americans, and they made me understand how commonplace was the raping of our women by white men, and they made me understand why. Under slavery, our women were common possessions to be used at the whims and fancies of whites. Their menfolk could do nothing. Think of the humiliation. After slavery it was a little different in the island where I came from; there were so many of us they couldn't use force and rape our women. But not so in America. There, almost to this day, the raping of our women is the other, and in some ways more cruel, side to the lynching of our men. There is nothing I can think of as brutal and savage as the rape of any woman by any man, even one of her own race and colour. When that particular savagery becomes racial, when it is used deliberately to inflict racial pain and racial humiliation, there are no words strong enough to condemn it. Yet this is what they have done to our women, and they call themselves followers of Christ. Now you say to me that because they have done this to you, because they have made you the victim of the ugliest and meanest form of racial violence, we must cast you out. We cannot do that and call ourselves followers of Jesus Christ. You were sinned against, you have not sinned."

"I should not have been where they could find me," Batari said.

"In your own land? No, child. Africa is the land of your birth and if you cannot move freely and without fear here, if strangers can come among you and force you into hiding from them to avoid rape, then you are back in slavery and emancipation is one great big fraud. You have done no wrong; you have been used brutally in order to try to humiliate your people. They feel comfortable when we ourselves come to see ourselves as they see us and want us to be seen. Lord, the self-denigration and the self-contempt they've inculcated! I find that hardest of all to forgive. . . ." Jacob lapsed into silence.

The evening breeze stirred the flame tree leaves. The world, in this green place, seemed tranquil. Only the man seemed distressed and disturbed by the thoughts he had spoken. Batari forgot her own distress in her concern for him. He seemed more humanly fallible now than in all the years she had known him and worked for him, more fallible even than under the stress and pain of the death of his wife. She reached out and touched his hand.

"I'm sorry I've upset you."

"Not you, Miss Batari."

Not his child now, she thought; not even his dear. He'll soon be in control again, benign and wise. But for a moment here he was, a very angry black man, and she would always remember that. How comforting to think of her bishop voicing the deep hurt and resentments she had thought a kind of sin against Christian charity, and giving it all this special and terrible meaning! If he's right. . . . Oh Lord that would make them so bad! As though divining her thought, he said:

"I do not think they do this out of wickedness or a special malice against us. It is the pursuit of power: the power of wealth, of authority, of control over others. This is a sickness which seems to have afflicted them more deeply than any other people in our age. For it they would kill and enslave each other quite as easily as they would kill and enslave us. What gives them this lust for power? It cannot be in their nature, for their nature is really no different from our nature. . . ."

Batari felt on safe ground now, her interest engaged on a matter which she could think and reason about, not some high spiritual or ecclesiastical matter.

"All people are like that," she said. "Even here the Baganda are stronger than the other people so they assert their power, and as they assert it their sense of self-importance grows." A hint of laughter crept into her voice. "Even your John Chitole. He holds himself up so straight and he has this air of authority because he's a Muganda, a member of the ruling kingdom. All the rest of us, except Michael Odera and a few students, are from lesser kingdoms."

"Me too," Jacob teased. "I'm not even from a kingdom."

"You're different," Emma Batari protested.

"How very familiar," Jacob laughed.

"You're the bishop," Batari insisted.

"Being different has a very special meaning where I come from. But no matter. So you think John a stiff-necked Muganda?"

"I don't think he's conscious of it; just born to it."

"Oh dear; is this what you have against him?"

"So you're back to that." She was more at ease now. "No, I don't hold that against him. I just never thought of marriage; not after what happened."

"Think about it now."

"I can't think about it. I feel cold inside. Even if you and the church forgive me it is hard for me to forgive or forget what happened."

"You don't have to forgive or forget; just think about it."

"I don't think I can be a wife to any man."

"John Chitole is not any man; he's a special man."

"All the more reason why he should have a special woman for wife."

"He thinks you are that woman. So do I."

"I have no feeling left. I cannot sleep with a man. It would be the nightmare all over again."

"Please think about it. Then tell him about it. Will you do that for me?"

She nodded, a world of doubt in her movement. He touched her hand and got up.

"Let us go in. Please stay for dinner. Just you and I. No John. And I will play some of Margaret's records of Negro spirituals for you. . . . As she used to do for you." He offered her his hand. She rose and he tucked her hand under his arm and they went to the house. Emma Batari felt safe and comforted and at peace.

And, in spite of herself, Emma Batari began to think about marriage. . . .

Emma Batari thought about marriage for nearly three weeks. During that time she avoided all social contact with both John Chitole and the bishop. At work she took their instructions, fulfilled their requests, then went to work, not appearing to note the usual personal pleasantries and courtesies which were, and had been, part of the office routine over the years. There was a new remoteness to her; she was at once withdrawn and more sharply alert than those who knew her remembered. She did not, after work, go to the small gatherings of friends at this or that person's home for an evening of talking or listening to music. She did not go, as in the past, to the bishop's Thursday evening Open House with its stimulating flow of ideas. She did not attend the student debates, held each Saturday night, as the climax of a week's activity. For more than three weeks she went home from work and stayed there, politely rebuffing all efforts to draw her out. All this time Emma Batari thought about marriage as dispassionately as she could. She wrote a long, careful, letter to the dear friend in faraway Salisbury. When she received the reply she read it, then put it into a mission envelope, sealed it, addressed it to the bishop and took it into his office and handed it to him personally.

They had not really spoken to each other for those three weeks, not since that evening under the flame tree and then later listening to Margaret's music. Now, having given him the letter, she turned to leave him. But this time he would not let her go.

"It's a long time, Emma. Time for us to talk again. John must leave soon. We can't give you any more time."

She turned back and took the seat opposite his great desk.

"Can't it wait till he comes back?"

"Without knowing your decision?"

"I don't know if I can be a wife."

"Do you want to be a wife? Do you want to be a wife to him? If he goes without knowing that he may come back married."

"I know."

"So?"

"What if I can't. . . ?" She choked on the words.

"What if you can't have normal sexual relations with him?"

"Yes."

"Do you want to? No, don't answer that. Do you want to be his wife?"

"I think so."

Jacob let out a sigh of relief.

"One thing at a time," Jacob murmured, half to himself, half to Emma. "Will you tell him so? Will you tell him tonight? And will you come out of that isolation of yours now?" He looked tenderly at her bowed head. "We've all been hurting for you; and stiff-necked John Chitole most of all. He feels personally responsible for your misery and isolation. Now we are going to have a good Christmas after all! Off you go now, and I want to see you at my house for dinner. That's an order, young lady!"

Suddenly, unexpectedly, Emma Batari felt the tears flowing down her cheeks, unbidden, inexplicably. She rose quickly, averting her head to try and hide the tears. She hurried to the door and rushed out of the office and out of the building into the late afternoon sun.

Emma Batari hurried home, feeling the weight of her burdens easing now that she had relaxed the tight control. Through blurred eyes she noticed how bright red the Christmas flowers were. But then, it was almost Christmas eve; and she had almost forgotten it.

Later that night, scrubbed fresh and in a pretty dress, she sat at the bishop's dining table facing John Chitole. Her eyes were still swollen from the weeping, but she did not mind now. There were only the three of them: the bishop at the head of the table, Missy's chair empty and unoccupied, a turned-down glass the bishop's sign of remembrance. They had finished eating. Jacob seemed preoccupied. Batari, once she realized how nervous Chitole was, had relaxed and even ended up telling a story that brought a brief smile to his face, her own nervousness more under control.

"You two go into the garden," Jacob ordered. "I want to sit here a while. You have things to talk about so that I can get things moving. And try not to fight. There is no stronger or weaker kingdom in these matters. And stiff-necks have to bend if they are to kiss ladies." He exchanged conspiratorial looks with Batari then smiled disarmingly at Chitole. "If you take too long you'll have to come and wake me in Margaret's garden."

They left. He poured himself a glass of wine and looked across the table to the empty seat and the turned-down glass.

"I know you're pleased with this," he whispered. "You always thought she was special. Well, he is special too. They need to be. I think it will be all right. I think she'll come alive again and give him wonderful children. And those old fellows in America will understand. I've decided to escort him personally and take her along as my secretary so that she can be formally introduced. It should inhibit anybody with designs and ambitions of their own finding him a wife over there. She and I will only be away for a week or so. He'll probably be there for three years. I wish you were here in person to share this moment with me. Our first native African bishop! Is it vanity that I should be so proud to be the first to have done it? If it is I hope the Lord will understand and forgive. It will make it easier for others. For if we don't do it, if the native Africans do not take over the affairs of the church in Africa, then we will be doing the same thing we fought against. We will become the new religious imperialists, black faces and all. So I'm bursting with pride over John. And now there is your Emma too. How I wish you were here!"

He closed his eyes and leaned back and the presence of his Margaret grew till it filled the room as it had done in life.

Jacob opened his eyes and the room was empty and silent and he was alone. He relaxed his body and allowed the terrible pain of loss to wash over him.

Mrs Kilu came in to supervise the clearing of the table. She sensed his mood and waved away the young person behind her.

"All right, sir?"

Jacob looked up and thanked her with his eyes.

"Yes, Mama Kilu. . . . Just remembrances."

She looked at the open French window. "The young people?"

"I think it will be well now," Jacob said, then added, "But it will take time and it may still be difficult. It is not easy for her."

"It will be easier in time as she learns to open her heart."

"Let us pray for that," Jacob said.

"We pray for you, too, sir; all of us."

"Thank you, Adina." He got up and touched her shoulder as he went out, passing the young helper waiting at the door.

"Come!" Adina Kilu's voice ordered the helper as Jacob went to his and Margaret's very private rooms.

He would rest a while before preparing for the midnight service. John and Emma needed to be alone to work out their problems.

313

Chitole said: "I'm sorry for the pain I caused you."

She said: "The bishop says the church says I have done no wrong."

"He's right."

"But I knew that all along. It does not end the shame."

"The shame is theirs, not yours."

"The shame was committed against my body."

"By force. Against your will."

"Are you sure? Will you be sure if a time comes when you are vexed with me and we quarrel and shout at each other and try to hurt each other: will you be sure then? Or will you remind me?"

"I don't know; I know I don't want to. If I do I will be wrong."

"Honest John," she said softly.

"Heh?"

"And if I cannot come to you, John? If I cannot be your wife with my body?"

"If you don't want to. . . ."

"Not want, John. Touch me and see."

They were alone under the tree, shrouded by the darkness. She willed herself to lean toward him, and as she did so her body shrank away instinctively.

A flood of understanding washed over Chitole. He turned to her and put his hands on her shoulders. He was not nervous or eager, no passion in him, only a great concern to help her across the chasm of dark fear that had been forced on her. He drew her body, stiff, resisting, to him and held her for a long time, in a calm, relaxed embrace, not speaking, trying to let the stillness that was in him flow into her.

After what seemed an endless silence, her body relaxed slightly. He felt it and released her. It seemed she emerged from a trance.

He took her hand and they resumed their walk in the cool quiet garden with all its familiar landmarks. And for Emma Batari other things than the lonely life she had foreseen for herself now began to seem possible.

"There is nothing between us to fight," Chitole said.

"There is my shame," she said.

"It is not yours, but even so, we will share it and wash it away."

"I would want to come to you clean."

"You are clean! Your own body has cleansed itself over and over again. It is only your mind that holds on to it. Count the number of menses you've had since! That is the number of times you have washed out whatever shame they tried to put in your body."

"The shame in the mind is not as easily washed away."

"Yes," he said softly. "But will you try, for me, with me?"

"If you will help me; if you will learn to love me."

"Then you want me!"

"Yes."

He looked at her, he began to reach for her and sensed her tensing. He let go of her hand, stared at her, then turned abruptly and ran laughing away from her, taking a huge leap every few steps; he kept up the running and the jumping and the laughing, moving in a wide circle round the garden.

After a while Emma Batari realized what was going on. The Reverend John Chitole, protégé of Bishop Jacob Brown, his right-hand man who would one day succeed him as bishop here, was doing an African dance of victory and celebration! Emma Batari started laughing, softly at first, almost under her breath, then more loudly, picking up the rhythm of his movement and the subtle timing of his laughter. Then she joined him and they did one large circular joyous victory dance together. Then she collapsed into the chair under the flame tree and waited for him to play out the dance of joy by himself.

The dance ended when John Chitole was exhausted and his shirt soaked in sweat. He collapsed into a chair beside her, breathing heavily. It was a long time since he had done this dance.

"You must change before you catch cold."

"It should be done without clothes," he gasped. "In true primitive native style! Did I shock you?"

"I'll never call you stiff-necked John again. Did he tell you?"

"Good. He told me. He would not be shocked."

"No, he wouldn't be. Come, change into dry clothes and take me home."

Chitole rose, took her hand and pulled her up. Briefly, he put a damp arm about her waist, and she did not stiffen or pull away.

When they neared the house he said: "May I tell him now you will marry me?"

"He knows," she smiled. "He gave me an ultimatum earlier today. Said if you left without knowing, you would come back with an American wife."

"So he forced your hand. . . ."

"He did indeed!"

"I still have to tell him formally."

"I'd like to be there. After all, he did most of your courting for you, John Chitole."

"Then we'll do it right now. I'll wake him if he's asleep."

"After you've washed and changed."

Jacob was not asleep. He invited them into Margaret's private garden where a bottle of wine was chilling on ice.

"I see," Emma Batari said, a hint of mockery in her voice. "More good Christian celebration."

"Hush, woman," Chitole said. "Bishop's wine is good stuff, not like *waragi*."

"Yes," Jacob said drily, his eyes glowing. "I heard the other celebration and took a peep. Savage business! And you, Miss Emma Batari, I saw you in it too!"

"He's not really stiff-necked," she said.

"I tried to tell you," Jacob said.

"I am too!" Chitole insisted, pulling himself up to his full slim five foot five and a half; then he grew serious. "It is settled, sir; she has agreed to be my wife."

"I'm very happy for you," Jacob Brown leaned down and casually wrapped his huge arms about Emma Batari and lifted her a couple of feet off the ground in a warm embrace.

There was no stiffening there, Chitole noticed; it was not the physical contact, it was physical contact with sexual implication. When Jacob reached for him, holding Emma in his one arm, Chitole offered his hand at long distance.

". . . And for the church," Jacob Brown said, putting Emma down.

He poured the wine and they drank a silent toast.

It was a good Christmas to round off a very good and profitable year for the mission and for the country. There were blemishes, of course, but on balance the good, here in the heart of Africa, still outweighed the blemishes that Christmas. The country was making steady progress. The economy was flourishing. The price of coffee and cotton were high on the world market and the small farmers were doing as well as the mission.

There was enough land here for everybody who wanted to work it; none was alienated to foreign settlers or giant international agricultural enterprises or mining companies as was the case in most of the countries bordering Uganda: Tanganyika, Kenya, Ruanda-Urundi and, above all, the massive Congo whose name had now become firmly prefixed with a European nation's identity. The *Belgian* Congo, not Africa's Congo: like the *White Highlands* and *White Africa* and *White South Africa*, vast portions of a continent alienated – such a pretty word for robbery – from the children of that continent. In this part of Africa, as in the south of neighbouring Sudan, the land was still the common right of the people. In Kenya they had taken up arms to recover the alienated land. In the Rhodesias and further south the day of battle seemed far-off and the prospects of success even further off.

The rays of hope for the liberation of a continent and its peoples shone brightest from the far western coastal strip of the continent where an angry, explosive, visionary with vast continental dreams was dragging the British colony of the Gold Coast at helter-skelter pace toward political independence.

But in Uganda, despite the restlessness among the upper stratum of his own people at the forcible removal of the Kabaka from his throne, things were relatively quiet and prosperous. The great dam at Owen Falls to harness the power of the Nile where it began its journey was near completion. Thousands of young men from all over Uganda and further afield had found work and earned many hundreds of shillings.

All this had gone into making for a particularly prosperous, happy and tranquil Christmas in the most stable, orderly and peaceful country in Africa.

Very early that Christmas morning John Chitole and Emma

Batari brought David's present to Jacob. It was a golden brown, soft-coated puppy, perhaps seven or eight weeks old.

"This is from David," Chitole said. "He said it had to be a she."

Jacob held the warm little bundle of fur against his chest in his left hand and stroked it gently with the index finger of his right hand. The name for it came to him instantly.

"Hi, Jane," he murmured.

The pup raised solemn eyes to the big face above her; she liked what she saw and tried to show it by attempting to lick the huge hand in which she was cupped. Her pink little tongue could not quite make it. Then, suddenly tired of all the excitement she had been through, and sure of being safe now, Jane closed her eyes and fell asleep.

Later, at the end of the day, Jacob thought, when all the visitors had come and gone and all the work was done, he and Jane would spend a little time at Margaret's grave and David would be with them in spirit. Not such a lonely Christmas after all.

6
David/Emma

David Brown stood a little distance from the official mourning party which was clustered about the President; and even here, at the place of burial, the President's bodyguard – young men with restless roving eyes and nervous hands which periodically patted the guns under their jackets for reassurance – stood out. No idle show of power this; two attempts had already been made on the President's life, and there was talk of another in the making whose origins were far from West Africa. Indeed, it was beginning slowly to come out that the man they were burying today had not been overthrown by a popular army and police coup as it seemed six years earlier. In this case too the true origins seemed to have been far away across the ocean. It was the age, now, not of direct conquest but of what they called covert operations, and destabilization, and disinformation; the true hand, now, was hidden. The agents of the new conquest came as bright, immensely friendly and generous young men with university degrees and large sums of the most desirable currencies and, quite often, with impeccable diplomatic, business, academic, journalistic or even missionary credentials. And where they passed, governments or leaders who were considered unfriendly or dangerous collapsed under sudden crises or political unrest, all co-ordinated by internal opponents of the regime with new subtlety, and with huge sums of money to spend. Often, too, the agents of the new conquest cultivated the key people in the security services of the targeted country. Third World leaders had been slow to recognize this new form of conquest; they had paid a bitter price. And so in the great African dream of freedom, which flowered so brilliantly after the man they were now burying had set the pace, nearly a score of African countries gained their political independence in one single year, unaware of the hidden forces at work. Nothing like that rush to independence had ever happened in the history of any other continent; but, then, no other continent had been as greedily dismembered. There had been talk of the African Decade: it seemed that all things were possible to Africans and to black folk everywhere. At last, the time had come for the Africans to put their own imprint on the pages of world history as had other people in other ages. They seemed, for a time, to dominate the United Nations and to make an irrelevance of the bitter power rivalry between the great power groupings. And the man who had been the quintessential symbol of that great African dream of freedom was now being buried in exile. That dream was turning into a thing of ashes, as was the companion dream of the earth's dark folk influencing the shape of the world by the moral quality of their leadership. He had shared that wider dream with Nehru of India, Nasser of Egypt, and Ben Bella of Algeria, who had that vision of all Africans dying a little so that all of Africa may be free. What a dream! What a vision those men had held before us!

"Why has it gone wrong?" David Brown whispered, half to himself, half to the man whose body was being lowered into the ground.

What had gone wrong could not simply be blamed on external interference, no matter how clever and devilish that had been. One precondition to any subversion is susceptibility, and susceptibility comes in many guises.

. . . The priest finished speaking the stark words: dust to dust; ashes to ashes. In his Jamaican childhood, David's father had said, they used to add, "If the devil don't get you, duppy must." The priest's fistful of earth thudded on the casket. Then the President, who had, symbolically of course, shared his Presidency with the dead man after his overthrow, shovelled in the first spadeful of earth. The President signalled to David and someone brought him the special shovel. He had known this man alive and in power; a complicated man with a confusion of motives and impulses but totally committed to African freedom. Not in the clear and starkly simple way of Ben Bella, or the visionary and almost religious way of Nasser, but totally committed. Of the four who had shaped the Third World vision and the non-aligned dream, Nehru had been the only one he had not known personally. There were of course two others among the dream-makers: the venerable Dr DuBois who had nurtured the dream longest of all, and George Padmore, the steady methodical organizer over the years. . . . He shovelled the earth on to the casket and listened to the heavy thud of damp earth on a box containing air. . . . Kwame dead in exile at sixty-three and his dream in ashes all about us. DuBois gone too, at the ripe old age of ninety-five; and Padmore too. Nehru a year after DuBois, and Nasser two years ago, in his prime. Only Ben Bella left and he and his dream under house arrest by men of a more practical turn of mind. DuBois must have died happiest of all. African freedom and unity still seemed to be spreading then, though there was, even then, a perceptible withdrawing from Nkrumah's strong vision. The hard and bitter problem with which DuBois had grappled all his life seemed to be moving to a successful conclusion. And he was home in Africa, a venerated elder among the leaders of the continent. Yes, perhaps he was the greatest of the dream-keepers because he was not directly involved with the day-to-day politics of power. . . . Must say this to Dad; might help wipe out that lingering memory of my stupid outburst at that last argument before Mother's death.

At last it was over. Kwame Nkrumah's grave was not in his beloved Ghana. But David was irrationally certain that one day he would be returned to Ghana.

The President came over to him; he knew David as the fighter-physician who had, at one time or another, looked after Ben Bella, Nasser and Nkrumah, and who had travelled with one or the other to meetings and conferences.

The President touched his arm lightly and murmured: "A tragedy for Africa, for him to die thus and without honour. They all fawned on him when he had power; they forgot him when he fell."

David thought, feeling unkind and not caring: And you expect me to say "Except you". Then he said it anyway; this one deserved that much, he had reached out to Nkrumah when things became awkward in Egypt.

"You will come back with us," the President said. "Dine with me this evening and let us talk. There is much to discuss."

"I regret, Your Excellency." He said it very carefully, very apologetically. Turning down this kind of invitation is tricky. "I have to arrange to move out immediately. I am worried about my father. I think you know he is a missionary bishop in Uganda. Reports are that the Nubian is turning against Christians and I have reason to fear that my father's mission has become a target. I fear for his safety."

The President clicked his tongue. "He's not a true Moslem, that one. He uses Islam. I've tried to warn my Arab brothers but he speaks anti-Zionism so they support him. The unity our friend –" his eyes swept over the grave – "strove so hard to fashion is rapidly falling apart. A great pity."

David thought: And you French-speaking blacks helped the process along. Aloud, he echoed the President: "Yes, a great pity."

"About your father?"

"I plan to fly to Addis as soon as I can get a flight. I have some connections at the Secretariat. I will try to get my father out."

"Not to worry," the President said. "You will get a flight straightaway." He signalled and an aide hurried over. The President instructed him that the doctor had to be on the first flight for Addis; the aide hurried away. "I will write a letter to the Secretary-General. It may be useful."

"And it may get you into trouble," David suggested.

"Oh?"

"If I'm caught, sir. You may be accused of complicity and therefore of interfering in the internal affairs of a member state which goes against the Charter."

"I see. Is it then your intention to attempt a coup? To overthrow the government there?"

"No, sir."

"There you are! How can I be interfering by asking the Secretary-General to facilitate your attempt to get your father, the venerable bishop, out of a country where he might be in danger?"

"I thought I should warn you of the possibility."

"So you have, doctor. And when your mission is over, could we persuade you to return here? We need doctors, and I need a doctor whose politics are beyond question."

David began searching for a way of answering graciously without committing himself. The President raised his hand.

"Do not answer now; you do not know what lies ahead. Just remember there is the offer and it is open as long as I am here. *Au 'voir*, my friend." The President walked away abruptly.

You could have been more gracious, David told himself. He's a good man, a caring man, who had comforted and sheltered Nkrumah in his hour of greatest need: of them all, he and Nyerere came closest to personalizing that co-operative spirit of a compassionate humanity in whose name we claim to make this African revolution, now so beleaguered. David resisted the sudden impulse to go after the President and tell him he would be happy to spend the evening with him. He knew he would not be. So he watched the President go, flanked by bodyguards, unable to move freely in the land he had led to political independence. Then he too walked from the graveside, limping slightly as he moved. A bullet in the left foot had caused that limp; a small price. Others, in their thousands, above and below the great desert, had paid with their lives for the African freedom now so deeply embattled, a little over a decade after its great flowering. . . . Where had we gone wrong? . . .

The smiling young fellow waited, leaning against his rusty run-down taxi on the other side of the security cordon. There had been more security than mourners: a small cluster of Ghanaians who had been the President's staff; a solitary veiled woman, apart from all the rest, who hurried away after the burial; and the Presidential party, itself bristling with security. More security than mourners. . . . This really what our struggle has come to? . . .

David got into the back of the taxi, avoiding the broad smile and the bright eyes.

"Back to the hotel?" the driver asked in his very clearly enunciated West African French.

"Go along the coast road for a while." David sensed the beaming smile grow bigger without seeing it.

325

The taxi lurched forward then settled to an even pace, travelling through the once fashionable residential section where civil servants from France lived in the days of imperial glory. They had built their villas on the coast of tropical West Africa as though they were villas on the French Mediterranean. Conakry was not quite as completely French as Dakar, but the district where the French civil servants had once lived was every bit as French as any district of Dakar other than the native quarter. And the sea air and the constant sea breeze made it cool and invigorating. Inland, it had all the scars and blemishes of a small industrial French town fallen on hard times. When the French had withdrawn because this President chose complete political independence rather than the continued association that other former French colonies had chosen, the departing French had taken everything with them, even inkwells from classrooms. Some of the French were back now, as the new technical experts and contract officers, and some of the neat little villas were again occupied by young French families. He looked out to sea, westward. The far islands of the West Indies lay out there beyond this vast expanse of water: Jamaica was out there somewhere, the place where his father and his father's people were born and called home, though their forebears had most likely come from somewhere along this Guinea Coast. If places could tell their tales what a story this Guinea Coast would tell! Then he began to worry about his father and ordered the cheerful taximan to drive back to the hotel.

The stern and proper and very black young man at the reception desk had no message from the airline office yet: too early, *m'sieur*, much too early; but they will call, have no fear. Then he leaned across his counter, David's room key dangling from his fingers: "A lady attends you," he inclined his head toward the darkest corner of the lobby where a woman sat.

It was the woman who had stood by herself at the burial. David walked down the narrow hallway wondering, what now.

The woman rose: "Doctor Brown – I'm sorry to bother you – if you can spare me a minute –"

He recognized the accent; she was a South African, he had encountered many such in exile in many parts of Africa. A woman in her thirties with the figure of a fashion model and a face

326

noticeable for the coarseness of the light-brown skin. But for that she would have been a most attractive looking person; as it was, she seemed withdrawn and forbidding.

"I was his secretary," the woman said.

Better sit, he thought and gestured for her to do so. He sat facing her across a little table. "Something to drink? A glass of wine? Coffee?"

She settled for coffee and David signalled the receptionist who sent over a young boy.

"How can I help?"

"I would like to get out," the woman said. She tried to sound calm but David heard the tension in her voice; she was under strain.

"Now that he's gone they're all going to help each other but not me. They resent me, always have, because I wasn't one of them – not Ghanaian – so they put out some awful stories about me. Even said I was his mistress. . . ."

Could be true, David thought, but held his peace.

"I know they will not want me around. In any case those who can go back safely are planning to do so."

"Why not try for a job here?"

"I don't speak their language, and the men in the government who will hire me will have one thing in mind. They don't really want a secretary. . . ." She turned her hard eyes intently on him.

"I'm a good secretary; I really am, even if I say so myself."

"Then what's the problem? Money?"

"No. I have enough for now. The problem is papers. I have no travel documents, no passport, nothing. While he was alive it didn't matter; nobody stopped me or questioned me when I travelled with him. They know you; they will let me travel with you; please! There are some South Africans in Addis and elsewhere in East Africa. If I could get there I'll be all right; please. . . ."

David thought for a while then shook his head. The coarse face crumbled but the woman held onto herself. A strong-willed one this, David thought. He felt overwhelmed by compassion for the terrible bleakness in this South African woman.

"Let me try something; what's your name?"

"Arends, Nora Arends."

"Wait here, Miss Arends."

"Mrs Arends; they killed my husband and banned me, which is why I have no papers."

David went to the receptionist. "Your telephone, please. Not this one; inside your office. I want to call the President."

The receptionist all but jumped to open the door into the small back office. He had known *m'sieur le Docteur* was a person of importance; but to be able to speak to the President on the telephone! He ushered David into the office, found the number and dialled. When someone answered he puffed himself up as though they could see him, and told them to hold on for *m'sieur le Docteur* who wished to have speech with the President; then, with a grand flourish, he passed the telephone to David and waited.

They kept David waiting a long time, passing him from one person to another, each wanting to know who he was, where he was from, why he wanted to speak to His Excellency. At last, after the fourth person, a fresh, young-sounding female voice said: "Doctor Brown? Hold, please – His Excellency." Then he heard the President's voice. While they exchanged pleasantries David made a gesture of dismissal to the receptionist who left reluctantly. Then David turned serious.

"Mr President, our deceased friend's secretary called on me."

"Oh so?"

"She's in some distress. There appears to have been some resentment because she's not Ghanaian, which could do her no harm as long as her employer was alive."

"They are very clannish, some of these people. There was talk of some sort of an affair. . . ."

"Isn't there always? About every leader?"

"*Touché*! Even I have been a victim of it and madam nearly believed it! But what of this one?"

"You know she's a South African?"

"Yes. So I heard."

"She has no papers. And they will not help her, or she thinks they will not, which is the same thing."

"She wishes to remain here?"

"She asked to come with me to Addis."

"Ah, so. And you need travel documents?"

"No, sir. I travel alone. What I may have to do requires it."

"My letter is on the way to you; and I understand the plane seat is secured though you will have to make two changes. Now this lady, what is her name? What do you wish me to do about her?"

"She's Nora Arends," David spelled it for the President. "I would appreciate it if she could be afforded a private person's one-way travel document to Addis."

"You do not trust her?"

"I do not know her; but we must remember our dead friend trusted her. That is in her favour."

"Is she a good secretary? Politically? Do you know?"

"I have reason to believe so. She speaks no French; I don't think she's young enough to learn easily and quickly."

"Good, my careful friend. We will help as you suggest. Tell her to come here and ask for my personal assistant. I will brief him now. Good luck on your mission; have a successful adventure and give my respects to your revered father, the bishop, when you see him. And remember my invitation. It stands." The phone went dead and David thought: wish there were more like you.

He found a piece of paper and wrote the name of the Presidential Personal Assistant on it; then he went out to where Mrs Nora Arends waited. He had many things to do, many letters and cables to write and dispatch before boarding that plane, so he dealt with Nora Arends with a brusque offhandedness he did not really feel. She seemed eager to show her gratitude and her face crumbled again when he refused her offer to cook a special South African supper for him and dismissed her with apparent cold casualness. Perhaps if they met again, in other circumstances, he would tell her why he had to be as he was this time. Now, he left her abruptly there in the lobby of the little hotel in Conakry and went to his room. From his window he watched her walk away along the dusty West African street in the late afternoon, trim body erect, head held high, an African exile a long way from home on her own continent. The occupiers were still in possession in some parts of Africa and Ben Bella's dream of us all dying a little to end it was under house arrest. When Nora Arends was out of sight David Brown settled down to his letters and his cables.

He worked for the best part of an hour and was about to try the airline office again when they phoned him. They had arranged his flight; could he please come in person to collect his tickets and pay for them? Could he make it immediately? The airline office manager would be glad to receive him personally.

David went out to where his smiling taximan was playing dominoes with another driver, also awaiting the pleasure of his customer for the day.

"The airline office, please."

After a few blocks the driver enquired: "*M'sieur* departs tonight? A pity. I planned to take you to a club in our quarter. Good wine and friendly people, nice women too; all proper. Perhaps another time, if *m'sieur* returns to Conakry."

"Perhaps," David murmured, wondering what he was going to miss.

"We are there, *m'sieur*."

Instead of being dealt with at the counter where two pretty young brown misses and one white and two black young men were in attendance, he was ushered into the manager's office where a suave and very beautiful young black gentleman in an impeccably tailored charcoal black suit and a dazzlingly white shirt and a red rose in his buttonhole came eagerly from behind a huge desk to receive David and lead him to a settee beneath the reproduction of a big Cézanne landscape which dominated the room.

"Ah, *docteur*! I am happy to report everything is arranged." He touched a buzzer on his desk. Almost instantly one of the pretty brown misses appeared from a side door with a small tray with two glasses of white wine: she made a pretty dimpled smile for David and withdrew.

"Your good health, *m'sieur*! A good journey!"

How complete the French conquest here, David told himself as he raised his glass and then sipped the excellent wine so perfectly chilled. Totally French minds in black bodies.

With the pleasantries over the business was quickly settled. The manager checked and rechecked his conversion of David's travellers cheques into francs. Then, for good measure, he telephoned a friend at the bank to ensure that he had used the correct conversion rate and that his calculation was right. The tickets were checked, the times of departures and connections rechecked and confirmed. Then the manager walked with David to his taxi, making of it the ritual painful parting of dear friends.

The messenger with the President's letter was waiting when David got back to the hotel. David noted the respectful, almost fearful, alertness of the receptionist in his dealing with this one. The man waited at the same shadowy table where the South African woman had waited earlier. Now, on signal from the receptionist, he came forward and made a small bow to David. The receptionist opened the door to his little office and stayed back till David and the man were inside, then he shut himself out of the little room. This he did not want to know anything about.

The man gave David a large envelope with the Presidential Palace heading on its face and a red official seal on its back. It was addressed to David. Inside was another, smaller envelope addressed, this time, to the Secretary-General of the Organization of African Unity by name, in the President's own handwriting, and marked "personal and confidential"; it had not been sealed. The messenger produced the Presidential Seal from a small briefcase he carried. An obviously very highly trusted one this: David waited for him to speak but the man held his peace and waited, seal in hand, till David pulled the letter from its envelope. As the President had promised, it was a request to his dear friend to facilitate the good doctor in a purely family and humanitarian enterprise which the doctor would himself explain, and which could in no way be regarded as political in any sense. A son was concerned for his father and was doing what any son, you or I, would want to do if our father were in a similar situation. The salutations and good wishes were flowery and were followed by the scrawled personal signature. David returned the letter to its envelope and stuck down the flap. The man took it from him, made sure the gum was holding properly then carefully stamped the Presidential Seal on it. He handed back the letter to David, put away the seal, made a small formal bow to David and left, passing the awestruck receptionist as though he did not exist.

It was time to go so David paid his bill and went to his room. He packed quickly, gathered up the letters and telegrams, examined the room for the last time to ensure nothing was left behind, and then he went out to the taxi, carrying his one suitcase. He ordered his taxi driver to go to the airport by way of the post office, and dispatched his cables and posted his letters. At the airport he boarded the plane which would take him to Accra where he would join another for Kano, then another on the long cross-continental hop to Khartoum on the eastern edge of Africa. With a little luck he should be able to get down to Uganda before the Nubian had time to give full rein to his murderous impulses against Christian missions in general and his father's mission in particular.

The airport at Accra depressed David and he was glad the change-of-plane delay was a short one. The place was almost deserted, not bustling with the colourful exuberant crowds of the Nkrumah era. He remembered the air of freedom about the place then, and the young folk who were always about in small groups, night or day, watching the planes come in and take off, recognizing and sometimes loudly hailing the popular heroes of Pan-Africanism who were constantly coming and going through this airport, often met by the great Kwame himself. Night life in Accra in those days was something he had, in common with most visitors, found exhilarating. But Accra then was the political nerve centre of Pan-Africanism and the dream-centre for all black folk aspiring to be free. It was here that the first manifestation of a reborn Africa, free of foreign domination was, for a startling historical moment, a glowing reality. Because of it the world will never again be the same for black folk, will never again look at black folk in quite the same way as before Nkrumah's revolution. Now the military and police who had seized power, and seized and re-seized it again and again, changing one soldier's name for another, the name of one committee or council for another while the land sank deeper and deeper into confusion, were the only ones out watching the planes landing and taking off from Accra airport.

Even though David was in transit, the young soldier-immigration inspector hurried into a private office with his passport and was a long time returning it; when he did it was with suspicion and an odd reluctance.

Then it was time to go, and David was glad.

The airport at Kano was charged with life and activity even though it was nearly midnight. This was black Africa with yet another difference. Not even the French would dare to think of this as Occidental Africa. Black Africa, here, had profound oriental overtones not even found on the east coast of Africa where Islam prevails. The Islam which dominated here was predominantly cultural with the African tribal content, still so strong in east-coast Islam, washed out of it. The oriental overtones showed everywhere, in everything: in the buildings, in people's bearing, in their manner of speech.

When David's plane landed, a young immigration officer, a bright-eyed Ibo from eastern Nigeria, singled him out and led him to the airport manager's office through a milling, noisy crowd of people on the first leg of the Nigerian Moslem holy pilgrimage to Mecca. The heat and the noise and the fetid smell of many bodies in a confined place was overpowering.

The immigration officer opened the door marked Airport Manager, and motioned David in: "Dr Brown, sah!" Then he saluted and returned to his hot duties.

David welcomed the cool freshness of the room. A thick-set man in his early forties rose from a couch and came forward, welcoming hand outstretched, a beaming smile lighting up his round bronze face.

"I thought it had to be you! You won't remember me: I dropped out of med school because I couldn't stand the blood. . . . And the pain. Remember the first year student who passed out at that operation you performed!"

David looked blank, trying hard to remember, and seeing the man's face fall.

"You don't remember. Never mind; it was a long time ago."

Suddenly, out of nowhere, a name flashed across David's mind: he said it out loud. "Mike Adibo."

"That's it! That's it! You do remember!" Mike Adibo let out a joyous roar and shook David's hand vigorously. "Sit down, man! Sit down! Good to see you! Let me get you a drink! Had any food?"

"I need to rest." David relaxed on the couch. "The Khartoum leg looks like being crowded."

"It always is." Adibo busied himself happily mixing scotch and soda; this had once been British West Africa, and scotch and soda and gin and tonic were as much the norm here as was French wine in Conakry. "We're on the way to Mecca, the starting point in fact for all West African Moslems, and this is our busiest route all year round. But don't worry, we'll make you comfortable." He crossed the room to his desk and spoke into the telephone, telling someone to make sure to let the pilot know that Dr Brown was on his flight and to take special care of him. He hung up and turned back to David, suddenly very serious. "We had a special flash from Conakry about getting you on this flight; said the President wanted it especially. Must be important."

"It is," David said.

Adibo waited a while then said: "Here's to seeing you again."

"I hope you didn't stay on just for me." David tried to make amends.

"I wanted to." Adibo stared into his drink. "I wanted to be sure it was you when we got the flash; it had to be. Couldn't just go off. You've been in touch with all these things – with the leaders, with what was happening – I wanted to ask you what was happening. What is happening to us? What is happening to Africa? I hoped we could talk a little before you moved on; nobody here knows what's going on or what is going to happen. . . ."

David sighed inwardly. So it's here too; up here in remote and politically backward Kano on the edge of the desert. It was, somehow, encouraging in a depressing sort of way that one person should be waiting up in the middle of the night to voice his concern and ask for answers and hope to find comfort in those answers. But how do you answer?

Adibo seemed to sense David's difficulty. "It's at least another hour to your plane time. Come home with me and have a bath and something to eat and we can talk a little. It's not far."

"Glad to." David was glad to be able to show appreciation.

"Good! Don't worry about your suitcase; it will be taken care of and given to you on the plane." Again Adibo spoke into his telephone before leading the way out to his car; he was clearly pleased for David to see the deference everyone showed the airport manager as they passed: even the masses of pilgrims seemed to know who he was and showed it by bowing courteously as he passed.

The journey to Adibo's sprawling house was a quick ten minutes' drive and David was soon luxuriating under a shower. Then Adibo lent him a flowing white robe and led him to an outside dining area of the walled-in compound where young men in white robes served the food. Adibo's wife, a tall, willowy and beautiful Fulani woman, came to pay her respects and spent a few minutes making awkward small talk in the very little, very poor Arabic she had picked up in her childhood; then, having done her duty, she said something very quickly and in a very different tone to her husband in Hausa, and withdrew.

In a worried voice Adibo asked: "What's going to happen? Everything looked so good in 1960. Now we've had a Prime Minister killed and we've had a civil war. Why are things not as they should be?"

"I'm not sure anyone can answer that," David said.

"We told ourselves that once we got rid of imperialism things would be fine and we would make Africa a great and glorious place for all its people. Instead we slaughtered each other. Why?"

"Not only here," David said. "Perhaps our notion of progress was at fault. Perhaps we tried too hard to move too fast."

"I sometimes wonder. . . ," Adibo lapsed into silence.

David completed the awkward thought, "Whether we can really manage our own affairs. That it?"

Adibo looked startled. "Yes."

"I think we can," David said. "What do you think?"

"I want to think so." Adibo sounded unhappy. "I know we have the ability. But look at what's happened and what's happening."

"And it leads to your doubting our ability?"

"No, not our ability; just that everything we do seems to go wrong. *They* managed things so well; why can't we?"

335

"I think we must keep asking that question till we find answers but I'm not sure we'll find those answers by looking back to how they managed. They were managing what was their own imperial thing, not our thing. We must ask why in our own context. Where did we go wrong and why? I think we want to go back and question all the assumptions on which our actions were based."

"How far back?" Adibo wondered aloud, and answered himself: "As far back as you have to go to find an answer. Yes, I think I like that. But what if you don't find the answer?"

"You don't begin your questioning by expecting not to find an answer. If you don't expect an answer it is foolish to start the questioning; if you start the questioning you must expect it to lead to answers."

"Where does one begin?"

"Where do you want to begin?"

"I don't know," Adibo sounded weary suddenly. It had been a long day, made longer by his waiting up for this man from the more optimistic past when everything seemed so much more clearcut and people always had answers, even if they were false answers. Now, after all the disasters, not even the great doctor David Brown, who had walked with Africa's leaders and travels on a diplomatic passport, could give him any answers. Only more questions to ask. Not what I had hoped for, waited up for, but the best there is. What was his question? Where did we go wrong, and why?

He's regretting all the effort he's laid out, David thought and wanted to apologize.

"I'm glad it *was* you and I saw you," Adibo said warmly. "We expect more than we should from old friends sometimes, and that is not fair. I was looking for easy and comforting answers. You know, like it was in the old days. But things have changed, haven't they?"

There was little further to say to each other till they got back to the airport, where they were told of another half an hour's delay in the flight to Khartoum. David declined Adibo's half-hearted offer to stay with him in his private office till departure time. Adibo tried not to show his relief as he shook David's hand. His face lit up, warm and generous as at their first meeting nearly two hours earlier. This, David thought, is something we have that few others have; and for all that has happened we still have it, this radiance from within at the meeting and the parting with those on whom we look as friends.

"When you find some of the answers," for all his weariness Adibo's eyes shone, "please let me know. Just address it to me care of Kano International Airport, Northern Nigeria; I'll get it, no matter where I am."

"I will," David said, knowing he would do no such thing, knowing Michael Adibo knew he would do no such thing.

For a few seconds Michael Adibo's and David Brown's eyes made four; then Adibo swung about abruptly and walked away.

There were five people in the VIP lounge: a man in the company of two women; a man alone; and a white man dozing, or seeming to, in the farthest corner of the lounge. The air-conditioning made the large room cool to near chilliness without freshening the air.

David recognized the white man immediately. He was a famous journalistic Africa hand, recognized internationally as one of the two or three current experts on Africa. He knew everything about Africa: its history, its politics, its people, its problems. He knew all its important leaders personally, and spoke on first-name terms about them on his highly publicized and lucrative lecture tours in the United States. His articles in a leading British newspaper were syndicated throughout the world. David had seen him at all the major Pan-African conferences and gatherings after the great upsurge of the 1960s, he had even been introduced to the man once or twice; but the man hardly noticed him, he had been interested only in talking to the leaders, in being seen talking to the leaders. David hoped the man would not recognize him now; he had had his bellyful of white experts on Africa, and this one had grown more authoritative, more oracular, with each crisis leading to the deepening of Africa's problems. He had advised this or that leader that this or that consequence would result from this or that action; now it had come to pass. If only they had heeded his advice! He knew all the answers, had well-reasoned explanations for every setback. Africa was still the white man's game and could

337

still be won for the West if everybody, black and white alike, inside and outside Africa, pursued the moderate and enlightened policies he advocated. And I don't want to talk with him, David decided, sensing that the half-dozing man was examining him. Apparently the man did not place him; the man moved his head slightly, as though adjusting his head in sleep, and the feel of being closely examined left David. He found a seat near the door and settled down to wait for the flight call, the din of the teeming crowd outside filtering into the air-conditioned lounge.

David dozed off and woke and dozed off again till it was time to take off for Khartoum.

COUNTY TIPPERARY JOINT LIBRARIES
County Library
Thurles.

2

Enid Kagwa, the bishop's office secretary, knocked on the door, entered, and shut it firmly behind her. John Chitole looked up from his papers.

"An officer from the barracks at Tororo to see you, my lord."

"What about, Enid?"

"He won't say, sir. I tried to make an appointment but he insists on seeing you now."

"These are the days of the soldiers," Chitole murmured.

"I pressed the alert buzzer so help should be outside by now."

"No," Chitole said firmly, "send them away. Let him in."

Miss Kagwa looked doubtful and unhappy but opened the door.

"The bishop will see you: Captain Musaka of the Tororo barracks, my lord."

The soldier marched briskly into the room and saluted. Chitole waved him to a chair, then looked at Miss Kagwa. "It's all right, Enid." She left unwillingly.

"She's suspicious." The captain made it an accusation.

Chitole looked at the captain, at the tilt of his head, the bearing of his body, the beginning of a bulge to his belly for all his youth. Not much more than twenty-three or -four but clearly enjoying the good life of an officer under the military rule of the Nubian. The captain tried to outstare Chitole and failed.

"Should she be? Suspicious, I mean."

"Of me?" The captain showed his teeth. "No, my lord."

"I'm glad to hear it; I'll tell her. Now, what can I do for you?"

"Don't you need your. . . ," Musaka paused deliberately, "your superior? Don't you need him here too?"

Chitole's smile did not reach his eyes. Want to play games, my young captain? All right. He said: "I can see you don't understand our church, captain."

"I was a Christian once," Musaka snapped, showing anger. "Before I saw it for what it was and is."

"And now you're a Moslem, like the President."

"That's right!"

"But that is not what you came to see me about, is it?"

Musaka calmed himself deliberately. "In a way it is. I speak for the officers at the barracks. We would like to have collaboration between your church and our barracks: for you to sort of adopt us and care for us. We know yours is the only truly black foreign church. The others have black bishops but white faces are in control in the back. We are told no whites control your churches anywhere, but it is still a foreign church and that is the part we do not like."

"So?"

"So we want to see how independent you really are. You are the bishop but the American stays here. Why? To watch you?"

Chitole casually touched a hidden button on the edge of his desk alerting Enid Kagwa to hear and take down what was said. Chitole chose his words carefully, spoke deliberately. "Bishop Brown stays here because this is his home. He is a citizen of Uganda who has been here longer than you have been alive, captain. He loves this place and this land and the people here; we want him to go on staying here because it is his home and because we love him and want him to stay here with us. Please understand that very clearly, captain, and please understand he is not an American. He was born in Jamaica in the West Indies, and Jamaica is part of the Commonwealth and the non-aligned movement."

"But not of the OAU!" Captain Musaka was really angry now; the encounter was not going as he had planned.

"Only because Jamaica is not part of the African continent."

"There you are! It is a foreign place! And nobody knows who is in charge of your church – you or this man from a foreign place! That is what I'm talking about!"

Looking for a quarrel now, my young captain: wonder why? But I'm not ready yet. "My dear Captain Musaka, no church, not even the white-controlled church, is run like an army unit or a civil service department, or even a government, where all authority and final decision-making ends up with one person – a Prime

Minister or President or. . . ." Chitole thought of the word "dictator" but did not say it. "So when you ask who is in charge it is rather difficult to answer simply. I am in charge of the running of the church, but then, the church is in charge of the running of me: the church is the congregation and the congregation is the church; and we are all subject to, and guided by, the will of God. Perhaps the best way for you to think of Bishop Brown is as the retired servant of the church who has been pensioned off and whom we are keeping here, as you do an honoured old father who can no longer work hard any more, so that he can live out his days in peace and happiness among those he has looked after and who love him dearly. That is not so hard to understand, captain; it is our way. He is like your father grown old, or mine, or anyone's."

In spite of himself the captain understood; to honour your father, to take care of your old, was a tradition that went deeper than his new militarism. And he knew the other officers at the barracks would see it in the same light. But was it really like that? Was this one really in control?

"Then it is you who get the instructions!"

Chitole floundered mentally for a while, confused by the notion of instructions. Musaka misread the confusion. Got him! He glowed inwardly.

"What instructions?" Chitole said at last.

"Come, bishop! You know. Instructions from your headquarters in America. Don't pretend you don't get any."

"I see. . . ." Chitole tried to contain the scorn that welled up inside him. "So that's what you think of me, of us, your own people? You see us as somebody else's tools. Oh my son, how could you? Can we never be our own people? Our own tools? Can we never belong to ourselves and do what we do because we do it for ourselves?"

Something about the bishop's quiet anger, something in his voice, the look in his eyes, disturbed and embarrassed Captain Musaka, made him feel small and shamed all at once. He jumped up from his chair, deliberately sending it crashing to the floor; he waved his swagger stick in anger and took two turns about the office; he set his face in an expression of rage, lips pushed out as he had seen the President do.

341

"I'm an officer of the Ugandan army!" he shouted, bringing Miss Kagwa rushing into the room. Chitole waved her out again. "I do my duty as an officer! I have no other business with you! You have not answered my question! Do not be impertinent with an officer of the Ugandan army!"

"If you stop shouting I will answer you, captain."

Musaka stopped, picked up the chair and sat down.

Chitole spoke into the little intercom box on his desk, finger on its key: "Miss Kagwa, please bring me the current file of communications from our headquarters."

They waited for about half a minute, the captain staring at a point above the bishop's head, the bishop watching the captain, till Miss Kagwa brought the bulging file. The bishop thanked and dismissed her with his eyes and placed the file on the desk in front of the captain.

"This is the file; examine it for yourself." The bishop's voice was cold and unfriendly now, the suppressed anger still in it.

Musaka hesitated for a second then briskly opened the file. He was more suspicious now but you can't refuse to look at documents when a suspect offers them to you. Of course they wouldn't offer it if it had anything incriminating, but you have to look all the same. He read the first document: a long and detailed quarterly account of happenings in the various sections of the church all over the world. This was followed by a lengthy business document dealing specifically with the affairs of the Uganda Mission: the amount of coffee, cotton, tea that had been shipped by the local co-operatives for sale on the American market; the volume and price of each item sold, to whom, and the total amount received. All deductions were itemized and explained. The money realized, less service charges and the cost of whatever the local church had ordered, was then transferred to the church account with its Ugandan bankers. The amount of money involved startled Musaka. This church was richer than those at the barracks thought; it was doing very profitable business.

Musaka looked up at the bishop, forgetting to make his show of anger, and grew embarrassed when he realized the bishop knew what was in his mind. But the question had to be asked.

"All this money? Who gets it?"

"Those who earned it," Chitole said. "All our business, our farms, our gins, our tools and machinery, everything, belong to those who do the work. Everything is owned co-operatively. I am sure you know that. Our co-operatives are all registered and legal business entities."

"I know." Musaka sounded impatient. His mind was on the money; the army could do with some of this money, the army could always do with money. He said, not looking at the bishop: "Then you could help the army with some of this money."

"In what way?" Here it comes, Chitole thought.

"Give us some of it for food and uniforms and arms and ammunition."

"We already do that through our taxes. Want to see how much taxes we pay? It's quite a sum."

"I don't mean like that. I mean as a personal show of your love for the army for the special protection your mission will enjoy."

He has the grace not to look at me. "We would have to have a special meeting of all members of all the co-operatives to discuss the suggestion and I do not think they would agree to just give away their money. Everybody here works for whatever they want. But I'm sure that if the army wanted to do some work with the co-operatives to earn. . . ."

"Don't you have some sort of special fund?" Musaka cut in quickly, still not looking at Chitole. "Some sort of bishop's fund."

"No." Chitole waited for the captain to look up.

It took time but at last he did: a quick, sidelong glance that slid over Chitole's face. Then the captain closed the file, pushed it across to the bishop and got up.

"So you have nothing for us, Lord Bishop, nothing to tell us and nothing to give us; and you will not let the American go. Is that what I must tell my superiors? I'm sure you've heard of Colonel Idrisi; is that what I must tell him?"

Chitole rose and offered his hand. "We have work, captain, and goodwill and friendship. You and your fellow officers and men will always be welcome to our church here and in every other part of the country."

343

"They want you to send the American home, if you are really in charge."

Suddenly Chitole resumed his seat and gestured for the captain to do the same. Musaka ignored him.

"Tell me, captain, why this sudden concern with a retired old churchman who can do you no harm and who has spent most of his life here?"

"He's an American!" Musaka snapped. "The President has warned the army to look for spying Americans who come as teachers or missionaries or journalists and try to destroy our nation's freedom and unity. What will you do if the President orders all Americans out?"

"He's a Ugandan citizen."

"Will you defy the President?"

"Nobody does that and it is not my intention or the church's."

"Everybody's a Ugandan – when it suits them. Americans, Englishmen, everybody. Even Asians."

Chitole rose once more. "Is there anything else, captain?"

"We will let you know, bishop!" Musaka clicked his heels, swung about and stalked out of the office.

Chitole resumed his seat and waited till he heard the roar of the military jeep going away. He let out a long sigh and touched his intercom. "Got it all, Enid?"

"Yes, sir," Enid's voice, seething with anger, came clear through the little box. "I don't like it, sir. There's talk about the Asians everywhere, and they say the two missing Americans are dead and buried."

"Who are 'they', Enid?"

"People everywhere, my lord; everywhere."

"Transcribe your notes for me now."

"Yes, sir."

What now, Chitole wondered; what is that violent and unpredictable man up to now? How did we get into this mess? How did a stable nation of sensible people allow this to happen? O Lord, help and guide us against this dangerous man!

Later that evening, as they prepared for the light supper they usually shared with Jacob, Chitole told Emma of Captain Musaka's visit and what had transpired. Emma realized that Chitole was more worried than he let on.

"How serious is it?"

"We'll know when he comes next; he or another."

"Then why are you so worried? Why not forget it until we see what happens next?"

"Because it may be too late by then. Enid says the talk is that the two missing American journalists are dead and buried and their bodies will never be found. If he has decided on a campaign against Americans we may have to act before it reaches here."

So that was it; she understood his agitation now, and tried to allay it: "He wouldn't dare touch Grandpa. . . ." They had taken to calling Jacob Grandpa for the sake of the children to begin with, but it had stuck and everybody now called him Grandpa or, when they wanted to be formal, the Old One, which also means the Wise One, the Father. . . . "He wouldn't dare!"

"Wouldn't he?" Chitole wondered softly. "He bombed the Kabaka's Palace; he seized power from the man who in his foolish arrogance made him what was supposed to be the puppet commander of the army; he used the Jews, then threw them out; he orders murder and plunder without hesitation; and you say he wouldn't dare touch Grandpa. When are we going to understand the wickedness of this man? What is an old missionary bishop to him? He *would* dare, my dear. My hope was that he would not notice us for a long time and that during that time things might change. Now it seems he has noticed us, and he would dare anything."

"Perhaps it is still only the people at the barracks," Emma suggested. "They sometimes do these things without his authority."

"I hope so." The muscle on his jaw seemed to jump. "If you are right it would give us a little time. But this young man also said something about the Asians and then reacted as though he had betrayed a secret. Then Enid said there is this talk about the Asians everywhere."

"They have behaved badly," Emma said coldly. "They have exploited and discriminated."

"We've known that for a long time so that cannot be the reason for this sudden upsurge of interest in them. Think, Emma: he ordered out the Jews when he couldn't get anything more from them. They had thought they were using him; it turned out he was using them. He quarrelled with the British because they would not give him a blank cheque type of aid, and he has killed or driven out all the people able to work up credible aid programmes for him; so he's gone to Libya looking for free money. What is to stop him just taking over everything the Asians have?"

"It's illegal."

"So is seizing power. Did that stop him?"

Emma gave up, stopped arguing. There was good reason for Chitole's anxiety but she found it hard and deeply disturbing to entertain the idea of the possibility that the inviolability of the church, her church, could be challenged. She had come to it for sanctuary in her time of greatest need when there was nowhere else to turn. And all the governments of Uganda, before and since independence, had always respected the inviolability of the church, not only this one, but all the churches of the land, whether they liked what went on or not. Now, her husband, John Chitole, bishop of the church, saw and feared the possibility of such violation. And even as she wondered why the usurper-President would do this, she knew the answer: this man had to control or destroy. Once she opened her mind to this she realized how wise Chitole was not to wait till something happened.

"What will you do? What can we do?"

"I must talk to Grandpa and Michael."

"He will want to leave to save the church."

"Will his leaving save the church? I doubt it."

Emma thought this through for a long while, then she exclaimed: "Oh, John! Is it really as bad as that?"

"I could be wrong; I hope I am. Let's talk to Grandpa."

Jacob was not in his study so they tried his private quarters. He was not there either but the door, as usual, was unlocked so they went in and through to the private little garden though they knew he would not be there.

They went back to the living room and out to the bigger garden. The old man and his dog could be taking an evening walk there.

Emma had made sure that the garden, and indeed the house, remained as his Margaret had conceived it.

"He's nowhere here." She had made a quick survey of the garden. "Let's ask Mama Kilu." She went back into the house, leaving Chitole by the door on the edge of the garden.

In the kitchen Mama Kilu sat in her rocking-chair at her table in the centre of her kingdom. Three much younger women were busy at the stove, the cupboards and the sink. Mama Kilu had grown heavy and slow with time, but she had firmly refused to retire as long as her bishop lived in that house. This, she had told Jacob and Chitole when they tried to persuade her that it was time to retire, was what she had promised her Missy and she would not break that promise. So one of her grandsons brought her to work each morning in the truck he drove for the Coffee Co-operative, and came for her each evening. And from her rocking-chair she supervised the work of the household: in order to ensure that this house would remain the same as it was when she first came here to work with Missy, to learn from her how to run this place and serve the bishop. For to Mama Kilu her bishop, the agent on earth of her God in heaven, and the holy man Missy loved, would always need to be cared for while he did God's work till it was time for him to join his Missy in heaven, and only the Great One knew when that would be. Till then, or her own time to die, it was her duty to stay right here.

Emma touched the old lady's shoulder; she seemed to have drifted off, as the old sometimes do. Now, at the touch, she came to with a startled little jerk.

"Heh! Oh. Ma'am, Miss Emma; what's it?"

"Grandpa is not here; d'you know where he is?"

"Should be back by now." The old lady sounded put out. "He said he'd be."

"Where's he gone?"

"To visit Missy. The dog's with him; he'll be all right."

"Walking this time of night."

"No, he's driving his little jeep."

"Oh, Mama! You know he doesn't see so well at night; why did you let him go?"

"I tell you the dog's with him; he'll be all right!"

"The dog can't help him drive, Mama!"

"Then it must be about the only thing that dog can't do."

The exasperation in the old lady's voice made Emma smile, despite her concern for Jacob. The old lady clearly did not share that concern. Emma laid her hand lightly on the old lady's shoulder: "You are right, Mama; Grandpa is safe with Jane." But the old lady had drifted off again, only half-aware of Emma now. Emma left her.

When she got back to the living room Chitole was still at the open window, but he was less preoccupied, more himself, more alert than when she had left him.

"Mama says he went . . ."

"I hear the jeep," Chitole cut in, a world of relief in his voice.

The strong emotions of a son for a much-loved father, Emma thought. How that old man has bound you to him! You and all of us.

Chitole took her arm and pulled her along. "Let's go and meet him."

Emma began her scolding before he was properly out of the jeep. "You know you should not be driving in the dark. The eye-doctor told you that. You should have had someone with you. We were worried." She stared up at the great looming shadow over her.

"All right, Emma," Chitole murmured.

She flung her arms about the great body and held tight for a few seconds.

"She's right," Jacob said to Chitole. "We had no business being out alone so late. I thought we would be back before dark but you know how time can pass unnoticed in a tranquil place. I'm sorry."

"Mama Kilu wasn't worried." Emma laughed and held on to his arm. "She said Jane was with you which made everything all right as far as she was concerned."

They went into the house and Mama Kilu, all there now, came to welcome Jacob and to take her leave for the evening. She moved slowly but surely, a helper a little distance behind her.

"There you are!" The old lady looked down at the golden dog. "I told Miss Emma not to worry. Your supper is ready in the kitchen; go." The dog tilted her head up to Jacob. He nodded slightly. The dog walked to the kitchen, pausing on the way to give a casual passing lick to the back of the old lady's hand, then she went to her dinner. Mama Kilu looked at Emma and not all the folds around her eyes could hide the wicked, mocking expression as she said: "Sure she can't drive?" Then the expression changed as the old lady touched her bishop's arm. "I must leave you for another night, old friend. If it is His will I will be here in the morning. Goodnight." She looked at Chitole, then Emma. "And you, my children; goodnight."

"Goodnight, Mama," Jacob said.

"Goodnight, Mama," Chitole said.

"Goodnight, Mama," Emma said, and added: "Who knows. . . ."

The old lady chuckled, turned and walked heavily but steadily out to the waiting co-op truck.

"I must try Jane at the wheel sometime." The vision of it made Jacob chuckle as he led the way into the dining room. They settled down and a woman pushed in the food trolley and the evening ritual began. Chitole prepared their three drinks; he knew what each one took. Emma served the food; she too knew what and how much each person wanted. Jacob was at the head of the table. The family circle was complete. Only the two young ones, Emma and Chitole's son and daughter, were not present. They had eaten earlier in the kitchen under Mama Kilu's supervision and then gone to their rooms.

Chitole brought the drinks, Emma passed the food; then Chitole took his seat on the right hand of Jacob. The seat that had once been Margaret's had long since become Emma's. They bowed their heads and Jacob said grace. As if on divine cue, the instant grace ended the telephone rang. Chitole answered; it was Michael Odera, Bishop's Secretary and the most senior administrator of the day-to-day affairs of the church. Chitole spoke for a while and then returned to the table and they commenced the meal.

"Michael," Chitole told Jacob. "He'll be here soon. I'm glad he's back to hear what I have to tell you. He's worried about something out in the country. We'll wait till he comes."

Michael Odera arrived halfway through the meal. The once skinny and very bright young man had matured into a tubby,

349

brilliant administrator with an enormous capacity for hard work. He had grown shortsighted with time and he wore very strong steel-rimmed glasses. This, and his balding head, had led a student wag to nickname him "bald eagle" and it had stuck. Thanks largely to Odera's organization and hard work the church had more than doubled its out-districts during the past decade; and its membership and its business ventures were flourishing everywhere. A great deal of Odera's time, these days, was spent in travelling to the out-districts to oversee church affairs. His latest trip to the distant western border area had been to both oversee church affairs and to launch a pioneering co-operative house-building venture to help cope with the growing numbers of refugees crossing the border from the Congo. The trip had gone well, but what he had heard brought him hurrying back, filled with concern and anxious to talk to Jacob and Chitole.

Now, between mouthfuls, Odera told his bishops the cause for his concern: "At first I did not notice it. All it was to begin with was a passing reference to this or that Asian shop or bazaar or house or piece of land or livestock or motor car or bicycle; and mostly from people outside the church. Then, in one small town to the north of Lake Albert I passed a shop and heard a man quarrelling with the Asian owner for not giving him credit. He shouted at the Asian that he, the one seeking credit, would soon be the owner of that shop, just as soon as the President gave the word. I went in after the man had left and spoke to the Asian. It was difficult. But in the end it came out, after I mentioned you, Grandpa. What came out was they had heard the President was going to give the word for all Asian property to be seized."

"With compensation, surely," Jacob said.

"Not as he told me; not as I heard from others," Odera said.

"Could be just talk," Chitole suggested, remembering Enid's words.

"I thought so at first," Odera said. "But then I asked our church people. They had all heard it: the priests, the deacons, the lay people, everybody. At first they, too, had not paid it much mind; the land is full of all sorts of rumours, and the idea of frightening the Asians is not unattractive to people who have been the victims of their prejudice. So it could be just talk to see the welcome new nervousness replacing the old arrogance in Asian eyes. But the talk persisted and was always the same: all Asians would be ordered to leave the country and to leave their possessions and property behind; nobody was to buy anything from the Asians even if they offered to sell at giveaway prices. The word was: Wait and you will get it all for nothing. When I heard it from two senior officials in the district I knew it was more than empty talk to frighten the Asians. And the idea of getting so much for nothing is spreading like strong drink among the people.

"Even if this were to happen," Jacob said. "Not everyone will get something; many will get nothing. How will they feel?"

"I had not thought of that," Chitole murmured.

"There is nothing that stirs up the moral conscience quite as much as being at the losing end of an immorality. I'm sure our church people have seen that." Jacob looked at Odera for confirmation.

"I'm not sure," Odera sighed, looking owlishly from Jacob to Chitole then back at Jacob. "The idea of a house or a car or a piece of land or shop being yours without costing you anything is dazzling. It stirs the greed in everyone, even some priests."

"Some of ours?" Chitole sounded distressed.

"Yes, I spoke to some of ours. It helped; some were shamefaced and honest enough to admit an ugly thing had been let loose among them. Others tried to hide what was in their minds but their eyes betrayed them."

"You have noted them? I mean the priests; ours."

"A passing temptation," Emma suggested. "They're human."

"We must stop it," Chitole said firmly, looking at Jacob.

"Not if the President orders it," Odera said.

"We can stop our own people, whatever the President orders."

"I agree with John," Jacob said. "But you must realize it could set us on collision course with the government, and that would mean trouble."

"We could do it quietly," Odera suggested. "The church of Jesus Christ is not unfamiliar with quiet underground activity in times of moral collapse and danger. There are ways in which we can spread the word without anything coming back to us."

"This may be a time for public witness," Chitole said. "The church of Christ is familiar with such too."

Odera lowered his head. He did not want to contradict his bishop and friend and mentor. "It is a question of what is best for the church and her people. This man would lead the country away from Christianity. If he had his way he would destroy the Christian church here, not only our church. In any head-on collision he could succeed, especially if he could keep his army happy and well-fed by giving them what he has stolen from others like the Asians. But one day he will run out of things to steal from others; he will run out of money to buy the loyalty of his soldiers and the misguided among the people. When that day comes people will see him for what he is. It is important that the church be not destroyed before that day comes. For if it is destroyed there will be nothing and no one to lead our people back to the paths of righteousness."

"I do not think we can avoid the collision you so rightly fear." Chitole used his voice to make Odera understand he did not mind being contradicted and that all was well between them.

"Tell them about the soldier's visit," Emma urged, certain that would resolve the issue between them.

Chitole told them all that had passed between him and Captain Musaka, using Enid's notes to leave out nothing. When he had done Odera nodded.

"Yes, now I understand; we cannot avoid a collision if they challenge us in this deliberate way. I see that."

Jacob said: "I think we have to do both things, my sons: we must bear witness, as you, John, want when the time comes; and in the meantime we must do as you want, Michael, and prepare for the survival of the church, no matter what happens. These are the two sides of the same answer to our problems. Do you agree? You, John?"

Chitole's face cracked in a warm smile. "Yes, Grandpa."

"And you, Michael? Don't hesitate to argue."

Odera took off his glasses and looked like a blind owl. He nodded, making it the gesture of a schoolboy. "No more argument, sir, Grandpa."

"Good!" Jacob said, growing visibly younger in bearing as Emma looked on. "Then let us conspire, my sons! Let us think our way through the troubles ahead; let us make plans and contingency plans and fall-back plans in case the contingencies fail. Emma, get paper and we will all make notes and all the notes must be destroyed once we have agreed and absorbed the details."

Emma went away and came back with pads and pencils. A young helper came and cleared the table; another brought a jug of fruit juice and glasses. Then they shut the door and began.

"Where do we begin?" Jacob asked.

Odera said: "They will want to seize whatever we have so we must put away whatever we can for later use. That means we must secrete away in safe places all the money we can lay our hands on; we can always bring it back if what we fear does not come to pass."

"It will come to pass," Chitole said.

"Then you, Michael," Jacob looked at Chitole who nodded, knowing what Jacob would say and agreeing in advance. "You'll begin immediately with the money and movable property."

"I'll work out a way for Emma to know where everything is if anything happens to me." Odera thought for a while. "I think a number of our women would have to know; the money and property would be safest with them."

"Next," Jacob said.

Chitole said: "My next meeting with the soldier, the Asians and you; in that order."

"All right. The soldier," Jacob said.

Chitole began to talk. They were, all of them, at the peak of alertness now. Emma looked at Jacob. For all his thinning white hair, for all the heavy slackness age had brought to his body, he seemed, suddenly, as he had been when his beloved Missy was alive, as she had first seen him when he was a man at his peak: clear-minded, in control. And so were her John and Michael Odera.

Emma thought: These men of mine, are using their wits to defend what is a lifetime's work for each of them; and they are doing it as calmly and without fear as though they did not know the terrible power and wickedness of the Nubian. Just one old priest and two not-very-strong younger ones.

A little after midnight Emma and the night-duty helper brought coffee and sandwiches. Odera made several telephone calls. One brought the mission chief accountant from his bed, another woke the transport manager who in turn woke a select group of mission workers who went out to the motor vehicles they drove.

When the first grey light of morning showed, Emma gathered up all the papers; she took them to the kitchen and stuffed them in the big range and watched till they were all burnt. Then Emma saw an utterly exhausted Jacob, grown very old again, to his bedroom, accompanied by Jane; and then she herself went to bed, leaving Chitole and Odera still refining a few more details of all the plans they had agreed on.

At last, as the sun rose, their work too was done and each went to his bed, worn out, but highly satisfied with the long night's work.

A few mission vans and jeeps, all the portable and readily available wealth hidden in them, took off for different parts of the country in the very early hours of the morning. The chief accountant went in person and woke the bank manager in Tororo before daybreak, who arranged that the money in the mission's account there would be out of reach of all unauthorized hands, even if the bank itself were taken over.

Over the next three days there was a great coming and going to and from the mission. Priests came from all the out-districts; they came mostly at night or in the very early hours of the morning and went straight into conferences with Odera; occasionally Chitole or Jacob sat in, but mainly this was Odera's business. Often, at odd hours of the day or night, Odera was away from the mission, somewhere on the road, with no one knowing precisely where he was or when he would return.

The officers and leading members of the women's guild gathered frequently and went on frequent trips to distant parts of the country, laden with presents for relatives no one had heard of before. For all these sudden new activities life at the mission continued in the old undisturbed manner; yet everybody knew their world was changing fast, and greater changes were at hand.

On the fourth day, which was a Friday, Captain Musaka of the Tororo barracks paid his second visit to Chitole in the late afternoon. Chitole met him at the door. The captain was dressed in his green parade uniform, not the casual old khaki of the last time. He had all his medals on his chest, his cap set at a jaunty angle, his highly polished shoes dazzled; he held his swagger stick so that the big gold signet ring on his finger could not be missed. This time he had not driven himself, he had sat in the back of his military jeep, erect and formal; the driver had a companion beside him with an automatic rifle cradled in the crook of his left arm, right hand near the trigger.

Captain Musaka entered the outer office with something of a peacock strut as if expecting Miss Kagwa's admiration. Instead, he read only resentment in Miss Kagwa's eyes.

In the inner office, Chitole said: "You're very formal today, captain."

"Any objections?" Musaka snapped.

Still looking for a fight, Chitole thought. "None at all; just a social remark, captain."

"My visit is not social!"

"My apologies; please have a seat."

Musaka remained standing, angry and fierce-looking. "I demand to see your bishop! I demand it now!"

"So be it, captain." Chitole depressed his intercom button. "Miss Kagwa, please call Bishop Brown for me. Tell him he is to leave whatever he is doing and come immediately. Tell him Captain Musaka demands to see him." He released the button. "There, he should be here soon, captain."

Musaka sat down abruptly, nonplussed, forgetting briefly to be the stern interrogating officer. "I thought. . . ."

"That I was trying to hide Bishop Brown from you? No, captain. I just told you I am in charge here, not he. You added the rest in your mind."

"And you will say this in front of him?"

"If you wish, yes."

"You have arranged it! You were not so eager to bring him in last time. You've talked it over and arranged it."

"To what point, captain? I still would prefer to leave him out. He's an old man, entitled to be left alone, like your father or mine."

"That's what you said last time to disarm me."

Wonder who told you that; you were disarmed so someone had to tell you. Aloud, Chitole said: "Well, he's coming now, isn't he?"

"Yes," Musaka said reluctantly. He was supposed to push this churchman into committing himself; instead this one kept making him answer questions to show civility and to think of family. Well, he would not allow it this time. He looked at the expensive gold watch he had frightened that Asian merchant into presenting to him, making it a show of impatience.

Chitole depressed his button: "What's happened to the bishop?"

"He's on his way!" Enid's voice was charged with anger.

Musaka tried to think his way through this one. If this churchman had persisted in refusing to let him see the old bishop he was supposed to take him back to the barracks with them for further questioning. That's what the Colonel, Idrisi Mohammed, had suggested; and Colonel Idrisi's suggestions were really orders. Now he would be forced to question the old bishop and go back without this one, unless he could trap either of them into some admission of guilt. He avoided looking at Chitole: he did not want to get into any conversation with him; he was too smart by far. Pretty little thing out there, but very hostile; he would smile at her on the way out and try and soften some of her hostility.

"The bishop. . . ." Miss Kagwa's voice, only slightly less angry, floated in the air. The door opened and the second biggest man Captain Musaka had ever seen came into the room and filled it with his presence. Only the President was, or appeared to be, bigger than this man. A very dark man, almost as dark as the President himself, but better-looking even though he was very much older; a very old man, as this one had said. Bigger than the President, it now seemed: just as overpowering, but in a different, more quiet way.

Chitole rose and in spite of himself Musaka found himself on his feet as well. The big man offered a huge hand, and again in spite of himself, Musaka took it.

"Bishop Jacob Brown," Chitole said quietly; "Captain Musaka."

"Glad to meet you, Captain Musaka," Jacob said. "Which Musaka?"

"John, sir."

"John; well, well. Same as our bishop here. Two Johns, what a coincidence. Then you must have been born a Christian."

"My family were Christians. . . ." Captain Musaka fought off the impulse to relax. "They did not understand how the Christian religion was used to exploit them."

"So you grew up a Christian boy," Jacob said softly.

"The army and the President showed me Islam is the true religion for our people."

"If that is what you believe then it must be good. Not to believe, not to have any faith, is the only thing that makes us lost souls. Once you believe there is hope. And there are many paths, very many more than most of us realize in our arrogance, that lead to the kingdom of God. Ours, and yours, are only two of the many though some among us, and some among you, a majority unfortunately, would claim that they have the one and only and exclusive key to God's kingdom."

. . . I must not allow myself to be trapped by this old man's way with words. I must not allow his peacefulness to drown me. I am a soldier. That is not what Idrisi sent me here for. The wrath of Idrisi is terrible. A soldier must not relax with our enemies, and I am a soldier and these are our enemies. . . .

Chitole said: "Captain Musaka dared me to say in your presence that I am the one in charge here, not you."

"And you are; and you have said it," Jacob said.

"But is it true?" Musaka challenged. "Is he really in charge or is he just the man in front? Some smart Asians are putting Ugandans in front these days: to be seen in the stores and bazaars; to have their names up as managers, while the Asians remain behind the scenes and pull the strings."

"And you think it is like that, here, at our mission?" Jacob looked from Musaka to Chitole, then back at Musaka.

"Could be," Musaka replied defiantly. "Why not?"

"So, the one John, the military John, sees the other John, the religious John, as the puppet." The old man pulled himself together and seemed to grow larger and younger and stronger. "Look at him, young man! Look at John Chitole, first Ugandan bishop of our church in your country; tell me if you see a man who can be used by you or me or anybody else to do what he knows to

357

be wrong or what he does not want to do! Look at him and tell me! Do you, John Musaka, believe in your heart he is anybody's puppet?"

. . . I will not capitulate; I must not capitulate. . . .

"He may not think so, and you may not think so; you may believe in what you are doing and still be used as a puppet."

"Explain yourself, captain," Chitole said coldly.

Musaka held on. "It is simple. You have been converted to their religion, you want it to be good so it is good for you; and so they use you to maintain their system through your belief. That is the best kind of puppet: the one who believes in what he is doing."

"You could say that about all religions and all faiths and all ideas," Jacob suggested.

Musaka felt more relaxed; this he could handle. "Yes, you could. The important question is whose religion or faith or ideas you say it about. Yours come from the white man. Islam is not a white man's religion. That is why they are against it. They fear it because they cannot control it; because it is the religion of dark people and will lead dark people to an independence that is free of them."

"I've heard the President say this," Jacob said.

"Was he wrong?" Musaka challenged.

"No," Jacob said and Musaka's face broke into a smile of triumph. "But it is not as simple as that," Jacob continued and the smile went from Musaka's face. "We face two things here, my son. We face the truth you spoke of: the use of ideas and faith and religion to gain domination over the minds of men. But we also face the other truth of an idea taking on a value and a life of its own, no matter who uttered it first, or in what land it began, or the skin colour of the person who first proposed it. And is it not interesting to note that all the really important ideas of the world began with one person. Not with committees, churches, armies, nor parties, but with one person. First there is the person; then the person has the idea; then, if it is a truly great idea, the churches, and committees, the parties and the armies will embrace it and institutionalize it, and, more often than not, distort it in subtle, clever ways that end up blunting the central point of that one person's idea."

. . . I will not let him mesmerize me with words. If he goes on with this I will call in the soldier with the gun to be witness and so that there will be two of us against two of them. He must understand the power is with us, not with them. . . .

Jacob continued: "And so it was that the central idea of the teaching of Jesus Christ, to love thy neighbour as thyself, and to have life and have it more abundantly, was distorted and institutionalized into a Christianity of burnings at the stake, of the mass murder of the so-called lesser peoples of the earth, of imperial plunder and domination, of slavery, and of the ugliest period of racism in the known history of man."

"Hah!" Musaka exclaimed, almost beside himself. "So you admit it! And admitting all this you still serve it! You're not a puppet, as I thought. You are agents! Agents and perpetrators of a rotten system to exploit the dark people!"

"Hear me out, young soldier, and then condemn and denounce. So we turn to your Islam. Did your Prophet really condone slavery? Yet it is in the lands of Islam that slavery still lingers. And it was the followers of Islam, members of the darker peoples of the earth, who opened the African slave trade. In what is this better than European imperialism? What kind of love for fellow Mohammedan is it to cut off a man's hand because he steals without knowing what drove him to steal? To pluck out a man's eyes because he looks on what he should not? To put to death young lovers who follow the impulses of their hearts rather than the decrees of calculating match-makers? Where is the love and the pity and the tenderness in all this, my son?"

"Islam did not do the same worldwide damage as your Christianity!" Musaka shouted. . . . He's convicted himself; why don't I call in the witness. . . .

"Only because it did not have the same power, my son. I think if it did it would have done just as much damage. Like our religion, yours became institutionalized and then the instrument of power-seekers. You're in power here now; the army is predominantly Islamic, so Islam is in control. We hear of terrible things which you know at first hand. Do you think the Prophet would approve of all the killings of which we hear, and you know? Tell us: Will he approve of the raping and degrading of our

359

women by your soldiers? This is what the Christian soldiers did a long time ago in the early history of an imperialist and marauding Christianity. This is what your soldiers are doing in your own country today. Would your Prophet approve? And to come back to your original question: are your soldiers puppets, and if they are, whose puppets are they? Whose interests do they serve in the brutalizing and degrading of your people? You are a young man of sense, Captain Musaka. I can speak to you like this because I'm old enough to be your grandfather. Please do not bury your feeling and your caring for people so deep that you cannot find them again. The darkness that is over this land now will pass one day and there will be need for decent people to help rebuild the land again."

"This is treason!" Musaka protested.

"Not to the laws of God," Chitole said.

"Treason!" Musaka repeated.

"And you listened to it," Chitole said. "You have your gun and you listened to it and did nothing. They have killed people for less, you know that."

"Stop it!" Musaka ordered. "I mean you no harm so stop it! Do not make it worse for yourselves. Give me tribute, something to take back: money and a promise of food – something I can take back – and I will try to get them to agree to leave you alone. Do you understand what I'm saying?" He was an earnest young man now: in the presence of wise elders for whom respect was an historically built-in tribal instinct which, for the moment, transcended the new militarism he wore so uneasily. But Idrisi would not understand that; if any of the others did, and many would, they would not show it in the presence of Idrisi. And these old men would be in trouble, for all their wisdom and understanding. The impulse to protect them was, for the moment, overpowering. "You must give me something to take back to them, for your own sakes!"

"We cannot give you anything," Chitole said coldly. "We will not bribe and we will not buy protection. It is wrong."

Musaka appealed to Jacob. "You understand, Old One. Make him understand. They will harm you. I may be in trouble if I go back with nothing. If you give me nothing I will have to take at least one of you back to the barracks to save myself. They do terrible things to people there."

"So we've heard," Jacob said.

"Then give me something; not too much, just enough to appease Colonel Idrisi."

"You heard the man," Jacob said. "He really is in charge and he says no."

"And you will not persuade him? Please, this is no trap."

"I know that, my son; and I will not persuade him."

"Then I must take one of you."

"So you say," Chitole said signalling Jacob with his eyes.

Jacob made a slight negative motion. There was a sudden flow of silent ideas between the two men. Musaka sensed it.

"What is it? Don't you understand I'm trying to help you?"

"Yes," Chitole was soothing. "We understand that."

"And you will not help yourself?"

"Not by betraying our faith, captain."

"I do not ask you to do that. Just to make a show of tribute for your own sake. You say you know what's going on; then do as I ask. For your own sake."

"To pay tribute is to condone what is going on and that would be betraying our faith."

"It is the same as paying taxes. You pay taxes. I looked at the records before I came here. We know your wealth."

"We pay taxes to the state because all people and institutions must do that. It is not the same as paying tribute to the army so that we are left alone."

Jacob joined in: "And the taxes we pay to the state are supposed to be for the services provided by the state for the people: the schools for the children and the hospitals for the sick."

"And for the army," Musaka added, then stopped abruptly.

Chitole nodded and smiled, making it a gentle friendly gesture: "Yes, captain, and if part of our taxes are already used to support the army there should be no need for tribute."

Musaka realized he had messed the whole thing up. He should not have argued with them. Idrisi had warned him: Don't argue with them, these old crooks are trained to argue; just slap your gun on the desk and raise your voice and frighten the hell out of them and they will give you what you want. Start arguing with them and they will make you fart and shit. And they were doing that to him all right. They're not crooks, Idrisi was wrong there; but you can't tell Idrisi he's wrong about anything, he's the man in charge. But he was right about the gun part.

Musaka pulled out his gun and laid it carefully on the desk. Would it frighten them? He made his face as stern as he could and looked from the old man to the other. The younger one really was in charge and neither of them was afraid. He had seen fear too often on too many faces not to know it. . . . There you go again. Idrisi had warned you about thinking too much; it screwed a man up, turned him into a mixed-up type who could not act, made him useless for the army. Stop thinking. . . .

"Which one of us?" Jacob asked quietly.

"Where is your safe?" He snapped it out.

"Which one of us?" Chitole repeated.

Musaka jumped to his feet and grabbed his gun.

"I said, where's your safe?"

"We heard you," Chitole murmured.

Musaka raised the gun and pointed it at Chitole's chest. Still no show of fear. . . . Stop thinking. . . . He turned his hand slightly so that the gun now pointed at Jacob's chest. He curled his finger around the trigger.

"Your last chance or the Old One dies. Where is your safe?"

No reaction.

"Get me the money from it. Now!"

Still no reaction.

Musaka pulled the trigger. The gun clicked harmlessly.

"A cruel joke, captain," Jacob said quietly, trying to contain a sudden wave of nausea.

"Not a joke, Old One," Musaka said equally quietly. "At the barracks they will do this to you over and over again until you are sick with fear. And just when you get used to it and stop being frightened they will wound you with a real bullet: not where it kills but where it hurts; and then they will play with you again until you are ready to do and say anything they want. Is that what you want?"

"I notice you say 'they'," Jacob murmured. "Why not 'we'?"

"Perhaps this is his first time," Chitole suggested.

"That must be it," Jacob nodded. "I hadn't thought of that. There has to be a first time for everything." His nausea was subsiding. His mind was clear enough for him to read the emotional turmoil in the young soldier's eyes, and to feel compassion for him.

"And there can only be one first time," Chitole said. "Are we going to be your first time, captain?"

"Fools!" Musaka exploded. "Stubborn old fools!" He swung about, gun still in hand, and marched to the door. "They'll be back! And they will not be like me! You'll see! You will suffer! Stubborn old fools!"

Musaka slammed the door behind him, then, after a few seconds they heard the door of the outer office crash shut, and the roar of the military jeep coming to life and moving off with screeching tyres.

Chitole sighed heavily.

"I didn't think he'd do it," Jacob said. "But I was frightened yellow."

"You didn't show it."

"Tried not to. I fear that young man is in trouble now. We may have dug a hole for him."

Chitole mused for a while then shook his head slightly. "I get the feeling that he was already suspect at the barracks and this was just a final test."

"Oh? Tell me more."

"When our people tried to find out what was going on after his first visit, there was this impression of someone rather brighter and more caring for others than the other young officers at the barracks; someone rather alone and not identified with the killings and brutalities going on there. It seems he was the only one the senior officers trusted enough to keep the books and the other records of their loot; and he was not usually sent on this kind of mission."

Jacob speculated aloud: "So they may have decided the time had come for him to commit himself to ensure their own collective security; like thieves and murderers hanging together and making sure there is no innocent one to tell the tale."

363

"Something like that," Chitole agreed.

"Then we *have* dug a hole for him."

"The hole was there. We only challenged him to look into it."

"We cannot escape the responsibility of having forced him to make a choice."

"That's true," Chitole said. "It's our job."

"A potentially good young man," Jacob said. "I hope he survives."

"I hope so too; I hope we all do. He said they'll be back. I think their officers' council will probably want to discuss us before they take any further action; I'm told they meet every Monday morning, so we have a little time and much to do."

Miss Kagwa brought in coffee and reported: "People have been phoning to find out what happened. Your wife too. I told them the soldiers have gone without either of you. Anything else to tell?"

"No," Chitole said. "To those who ask, everything goes as planned."

After Miss Kagwa had withdrawn Jacob asked: "Everything, John? What if I refuse to leave?"

"I would have to order you and that would hurt deeply."

"I do not want you to face this alone."

"You saw Musaka's demonstration. You heard what he said. Would you want me to watch them kill you slowly in order to break me?"

"They may do it to you if you can't deliver me to them."

"You are our symbol, more than just a man. You are our founding father, our inspiration; they must not lay hands on you and break your body."

"I will not betray the church. I will find the strength."

"Shame, Old One! I know that! We all know that! It is the symbolism of your untouched person that we are concerned with. The church must survive these evil days: and you must be the symbol of that survival so that there can be a new beginning as well as continuity. All this you taught us, so why make me teach you what you have taught us? You know, better than any of us, what has to be done."

Jacob sighed and felt old suddenly. "Oh John!"

Chitole closed his eyes and allowed the wave of love and affection to sweep over him. Then he opened his eyes and straightened his back. "Your draft of the 'Bishops' Letter to our Congregations' was approved by everybody last night. I think it should be read in all our churches this coming Sunday, and every Sunday for a month or until we are stopped."

"You say everybody? Michael and all the others?"

"Yes, father, everybody. You taught us well."

"It was easy," Jacob murmured, taking a second cup of coffee from Chitole. "You were wonderful students, eager to learn, all of you."

"Even the rogues and thieves who came among us from time to time?" Chitole laughed; and suddenly the little office was a sea of remembrances of the scores and scores, some of them charming rogues and vagabonds and downright crooks, who had passed through this place and the quiet but firm handling of this old man.

"Yes, in retrospect, even those."

Chitole's mood changed; Jacob recognized and shared it. The intimacy between them was at a level, now, where they could reach each other's thoughts and feelings without words.

"What troubles you, John?"

Chitole closed his eyes and raised his chin; "I want you to take Emma with you, father." He opened his eyes. "I fear what might happen when next they come. She must not go through another bitter experience."

"Does she know?"

"No."

"Don't play God, John. She will want to stay. She's no symbol. She's your wife."

"She must go with you. That is the only hope of safety. If nothing terrible happens, if things turn out better than we fear, she can come back. We will soon find out. Probably before you cross the border."

"And the children?"

"They've gone. They left this morning for the far west, near the border. They'll be safe there with my relatives."

"And what if Emma refuses?"

"I will order her to go."

"You are not only her bishop, John; you're her husband."

"Don't make it any more difficult, father! In my place, would you do any different if it were your Missy?"

"I don't know. You can't know till you face the choice."

"I know what you would have done. I'm doing it now."

"Then come with us too – till we see what happens."

Chitole's face softened, reminding Jacob of how he looked as a shy young man pretending self-assurance. "You know why not."

Yes, Jacob thought: The shepherd does not leave his flock in times of danger. And my John is the shepherd now. Where are you, Oh Lord, to allow these things to happen to the good and the useful and the beautiful ones of this earth? Where are you?

"Come, let us go home," Chitole pulled Jacob out of his reverie. "And please help me with Emma; it won't be easy." Then his mood changed again as they got up to leave. "Michael is due back this evening. I worry each time he's away these days, like a conspirator. It will be good to see him and hear his news; and my mind will be at ease till he goes again."

"Someone has to do this: Michael has a natural feel for it, and he's careful."

"I know; and still I worry."

"Because you're a good shepherd."

"Come, Emma's waiting and we both need to rest a little for what lies ahead."

They were aware, as they strolled home in the very late afternoon, of groups of young men hanging about in pairs at odd intervals along their route. Each young man had a wooden club. These were the unofficial security guards of the mission. Nobody had appointed them so they broke no law; they had just come together and agreed among themselves to protect their people and their property.

Jacob recognized most of the young men they passed; he and Chitole exchanged words with them. And Jacob's heart went out to them, these brave young men with only wooden clubs.

The dog Jane, as usual when not with her master, was waiting for him just inside the stone gateway with no gate which led to the sprawling house.

Now, at last, she saw Jacob and Chitole in the distance and the long afternoon's wait was over. She got up, stretched herself, cocked her head to one side and let out a sharp piercing sound, half yelp, half hysterical scream, but she waited, listening intently till she heard the familiar sound: a sharp, high-pitched whistle. She shot forward like a bullet and raced to meet her master, taking long bounding leaps while her tail made circles. She reached him and slithered to a stop, raising a small dust cloud. She danced out her welcome, back arched, body twisted in a constantly moving semi-circle of quivering excitement, all the while making small sounds of welcome. Jacob went down on one knee and man and dog embraced. When it was over Jane was calm and sedate once more. Only the gentle softness of the eyes now showed her happiness.

Jacob got up, brushed a bit of earth from his knee and said, without looking at Chitole: "You know I can't leave her."

"Of course," Chitole said.

The two men and the dog continued their slow walk home in the gathering dust.

Jacob looked down at the congregation, his congregation, and felt the specialness of the occasion. All the old ones were there; a few of them, like Mama Kilu and the blind and toothless old man who had been head gardener, went back to the very beginning when he, Jacob, then a young man in his late thirties and his young bride had come here to start this mission. The service John had conducted, the sermon he had preached, had been most eloquently moving. The theme of love and farewell had run through it all. These people here, these old friends who had shared in the long years of labour and of building, had come to share in this moment of love and farewell. And throughout the sermon Emma had sat beside him, her hand in his, but otherwise without any outward show of feeling. It was farewell for her as well. She had argued passionately against going but John had insisted; in the end he had used the unfairest but most effective argument of all. He had said: "If you do not go with him, who will look after Grandpa? He's an old man; we cannot send him out to find his way to the border all by himself." Jacob had protested but

Emma had given in to it. Now they were all here to say farewell and to hear the letter which would be read in all their churches at the same time, a little from now, on the hour.

Jacob spoke to his congregation: "Dearly beloved –" And his mind said how very dearly beloved they were to him and his heart ached. "The Good Book says, 'To everything there is a season, and a time to every purpose under the heaven.' This is the time of the parting of old friends. I hope it will not be for long, for so much of me is here and will always be left here. I hope I will be back here among you when it is for me a time to die. I will not want to die far from you and in a strange land; but if I do I will want my remains brought back here so that I may be buried with my wife and among those I loved and so that my spirit will be among you always; that is the only way my soul will rest in peace. I see some of you weeping and I understand it for I too feel like weeping. When old friends part without knowing when they will meet again it is a time to weep. But if we remember the other side of it, if we remember what we have done together, what we have shared together, what we have built together, then it is also a time to laugh and be happy, a time to take stock and to rejoice. So weep not, my dearly beloved! Rejoice instead in the good works we have together succeeded in accomplishing. Remember the good works in the morning and when the sun goes down; and in remembering the good works, remember the faces of those who shared the good works with us. Remember that and you will remember when it was a time to laugh and a time to plant, a time to love and a time to dance. In times of war and times of hate and times of killing it is wise to remember the times of goodness and to be made strong by remembering the work in which we all shared. We must hold on to that in the darkest hours. That is our Christian witness through the ages." Jacob paused. "It is time for the Letter." He looked up at the big clock over the great doors and waited for the coming of the hour. The vast congregation waited with him. John Chitole came and stood on his right hand. Michael Odera came and stood on his left. Then it was the hour and Jacob put on his glasses and read the same words that priests in all their churches were reading to their congregations at this same time:

"From the Bishops of our Church in Uganda to all the congregations of our Church in Uganda, in the name of Our Lord Jesus Christ, greetings. It is the duty and the responsibility of the Bishops, after consulting with all the groups and sections and associations and parts which make up the Body of the Church of Christ, to issue from time to time guidance on matters of important religious or moral principle. Such Pastoral Letters are always addressed to the church itself, to our own, not to others. They are not addressed to governments or princes or principalities; they are not even addressed to other denominations of the Christian Fellowship; they are addressed only to our own members for it is only over our own members that we have the authority to instruct and give guidance. It is so with this Letter: it is for our people only, for their guidance only. It seeks to challenge no other authority. The things that are Caesar's remain Caesar's; the things that are God's must likewise remain God's. The spiritual and moral guidance of his people is God's business, entrusted for the time being to those who are his shepherds here on earth. It is in this spirit, no other, that we, the Bishops, address this Letter to all the congregations of our Church that they may know how to comport themselves on the matter set out hereafter.

"Dearly beloved, it has come to us and we have confirmed it, that a day will soon be appointed to order the Asians out of this country. They will leave all they have behind them; they will not be compensated. Their goods and chattels, all they have, all they have built, all they have acquired, whether by honest or not honest means, will be seized and will be shared out among the people. This means that, on that day, where there is, say, one Asian-owned shop or bazaar, and one farm and two factories in your town or near your town, and if the owners and managers of these places who are Asians have ten or twelve houses, and their children altogether have thirty or forty bicycles, and there are a dozen or more motorcars among the adults, all these things would be taken from them and given away freely to the people. Their clothes and their food and their livestock, everything they have, will be taken and given away by those who are not the rightful owners and so have no moral right to do the giving. A man can only give that which is his. He cannot take what is

369

another's and give it away as an honest man. When a man or a woman or a child takes that which belongs rightfully to another, we describe that as stealing, no matter what he or she does with it. And for us the instruction and the Commandment is clear: *Thou shalt not steal*.

"Many among us, dearly beloved, will be tempted. Others may have just grievances against some Asian shopkeeper or merchant or manager. Many will say the Asians discriminated and behaved as badly and brutally toward us as did the whites because we are black. This is true. But it does not give us licence to go against the Commandment: *Thou shalt not steal*. Our first concern is not with the Asians but with our own people; it is a matter of how we conduct ourselves, of how we deal with others, of whether we steal and rob. That others behave with wickedness may be excuse for wickedness against them; but excuse does not justify. To take by force what is not yours, even from the wicked, is to steal. The Commandment says: *Thou shalt not steal*.

"We draw one important distinction, dearly beloved. What has been taken from us unjustly, that is, what is stolen from us, and we can identify clearly, that we have a right to take back, but only as a collectivity. Traditionally we held land as a collectivity, even as we now do with all our mission property and other goods and chattels. This is one way in which our church is different from others. You know the many ways in which we have blended the traditional ways of our people with the universal teaching of Our Lord. So we accept that the land is the people's as a collectivity to be worked and shared together: it is not the government's to buy or sell or give away in exchange for favours; it is not even one man's to do so outside of the collectivity. For land is the life of a people, a trust which each person enjoys and benefits from and serves and safeguards for the generations to come. So taking back the land which was taken from us is not stealing. That is the great exception. But what is on the land, what a man has built up from his own sweat and effort and from that of his family, even if he often used crooked means, that should not be taken from him except for fair and honest compensation. That is the right and proper way, the honest way. To do it any other way is to steal, and the Commandment is clear: *Thou shalt not steal*.

"So, dearly beloved, it is our solemn injunction to you to honour the Commandment and take no part in the sharing out, or the seizing of, Asian property. There is no profit in gaining the whole world if we lose our bearings as Christians and cease to draw a sharp line between what is right and what is wrong. The exodus, the driving out of a people and the seizing of what is theirs, was wrong in the beginning, is wrong now, and will always be wrong; and even if we do not have the power to do anything about that wrong, we must not be a party to it, and we must not condone it.

"We end as we began, dearly beloved: this injunction is to our own. If others choose to heed our words and follow our example we will be greatly heartened; but we do not call for this. We tell only our own, as is our duty and our responsibility, how we must conduct ourselves in trying to follow the example of our Saviour. Peace be unto you, and the blessing of God go with you through all the days of our life."

Jacob Brown stopped reading, felt the charged collective emotion of the hushed congregation, and said: "The Letter is signed: John Chitole, Bishop-in-Charge; Jacob Brown, Bishop Emeritus."

A big man in one of the front rows of the church, his big voice made small and faint, started singing "Onward Christian Soldiers". Chitole made a sign to the choir leader and the choir, with its elaborate amplification system, joined in and filled the vast place with the stirring hymn. The congregation rose to its feet and joined in the singing.

Jacob put his lips close to Chitole's ear; "Didn't sound quite as unprovocative as I hoped and tried to make it."

Chitole's lips curled; he stood on tiptoe and Jacob bent low to hear him: "It isn't easy to make the message of the greatest revolutionary of them all sound moderate."

The singing came to an end. The congregation remained standing. This was the moment of parting. Their old bishop had to flee this night to avoid the coming of the soliders. The plans were laid: many others would leave too, travelling to different parts of the country to take refuge and wait out the storm they feared was soon to be let loose on them. After the storm those who survived would return and put together what had been broken and resume their lives. That was the plan.

Chitole replaced Jacob at the pulpit. One last ceremony had to be performed to ensure apostolic continuity before the dispersal and the coming of the soldiers in the morning. For after this Letter they were sure to come early. Some feared they might even come this night, so a warning system was in place.

Chitole said, "We will now proceed with the last and most important piece of our business." He turned to see if Jacob's robing was completed, then he stepped back from the pulpit to be robed himself by three waiting priests. When it was done Jacob and Chitole conducted the historic ritual of the laying on of hands. Michael Odera was enthroned as a bishop of the church and two other priests were made auxiliary bishops. The plan was for the two auxiliary bishops to go underground immediately in case there was a stepped-up war against the church by the Nubian and his predominantly Islamic soldiers.

When the ceremony of enthronement was over the leave-taking commenced. Jacob, Chitole, the newly enthroned bishops, and Emma, walked down the aisle while the singing congregation turned in their places and watched them pass. They lined up at the great carved doors and the congregation started the slow, singing procession, moving row by row from the front of the church. Each person shook the hand of Emma and each of the bishops waiting at the door, Jacob being the last one. The singing, now turned into a haunting vernacular hymn of parting, filled the great church and spilled out into the cool cloudless night.

An old woman took Jacob's hand and he could feel the trembling of her body though her face showed no expression. She was one of those who had been here at the beginning: she too would leave for safer sanctuary. Jacob remembered her as she had looked more than thirty years earlier: upright and square-shouldered and big, with a child strapped to her back; in the prime of her life then, with several children still to be mothered. Those children were adults now, and she was old, old as he himself was. He felt just a little weary in spirit suddenly; this parting was hard.

"So we part, Old One." Her voice was raspy and rusty.

"We part and my heart is heavy."

"We have shared much and I will not see you again, but your spirit will be with me always, even unto death."

She offered him her cheek and Jacob bent down and kissed it.

"And yours with me," Jacob said.

"This evil thing will pass from the land but the young will suffer before it passes."

"It is our shame that we allowed it to come," Jacob said.

"But it will pass, after the suffering, as all things must."

The processional line had come to a halt but Chitole refused to interrupt the two old friends. At last she let go of Jacob's hand.

"Go well, good shepherd."

"Go well, beloved sister."

She walked away heavily and Mama Kilu came, tears flowing unchecked down her cheeks. She had insisted on remaining behind with Chitole to take care of him and of Missy's house until her bishop's return. Again the line was held up. Then another old friend, and another and another. The line moved very slowly till all the old friends had had their parting words with Jacob; then it speeded up, but still the parting and the touching of each other did not come to an end till well after midnight, when a fleet of trucks and vans and landrovers and cars and jeeps moved in a steady procession to pick up people and depart. Young men and women from the school and the seminary and mission business enterprises used long lists to identify and help people into their assigned transport. The vehicles moved off in small convoys going in the same direction. When more than half the vehicles had gone Jacob and Emma were helped into a covered long-bodied landrover which had been prepared for a long journey and stocked with food and drink and their personal belongings. And Jane was waiting inside, curled up on one of the two narrow sleeping bunks.

The parting with Chitole was quick and painful. All the words had been spoken between him and Emma, and between him and Jacob. Emma had done her weeping in private; Jacob had shown his fatherly feeling in private. Now, in the presence of others, Emma kissed Chitole and turned away and Jacob shook his hand and blessed him and went into the landrover, which moved off with the convoy going to the foothills of Mount Elgon, where some would leave the convoy; then on, further north, to Moroto where the last group in the convoy would disperse and Jacob and Emma would make for the border on their own.

Jacob remembered the last intimate moments with Chitole, just before they had gone to the service. Chitole had taken Emma's hand in one of his and Jacob's in the other. He had said: "Thank you for being a father to me, the most wonderful father a man could have; for showing me the way. And you, my Emma, for being the best wife a man could have. You have filled my days with blessing – both of you. Thank you; pray for me."

And remembering it, and hearing the last faint sounds of the hymn of parting, tears sprang to Jacob's eyes. Emma took one hand off the steering-wheel and felt for Jacob's hand. She too was weeping silently.

The army came early next morning, just as the sun was rising. Colonel Idrisi himself led the column of army jeeps and trucks which swarmed into the mission grounds and fanned out in every direction in what appeared a well-rehearsed operation of occupation. Soldiers surrounded the administrative block, the church, the dormitories, the factory and warehouses area; all at once they were everywhere, outnumbering what remained of the mission's population, their shining guns on show. They hustled people out of the buildings and ordered them to the church. A score of machine-gun-toting soldiers stood guard over those hustled into the church. John Chitole was marched from his home to join those in the church. He had not been allowed to complete his dressing; he wore a pair of trousers held up by braces, a collarless shirt and a pair of soft house sandals.

Colonel Idrisi was waiting at the church door. He was a big man with a near jet-black face and the slightly Arabic features of some of the southern Sudanese; his strong body was going to fat.

"Where are the others?" Idrisi demanded of the officer who had brought Chitole.

"Only a very old woman and two girls in the kitchen," the officer said. "My men looked everywhere, even the garden. No one else."

Now Idrisi looked at Chitole. "You, who are you?"

"I'm the bishop of this church. John Chitole."

"Ah. The one Musaka tried to phone last night. So he did get word to you. Where are you hiding the American?" He waved Chitole into the church. "Your kingdom, your people are in there, all of them we could find."

Chitole went into the church, followed by Idrisi and his soldiers.

Chitole said, "Captain Musaka did not phone me."

"I ask you once more: where is the American?"

Chitole felt the hard point of a rifle in his back. "He's gone; and he's not an American. He's a Ugandan citizen."

Idrisi took a step toward Chitole and casually slapped him across the face, not hard. "You see I'm not afraid of hurting people because they are called bishops." He turned to the small crowd gathered near the door of the church. "I'm not even afraid of killing people because they are called bishops. Answer! Where has the American gone?"

Chitole kept silent and braced himself. Idrisi's eyes blazed with explosive anger. A man moved out of the small crowd.

"I will tell you, sir. The bishop, the old one, left here three-four days ago to go to Entebbe. He has not returned and our bishop's wife went with him."

"You lie, man!" Idrisi roared.

"No, sir. I tell the truth."

"It is the truth," a voice in the crowd said. Other voices took up the affirmation.

"So," Idrisi turned to his young officer. "Musaka's treachery began earlier. The American left shortly after his last visit." He stared at Chitole. "You bribed him. How much? What was his price?"

"We did not bribe him," Chitole said. "We gave him nothing."

"We found nothing on him," the young officer confirmed. "And the soldiers who were with him say he came straight to the barracks from here."

"Then you promised him something to collect later."

"We gave him nothing and promised him nothing," Chitole said.

Another officer, a senior man, came in, saluted and led Idrisi aside. They conferred in whispers then the man saluted and left.

Idrisi took a document from his pocket and read out loud from it: "Fifteen jeeps, twelve trucks, twelve motorcars and one special limousine, fifteen motorcycles, seven with sidecars, thirty bicycles. This was your mission's transport stock according to your last tax returns. Where are they, Mr Bishop?"

Chitole remained silent.

"We opened your safe, Mr Bishop. There was nothing in it. What have you done with the money? Where are the farm animals? Why are your warehouses empty, Mr Bishop?" Deliberately, slowly, Idrisi pulled his gun from its holder. "Is this part of your letter of not taking anything from the Asians? Are you agents of the Asians then? Speak up, Mr Bishop, before I take the pleasure of killing you slowly. Where have you hidden all these things? Where is the money?" Idrisi raised his gun and took careful aim at Chitole's left thigh.

Someone in the crowd began to moan.

"Look out of the door!" Idrisi yelled suddenly. "Let them all see! Let them see their bishop's house burning! Drive them out!"

The soldiers drove the people to the church door.

"And if they do not tell us where they have hidden the money and the other things, then this church and every building on this mission will burn as the bishop's house now burns! Did I tell you, Mr Bishop, how angry the President is about that letter you and the American sent to your churches? I didn't? Well, he was so angry he wanted to come up here and burn you down himself! I promised to do it for him, Mr Bishop, so that the foreign press will not have another thing for which to blame him. Speak, Mr Bishop! Where have you hidden everything? Where are your people? Where's the money?"

Chitole remained silent.

The sound of Idrisi's first shot entered the church and came back as a vast boom. The force of the bullet knocked Chitole to the ground just outside the church doorway. At first he felt only numbness, then the pain in his thigh began to spread through him as though his whole body had been shattered.

Those who had been driven out of the church to look at the

growing cloud of smoke from the bishop's home retreated back inside the doorway for sanctuary. One woman, big and strong and perhaps braver than the rest, went toward her bishop to help him.

Idrisi roared "Stop!" The woman kept going, so Idrisi aimed for her head and shot her dead. Chitole got to his knees and crawled to the dead woman. He fought against the terrible pain and the mounting panic inside him. He looked at the cold faces of the soldiers, then at the frightened faces of his own people. He summoned all his strength and said: "The Lord is my shepherd; I shall not want." Then he heard the voices of the members of his congregation coming to him, and the panic left him despite the pain. His voice, in union with theirs, grew stronger: "He maketh me to lie down in green pastures; he leadeth me beside the still waters. He restoreth my soul: he leadeth me in the paths of righteousness for his name's sake. . . ."

"Silence!" Idrisi shouted.

They ignored him. "Yea, though I walk through the valley of the shadow of death, I will fear no evil: for thou art with me."

Again Idrisi shouted "Silence!" And then he fired into the body of the kneeling John Chitole. He kept on firing even after Chitole collapsed sideways and died; he fired till all his bullets were spent.

The stunned congregation paused momentarily, then, first a woman's voice, then all the rest, picked up and completed the words of the psalm.

In the silence that followed Idrisi stared angrily at the dead man and the dead woman on the ground. He took a step toward the dead bodies then abruptly swung about and stalked away, shouting, "Burn it to the ground! All of it! That's an order!"

They watched him get into his jeep, watched the jeep roar away. Then the congregation moved forward to take up their dead. Some soldiers raised their weapons menacingly; the young officer held up his hand: "Let them be!"

They took up the bodies of John Chitole and the woman and carried them into the church. The young officer signalled his men to withdraw. The rest of the place was burning; now these people could be left their church to do their mourning.

Fire and smoke were everywhere as the soldiers carried out Idrisi's orders to burn it all. The home which Jacob and his Margaret had built those many years ago, and to which Emma and Chitole had added later, was now blazing fiercely. Mama Kilu, supported by two helpers, sat on a stone, out of the danger range of the blazing fire, watching the place she had come to as a young woman perish in the flames; she moaned desolately, rocking from side to side.

David's party of two militarized jeeps, one large personnel carrier and a dozen seasoned fighters, crossed the border into Kenya above the western end of Lake Rudolph, close to the border of the Sudan and near the town of Lokitaung. David had picked up the news of the death of Chitole and the burning down of the mission on Radio Uganda two days earlier. According to the short-wave broadcast for external consumption, Bishop Chitole had died in a supposed shoot-out with soldiers who had come to investigate reports of subversive activity at the mission. Large stocks of arms had been found. But the American who was suspected of being behind it all had escaped and was being hunted. The President, the radio report had said, had wept when he heard of the death of Bishop Chitole, a good man who had been misled by American agents masquerading as missionaries. The reference to the missing American suspect meant Odera's plan was in progress. The thing now was not to lose the old man in the great Rift Valley below the lake.

The plan was for Jacob to cross the border into Kenya at a point to the north of Moroto and to make for Lokitaung, without being spotted by either Kenyan or Ugandan border patrols. If he were spotted he was to make a dash for the Kenyan side; Kenyatta's people would deal more kindly with him than the Nubian's, and church and diplomatic pressure could then be used to gain his release. No such pressure would work on the Nubian, especially after the story they had put out: chances were they would do away with the old man if they caught him and talk of another shoot-out.

David led the party off the dirt road as they skirted Lokitaung and bumped and bounced across the dry rocky scrubland. The local people would not be able to distinguish them from Kenya's own border patrols: the danger was of their running into one such patrol. So they travelled far from the populated centres near the lake with its shady trees and cooling breezes, and made their way slowly across the vast dry African landscape.

They had crossed the border early in the morning, before sunrise; they had travelled steadily through the day, not stopping, as though on a forced march, munching what they had to eat on the move, the men peeing from the moving vehicles when they had to. There was a driver and a companion manning a mounted machine-gun on each of the two jeeps; and there were eight men, two mounted machine-guns, a small cannon, several automatic and assault weapons and a vast supply of ammunition as well as food and fuel on the carrier. None of the men was under thirty; they were all tough seasoned fighters, all companions who had shared in other battles. Their commander on this mission, who drove the second jeep, was a battle-scarred brown Algerian called Hassan. David had fought with Hassan in Algeria and had cabled him from Conakry to assemble this fighting group. Hassan and the men had been waiting when David reached Addis, and in three days they were crossing the Ethiopian border into Kenya.

Toward sundown the party stopped on high rocky land which gave them a clear view of the surrounding country for miles in every direction.

"A good place to stop!" Hassan shouted to David in Arabic.

"Then we stop!" David yelled back.

Hassan signalled and the vehicles drew closer together, slowed down, then stopped in a small crude circle. The men tumbled out of the carrier and set about preparing for the night; two serviced the jeeps and carrier; one started a fire while another prepared a large pot of coffee, huge slices of cold spit-roast sheep, and doorstep slices of a round brown bread. Two went off to the highest point of the land to examine the southern and western horizon through binoculars. All worked with their firearms either on them or near them. They spoke little and there was none of the banter usually associated with men in arms.

When the coffee was ready Hassan and David walked a little distance from the camp with a huge mug each.

"I'm worried," David said. "We are near Uganda's border."

"We cross it if we have to," Hassan said.

David shook his head. "We may have missed him. He's supposed to have started out three nights ago; should have been across the border by now."

"You said he's an old man."

"Not that old; he's strong and clear still. . . ."

One of the look-outs on the highest land whistled twice. Instantly the air of relaxation vanished: the fire was put out; the food put away; the tools, petrol, grease, oil stored back in the carrier. The men took up their arms, checked them, and waited. David and Hassan joined the look-out, who pointed and passed the binoculars.

After a while Hassan said: "Yes, a big jeep, moving slowly." He made a wide circle, scanning the horizon. "Nothing else, but you never can tell; a plane could be overhead in a few seconds if it is a decoy."

David looked through the binoculars. "Too slow," he muttered. "Will not reach here before dark at that pace."

"And if it is him he may miss us in the night," Hassan said.

"I'll go out," David decided. "If it is mischief. . . ."

"If it is mischief we fight," Hassan said.

They sprinted to their little jeeps, leaving the look-out in place. Hassan told the men of the slow-moving vehicle and David's plan to go out and meet it alone in case it was a trap.

"Not without me," the one who manned the machine-gun on David's jeep growled. He was a small, very muscular, very black little man with many scars on his face.

Hassan made a small shrug. "It's his gun; a man and his gun."

"Then come!" David knew the time-wasting futility of arguing. They got into the jeep, the little man in the open body, swinging his machine-gun from side to side, testing to ensure the ammunition belt would not jam. Hassan made a half-salute and the little jeep came alive and sped southward to meet the distant landrover before darkness fell.

. . . If it is not the old man. . . . He touched the gun in his belt.

It took half an hour of fast driving before they came into clear unassisted sight of the crawling landrover. But now those in the landrover had also seen them and come to a halt. At a little over two hundred yards David pulled up and used his binoculars to make out the figures in the landrover: there were two, but not enough light to identify them. Then he caught the shadowy outlines of a dog between the two figures.

"It's them!" he exclaimed softly. "It has to be; it's him and another. Only he would think of taking a dog even when escaping from death."

"Careful, Commander!" the little man warned as David shot the jeep forward; he settled into fighting position, kneeling on his left knee for better balance and stability against the swaying of the jeep.

They stopped at twenty yards.

"Ready?" David whispered.

"Ready."

David jumped out of the jeep, gun in hand, and ran in a crouching zigzag toward the landrover. At ten yards he dropped to the ground and shouted: "That you, Dad?"

There was a pause then the reply came: "David?"

"Yes! Who's with you?"

"Emma – you know her, John's wife – and the dog, Jane."

"That all?"

"Yes."

"Nobody else?"

"Nobody else."

"It's all right," David called back to the one at the machine-gun.

"Make sure, Commander! We say anything with a gun in our back."

"I will," David replied.

"What now?" Jacob called, not understanding Arabic.

"Stay where you are," David shouted in English. "Don't get out and don't move! If anybody else is with you we will find them and destroy them! Tell them that! Tell them they are surrounded."

He made a sudden dash for the landrover, and before Jacob and Emma realized it, he was looking at them from the back of the landrover, gun pointing menacingly. Jane, first to sense the intruder, crouched low in the confined space, ready to leap.

"Down, Jane," Jacob commanded; Jane relaxed. Jacob peered at David. "Glad to see you! Thought we'd lost you or something had gone wrong."

"Hello, Dad. Hello, Emma." He wondered if they knew about Chitole; not likely. He would have to break the bad news. He leaned out of the landrover, cupped his hands to his mouth and called out in Arabic: "It is my people! All is clear!"

The little man left his gunpost and drove the jeep alongside the landrover.

David said: "Back to camp. You lead; I will drive this and follow."

The journey back to the camp was fast but it was quite dark when they got there. Hassan insisted that they broke camp immediately and make the journey back out of Kenya and into Ethiopia without delay. The most dangerous part of any mission was its winding up after success; that was when people tended to relax and were in most danger of running into trouble. They had been lucky this far, everything had gone their way; it would be dangerous to push that luck. Any incident now between them and the Ugandan army or Sudanese forces or Kenyan border patrol, with the bishop in their company, would cause uproar in the ranks of the Organization of African Unity.

Hassan assigned a driver to the landrover; David advised Jacob and Emma to get some sleep. The convoy started the journey back, travelling at a fast pace across the harsh landscape, and showing light only where they had to. With a little luck, and if they could keep up the fast pace, and if they did not run into any Kenyan patrol, they should be on the Ethiopian side before daybreak, and be safe.

Inside the landrover, on their narrow bunks, Jacob and Emma let go of the tension which had driven them these past two days. They had found David, they could relax now; David and his friends would ensure their safety.

Before she slipped into a dazed half-sleep, Emma said: "Strange to see David as a soldier; never thought of him like that."

"I find it hard too," Jacob said. "If he were not we would not be here now."

"We would be back home with John," Emma said, aching for Chitole and wondering how he was and wishing they were with him.

"We would not be safe," Jacob said.

"Is he safe?"

"Pray God they all are."

Silently, Emma prayed for the safety of Chitole and those they had left behind. Take care of them, Lord, and let there be someone like David to come to their rescue as he has come to ours: Amen.

Jacob remembered Emma had done most of the driving this day, from early afternoon till David found them, so he said: "You must rest, Emma, even if you can't sleep. Let your mind and your body rest."

"Yes, doctor!" She tried to make it sound light and flippant.

Ritual always helps, Jacob thought and said: "Goodnight, Emma."

She had heard him talk of the value of ritual many times so she said: "Goodnight, Grandpa."

Then they lay awake in silence through the long journey of what seemed an endless night.

In the morning, on the Ethiopian side of the border, and a good twenty miles inland from it, they had breakfast on a broad flat hill overlooking a village on the banks of a small river which flowed into Lake Rudolph. The village was roughly twenty miles from the Sudanese border too; and just about four or five times that distance and you were in northern Uganda. The people of the village had witnessed the coming and going of all manner of people from those borders; they had grown used to it and they had profited from it, and they had learned not to ask or to answer questions about those comings and goings. They had turned the hill into a compound where those who came and went could rest and eat, and wait for others who would come to take them on the next stage to wherever they were going.

The village headman, who embraced Hassan as an old friend, joined them for a ceremonial cup of coffee. Then Hassan, carrying a pouch of David's money converted into local currency, led the headman some distance from the others to settle their payment for food and drink and the secure shelter supplied. The payment settled, the headman returned to the group with Hassan to make a great show of taking his leave; then he made his way down the hillside, back to his village, in the long, loping strides of a person used to walking great distances in high mountain country.

There was awkwardness between Jacob and Emma on the one hand and David on the other. They had not seen each other for many years. Letters, no matter how frequent or intimate, never quite bridge the gap of change wrought by a long absence; and the letters, during those years, had not been many, had not been intimate. So Jacob found it hard to reconcile this aloof, greying, cold-eyed and controlled military man with the rebellious and volatile boy and young man who had been his and Margaret's son. Almost, this man was an Arab stranger to him; he spoke Arabic as though it were his native language, and English, his true native language, as an Arab who had learned it might do. And that gun at his waist was a natural part of him: yet the voice was his David's and the deed of rescue the expression of a son's love.

Emma's mind could not get past the reality of David the soldier, the man with the gun, at ease in the company of men with guns. Her life, most of it, had been spent with men of peace and love; with Grandpa and John and the peaceful workers at the mission all about them all the time. This David was clearly a man of war and violence, respected as such by these men around him who called him 'Commander'. This was not the young David she had known in those early years at the mission. So Jacob and Emma were ill at ease that morning in the presence of people who all seemed strangers, even David: armed strangers, which made it worse.

Hassan got another mug of coffee and settled near David.

"You look troubled, my brother. No need for it; your transport is on the way."

"They do not know of the destruction of their mission; she does not know of the killing of her husband."

"And you must tell them. Is that it?"

David nodded. "And I don't want to."

"I've seen you tell people of death and destruction before, my brother."

"Not these people."

"Ah, they are close. Remember I was with you, David, when you had to tell your wife's father of her killing. . . ."

"That was in battle."

"Yes, of course; the fortunes of war." Hassan was bitterly cynical. "If only we could isolate the killings and the horrors of war to only the freedom-fighters and the soldiers they oppose."

"I didn't mean it like that."

"That's how it came out, David."

"Sorry. I have to tell them."

"Then get it over. Do it now!"

David rose abruptly, unbuckled his gun-belt and handed it to Hassan. He said in English: "Dad, Emma, come with me. I have something to tell you." Then, without waiting or looking at them, he walked briskly to a small cluster of rocks on the far side of the hill. Jacob and Emma followed him more slowly and they, in turn, were followed by Jane.

When they reached him, David looked searchingly at each of them in turn. He motioned them to sit on a smooth rock. The realization of how old his father really was, and the seeing of the setting in of physical decay, had come as a bit of a shock. How would he, this old man, stand up to the news? How would Emma? He hardly knew her any more.

Emma read the compassion in his eyes and thought: He is less cold without his gun; almost human like the old young David.

Jacob braced himself: "What is it, David?"

"They burned down the mission; we heard it night before last over Radio Uganda."

"And the people?" Jacob's voice was a whisper.

"They killed John and a woman. . . ."

Jacob put an arm about Emma and held her tight, feeling her body stiffen. He's not so frail after all, David thought; they had prepared themselves for it, as soldiers prepare themselves to die. Emma too; both stronger than I thought.

David said: "No word of Michael, which means he's gone to ground. They say you and Emma slipped out of Entebbe with the help of a traitorous army captain."

"Captain Musaka," Jacob said softly. "I'll tell you about him one day. And about my John, our John, Emma's John, the church's Bishop John Chitole. He knew what would happen, what had to be done."

Emma began to moan, her head buried against Jacob's chest.

"Please leave us for a while now, David. We need to be alone."

He left them, and the old man and the woman remained on the rocky spot for nearly an hour; they remained till the distant hum of an approaching helicopter drew nearer and nearer, till it hovered overhead and came slowly to rest on a cleared spot. Then Hassan came to them and said in English, with the slightest hint of an Arabic accent; "It is time for the next stage of your journey, my lord. My men and I are glad to have been of help to you this far. That monstrous Nubian will pay for his crimes one day, believe me."

"We are grateful for your help," Jacob said.

Hassan looked into Emma's eyes, hesitated, then said softly: "I, we, my men and I are all sorry about what happened to your husband and your mission. David will tell you," he made David's name sound Arabic, "that one is not representative of the best in Islam. You have bad Christians, we have bad Moslems; that one is worse than a bad Moslem. Islam does not make war on the peaceful and the defenceless; David will tell you; he knows us."

"This is the way of our world," Jacob said. "Do not reproach yourself." He took Emma's hand. "My daughter and I thank you for helping us."

Emma held on tight to Jacob's arm. It was the first time he had called her his daughter. She fought down the strong impulse to lean against him and bawl. This old man, now, was her only family. Her children, Chitole's children, would stay in the protection of Chitole's family and would be raised as the children of one of his brothers, comforted by a large family and many brothers and sisters and uncles and aunts and grandparents; better than being children without a father and only a mother. So, unless she joined her children in the shelter of Chitole's family, this old man was all her family now.

Hassan said: "Come, please," and led the way to the helicopter where some of his men were lifting Jacob's and Emma's possessions from the landrover into the helicopter.

"My papers," Jacob said anxiously. "In the box; they're important."

David came to them. "Don't worry, Dad. We'll take care of everything."

386

"I'll go and supervise them," Emma said, going to the landrover.

David looked into his father's eyes. "Where do you want to go, Dad? Back to the States?"

Jacob shook his head. "No, there's nothing for me there. I'm retired. Emma and I will go to Jamaica and wait there till we can come home and pick up our lives again. Michael and the others will keep things together till then. You know Michael?"

"He's been my contact all these years, Dad." David wondered if the old man's memory was fading; he knew the three of them, Michael, Chitole and the old man himself, had thought out this contingency plan; Michael had written him about it. "He was the one who advised me to set up this operation."

"Of course," Jacob said absently. "I didn't always know the details." Then he looked at David, suddenly all there, fully alert. "Will you come with us to Jamaica? For a while, perhaps? I'd like that. I'd like to show you the hills where I grew up and the home and land your great-grandparents built out of the wilderness. I want to show you the place where the church was burned down. Ours was not the first church to be burned down; it will not be the last."

"And God's children who love and fight for freedom will overcome," Hassan said.

"He sounds just like a brother," Jacob smiled despite his grief.

"He is a brother," David said. "One day I'll tell you just how much of a brother."

"And you will come with us?"

"For a time at least," David said and felt hugely rewarded by the sudden glowing warmth in his father's eyes.

. . . I must stay with this old man now; until he dies. . . .

It was time to leave and the men who had been prepared to risk their lives to rescue them stood in line for Jacob and Emma to shake each by the hand before climbing into the helicopter. Then David had a farewell word with each. He had fought beside these men; they were comrades. Then he embraced Hassan with the feeling of parting from a brother. All had been settled: the payments to be made, and the contact with Michael in case of need with David not on hand.

The helicopter rose, veered right, and sped northward.

3

Emma sat on the long verandah watching the Blue Mountains turn a hazy purple against the darkening sky. It was quiet, so quiet the whole world seemed hushed. The sense of the tranquillity of this place, which she had first felt nearly seven years earlier, was all about her. The letter with its postmark, Kampala, Uganda, lay on the crude wooden table beside her. They had received several letters from Uganda over the years, but all those had been postmarked Nairobi, Kenya; or Dar es Salaam, Tanzania; or Addis Ababa, Ethiopia; or even London, England. For many of the best sons and daughters of Uganda were scattered all over the place, like dry leaves in a strong wind. So the Kampala, Uganda postmark made this one special. And it was addressed to her, not to Grandpa as was usual. To Mrs Emma Brown, so whoever had written knew what had happened. That was what made her afraid of opening the letter. She would wait till David returned from the city down there, and until Grandpa and Jane returned from their long walk across the valley of Mount Zion. They were forever exploring, those two. After one such exploration Grandpa had come back in high excitement. He and Jane had come upon a very old man who lived alone in the remote bush, who claimed to be a descendant of someone called Noname Brown, one of the group of runaway slaves with whom Grandpa's and David's ancestors had first come to this place. Emma knew all about that story now. Much of it in Grandpa's notebooks and journals and in some of the older papers he had inherited from his Grandma Sarah. Emma and Grandpa spent most of their mornings working on those notebooks and journals, transcribing them, editing them, typing them and then revising them, then typing them again. This work had been good for both of them. It had given Grandpa something important to do; seeing him happily at work again had made life happier for her and she had thrown herself into the work. Now the manuscript was near completion. It would make a wonderful book, a fine record of Grandpa's work as a missionary, of the origins and outlook of his church, of the many-sided struggles of black people in the twentieth century, and the role of one particular black family in those struggles. Emma had come to know and to love the slave girl who became the matriarch of Grandpa's childhood and youth. Yet David who was part of that struggle – an unfamiliar military part, to be sure – was curiously unwilling to take part in the planning and discussion of this book. He said he did not want to influence its shaping in any way, and that discussion always influenced people's thinking or perspective, whether they were aware of it or not; he said he was anxious that Grandpa's last important work be truly his own.

"What about me?" Emma had asked. "What about my influencing him by our discussion?"

"That's different," he had said. "You and he share the same perspective; the interaction of your ideas deepens the work without raising questions about fundamental assumptions."

"In other words," Emma had pressed, "you disagree with our fundamental assumptions?"

Jacob had cut in then: "I don't think he so much disagrees, Emma, as wants to avoid getting involved and perhaps having to face up to the challenge of our fundamental assumptions. Right, David?"

"I have no problem with that, Dad. I just think that after nearly a century of us tearing each other apart, usually for the applause or approval of white folk, it is time for us to stop putting down each other and to put down our enemies instead. As I say this I realize I'm being sucked into an argument I want to avoid, because I know you dislike the concept of the enemy."

"That concept has been forced on us, son, and regardless of colour. We saw it in Uganda. I don't like the concept but the enemy is real and pretending otherwise does not help."

"So we are a little nearer, which I didn't expect. But my point is not racist, Dad, though it goes right back to your friend DuBois and his statement about the problem of the twentieth century.

The relationship between the lighter and darker races of mankind of which he wrote has been so unnatural, so ugly, so destructive of one side as to have become diseased. For the best part of this century you have all worked and hoped for the disease to go away and for the relationship to grow healthy and clean. And because this has in fact happened between individuals from time to time you have seized on it with hope and seen it as symptomatic of what would happen between societies. So your friend, DuBois, almost to the very end, argued with brilliance and passion for an understanding and a coming together. Your church fought nobly for autonomy on the assumption that once your capacity for self-rule was beyond doubt other good Christians would abide by the reality that your Christ is of all colours, for all men. . . ."

Jacob had cut in to ask: "Do you believe in that Christ of all colours, for all men?"

And David had thought for a while then answered: "Which one? The one who orders submission and obedience in the face of cruelty and injustice? The one whose agents are part of the machinery of colonial power and domination? Which one, Dad? The Christian churches have so confused his image."

And Jacob had said: "Try the greatest revolutionary who ever lived; try the Christ who taught love and kindness and compassion."

There had been one of those sudden waves of intimacy between father and son, and Emma had been enveloped in it. Then David had made a small gesture of impatience.

"You are sidetracking me, Dad. Let me make my point. What if the man to whom you are always reaching out, for whom DuBois wrote those brilliant books, what if he does not want any change in the relationship? What if he wants to continue to discriminate and exploit because that is of more benefit to him that the equality and friendship you demand? What if his show of friendship, where it exists, is only in order to get your raw materials, your oil, your minerals, your agricultural produce? Please let me finish. On the hard evidence, that is all he wants by way of his trans-national operations. So why should my heart bleed if those trans-nationals also exploit their own white people savagely? That savagery is not half as great as the savagery they visit on the so-called Third

World whose workers are less organized and less able to put up even the limited resistance of the white workers of Europe and America. And still there is this talk of solidarity. What kind of solidarity? Even Garvey seemed to think that if we had our navies and our armies and our black kingdoms and emperors, they would somehow learn to respect us and accept us as equals. Always, we think of them accepting us, of them respecting us; never of us accepting them, never of us respecting them. Both they and we see the whole relationship flowing in one direction only. You see, you've made me say things I have not yet completely thought my way through. Fanon began the process but even he seemed a little afraid of the line of thinking he had opened. . . ." David had paused for a long time.

"And you," Jacob had challenged. "Afraid too?"

"Out of my wits," David had said and laughed, bringing about a sudden mood change among them.

Emma had watched, with growing happiness, as over the months and years, Jacob and David grew closer and closer to each other. The distance between them, at first, had been awkward and she often had to play the difficult role of go-between. That had, in time, made things easier between David and herself and had led, ultimately, a year after their arrival, to their marriage. At that time she was not quite sure why she had agreed to marry him, or even why he had asked her to. Love came later, slowly, imperceptibly; then grew deep.

The worst time for all of them was the first six months when Jane was kept in quarantine and she and Jacob had to go daily on the long drive to the quarantine station on the Palisadoes to visit her. David, meanwhile, had to spend most of his time in seemingly endless wrangles with lawyers and builders to get his special piece of land and get his house going. They had rented a small house at the foot of Red Hills in a drab and dirty little cul-de-sac which depressed Emma terribly, especially when she remembered the beauty and cleanliness she had left behind in Uganda.

But at last the dismal six months passed, and on the same day that they moved up into this then-not-completed house, she and Jacob made their last journey down to the quarantine station to collect Jane and bring her to their new home in the high hills.

Jane had been beside herself with relief at being free and with her owner at last; she could not stop shaking and whimpering. Jacob got into the back of the car with her so that Emma could drive through Kingston's heavy traffic without distraction. David had overseen the moving and then gone down to the clinic in West Kingston which he and a recently qualified young doctor, a very pale, middle-class young man who had joined the Rastafarian sect, the Twelve Tribes, had taken over from an old Syrian doctor who was retiring.

When the car started the climb up into Red Hills, Jacob said: "We'll go to Cyprus, Emma!"

For six months he had thought only of Jane and of putting his papers in order. Now that Jane was free and they had moved up into the new house, there was time to think of the family he had not seen for more than half a century. Cyprus was the starting point for the finding of that family. He had been born there; he had talked often of seeing it again; now they were going to Cyprus, and Emma was as eager as Jacob himself to see the place.

Emma had grown familiar with the road to Red Hills, and to Rock Hall further up. They had made the journey often while their house was being built. This was the road which, according to the earliest of Jacob's papers, was once the cart road to and from Kingston. Now it was wide and well-surfaced; where there had been bush, big well-built suburban houses now stood in spacious grounds on both sides of the wide road. Kingston's affluent, the merchants and the professionals and the senior civil servants, lived in these fine homes on the lower slopes of the hills, away from the noise and dust and fumes of Kingston but within easy reach of it. Further up at Limes Kiln and Padmore and the areas beyond, the land was still in the hands of the descendants of those who had moved up into the hills in the days of slavery and immediately after and in the period of apprenticeship. Now they were the independent peasant smallholders who worked for themselves and who wanted to have as little to do as possible with the government down in Kingston, and its taxes and its police.

But the small peasants were losing out. Each year fewer of them worked the land: the young deserted the land for Kingston; many whose land commanded one of the magnificent views of the city, the sea and the mountains sold their land for what seemed large sums of money. Those looking for such land came in fine big cars and spent generously at the local rumshops, at Bagley's in Red Hills and Curtis's in Rock Hall. They spent lavishly until they got what they wanted; then the lawyers took over, and some of those who had made their marks on what they thought, under the influence of strong rum, were receipt papers for generous deposits on their plots of land, discovered that they had sold their land outright for five or ten or twenty pounds an acre. And so the ownership of the land, and then the land itself, changed. The village of Red Hills changed until it had its own post office, police station, supermarket, funeral parlour and filling station, and electricity and running water and local branches of the two main political parties. Strangers moved in till they outnumbered the descendants of the original small peasant farmers. The political parties divided and then polarized the community. Elections and electioneering became so fierce that old school friends were pitted in bitterness against each other; families were divided along party lines, with those supporting the winning party getting the scarce jobs and the small road maintenance contracts, while those of the losing party "sucked salt" till their time came around. The fierce party politics became a matter of survival for many of the poorest up in the hills, as it had long been in the ghettoes of Kingston. It systematically eroded the tradition of independence and self-sufficiency the hill-folk had built up over the hard years of their past. The little that still remained of that tradition was dying visibly. It showed in the Cyprus Jacob and Emma entered by way of the narrow stony dirt road over which their car slithered and bumped.

The once lush green land had been burnt and burnt again, generation after generation, for quick and easy clearing. The forest of old trees on the gently rolling hillsides had been cut down for charcoal till the hills were bare and barren as though no big trees ever grew. Bad husbandry and the sun and the wind and the rain had, over time, turned much of the once fruitful green hills into poor dry shrubland.

Emma sensed Jacob's dismay as he looked at the changed landscape of his childhood and youth. This was not as he remembered it. Jane too, it seemed, sensed Jacob's distress and rested her chin on his knee, quiet and subdued.

"What have they done? It was not like this, never like this; they've destroyed the land."

Emma kept her eyes on the dusty dirt road. "Things change, Grandpa. It's a long time since you were here."

"Time has nothing to do with it!" Distress was turning to anger. "It's how you take care of the land!"

"If you know how." Better anger, she thought.

"They knew how! We all knew how! Grandma Sarah and Grandpa David taught everyone who came on the land how it should be used! They taught us. If you cut down one you plant one to take its place so that the species continues; if you want the species to grow and multiply then you plant two for every one you cut down. They have destroyed it all!"

"Perhaps they forgot and grew lazy; it is easier to burn the land than to bush it!"

"And it takes so very long to restore it," he said bitterly. "So very long."

They travelled in silence after that till they approached the first building on the outskirts of Cyprus. Emma grew apprehensive at the sight of the little shop on a piece of rising land on the edge of the road. Across the road from the shop two men wielding pickaxes were digging at the raw face of a partly gouged-out marl hill. Three men sat on a long bench against the wall of the shop watching the marl-diggers work. How would Grandpa react to those men tearing down that marl hill?

Emma stopped the car near the shop. Jacob ordered Jane to stay and got out and climbed the small rising to where the men sat. When he reached them he turned and looked deliberately across the road to the ravaging of the marl bank, then he turned to the men on the bench. "Morning."

The oldest one sitting in the centre of the bench answered for all of them: "Morning." It was cordially noncommittal.

"We're looking for the place where the Browns lived; near the old church ruins."

"You built the new house on the hill at Mount Zion?" There was interest now, and it showed in the way they examined him.

"Yes; my son supervised it, really."

"The doctor-man," one of the younger ones said.

"Then you the bishop?" the eldest half-asked, half-stated. "One of the Browns who had control of all the land here once ago?"

"Yes," Jacob said. "We took care of it then."

"Hear say them all scatter; some gone a foreign; them sell off all the land except for a small piece where you find the old man. Go down so to the other side of the village by the river."

"Anybody there now? Any of the Browns? Is the old man a Brown?"

"Doan know; doan think so; better you check him."

"Thank you." Jacob returned to the car.

They drove through the village, the land sloping downward. There were small houses and small-holdings all about, all fenced-in, nearly all too small for viable economic farming. The few exceptions went to the other extreme with vast stretches of land unoccupied and apparently unused. They stopped at the far western end of the village and heard the sound of water. They left the car and walked across a large fenced-off field which sloped steeply down to the river. The river seemed to have gone deeper into the ground than Jacob remembered; the river was much narrower; the way down to its banks much steeper.

"It has dropped greatly."

Something in his voice made Emma want to turn back. She touched his arm. "Let's go back; there's been too much change."

He stopped abruptly and turned to her; he put his arm about her shoulders and held her tight for a moment. "Forgive me, Emma. I've been thoughtless."

"You've been upset."

"No excuse." He leaned down and rubbed Jane's head. "And of you, too, old lady. Forgive me, both of you."

"Perhaps it's better for us to go back," Emma said.

"Perhaps it was foolish to start but it's too late to turn back now. I must see it through."

"All right."

They crossed the river and found the old man in the ruins of what had once been an outhouse of the home in which Jacob was born. A few of the old trees were still standing, and the land was as lush and green as Jacob remembered it. But there was no sign left of the sprawling house or even of the ruins of the great church which had been burnt down. All this land now, across the river and up to the road in one direction, and beyond where the church ruins had been and away to the distant horizon in the other direction, was part of the farm of a prosperous Kingston merchant who spent his weekends here. The old cutstones had been used to build his weekend home, a vast two-storeyed mansion with swimming pool and tennis court, its own electricity plant and water storage tanks. The rest of the land had been cleared of all the old relics and turned into a very prosperous farming enterprise.

The old man was not a Brown; Jacob did not recognize him. He had come to work for the Browns after Jacob had left for America. He could tell Jacob nothing about the whereabouts of the rest of the Browns. All he could do was express his bitter resentment for the way the Browns had treated him after a lifetime of service: when they sold off the land and moved away all they gave him was this square of land with this old house on it; no money, just this square of land. Jacob gave him a few dollars and they left him sitting at his table, cursing the Browns for not leaving him money.

With the permission of the Kingston merchant's overseer they spent an hour wandering across the land. Where the church ruins had been was now part of a vast and highly organized piggery. Beyond it, on the higher hillier land were equally well-organized goat pens. Unlike the peasants, the Kingston merchant seemed to know the importance of a good and abundant water supply for goat-rearing; he had installed large tanks and an elaborate pumping system to bring the water up from the river.

Jacob talked to Emma about the goats and pigs the Kingston merchant was raising on the land, and about how well-fed his dozen or so workers seemed to be. He talked as though talking would somehow ease the sense of desolation and the emptiness of mind and spirit he felt.

Emma listened and felt the pain in him and thought again what a terrible burden men had put on themselves by suppressing their natural capacity to weep. So she let him talk and clung to his arm and let her own tears flow for him.

Later, at home, and while Jacob and Jane were out walking, she had turned to the telephone book and gone through the listings under "Brown": there were seven columns of Browns in Kingston, and four columns in the country section. How do you find a family after fifty years and more? She abandoned the idea of trying it by telephone.

When Jacob returned, still depressed, Emma said: "I looked up the Browns in the telephone book; there are an awful lot."

Jacob smiled wanly. "They would be strangers, even if we found them. I haven't the time left to start anything new."

Not knowing how else to comfort him, Emma went and brewed a pot of coffee; they sat on the long verandah looking at the city far below, and watching the Blue Mountains to the east turn a glowing purple under the light of the setting sun; and waiting for David.

After a time the tranquillity of the place crept over them and made them tranquil too. The heaviness went from Jacob's spirit. Emma was silently grateful for the moment and for this place which made such moments possible when the need was greatest.

It took Jacob nearly eight months to recover sufficiently from the Cyprus experience to talk about it. He did so one late afternoon on the verandah when they were again waiting for David to come home. They had sat in silence for almost an hour. Jane had been asleep under the table, snoring rhythmically, and every now and then acting out some dream in her sleep.

Jacob had turned his head to look directly at Emma, an odd little half-smile of self-reproach on his face. "Remember that day at Cyprus?"

"I'll never forget it."

"It was a foolish impulse. Home is not always where you are born; family is not always a line of blood alone. You and the people of the mission were and are my real family. This was just an old man's foolish dream; a foolish attempt to reach back to a dead past."

She had said, very softly: "Dreams have to be played out sometimes. Nothing wrong with that."

"This one was forced on us. We came here because we had to go somewhere and I did not want to go to America or Europe; I was weak and needed comforting so I thought returning to where I was born would do it. But it isn't home any more, had not been for a very long time. Did you know I would find nothing?"

"I feared it."

"And still you came without a word."

"I needed comforting too, remember; and where else could we go?"

"I never asked you: where did you want to go? I mean, when we first left and you heard about John. Where would you have preferred to go at that time?"

"Wherever you went." She remembered how empty she had been at the time: too empty even to think of John's children, about whom she now thought so often with longing and curiosity, but without worry because she knew they were safe. "It didn't matter where I went as long as I was with you. John's last wish was for me to look after you, to be with you."

"That was before you married David."

"David wants the same thing. We will stay with you. . . ."

"Until I die?"

"Yes, Grandpa."

"And after I'm gone, what then?"

"I don't think he married me just to keep me looking after you!" Her eyes were laughing at him now, making her small round face look very young despite her greying hair; there was a teasing smile on her lips. "We are going to stay together forever. We'd like to take you home when the time comes; and if you must we would like you to die there and be buried beside your Missy."

"You don't have to tempt me! I want to live till then. I'll try."

"Good!"

"But if I don't, promise you'll take my ashes home for burial."

"I promise."

"Good for you. Now let's talk about you and David; he doesn't talk about himself and you tell me very little."

"What do you want to know?"

"I know he was married before; I know his wife died; I know it was in that war; I know they had no children. I don't know what she looked like and what he feels about her. And now there's you whom I know and you don't tell me what kind of man this son of mine really is."

"Where do you want me to begin?"

"First, do you love him. . . ," a long pause ". . . as you loved John?"

His expression had stopped the flippant reply she was about to make. Oh lord, Grandpa, how could you! But then, you love him too, and you loved John; so you need to know. She chose her words carefully. He had backed himself into an emotional corner of split loyalties to the living and the dead.

"Yes, at least as much; but it is different too. John was both my husband and my bishop. It made a difference, I think."

"To your sex life?" He looked at a distant John Crow floating on the air as no man-made bird ever could. "I was a bishop and I had a healthy, you might even say, robust, sex life."

"Easy, Grandpa!" How I wish David were here now! "It has nothing to do with how good sexual partners bishops can be. Let me try and explain. David's first wife, the Algerian – you know she was a doctor too and died in the fighting; he told me Hassan, who helped in our rescue, was with them in that fight in which she died – well, she had been circumcised. David said they cut off her clitoris, which is the equivalent of cutting off a man's penis."

"And you talk about these terrible things in bed?"

"Hush, old man, don't heckle! You asked: now listen. David's wife was mutilated like that so that for all their love for each other they could never have a really warm sex life which satisfied them both. Sex was an ordeal for her. And because he is the kind of man he is, they had almost no sex life at all. John and I had more of a sex life; we produced two children to prove it but. . . ."

"That bad experience you had," he prompted. "Is that what spoiled your sex life?"

"Not so fast, Grandpa. John's gentleness and my love for him soon overcame the panic fears bred by that experience. So it was not frightening or unpleasant. David says the world is full of women for whom sex is just that: they live with men whom they love, and bear them many children, and are happy, without ever having a complete sexual experience."

"And this is the difference you're talking about? Did John know it?"

Emma shook her head. "He didn't and I didn't till David explained it to me and helped me experience it."

Jacob stared out at space. The John Crow had gone. The sky was clear, though the speed of a few thin fleecy clouds, very high and travelling north-westward, suggested a high wind in space. He wished he had not started this conversation.

Emma said: "Don't be disturbed, Grandpa. It is not disloyal to John's memory for you to be happy to know I am fulfilled. You wanted to know; now you know. I loved and respected and looked up to John; I love and respect and look up to David, and David is also my lover and my friend, which makes him very special. Next question?"

Jacob had looked into Emma's eyes and shaken his head. And then, spontaneously, they had been enveloped in a wave of joyous laughter which disturbed one of Jane's happy dreams and she had woken bad-tempered.

The Maroon woman, Eliza-May, who came three days a week to help Emma with the cleaning and ironing, pushed her head through the open sitting room window. "Miz Brown, Miz Brown! Miz Emma!"

At last Emma was startled out of her daydream.

"I'm going now," the woman said. "Everything done."

Emma got up and picked up the letter postmarked Kampala, Uganda, then she went into her bedroom and got Eliza-May's money. She left the letter from Kampala on her dresser and went back to the verandah to see off Eliza-May, who, as usual, was reluctant to leave Emma alone in the house. So they stood on the verandah looking south at the winding road on which the bus to Rock Hall would come, and west into the valley of Mount Zion from where Jacob and Jane should come.

"Them late tonight." Eliza-May's concern was for the old

400

bishop who was growing weaker every day. In her Maroon community when people got this old a young boy or girl always walked with them "just in case".

"He's got Jane." Emma had a sudden aching remembrance of Mama Kilu.

"She old too," Eliza-May objected. "Two old ones together; not right."

Then they saw them, far down the slope of the land, coming home slowly, an old man using a long staff to aid his climbing; the old dog, grown thick-bodied, moving equally slowly beside him.

Emma opened the verandah gate. "I'll go and meet them. You go home now."

Still Eliza-May hesitated. "You need someone here when doctor not home, just in case."

Emma looked back from the bottom of the steps. "Go on or you'll miss your bus!" The five-thirty bus announced its coming with a long shrill blast. Eliza-May scampered down the steps and then down the long driveway to make sure she caught it.

Emma met Jacob and Jane about a hundred and fifty yards from the house. Jacob paused for breath; he was puffing; the going was becoming more difficult each day. One day neither he nor Jane would be able to take these long, regular, twice-a-day walks. When that day came, Emma knew, life would become more difficult for all of them. As it was, the work on his book was pretty much over with only odd bits of tidying and typing remaining, which she could do without his guidance. Without his book to work on, without his walks with Jane, life would become empty, and Grandpa was not a man to lead an empty life; the will to life itself would go. She remembered how David had tried to prepare her for this by talking regularly of the time Jacob would not be with them. He was also, of course, preparing himself; but she knew that when death came it would be unexpected, no matter how thorough the preparation for it.

She slipped her arm through Jacob's and he offered her a white wild orchid of exquisite beauty. "We found a whole cluster of them growing out of a cracked red vein in a marl bank, back there past the old ruins. It was a shame to pick any more than just this one to show you."

401

She held the orchid to her nose and got the faintest whiff of its elusive fragrance. "You shouldn't go so far any more. . . ." and to forestall protest she added: "I'm not sure Jane's up to it."

"We can still do it." He looked at the dog, "Can't we, old lady?"

"Shame on you, Grandpa! You know she'll do anything you want. Just don't overdo it and kill her."

"Oh all right, we won't go that far any more; but you ought to see those orchids."

They resumed the walk to the house. They were into the dry season and all the hills about looked brown: the trees and shrubs starved for moisture, the land bleached and leached by bad use, wind and sun and little cover. There was no water in what had once been the deep pool in the Mount Zion valley; just a very deep hole, with only signs that there had once been water.

They walked round to the back of the house so that Jacob would not have to climb the steps to the verandah. While Emma prepared a jug of fruit juice they heard the familiar signal of David's coming: three short and one long blast on his car horn. Emma added a bottle of his favourite rum and a jar of chilled coconut water to her tray and they went out to the verandah to wait for David.

David came in so angry that he ignored Jane's welcome and did not rub her tummy as she rolled over for him. She crawled under Jacob's chair, making herself as inconspicuous as she could. Emma and Jacob waited till he had settled down with his first drink.

Then Emma said: "Really bad today?"

"Bad as can be." His face was bleak. "They're now using M16s to kill each other. Unless you've used an M16 you can't know what a deadly thing it is. And poor hungry ghetto blacks, mostly teenage youngsters, are killing each other and their communities with these things. You can kill ten, twenty people with one random burst. A little over an hour ago I examined half a dozen bodies after a so-called shoot-out. They were mostly children; only two, the ones they describe as top rankings, could have been as old as thirty. God! A bunch of dead undernourished kids with shining, high-precision instruments of death! Democracy at work!"

"How do they come by these things?" Jacob looked at David's grim face, then down at the toylike city where the lights were being turned on. So peaceful-looking from up here; so pretty with all those lights and the dark sea for backdrop. "Aren't they very costly? Hard to come by? Where are they from and how do they get them into the country?"

"The ganja trade," Emma suggested.

"No," David said. "Ordinary hand-guns, yes; but not these. These are military weapons and you have to have some sort of military connection to lay hands on them. They're not easily available to even the smartest street hustlers of Miami."

"They're American?"

"Yes, Dad; M16s are American weapons."

Emma said: "I read the Vietnamese captured many of these guns after the defeat of the Americans."

"I expect they did. The question is: did they then ship them to Cuba to ship to Jamaica in order that ghetto youth should kill each other? Could be; but it is much more likely that they came from a stockpile in the Florida area. In these things you must always ask the central question, Emma."

"And what is that central question?"

"Who stands to benefit from what we have witnessed unfolding over the past couple of years? We've watched the systematic undermining of public confidence in the present government; the steadily escalating violence is part of that. All the signs, all the opinion polls, the general mood in the country, say the government will lose the next election; and the government has publicly committed itself to such an election. . . ."

"Hold it, David," Jacob cut in. "If all this is so, then there is no need for those opposed to the government to continue what you call their systematic undermining of confidence. As far as I can see it public confidence has collapsed; there will be a new government after the election. So why the escalating violence?"

"Because this is not a simple straightforward parliamentary election to decide which of two parties should run this country. It is that, of course, but much more too. This is political warfare for ideological supremacy. You two have been a little distant from it up here, as have been many others in the rural parts. Down there

403

it is naked war; I've watched it daily, and I know something about these things."

"Elections here have always been a little violent," Emma said. "The papers say so; the only new element are the guns."

"No, dear; the new element is the determined and carefully orchestrated campaign to demoralize the population by the excessive use of violence in its most brutal forms: more violence than is needed to achieve a specific end; horror upon horror for its own sake – torturings, decapitations, mutilations, burnings. Why? Why pile up the horror? To underscore the inability of those in control to control the situation. The basis for acceptable government, whatever the ideology, is that the government is able to provide security and stability. Any government that cannot provide these, that cannot enforce these, if need be, has no business to be in government. And all the horror is to convince the people, even those who support the party now in power, of the incapacity of that party to govern."

"No!" Emma protested. "They all say they want the two-party system to continue."

"They also say the government is turning communist and so destroying the two-party system. It is not a big step from that to saying that, if the two-party system is going to be destroyed anyway, then let it be in our interest rather than in the interest of the communists. But they are not saying that. They say that once the communist threat has been defeated, democracy will be restored. So all the horror is in the name of fighting a perceived horror."

Emma was not satisfied and it showed on her face. "You make it all sound so simple, black and white, good and evil; are they really such simple people?"

"Who?"

"Those you think responsible for the horror."

"Not simple, Emma; simply brilliantly schooled by experts in the business of how to conduct a two-pronged operation: one prong, psychological warfare; the other, a limited and carefully contained military-type terror operation. It is a perfect synthesis of the use of the ballot and the bullet to achieve the desired end. It is a familiar method used wherever there is a profound struggle to change, or to re-order, existing power relationships. In Algeria, and wherever else people were engaged in a real power struggle – rather than in the shadow-play of Tweedledee and Tweedledum parties pursuing the same objectives and differing only in style and personality – you have had this kind of political warfare. We used it in Algeria; and they used it against us. The simplicity here lies in the fact that the front-line troops, those undernourished ghetto youngsters, who do the fighting and the killing and the dying, do it without any clear understanding of what it is they are doing or why."

"On both sides?" Emma's curiosity was fully aroused now.

"They're shooting from both sides, whoever started it. It would be suicidal for one side not to shoot back. It is a rule of war that you shoot back or die like a sitting duck."

"No! Not that. About them not understanding what they're doing. D'you say this applies to both sides? The government side as well?"

David poured himself a second rum and coconut water; Emma refilled Jacob's glass and hers with fruit juice.

"If you are right," Jacob said thoughtfully. "And if your answer to Emma is that the ghetto youngsters of both sides do not understand what they are doing or why, then you must tell us who is manipulating each side; you cannot have one puppet master for two sets of puppets."

"The puppet imagery won't work, Dad. There is conscious choice at work here, and there is the power and the option of conscious choice on both sides. The party politics is probably the most sophisticated in the Third World. The one side chose one line of action, the other side chose another. The great manipulating world powers side with what suits their own geopolitical interests. Neither the CIA nor the KGB can operate effectively in a country unless they have friends or agents among the local people to facilitate them in whatever their paymasters want them to do; willing native collaboration is essential. No simple puppetry involved here."

Old Jacob smiled appreciatively and nodded. "I was only going along with your unexpressed idea of manipulation."

"Not unexpressed," Emma said. "Strongly implied."

"You two really think in tandem. Let me see if I can formulate my thoughts more clearly. I think there is something odd about a government setting out on a course of social revolution in the way this one has. No government of a society as divided by deeply entrenched colour and class interests as this can seriously expect to transform that society by way of consensus. It cannot be done; dominant people and classes always fight to hold on to what they have, no matter how it was acquired. Not to see and understand that reality and still to embark on the politics of revolution is at once romantic and brutally cruel to those who are the foot soldiers of that revolution."

."Perhaps so," Emma interjected. "But that is not the same as saying they have no clear idea of what they are doing and why. That was uncharacteristically arrogant for you." She sensed him grow angry and softened it by adding. "I'm sure it was because you were upset."

"Upset and angry; yes. But not enough to cloud my judgement."

He is angry now, she thought. "Oh, David. I didn't mean. . . ."

"Let's think it through." His anger was cold now. "They started out with a massive electoral mandate for social change. In less than ten years it has all been systematically eroded by the steady war-politics I've just described for you: unless you and Dad still believe that the violence and the killings and the burnings, the flight of capital, the finding of a secret prison and a secret hospital with a stockpile of drugs and surgical tools, and the inflow of M16s are all random, unconnected happenings; if you do, then I must sound arrogant."

"Come off it, David. So the anti-government campaign has been systematic and in all probability helped from outside. Emma's question still remains."

David's anger eased somewhat and Emma thanked Jacob with her eyes; that old mind could still work with precision.

"All right. You accept that it at least looks like a systematic campaign of destabilization. I think you agree that no foreign power can come in and destabilize a country unless it has the support of a significant group in that country; so the point is not to look for external villains. In any case, they are expert at leaving no evidence behind and their beneficiaries do not talk. So forget them and look at the victims. If a victim understands what is happening, he acts to protect himself and to prevent the same thing happening again."

"You yourself said they are shooting back," Emma whispered.

"True; and being out-gunned and out-killed at the level of the ghetto. Four of the six who died today belonged to one side. What did they die for? When the next election is over there will be a new government; the people will have transferred the mandate from the present lot, who cannot defend it, to those who are proving themselves strong and ruthless enough to go after it by all necessary means. The gentlemanly parliamentary game is only the surface show. When hundreds of people die in what is supposed to be an election campaign you are into war-politics. And the victims do not seem to understand this. So they will see their loss as a temporary setback, and they will try again, the next time around, in exactly the same way. The catch. . . ." He paused, all anger gone now, replaced by that air of quiet sadness with which he had on rare occasions talked to Emma of war comrades who had died, or of the terribleness of killing.

She resisted the strong impulse to reach out and touch him.

"Shall I complete it for you?" Then, not waiting for his answer, she did. "The catch is that if they are re-elected and set out on this same path again, the same force will rise against them and they will again end up as the victims of your war-politics. Is that it? Which makes it almost pointless, and makes you say they don't know what they are doing?"

"Yes, that's it."

Jacob tried to change the sombre mood. "So we do understand, after all; don't underrate us, son; our church has had similar experiences."

"Not quite, you always knew where you were going; you and the communists have that in common. When their people – their soldiers – and your people die they always know clearly what it is they die for: you die for Christianity, they die for communism. You think you will triumph in the end, they think they will. Will that be the last great ideological encounter?"

"If it comes," old Jacob said softly, "I rather think our Christ, not the one taken over and institutionalized by the power-brokers, will prevail. His is a revolution of love, not hate, and love is stronger than hate. Surely you see that."

"I hope so."

It was there again, that sudden and strong bond between father and son. Emma felt it as they looked at each other in the gathering darkness. Then, as quickly as it came, it was gone.

"Anyway," David said. "The people who fought and died in Algeria did so for a very specific purpose; not as long-term as your religious purpose, or the political purpose of the communists, but very specific all the same. And each one knew that those who survived would ensure that his or her death was not a pointless waste of life. The independence of Algeria justified their deaths. The greatest crime, the greatest tragedy, is to kill pointlessly and to die pointlessly. Just to die is tragic enough; the other is worse, it is wanton waste. What makes this thing here so terrible is its pointlessness: it leads nowhere, serves no over-riding idea or clearly defined purpose. And promising to repeat the process is simply promising a repeat of the cyclical wave of slaughter each time the so-called progressives try to alter the terms of power. The question they have not faced is whether any Third World country like this one can achieve even the mild West European type of socialism while the old ruling class and all its instruments of power remain intact."

"Surely they will not always lose," Emma said.

"They won here and you've seen what happened; it will happen again if they win again under the same terms."

"So give up all hope for socialism?"

"As long as the great power to the north will not tolerate anything labelled socialist which tries, however moderately, to live up to the implications of the label, they will ensure that it is put down every time. How long do you think the Cuban revolution would survive without the protection of the Soviet Union? Just as long as it takes for an American army to crawl all over it. The Soviets are Cuba's security shield. That is the reality. Those who seriously want to alter that reality will need much more than fine speeches, they will need what the peasants here call 'backatif'. Without that, without superior firepower to put

408

down the fire of your local enemies, and without some form of protection against an outside enemy, or a simultaneous political upheaval throughout the Caribbean and Central America, or a combination of the most important elements of all these, there can be no radical change in this part of the world. Even the churches here, unlike your church in Uganda, act like partisans in the power game between the superpowers."

"You make it sound hopeless," Jacob said thoughtfully. "Are these people then to give up and not struggle for justice because the odds are too great?"

"You know they are politically freer than any group of people you care to name in Africa. They elect and reject their rulers. How many exercise that same freedom in Africa, with or without the help of the gun?"

"Now I'm lost," Emma protested. "What are you saying, David?"

"I'm saying you have a model parliamentary democracy here, better than anything in Africa. In theory the people have control of their own destiny; in theory they can make all sorts of political and economic choices. But it is all theory for most of them."

"There are limits to all freedom," Jacob said.

"True; but who sets them? In whose interest?"

"I really am lost." Emma was feeling a little angry now. "You say they have more democracy than we have in Africa; you're angry because they slaughter each other in pointless party politics. And when we ask you what is the way out you make it all seem hopeless. How can they be both freer than people in Africa and also hopeless? There are many things I don't like here. I don't like the racism which everybody pretends does not exist; I don't like the self-contempt which comes out in the white bias of most black Jamaicans and in almost every brown Jamaican; I don't like the brutal callousness they show to the maimed and the sick and the old and the helpless. But I do like their democracy and I would have thought you would too; I thought we agreed that the only things which marred that democracy are the gross inequalities and cruelties in the society and, of course, the political killings. Now you make it sound as though they have nothing to hold on to and nothing to offer. I really don't understand you, David!" She did not care whether she angered him or not.

There was a long silence on the verandah after that. A cool breeze blew through the grapefruit and navel orange trees immediately below the verandah, making a soft, steady rustling sound. Far down in the valley of Mount Zion a John Crow made a sudden swoop in the fading light.

Jacob looked from Emma to David. "Cool enough?"

Emma looked at David, willing him to look at her, and smiling warmly when he did. Their eyes met and embraced.

"Cool enough," Emma said.

"Can we understand each other on this one, or put it off?"

"I'd like to finish it, but I'm upsetting Emma."

"Not really, not angry upset; it's just. . . ." the words seemed hard to find.

Jacob helped out. "Now, where were we? Let me see if I understand you. Your point is that the limits on their freedom are not set by the Jamaicans themselves or by what you would accept as reasonable external factors."

"Please bear in mind the context, Dad. A strategically placed little island wanting to assert its independence of both the American Eagle and the Soviet Bear, get aid from both sides, and go its own sweet way. In the real world of today's power politics it can't be done: not here, not at this time, and certainly not without the kind of understanding that would make possible the long period of austerity and the will to struggle which ultimately drove the French out of Algeria, the British out of Kenya, and both the French and Americans out of Indo-China. There is no perceived reason for it: Jamaicans have their political democracy; they don't have to fight to gain that. And economic democracy is just about the trickiest to fight for at the political or any other level. The vast majority of the people of the most advanced Western democracies do not have economic democracy, except perhaps in a most limited form; the welfare state is the nearest thing. My point is that this government of Jamaica seems to think it can have it both ways: be a Western parliamentary political democracy and an almost Soviet- or Cuban-type socialist economic democracy with its own brand new twist: a pattern of worker ownership and

410

management which I'm not sure even the Soviets would tolerate. There is, in Marxist terminology, something wildly utopian about it all. And it is for this that the youngsters of the ghetto down there are spilling out their guts and dying by the hundred. I find it intolerable! To repeat the waste in five-yearly electoral cycles makes it worse. That's all I'm saying.''

''Then what is their future?'' Emma asked.

''It will largely be determined by what happens outside: in the region around, in the twists and turns of the cold war, in the internal politics of the United States.''

''So what can they do?'' Emma persisted. ''Those who want to change the system?''

''I suggest they learn from you, from your church, the other way of long-term historical struggle. You are the people who elected not to be part of a religious system which had ceased to be revolutionary and become counter-revolutionary; you kept your way alive and strong at a time when there was no hope for black independent churches. To change systems you must understand the play of time on history, and then you will know how to choose your moment.''

Jacob's eyes glowed suddenly, and he was glad of the fading light. ''I see someone has looked at my manuscript.'' He tried to sound offhand.

''I like what I've read; it's helping me to see things.''

Emma reached out and took Jacob's hand. ''Well!'' She could not hide her excitement.

''How much have you read?'' Jacob was still casual.

''A little more than half. I'm nearing the end of your Liberia spell. I like your people, Dad; especially that Dr Lee with whom you were so close, and Mrs Willis and the Jones couple who started the school in the bush.''

''I thought. . . .'' Emma hesitated. ''We thought. . . .''

David smiled, knowing what was in her mind. ''Reading it is not the same as discussing a work in progress; there's no influencing possible.''

''So they can learn to survive,'' Jacob said. ''No big thing. You don't need the church to survive.''

''It is the quality of the survival, Dad, and you know it. What your ancestors did here, and what the blacks did in America which you

411

write about so beautifully, was the quality of that survival, the refusal to be debased into savaging each other; holding on to your humanity when everything conspired to dehumanize you. Reading your book made me wish I had known your Grandma Sarah and Grandpa David. Did you name me after him?''

''Yes.''

''Well, those two found a way of survival in a hostile world, and so did your church. It is more complex now, but I feel their basic solution still holds. I think it will be easier to apply in Africa than here.'' Then David shook his head. ''No, I don't know that it will be any easier there than here. I don't even know that it is possible in today's world. What I do know is that your people, your church, have always had the answer to the problem which obsessed your friend DuBois and so many generations of black folk.'' He lapsed into thoughtful silence; his mind worked rapidly, with growing excitement.

Emma watched him. She felt very close to him, very close to both of them, the father and the son who were now the cornerstones of her life.

Old Jacob leaned back in his chair and closed his eyes, feeling good and almost young again. David's reference to him had triggered remembrances of his old friend Dan Lee. Dan's hospital, and Mrs Willis's girls' school and Nurse Symes's properly trained nurses, were all there, memorials to them, on that Liberian hill. They had their monuments; only his, the place he and Margaret had started from nothing, was no longer there. But perhaps Emma was right: the manuscript made into a book would be his monument, and a monument to all those others with whom he had worked over the years. They would live and be remembered as long as that book is read; and the Chairman of the Bishops' Council in Atlanta had written to say the church would itself publish the book to ensure its widest circulation. So it will be read by many. . . . He shook himself free of his memories and dreams. ''Well, aren't you going to reveal the secret you found?''

''Give me a little time,'' David replied. ''Words are your business, not mine; I have to work at organizing them.''

Emma got up and gathered the glasses, bottles and jugs on to her tray. ''I'll get the food ready while you grapple with words.

We have jerk pork, fried chicken *à la Brown*, rice and gungo peas *à la Eliza-May*, and a dish of southern mixed greens in poor man's butter!'' She left them with a little dancing flourish.

David was under the shower when the telephone rang. He knew Emma would pick up the extension in the sitting room; he hoped it was not any emergency at the clinic. His young Rasta partner was an able doctor who would only call him in case of some grave emergency. He and his nurse girl-friend were as accustomed as David himself to the bullet wounds and stab wounds and the battered bodies of their ghetto patients.

Emma came into the bathroom carrying the telephone with its long extension. David turned off the shower and dried his hands.

''One of those funny calls.''

David took the receiver. ''Hello? Yes?''

''That you, doc?'' It was a husky whisper.

''Yes, who's that? There's a doctor at the clinic if you need help.''

''Is you we want, doc. Stay where you are; don't call anybody.''

The phone went dead.

''Looks like we'll have visitors.'' David handed the phone back to Emma.

She watched his eyes grow cold and distant, felt him withdraw into himself. They had had this kind of experience before. Once three young men came looking for firearms; another time it was an attempted robbery by an elderly man who looked half-starved; once two men had tried to steal one of their cars; twice men with gunshot wounds had sneaked up looking for medical help.

''What do we do? Call the police?''

He shook his head. ''They may only need help.''

''Or be up to mischief, be killers.''

''We must risk that.''

''Oh, David, why? What if they are killers?''

''What if they are not? What if they are only part of that pointless foolishness going on down there?''

"So we just wait?"

"And be ready."

He finished drying himself and wrapped the towel about his waist. She led the way into their bedroom and sat on the edge of the bed while he dressed.

"I think I'm carrying your child," she said, startled because she had not intended to tell him, not like this, not now. Perhaps the desire to blot out what they were waiting for made her do it.

He stopped in the act of buttoning his shirt. "What?"

She laughed. "I know; you don't expect an old lady of forty-plus to get pregnant."

The cold distant look went from his eyes, his excitement was palpable; a warm glow replaced her anxiety.

"Sure?"

"Yes."

"Oh Emma!" He gathered her up in his arms and kissed her tenderly. "Told Dad?"

"No."

"He'll love it!"

"Better confirm it first."

"Miss one period?"

"My second is two weeks overdue; but it's more a feeling of being pregnant, a woman thing."

"I trust your woman thing, my love. Tell Dad; he'll be happy to be a grandfather!"

"And you, David?" This was what she had not been sure of.

He held her lightly, close against him, her head reaching up to his chest. He tilted her chin up so that she looked into his eyes. A sea of tenderness washed over her; he kissed her and the tenderness overwhelmed her, brought tears to her eyes. Then he pushed her away to look at her at arm's distance.

"What do you think?"

"I'm so glad, my darling." Tears ran down Emma's face. "Come, supper and Grandpa and Jane are waiting."

They had finished supper and Emma was about to get the letter postmarked Kampala, Uganda, when Jane told them someone

414

was coming. She crawled quickly from under Jacob's chair, cocked her head to one side, listened intently, and growled softly, deep down in her throat. It took at least another minute or so before the people at the table heard what the dog had: the distant sound of a car, nearly half a mile away, starting the long, low-geared struggle up the steep and narrow driveway.

David got up briskly and went to their bedroom. That gun, Emma thought. His sudden transformation always meant the gun and a man as alert as an animal in the wild. When he returned she knew the gun was on his person though she saw no sign of it.

"Stay here, all of you; you too, Jane." He crossed the room and shut the two big windows opening onto the verandah. The sound of the struggling car was louder now. "If you hear any shooting dial the police emergency number; then get out by the back way and hide in the bush till the police come, if I don't."

He tested all the doors, making sure they were locked, then he went to the one nearest the verandah steps. He looked back at them, first at the dog, then at his father, then at Emma. "Lock it behind me," he ordered and went out.

Emma locked the door, then she went close to Jacob, by his favourite easy chair. Jane curled up at his feet on her special piece of carpeting. Jacob offered his hand to Emma. They sat holding hands, alert, waiting. Emma felt the terrible trembling of Jacob's hand.

"It's all right, Grandpa. David will take care."

"I know, I've seen him do it. He's good at it."

"Then stop trembling, dear."

"I can't." His voice was suddenly very weary.

David went quickly down the steps leading to the driveway which was a good twenty feet below the verandah. He crossed the driveway and took up a position behind the huge banyan tree which overshadowed everything, making the place an area of darkness. The gate leading to the back of the house and their carport was shut; the approaching car would have to stop in the area of darkness. When the car headlights swung into view and lit up the dark area, those inside the car saw no sign of the man behind the trunk of the massive tree.

415

The car pulled up near the gate. A voice inside said, "Turn the car; douse the lights." When that was done the same voice said: "Blow the horn." It was a loud, squeaky noise. When nobody appeared on the verandah the door on the passenger side opened and a tall shadowy figure got out. "Gimme the gun."

"You going up there?" another voice asked. "Me no like that."

"Want Joe fe dead?" The first voice was impatient. "Gimme the gun."

A long gun was passed out of the window.

"Joe bleeding bad," a third voice said.

"You sure 'bout this man?" Second voice was worried.

"Stop this foolishness before Joe dead." The first one now had the gun at the ready and turned to climb the steps. "I hear about him; they say he was a freedom fighter in Africa."

David's voice, cold and threatening, came at them as from nowhere. "You with the gun! Stop! Don't move or I drop you on the spot! I'm the doctor. What d'you want?"

The tall one started to turn in the direction of the sound.

"I warn you!" David snapped.

"Peace, doc, peace," the tall one pleaded. "We only looking help."

"With guns? Put down that gun! Carefully!"

"No, sah!"

"Then you and your bleeding friend and the others die!"

"They going kill us if you turn us in."

"That what you heard about me?"

"No, sah."

"Then give me the gun. Walk to the tree; don't point the gun."

The tall shadowy one hesitated then approached the tree slowly, carefully, the long gun pointing downward. One instant he was near the tree, the next he was on the ground, disarmed, his high-powered rifle pointing at him, a big man towering over him.

"Get up; warn your friends not to try anything."

The tall one got up, utterly bewildered by the suddenness and ease with which he had been disarmed. Always, in the past, all you had to do was point the gun at a person and they did exactly what you wanted.

"We not try anything," second voice said from inside the car.

David put two fingers to his lips and let out a sharp whistle. Inside the house Emma and Jacob reacted with relief. Emma rushed to their bedroom from which she switched on the outside lights to flood the dark driveway. Then she let herself out onto the verandah and looked down at David with the long gun in his hand and one of the strangers beside him.

"All right?" she called.

"Yes. Tell Dad and light up the back; we're coming round."

Emma withdrew.

David looked at the tall thin one beside him. In his early or mid-twenties, bright looking, obviously the leader of this lot; three others in the car, one wounded: brave and foolish and now frightened tools of a cynical political system.

"What happened? You tangled with the police?"

"No, doc, is gun battle with the other side; politics."

David opened the gate, then turned to the driver of the car. "Drive up slowly and wait." Then he and the tall one followed the car. "You know I have to report this to the police."

"Yes, doc, but you not holding us. You fix him first and then we go and then you report. So it go, doc?" A note of pleading in his voice.

David gestured with the gun. "I'll keep this thing till you are ready to go."

"We hear right about you, doc." The tall one was relieved and trying to be friendly.

"Did you also hear that we did not play foolish political games with life?" David was angry. "What's the difference between you and what you call 'the other side'? You are poor and black and so are they; you are hungry and unemployed, and so are they; you are all hell-bent on killing each other. Do you know why, what for?"

"For power, doc." The tall one was sure of himself now, clear about the politics behind their deadly game. "See, doc, if we have the power we get the benefits, if the other side get the power they get the benefits. Middle-class people don't understand this, doc; they're all right, you're all right, no matter who is in power. Not so in the ghetto; in the ghetto who is in power decides who eat and

417

who suck salt, who get house or a work or a money and who don't."

"And for that you kill each other! Why don't your leaders also kill each other?"

"That different, sir; if they kill a leader that's war and the whole country mash up; so they don't."

"So it is all a well-thought-out game of knowing who can and who cannot be killed without upsetting the show. And you, you people from the ghetto, you approve of it?"

The tall one showed his teeth in a grimace David recognized from his African childhood. The tall one's voice was almost gentle as he turned the question back to David. "What fe do, doc?"

David's anger evaporated. How do you answer? What do you say? You are caught in an historic trap, and the most heroic thing may be to bide your time and prepare yourself and stay alive until a more opportune time. Can you tell that to the hungry and the homeless of the ghetto? David shrugged and turned to those waiting in the car near the kitchen door. He stood over them while they carried the wounded man from the car, through the kitchen and into the small room which he used for weekend emergencies from the surrounding villages, when little or no medical services were available.

David removed three bullets from the young man's body, all in non-vital areas; but he had bled heavily, and the danger was his weakness from loss of blood. Emma helped him stop the bleeding. Jacob and Jane waited in the sitting room.

At last it was over. David turned to the tall one. "He has lost much blood. He could still die if he does not get proper attention; hospital is the best place for him."

"No hospital." The tall one was firm.

"Wanted?"

"They framed him for murder. I know him; I know he won't murder women and children. We know who did it and framed him; we'll settle it."

"So what will you do?"

"We have a safe place. Now that you fixed him up we'll take him there; we'll care him good."

"The wounds are going to have to be cleaned and the bandages changed every day."

"We have someone."

"And proper feeding; he's very weak."

"We'll feed him."

"Then what? Back to the street war if he gets well?"

The tall one shrugged. He pulled a fat wad of money out of a pocket of his tight jeans.

"Keep it!" David snapped.

The tall one stuffed the money back into his pocket and smiled with a hint of irony; he looked at Emma. "Doc's all right, ma'am, but too soft; they ginnel him; anyone else would take a heap of money for this job."

Emma tried to look forbidding, not knowing how to answer, but she was secretly amused by the idea of David as a softie.

David finished his final injection. "Take him away and take care of him. Remember I have to report this."

They lifted their wounded comrade and carried him out to their car and arranged him on the back seat, one of them supporting him. The other went into the driving seat. The tall one, almost as tall as David but less than half as broad and big, looked steadily at David.

"The gun please, doc; we need it, must have it."

David nodded, went back into the house and came back with the gun. "Know how to use this thing?"

"Yes, sir, doc." The tall one was solemn now, with the intense seriousness of the very young. "We don't shoot except they shoot. We are not gun-happy."

"Weapons of death attract death."

"If we don't have them, we don't live."

"But this way is wrong, young man, both for you and for the other side. Neither of you will get any long-term benefit, Jamaica will not benefit from your slaughtering of each other. Others may benefit; not you; not Jamaica."

The tall one shrugged, investing the gesture with a hint of resignation, as if saying "Wha' fe do?" David handed him the gun.

"Thanks, doc. Thanks for everything." He got in and the car started down the steep driveway.

Emma came and stood beside David and they watched the tail-lights till the car went out of sight round the first bend. She took his hand and they walked to a point of the land, under the

419

avocado trees, from which they could see the lower part of the steep driveway. They heard the engine in low-gear compression, loud and coughing, as though needing a tune-up; then, a while later, they picked up the red glow of the tail-lights and followed them till the car reached the flat land and disappeared in the citrus grove. Then they watched it reappear, crawl to a halt, and join the main road, turning left. The way to Kingston was down to the right; they were going away from Kingston, further up into the hills, probably somewhere in St Catherine, or turning off higher up and doubling back to confuse any likely pursuit. That would be obeying the first rule of war: trust no one.

"What now?" Emma sighed.

"For them?"

"Yes, for them. Where will it end?"

"Another gun fight another day and they may not be as lucky as this time. Sooner or later those young men, probably all of them, will die by the gun. That is the price they pay for their much vaunted parliamentary democracy which can be so cynically manipulated. What a different place this would be if the leaders were the ones who had to go out and gun each other down! You'd soon have an end to the bloodletting then!"

She tucked her arm into his. "Come, we've neglected Grandpa long enough." She pulled gently and they went back to the house. "I have special news for him, and there's that letter from Kampala."

"Have they gone?" Jacob sounded breathless.

"They've gone," Emma said and went and sat beside him, took his hand, felt his galloping pulse; David must do something about this.

"I must call the police." David went quickly to the study, picked up the telephone and dialled police emergency. There was an instant answer; he identified himself and asked for the Superintendent in charge. The Superintendent came on within seconds. David and the Superintendent had shared many moments and after-moments of ghetto violence.

"Hello, Doctor Brown?"

"Superintendent Marks, thought you should know I just

420

removed three bullets from a man: nothing serious, said to be after a gang fight.''

''He with you now?''

''No, he was brought by friends who took him away.''

''At gunpoint, of course.''

''Of course.''

''Please describe the man, doctor, and his companions. Are you at your clinic?''

''No, at home. They looked just like all these youngsters killing each other; you know, like the ones we looked at earlier today. Same sort of political gang warfare, from what I got out of the leader.''

''Oh? What did he look like?''

''Very tall, very thin, long face, intelligent, educated.''

''Soft voice and Rasta locks and blue jeans?''

''Yes; all except for the locks.''

''Must have cut them off then.''

''Sounds like you know him.''

''I think so. Bright boy; might have been different if things were different.''

David knew the conversation was being taped so he was surprised at Superintendent Marks being so forthcoming.

''Sounds as though you like him.''

''If he's who I think then he came from a good home and his father was a friend of mine, a decent sort who was killed in a political accident a couple of years back. Anyway, they were armed, you said.''

''An M16.''

A long silence, then. ''The tall young fellow had it?''

''Yes.''

Another long silence, then: ''Know which way they went when they left you?''

''Further up into the hills, away from Kingston. And I didn't see the number of the car, or if it had any.''

''Witnesses?''

''My wife and father.''

''You could have refused to help them till you called us.''

''And risk my wife and father?''

"All right, doctor; thank you for calling; sorry about the experience. Someone will come and take a statement from you at the clinic in the morning, if that's all right."

"That will be all right." David hesitated then added: "The shooting eased up down there?"

"Yes, it's much quieter than earlier. But they are now setting buildings to the torch and keeping the police and firemen at bay from rooftops. Quieter but still bad. Want me to send a couple of men to guard your home? They'd be glad of the peace and quiet."

"No need to; I don't expect anything further."

"Then you expected this one? A phone call perhaps?"

"Come, Superintendent Marks! Just not likely. Tell me: when will all this foolish bloodiness end?"

"Your guess is as good as mine, doctor; probably after the election."

"When there'll be no more need for it?"

"As you say, when there'll be no more need for it. A bad business. 'Night, doctor."

"Goodnight, Superintendent."

David joined Emma and Jacob in the sitting room. Emma had tried to persuade Jacob to go to bed, promising to come and read the letter from Kampala as soon as David finished his phone call. But Jacob would have none of it. He had brought out his special bottle of hundred-year-old brandy which he dispensed by a few drops on rare and important occasions. Now they were about to toast Emma's unborn child, and then she would read the letter, and then he would go to bed. Not before.

Now, with David present, he poured small amounts of the special brandy into three small barrel glasses; his hand shook but he did not spill a drop. One glass to Emma, one glass to David, and then he raised his own.

"To dear Emma who is making me a grandfather and who is nursing your child, my son; and to that unborn child. May he walk straight in the ways and service of his people and of his God; you will see to that, Emma. And you, David. That is my charge to you. And I am so happy, my children."

They drank, and then they embraced; and Emma used her eyes to make David aware of her concern about old Jacob's trembling.

"Now the letter," Jacob said. He took it from Emma and peered through his thick reading glasses at the outside of the envelope, trying to remember and to identify the handwriting. He couldn't decide if it was Michael Odera's; such a long time since he had last seen Michael's writing. Now if it had been John's he would know it straightaway.

Emma took the letter from Jacob and opened it. David sat close beside her, so close their bodies touched. He put his hand on her thigh, caressing it gently. Unusual for him with his strong sense of emotional privacy. It's the thought of the child in me that makes him do this. Whatever they say, most men want the woman of their choice also to be the mother of their children: a sort of visible and outward symbol of commitment and surrender. It had seemed not having a child did not matter to him. Now she knew how important it was. Then she flipped through the pages of the letter.

"It's from Michael Odera," she said.

"Read it, woman!" Jacob was getting testy with tiredness and excitement.

She read in a measured voice, loud enough, and slowly enough, for an old man going deaf to hear it all, conscious all the time of David's hand on her thigh.

"Dear Sister Emma: Greetings to you and to our revered Bishop, Grandpa, and to his son and your husband our brother, David. This letter is one of joy and good news. The tyrant is still here among us but his days are numbered and the land will soon be free of him. It is only a matter of weeks, if not days, before the soldiers from Tanzania will be here. We know the outside news you get of what goes on here may be twisted because there are some who are powerful who do not wish to see the tyrant's fall, especially with the help of Tanzania whom they damn and fear for putting the land and the power in the hands of the people. So, whatever you hear or read, we know, and we tell you with great joy, that the tyrant's end is near. You know our people are everywhere and know everything; that is how it has always been since the days of our beginning with the Old One, and the time of our glorious martyr, John Chitole, Bishop of our Church and beloved of our people. We have lost many of our good brothers

423

and sisters, but many others have come forward to take their place. As two fell, four stepped forward to take their place and the Church has grown stronger: so we are everywhere and know most things. We know the dark days of the tyrant are coming to their end, and we know the time is at hand for our Church to come out of the dark shadows into which we have been driven. The word has gone out to our brothers and sisters who have survived that it is the time to return, a time to rebuild, and a time for all those who have been scattered to return to their villages and their communities and to rebuild the Churches and the congregations. And we of the centre where it all began are returning too. Indeed, some are already there; many of our vehicles are back, the men are rebuilding, the women and the children are out in the field. Soon the Mission will live again. But it is not of these things that I wish to write now, though we know they will be good tidings for Grandpa and your good self. The purpose of this letter concerns Grandpa.

"We know he is very old, but we also know he is well in body and spirit, and it is the wish of his church that he returns to his people and his home as soon as possible so that our minds may be at peace because our father is among us. . . ."

Jacob let out a choked cry compounded of pain, joy, love. He broke down and wept for a long time. For a while they let him be. Then Emma cradled his head on her breast, rocked from side to side, and stroked the thinning, fleecy white hair and murmured the ageless comforting sounds mothers make to calm disturbed children.

Old Jacob's sobbing subsided; still Emma kept up the rhythmic swaying and the comforting sounds. He fumbled in his pocket, brought out his handkerchief, wiped his face, blew his nose. Jane came and sat in front of him, head cocked to one side, eyes questioning.

David took Jacob's wrist and felt the racing pulse. Jacob straightened up. "Now the rest of the letter!"

Emma composed herself and resumed reading where she had left off: ". . . so that our minds may be at peace because our father is among us. So will you please bring him home to us. If you yourself or your husband cannot do it because of commitments, let us know as soon as possible and we will send one or two people whom he knows well to travel with him. As you know, our Church is not poor so money is no problem; the tyrant and his people never found what belongs to the Church. We made sure of that. So we will take care of all costs, whether you bring him or we have to send people to bring him home. Tell him the women have restored the damage done to the grave of his beloved wife and it is now as beautiful and filled with flowers as when he last looked at it. . . ."

Again Jacob let out a cry; but he contained himself this time and Emma paused only briefly before continuing.

"Tell him by the time he gets here his section of the Bishop's Home will be ready; they are already at work to ensure that. The work will move faster as soon as the tyrant is overthrown.

"You and your husband must forgive the inconvenience this may cause but we need to have our father here in his home, we need his spirit here, and we need to bury him here when the time comes so that his spirit will always watch over us as we move and work in the way he taught us.

"We will understand if you and your husband have made a new life in a more peaceful place and do not wish to return. But he who was our inspiration and our father and leader must not be buried in a strange land, far from us, so that we cannot go and sit by his grave and commune with his spirit.

"We ask this of you in the name of our Church and all its branches and all its congregations.

"The Lord bless you and keep you. Michael Odera, Senior Bishop."

Old Jacob said: "Amen!" He looked at Emma. "You will come with me!"

"Oh yes, Grandpa!" She said it quickly, excitedly. Then she thought of David. "Oh, David! It's all right, isn't it?"

"It is all right."

"There!" Jacob drew Jane to his knees. "We're going home, old girl! We're going home again!" He was breathing fast, gasping a little with each intake of air. "How long, David? How long will it take? A week? Two? Emma, let's send a telegram to Michael! Say: 'Coming home as soon as possible stop will let you know date. Grandpa.' Can you phone that through now?"

"We'll send it in the morning," David said softly.

"We can fly! That will make it quicker! We can be there in a week! Can't we, David?"

David took his father's wrist and felt the racing pulse.

"Easy, Dad. We'll make it as soon as possible, but there are quite a few things to be done. You know, papers to get in order, plane seats to book, my practice and this place to think about."

"We'll go ahead and you can follow us when things are wound up, can't he, Emma?"

Emma looked at David who nodded imperceptibly.

"Yes," Emma said. "Yes. But there's Jane. . . ."

David rose and hurried out to his little emergency surgery.

"Oh Lord, yes, Jane!" Jacob's excitement mounted. "Can we get her on a plane? We can't stand another long quarantine. No! We'll have to do something about that. You're the doctor, David!"

He's not even aware that David has left us: Emma was dismayed. She jumped up and ran to David's little room. The old man continued talking with mounting excitement.

David was rummaging in his medicine bag. Emma touched his arm. "What wrong with him?"

"I've got to slow down that pulse rate before it forces an attack. Trouble is I can't use anything strong; he's too old."

"Does that mean he – we – can't go?"

"We may be able to, if we can control this. But he's very old, dear. His heart won't take much. We must be careful." They returned to the sitting room when David had found the little pills he wanted.

Jacob was still talking, remembering home and people and places and the things that would have to be done and the plans to be made; now talking to Jane, now to Emma, now to David.

David made him swallow two little pills with water then tried to help him up.

"Time for bed, Dad. There'll be much to do tomorrow."

"Yes, of course, you go off to bed. You are going to do most of the preparing; not much good at that any more. Emma and I will sit and talk a while, make a few plans like in the old days. It's going to be difficult without John. He was the best planner and manager we ever had; I taught him but he became better than me

426

at it. Of course, Michael's good too, but it's not quite the same as with John. . . .'' He talked on and on till the pills took effect. Then he stopped talking abruptly, his excitement abated. He looked at them as someone coming out of a trance; his lips curved in an apologetic little smile. ''I got carried away, didn't I?''

David looked at his watch; it had taken twenty minutes for the pills to work; now to see how long their effect would last. He felt Jacob's pulse again; much slower, but not quite down to normal yet.

''Those little pills,'' Jacob said. ''To calm me? They work, all right. What's wrong with me? Is it serious? Must be to make you both so worried. Tell me, what does it mean? Tell me straight. Emma noticed it. What does it mean, this excitement that I can't control?''

''Like a machine running down.'' David made it sound casual, off-hand, professional. ''Like an old machine that needs special care and attention.'' He warmed to the idea. ''The body is a machine, you know; the best and most sophisticated ever made, self-renewing and self-servicing and self-healing if you handle it with reasonable care; it's only when it gets old and parts get worn out that it needs patching and spare parts; and the older and more worn out, the greater the need for spare parts.''

The idea amused Jacob. ''What parts for excitement?'' He saw the sudden contortion of Emma's face and offered her his hand. ''Come, child. I am very old, you know, and the old machine does run down. Don't be afraid. Which parts, David?''

''In your case, no special parts, Dad; just wear and tear.''

''Just time?''

''As you say.''

''And pills and drugs can't overcome time and wear and tear.''

''Stop it!'' Emma jumped up and stormed weeping out of the room.

Jacob called after her: ''Come Emma, we must talk about these things.''

''Let her be,'' David said softly. ''It takes time to adjust. She will be back.''

''Poor Emma,'' Jacob said. ''Always losing those she loves and depends on. You must not let her lose you too, David. I don't think she'll be able to bear that.''

"I'll do my damnedest not to."

Father and son looked steadily at each other, all barriers down now.

"And you, son, are you adjusted to the idea of death – my death?"

"It's part of the process, Dad; you get adjusted in my work. But still it hurts, each time."

"Do you mind talking about mine? I'd hate to have to do it with a doctor who's a stranger."

"No, not now, so let's talk."

"Good; about the overheating and the engine cracking, how near am I to that?"

"Hard to say, Dad, too many variables; never quite the same from one person to the other, or one case to the other."

"All I want is your guess. You understand I don't want any long-drawn-out effort to keep me alive; none of those transplants or fancy new organs. Of course I'd like to see home again before I die, but it is not all that important now. Things will begin again, whether I'm there or not; all is not lost; Michael's letter says. If I can't make it I will die in peace knowing that you and Emma will see that my ashes are buried with Margaret, and that my spirit will be among my people. So what's your guess, doctor?"

Emma came quietly back into the room and composed herself on the small divan in the shadowy corner near the door, away from them. Jacob held out his hand, beckoned.

"Come, Emma, you must share this with us and we must make plans together; it is better that way. Don't be afraid of the idea of death, my child. Don't push it away."

She came reluctantly out of the shadowy corner and sat beside Jacob and took his hand, her eyes puffy from weeping. David caressed the back of Emma's neck.

Jacob said, "David was about to give me an educated guess of how much time I have."

"It's not the sort of thing you can date."

"I know that, quit stalling, guess!"

"Oh, let it be!" Emma protested.

"He's right, Emma," David said and Emma nodded unhappily.

428

"Well?" Jacob was tiredly relaxed now, fully under the effect of the pills.

"It could happen any time," David said. "It could be triggered by any moment of tension, tomorrow, next week, next month; or you could go on for months or even years. So I think we go ahead and start planning for the journey home as from tomorrow morning."

"I like that." Jacob smiled at Emma, trying to coax a responding smile out of her. "Who was it said we must carry on as though we are immortal, even in the face of death? Whoever it was, one thing that poor soul didn't seem to realize is that we really *are* immortal. Oh, not in the way those involved in what my old friend Dan Lee called the God business think, but in the way it really is, in the way our congregation and our people understood so well without the help of any intermediary. If you listen to the wind, or the sound of the trees and the leaves, if you listen to the rain, if you walk on a special piece of earth and sit in a certain place on a certain rock, and if you are quiet, and if your senses are responsive, you will feel the spirits of those who have been in those places before; and if you learn to listen you may even hear them."

"A kind of reincarnation," David teased.

"Spirits in rocks and trees and rivers," Emma said.

"Mock if you must. My old Grandma Sarah often heard them. I know now it was no vision." He beamed at Emma. "For all your mocking, you've heard them, too, haven't you, Emma? I've seen you when you were with them."

"Oh come, Grandpa! I was only immersed in the peace of this place, I heard no voices."

"Didn't you? Didn't you, really?" He stopped and sighed, utterly exhausted suddenly. "I want to go to bed."

Emma and David helped him up and on the short walk to his room. This night, for the first time, they helped him undress and into bed.

"'Night, Grandpa," Emma said; but Jacob was asleep already. David turned off the light and shut the door.

They sat on the verandah looking at the twinkling lights of Kingston, more than two thousand feet below. Jacob was asleep with Jane on guard at the foot of his bed; she would let them know if he woke in any kind of distress. The strong south wind which had blown in from the sea for about an hour had abated; the world, from their verandah, was calm and peaceful now. The distant city was a thing of fairy-tale quality, a piece of starlit earth framed by the dark mountains to the east and the darker Caribbean Sea to the south and south-west, and by the clear moonlit sky above. This they would miss. This they would carry with them wherever they went; this they would remember with a quiet ache when they thought or talked of Jamaica.

They had gone to bed after taking care of old Jacob, but neither could sleep. After the high wind had passed they had put on pyjamas, got themselves a jug of grapefruit juice and gone to the verandah and the view.

Emma knew that of all the things she would miss about Jamaica, this place, this view, especially on clear nights like this, the very feel of the place, the atmosphere it radiates, would be greatest. She had sunk much of herself into this piece of earth over these past seven years. Now she had to prepare herself to leave and forever after to have only its memory. She had, too, all at the same time, to prepare herself for life without Grandpa at its centre; to prepare to lose both at the same time perhaps. . . .

She said, "I'm writing Michael in the morning. What do you want me to tell him?" She thought: Not both at the same time, please Lord, give us a few years between one and the other; is that too much to ask?

"What we agreed: we're all three preparing to come together as soon as we've wound up things here. I don't see us doing it in under a month, but we'll try."

"And about Grandpa?"

"That he could go any time, though we hope careful medication will buy time. They must prepare themselves too."

She looked steadily away from him, at the invisible distant world beyond the dark sea. "Then what, David? What for us? We'll take him home, one way or the other, him and Jane. Then we must plan for you. Where do you want to go? Where will you do what you want to most and be happy? North Africa? Algeria? You were happy there and your friends are there. Shall we go there?"

He took her shoulders and turned her and made her look at him.

"Where do *you* want to go? What do *you* want to do?"

"Thank you for asking; I appreciate that very much, more than I can say." She had thought her answer out long before this bitterly painful night, not consciously perhaps, not even expecting the question to be asked, but she had thought it out; now the answer was there. "I want to go home, of course. I would like to see the children again, John's children; they'll be quite big now and integrated into their extended family." She smiled. This was one of the great African virtues and it had taken Grandpa to make her see it. "But I'll go wherever you want – if you want me to." She knew, she was cheating with that last bit. "I'd stay here if you were happy but you are not; the politics here distress you; I'm sure it's not just the violence and the waste of life you're so angry about."

"And you, Emma, could you really be happy here?"

"The roots of my happiness are rather different from yours, dear. Ruth, the woman in the Bible, said it."

"But after Dad's gone. . . ."

"There'll be you; you've been at the centre too, you know."

"Not like him."

"Only because he needed me more and you understood. When he's gone you will fill all my life. And if you'd be happy here, you and this place and the land would be enough. I could never be lonely here; but I'll go wherever else you want if you let me have a piece of land – and your love."

He put his arm about her shoulder and they leaned against the verandah rails, looking at the twinkling lights of the city.

"Do you remember our talk before the young gunmen came with their wounded comrade?"

She thought back to how nearly they had quarrelled and how wise old Jacob had eased things. "What has that to do with our future?"

"Everything, my love. I wish I were as good with words as Dad. Think about those youngsters and the deadly game into which they have been manipulated. We can't see it from up here, and we can't hear it, but right now down there they are killing each other and burning down their homes in the name of their precious two-party parliamentary democracy."

431

"What we fled from in Uganda was worse, much worse," Emma said.

"To be sure; but are those really our only options? Must we have either that brutal and bloodthirsty dictatorship or this more democratic elective bloodletting every five years?"

She said, very carefully, trying to be clinical: "Why ignore the Cuban or Soviet alternatives? We talked about them too."

"Cuba's communism can only last as long as she has the protection of the Soviet Union; take away that protection and it collapses, with American help, of course. Any deal between the Americans and the Soviets, any change in the terms and nature of their relations which makes Cuba expendable in the interest of some higher national Soviet objective, and that noble attempt at schools and jobs and homes and health for all and pride and self-respect and sense of sovereignty would be wiped out as though it never existed; all the effort and sacrifice would be cancelled as though it were never made. Ultimately Cuba's freedom of choice is as restricted and dependent as is Jamaica's freedom of choice. To be sure, the making of their revolution was their own choice, but now, for the survival of that revolution they must depend on the Soviets to shield them against an American overthrow of their revolution. And in order to survive, in this context, you must adapt yourself to the thinking and the desires of those on whom your survival depends; you are, in short, dependent."

"Oh, David, anything else would, to use your own word, be utopian! We are all dependent on each other, nations, groups of nations, families, individuals. You know that."

"No, Emma, you are confusing interdependence and dependence; they are not the same. The child is dependent on the parent till he grows to adulthood, then the relationship changes and the parent, grown old, becomes the dependant; the process is dynamic, not static, and is an ever-changing pattern of interdependence. There is very little such interdependence between the Soviets and their client states, or between the Americans and their client states. It is really all a question of your angle of vision, darling: of whether you have always to tilt your head and look up and choose your words with care not to offend, or whether you can look straight ahead into another's eyes and turn your back

432

and say no and walk away and still survive. It gets worse when the dependence has gone so deep and for so long that you are conditioned by it and cannot see yourself surviving without it. At that point you become the first agent of dependence. The real tragedy is what has happened to our minds. Our minds have been so colonized that we are ourselves the most effective propagandists of the process which sets other people's limits on our own thoughts and options. You, my love, could not think of survival options other than those which evolved from the great Western European awakening. And yet there were great political systems and great philosophies long before the rise of Western Europe to its dominant position."

"But no such great worldwide imperialisms."

"Probably because those others did not see the terrible useful-ness of colour difference as a power tool. Others did not put quite the same premium on aggression and conquest. And it was out of that aggression and conquest, and out of lust for greater and greater power, endlessly, that we have come to this point where all the world and its people are now seen as pawns in the great rivalry between the two Western technological giants for ultimate power and control. This is the road to a new technological barbarism which threatens to engulf the whole world, if the Russians and Americans do not wipe us out first in pursuit of a so-called winnable nuclear war. There is no need for us to follow them down that path. This is their dead-end if we can't show them another way."

"Why we?" She went to the table, sat down and poured herself a drink. He remained standing at the rails, caught up in his ideas, which now depressed her by the future they conjured up.

"Because it's our obligation, our debt to life and this world which is so beautiful and which we have so abused. They carried the burden of enlightenment when there was the historic need for it. I think we are approaching another such moment of historic need."

"Another cross for black folk, David? Haven't we suffered enough and paid enough?"

"They've run out of steam, darling; they've lost their way and will smash us all up with them if we don't take a hand and save ourselves and them. Life is more, much more than wars and dominations and vast material holdings. We do not want this world to end up as another barren, lifeless planet floating in space. And this is where it has to do with your future and mine, and the future of the church to which Dad and so many others devoted their lives in the long struggle for survival. This has to do with DuBois' vision and Garvey's dream."

He came to her and pulled a chair close up and sat beside her. He gave voice to his thoughts again and she listened closely, mentally wide awake in the deep of the night.

"The people of the East – the Indians, the Chinese, the Indo-Chinese, the Japanese and the people of the Indonesian islands – and, to a lesser extent, the people of the Arab world, have somehow succeeded in surviving this great Western onslaught without having their minds occupied. Even those who went to school in Europe somehow survived psychologically intact. Some of the more inaccessible African tribes did too, but their numbers are too small to be of any significance. In the main it was only the sub-Saharan African mind which was so completely colonized that we ended up as the principal instruments in our own continued domination by others, even after most of us gained political independence; nowhere was this more pronounced than in the black diaspora. And so we saw the whole world through the eyes of those who had colonized our minds, as they saw it or wanted us to see it. The only options were their options, the only possibilities their possibilities. How to break out of this mould was what I could not see till I read Dad's manuscript. I suppose I was looking for some political or economic or military formula-tion. . . ."

Emma's mind was in tune with his now. "But David; Grandpa's manuscript is a Western document."

"Yes," he said. "Like I am a Western product. Does that disqualify me from exploring non-Western ideas? I'm also a product of Africa, Emma, in some ways more so than you. It is not surprising that the children of the black diaspora born outside black Africa were more concerned about this problem of our colonized minds. I think they had to be Westerners to look critically at this problem. So I'm not interested in rejecting Westernism. We must come to terms with it, and before we can do that we must know who we are and what we are, and that the

434

thoughts we think are our own and not knee-jerk responses to conditioning. Do you see, darling? It is not being against anything or anybody; it is not anti-Westernism, not anti-capitalist or anti-Marxist. It is, quite simply, being for us, first, second, third and last. And to be for us, we must withdraw from all this as fully as is humanly possible, and for as long as it is necessary, in order to free ourselves from that long occupation of our minds.''

"Withdraw from all what?''

"Don't sound so shocked! In your manuscript those early slaves, Dad's ancestors and the one called Samson who led them to this place, they withdrew.''

"They had no option.''

"That's my point. We are back to the question of options: the brutal dictatorship, or your murderously manipulated parliamentary democracy, or the variations in between – which the Chinese so rightly, if indelicately, call the 'running dogs' of this or the other superpower's hegemony.''

Emma cut in quickly: "Or the bobbing and weaving and snatching of advantage from one side or the other in their cold war. That is the non-aligned way.''

"Until they outwit and out-manipulate even non-alignment. They do it with everything. It took them a few years to get the measure of OPEC, and then they did it with CPEC's money. They will go on using their wits and their money and the stranglehold of their trans-nationals to ensure privileged access to the world's resources. For all your many sovereign states, they have a tighter grip on the world economy today than ever before; and they have devised new ways of smothering you with loans and tying you up in debt. No, love, all your bobbing and weaving and snatching of advantage will only end in your further impoverishment, your further dependence. This is, after all, something they have developed and refined over a long time. And what they do to us, they do just as ruthlessly to each other; all without malice. It is pure foolishness for Third World countries to think they can outmanoeuvre the West at its own game. Just watch them undo the efforts for a more equitable sharing of the resources of the oceans!''

"So we withdraw." Emma sighed. "Where to? Africa? And why should they leave us alone there? And how many from here will want to go?"

"Not many; and they will not leave us alone. We will have to insist, and you cannot insist on anything if you cannot enforce it and defend yourself."

"You will do without their loans and technical assistance?"

"We will do without anything we cannot pay for in cash or kind; we will do our own training, as you did in your mission and your churches. You've done it, Dad and his ancestors, generations of black folk have made life for themselves, by themselves, under the most unbearable conditions. It can be done; all we need is to organize it carefully and do it on a bigger scale, not defensively but as an act of self-discovery and self-assertion, on our own terms."

"On a national scale? A continental scale? Oh, David! You are dreaming, my love. Your father spent all his life creating one small mission which tried these things. One dictator came along and burned it down in one night."

"And before that they burned down his grandparents' church. And before that they burned down other so-called primitive temples, and even cities and towns and villages and whole communities. They even burned people. What's the matter with you, Emma? First you and Dad make me see something in a new way, now you try to cast doubt on it. Do you give up because a dictator comes along and burns down your work? Your people are rebuilding it."

Emma had to go on arguing against this overpowering idea. She thought of the young gunmen and their wounded comrade who had been there. "Those who came here with the wounded comrade, would they have the patience to make the sacrifices demanded by your withdrawal?"

"They would not; even if they wanted to they would not be allowed; but they wouldn't want to. That is part of the occupation and corruption of the mind. They want what New York and Chicago have to offer, no fault of theirs, just fact."

"Then it is only the Africans."

"And those very highly conscious of the diaspora; and not all the Africans, but I think enough to make a beginning. It can be done, Emma. The whole history of black withdrawal says that it can be done. What is urgent is to lay the groundwork and set up the new structures, and give them time to root and grow."

"What new structures, David? Back to the tribal village council in which only the old men talked and the women had no say?"

"You were at the centre of the structures created by your church. Was it like that?"

She remembered how it was and her impatience vanished.

"A synthesis," she said softly.

"A synthesis which came out of two things," David said, and now he, too, sounded soft and at ease, knowing that he had won her over at last, knowing that all this long night's talk would repeat itself over and over in her mind; its ideas would be questioned and explored till they became part of her mental baggage, a frame of reference for all her thinking about life and the world. "First, out of people's need to worship in freedom and in their own way, and secondly, out of the need to create structures to make that possible. Out of these came the kind of love that made my father go to Uganda to start his church; and people like John and Michael and you and all the others found their way to that church out of their need. You all found love and self-awareness there, a sense of belonging together and being creative and useful to your world. All I'm saying my love, is that we must enlarge that and make the self-discovery national in scope."

"And the beginning of this has to be withdrawal?"

"I see no other way. They will subvert the effort if they are not excluded; they will try to take it over and redirect it."

"If it can be done, how long must this withdrawal last?"

"Only as long as it is needed. Those who have gone through it will know when they are their own people and their minds are their own, no longer colonies of other minds. One of the most terrible things about the Westernism from which we must withdraw to find ourselves is its loss of faith and direction, of the capacity to know, instinctively, the true imperatives for historical survival. To be of any use to ourselves, and to the love and humanity of your vision and your God, Dad's God, we must separate ourselves from this destructive Westernism.

437

"You keep saying my God; is he not your God too?"

"The way I see it now, yes; my God too. He's not the God they used as an instrument for conquest and power. He's Dad's God who is in everything, the wind and the air and the earth and the water. Yes, that's my God too, though it's still a bit awkward to say it. I had, and still have, many things to discard from my own conditioned mental baggage. It is not going to be easy for any of us."

They were silent after that for a long time. The moon was very big and hung low in the sky, very near the earth, seeming not much more than an hour's flying time from earth. David remembered the total scepticism with which a group of men from Rock Hall had rejected the reports of the first men who had landed on the moon. All lies, they said; the television pictures of the event were faked, they said: man could never walk on the moon. That was that. What made for this scepticism, this gulf of distrust?

Emma thought of the tranquillity of this place as she felt it again. David had come close to Grandpa's vision of the connection of all things in our world. Was the absence of loneliness because the invisible spirits were all about, sharing her work and thoughts with her? And did they influence those thoughts? And were they part of this night's thinking and talking and working out of things, influencing them without our knowing? Where will what David now plans lead?

At last Emma broke the silence. "I think Michael will agree with you, and he is key; but it is a long work that you are planning. Can you work for something that you will not live to see the end of? It is not like you, you don't have the missionary training."

"I'll be a medical missionary."

"I don't mean that, darling. I mean the special kind of patience and vision which makes the missionary work all his life for something he knows he will not see. Can you do that, David?"

"I must try; not to try would be a betrayal. There is the mission as a starting point. We won't be starting from scratch. But let me warn you, there will be more crises and upheavals in Uganda; things will be unsettled for a long time, which is both the challenge and the opportunity. We are going to have to train our young people to use guns to defend what we have and what we stand for. If we don't, we are exposed either to another dictator or to intervention from outside."

"A Christian church with guns!" Emma was appalled.

"Dad might call it the Church Militant."

"Michael will. But I don't like guns, David; I never have, I never will. That is the one thing between us."

"I don't like guns either; you know I don't like killing. Does that mean we must be defenceless against those who would kill us? No, love! Those who would destroy us will not be restrained by our defencelessness. Listen, Emma. I learned the Ten Commandments at Dad's knee. I know the Commandment says, 'Thou shalt not kill.' But what if our enemies would kill us?"

"All right, David." She did not hide her unhappiness. "I'll accept it but I don't like it; please remember."

"I'll remember, my dear."

"Then it is settled. We'll go home as soon as possible and if Michael and the others agree, this will be at the centre of our work."

Emma got up and moved to the edge of the verandah, a mood of sadness over her. David came and put his arm about her; the long night was imperceptibly changing to a new day. It showed in the changing quality of the darkness of the mountains whose outlines were now sharply etched against the sky.

David said: "And you Emma, is it so difficult for you to embrace, not just accept, the idea of a withdrawal inward in order to find ourselves and become our own people?"

"No, it's not all that difficult; I just need to get used to the idea, which will take a little time."

"Then what is it? Why are you so sad?"

"It is the hurt of the thought that it should be necessary. It makes me understand, suddenly, how hurt all those others through the generations must have felt to want to withdraw. The pain of it, David. Think of it: generations of black people trying to escape to be themselves. It's awful and depressing. And now, a hundred years and more later, we must do the same thing. How can I not be sad?"

"It may be the last withdrawal, my dear. If we succeed we may free ourselves in time to point to a new way of seeing our world, a new way of living with each other and understanding each other;

439

we may all learn to co-operate instead of compete, to share instead of grab. But it will not come by itself or through pious words and hopes. There have to be the hard times first, the hard decisions and the hard actions necessary to save ourselves. You have to save yourself first before you can hope to save anybody else. A healed people, a whole people, freed of the bitter historical scars, may have something rich to offer the world.''

''Pray God you're right, David.''

''Dad's manuscript says I am. Please don't be sad.''

She took his hand and pulled him to their bedroom door. ''Then come and comfort me. I need to be comforted.''

David held back. When she turned to him to seek the reason he averted his face and looked instead at the twinkling city far below.

''What is it,'' she asked.

''A small foolishness.'' He sounded acutely self-conscious.

''Tell me.''

''You will find it foolish; a thing of symbolism I have long thought of.''

Her sadness lifted a little. ''All right! So I'll find it foolish. But you think it important enough to want to tell me, so tell me!''

''Batari. That was your maiden name. May I use it?''

''Oh, David!''

She flung her arms about him and held him tight, head against his chest. ''Oh, David, oh, David, oh, David!'' she said softly, so that he just heard it: ''Doctor David Batari of Uganda; Doctor David Batari and Mrs Emma Batari! Oh, David! I love it and it's not foolish. I give it to you with all my love and you can give me back my own name. I love you!''

This, she knew, was the first step in the withdrawal. If the others were half as rewarding. . . .

They went into their bedroom.

Suddenly, a shaft of light hit the mountains, transforming the view from Coyaba.

COUNTY TIPPERARY JOINT LIBRARIES

County Library
Thurles.

440